Praise for *The Quiet Girl*

"*The Quiet Girl* is brimming with twists and turns from the first page to the last. It's a story that will keep you reading well past your bedtime as you try to unravel truth from fiction in this clever novel. Chilling and shocking, *The Quiet Girl* is sure to stick with you even after the last page has been turned."

—Gina LaManna, author of *Pretty Guilty Women*

"Prepare to be enthralled—*The Quiet Girl* will grab your emotions and then hang on with a death grip. Atmospheric and twisty enough to deliver whiplash, S. F. Kosa writes with a keen eye for detail and surprise endings. A compelling narrative that hums with momentum long after the reader is done."

—Maureen Joyce Connolly, author of *Little Lovely Things*

THE QUIET GIRL

THE QUIET GIRL

S. F. KOSA

sourcebooks
landmark

Published by Sourcebooks Landmark, an imprint of Sourcebooks
P.O. Box 4410, Naperville, Illinois 60567-4410
(630) 961-3900
sourcebooks.com

Library of Congress Cataloging-in-Publication Data

Names: Kosa, S.F., author.
Title: The quiet girl / S. F. Kosa.
Description: Naperville, IL : Sourcebooks Landmark, [2020]
Identifiers: LCCN 2019056944 | (trade paperback)
Subjects: GSAFD: Suspense fiction.
Classification: LCC PS3606.I5337 Q54 2020 | DDC 813/.6--dc23
LC record available at https://lccn.loc.gov/2019056944

Printed and bound in the United States of America.
VP 10 9 8 7 6 5 4 3 2 1

For Peter, who held my hand
as we leapt into the unknown together.

MONDAY, JULY 27

The batter flowed in undulating ribbons and melted into a smooth, creamy lake. Mina scraped every bit from the bowl before shaking each cake pan to settle the contents. Everything had to be perfect.

When the pans were safely ensconced at 350 degrees, she moved to the next step. Humming a long-ago tune, she poured the premeasured and sifted powdered sugar into the mixing bowl over the softened butter and the extract, just enough to do the trick without overwhelming the flavor.

Baking was chemistry. Baking was precision. Never more than today.

When the frosting was the right consistency, she separated half into three bowls and used the droppers to apply the colors. Blue for innocence. Yellow for youth. Pink for so many things. Love. Warmth. Pain.

The effect would be neat. Cheerful. Enough to leaven a sultry summer night, draw the hands to the plate, the fork to the mouth, a smile to the lips.

Once the frosting bags and tips were assembled, she sat on the floor in front of the oven. The cakes had turned golden, but she would wait for the timer. She'd learned to trust herself in most things, but time was an entity she'd never mastered. She was always losing track. She couldn't keep it still or reliably pin all the bits of her past into proper temporal position. Even now, now of *all* times, she could feel it turning slippery.

She closed her eyes. Not long now.

The timer went off. She jerked, startled even though she had known it was coming. Wasn't that always the way of it?

Waiting for the cakes to cool was the hardest part, but she filled the time with cleaning. She was so good at it, good at making things pristine. The dishes. The counters. The floors. Herself. She smiled as she remembered how recently it hadn't been necessary. Every second of messiness, at once hard-earned and effortless, had been worth fighting for. It had given her hope. But she'd been foolish to think she could escape that easily.

Once the heat had bled from the layers, she placed the first on the plastic base and topped it with a generous layer of icing, to be sandwiched between slabs of cake. Of course, that part had to be pink. A nice effect during the cutting process, like slicing deep enough to reach a vein.

After adding the top layer and completing the crumb coat, she applied the white outer layer. Thick and even like new snow, covering all that lay soft and fragile beneath. Next, the frosting bag and Russian piping tip. It had taken a lot of practice to keep the flowers from looking like spiky piles of chaos, but now she was a pro. Soon, the cake was a garden of delight, a riot of color, a treat for the senses.

She donned dishwashing gloves and washed all the extra frosting down the drain, then cleaned the bags and tips by hand, lots of soap, once, then again. She tucked each piece into her decorating kit and slid it into its slot in the cupboard. Alex complained that she didn't put things away properly, but he was wrong.

She did, when it mattered.

The cake was perfect. She turned it this way and that, making sure it didn't have a bad side. Just like she'd been taught. Then she trapped it under the floral tin dome and attached the wire handles. Ready for transport.

She poured herself a glass of wine and drank it down. One for the road. It unfurled in her bloodstream, loosening knotted muscles, allowing her to breathe, allowing her to move.

She reached for her keys, then caught a glimpse of her hands. No, this wasn't right.

He would never understand, but he didn't need to. Because he would never know.

She made the necessary adjustments and stepped into the bathroom. That face in the mirror. *Her* face, every feature and flaw. And then she recited the line, the one that resonated even now. Especially now. "I know who you are," she whispered.

The minutes were slipping away, but she allowed herself to stare until her eyes shone.

Then she blinked.

Time to go.

WEDNESDAY, JULY 29

I make it to the pier with five minutes to spare, thanks to the driver's valiant swerving along Seaport Boulevard. With a quick *thanks*, I'm out of the Lyft and charging for the Bay State ticket booth, phone chiming in one hand and a backpack clutched in the other.

"Zarabian," I say to the attendant before he has a chance to ask. "Alex." After glancing at the screen of my phone and seeing it's not Mina, I silence the damn thing. Everything else can wait.

God, how I wish that were true. I set the phone on vibrate, and it instantly buzzes against my palm. Still not Mina. It's going to take more than a slew of conciliatory texts to fix this, and that's why I'm skipping town forty-eight hours early. "I called this morning," I say to the guy in the booth. "To change the ticket."

He squints at his screen and hesitantly types a few letters. "Arabian, you said?"

I say my last name again, then spell it. "I'd hate to miss the boat," I add, as if that's going to make a difference to him.

He shifts his weight as he taps the keys. "Round trip. Coming back Sunday."

"Yeah. Yeah." I watch as the printer extrudes my ticket, as he plucks it from the slot in no apparent hurry.

"Make sure you keep the return part," he drones. "You'll have to pay if they need to reprint it for you in Provincetown..."

I've snatched it from his fingers before he's finished talking. His voice fades as I jog down the walkway. The usual line has dissipated; everybody else is already on board, and the boat's engines are running. I offer my ticket to the guy standing near the gangway, and he tears off the top and hands me the rest. He's a young, bored bro sweating under the summer sun, and as my phone buzzes again, I feel envious of him and the job he can simply leave behind at five every day.

"Have a great trip," he mumbles.

A tangle of bikes clogs the bow, and the strap of my pack catches on a handlebar when I try to edge by. My T-shirt is sticking to my back, and the bar is singing my name. I duck into the first-floor cabin and toss my bag onto one of the last available seats. It's a booth, and there's a couple already sitting there, two guys with their tans and their polos and their boat shoes and their shorts, one pair pink with embroidered skulls and crossbones, the other yellow with martini glasses.

Yellow Martini looks startled when my bag lands next to him, but Pink Pirate smiles. "Plenty of room," he says. He sees me eye the line stretching from the bartender to the bow, then lifts his own Bloody Mary. "Not gonna win any awards, but still worth every penny."

I give him a quick nod, already contemplating standing on the top deck for the ride. Not in the mood to make new friends. There's been a knot in my gut since Mina left Monday morning, shoving her laptop and legal pads into her bag, murmuring that she needed time while I sat at the table with my lukewarm coffee and my tongue cocked, ready to pick up the fight where we left off.

With every hour between that moment and this one, all my righteousness has been sanded off. I'm raw now, stinging with the memory of the words I spat at her and the way she looked as they struck home, eyes wide and vacant like her brain was already on Route 6, miles away from me, from us. I pull out my phone and tap the messages icon, then her name.

Monday, 12:53 p.m.: Mina, we should talk. I was too harsh last night.

Monday, 11:17 p.m.: I love you. I don't like the way we left things.

Tuesday, 8:01 a.m.: Please respond. I'm sorry.

Tuesday, 11:42 a.m.: Don't punish me like this. I asked when we could start a family and you're acting like I ordered you to murder a puppy.

Tuesday, 4:35 p.m.: Sorry for being a dick. This is difficult for me. I'm trying to give you space. I love you.

Tuesday, 9:26 p.m.: I love you. Please let me know how you're doing.

Tuesday, 11:48 p.m.: Mina?

I'd be more worried about her, but she can be this way, especially when she's on deadline. She disappears into her stories, her characters. She goes off to her cottage, lets her phone die, and sometimes forgets to eat. I knew this was part of the deal, and I do my best not to take it personally, but Jesus. This time, it's hard.

The ferry lurches into motion and glides through Boston Harbor, beginning its swoop along the South Shore before angling toward the tip of Cape Cod. Ninety minutes to MacMillan Pier, less than two hours to Mina. As the line for the bar inches forward, I consider texting her one last time to let her know I'm on my way, but then I think better of it. Though I'm not great at romantic gestures, this situation seems to call for one, and my texts haven't yielded results thus far. I pull up a browser, find the florist closest to the pier, and order a bouquet. I'm not even off the phone before it buzzes with a text.

Not from Mina, but just as good, which is a weird thing to say about a message from one's ex. I smile as a picture of my daughter fills the screen, gap-toothed grin, dark eyes bright, hair wet, and skinny arms encircled with orange floaties. She ducked her head under water today. She wanted me to tell you that she's not scared anymore!

I run my thumb across the image of my kid—this perfect little person who inexplicably thinks I know everything and am the best person in the world, who has my eyes but her mother's dimples—and tap out a reply. Tell Devon I'm proud of her. I'll take her to the pool next weekend.

Caitlin's response comes within seconds, leaving me to wrestle aside the irony that my ex-wife is speaking to me when my current wife is not. You should have seen her today. It all just clicked and now she's like a little fish. The instructor is great. You were right that we shouldn't let her avoid the water.

"You were right." Why didn't you realize that when we were married? I add a winking emoji to convey the obvious, which is that even if she had and despite the fact that we seemed to have everything in the world going for us, we were probably doomed from the start.

Very funny. See you on Monday? Or is Mina picking her up next week?

My stomach goes tight. Not sure yet. I'll let you know.

I've only just gotten my beer when the phone buzzes yet again, and yet again, the text is not from my wife.

It's from my boss: Hey, asshole.

My reply: Why are you bothering me right now?

He's also my best friend. My phone rings a second later.

"Our new assistant was just dippy enough to tell me you were headed out of town."

I roll my eyes. "Please fire him. Harvard doesn't make 'em like they used to."

"Says the guy who went to BU. Everything okay?"

I take a gulp of my beer and step out onto the rear deck of the ferry. "I'll do the board meeting by phone tomorrow."

Drew is quiet for a moment. "You didn't answer my question. Is it your mom?"

"Nah. I talked to her yesterday. Her scans still look good. She wants to take Devon for a few days next month."

"Caitlin's on board with that?"

"Hell yeah. She wants to take off for a week with her new guy."

"Brad?"

"You're behind the times. Ryan. I met him a week or so ago. Quite a beard."

"Sounds like a dick. And speaking of—you have to be on top of your game for the Pinewell meeting tomorrow."

I bow my head. "I had Raj reschedule for Monday."

"Alex. What the hell. *Now* I'm worried."

"Don't be." I'd never get away with this if I hadn't known Drew since we were in diapers. Any other CEO would be screaming. "I'm on this."

"I'm still wondering if there's a way to do this without VC funding. Those smug bastards undervalued us by 90 percent. They're fucking sharks."

I keep my voice level as I talk Drew off the ledge for the hundredth time. "We're never going to get CaX429 to the clinic without learning how to swim with them. And if they do walk, that's it for Series A, and we're not the only ones who'll be fucked." My mom will lose her investment—along with about twenty other family members and friends we convinced to hop on board. Guilt rises like bile in my throat.

"How about I meet with them in your place?" he suggests. "Try to get through to them. I'm the fucking CEO! And I'm—"

"Drew." I bark his name loud enough that it swivels the heads of a couple leaning against the rail in front of me. I turn away and lower my voice. "The meeting is with their number cruncher, not the partners. It's below your pay grade, and they were fine when I asked them to reschedule." Not to mention, if Drew goes in there and acts all outraged that they don't think we're a unicorn that shits diamonds, it could actually finish us off. We've struck out with every other VC firm in Boston, and we'll burn through the last of our angel funding by January, easy.

"I've gone over my model a thousand times," I tell him. "It's solid. I'll call in tomorrow for the board meeting. Everything's fine. I just needed to step away for a minute."

"Something going on with Mina," he says. It's not even a question.

"It's fine." With my eyes squeezed shut, I add, "It's probably fine."

"You guys'll settle into it. You knew it would be an adjustment." He's too loyal to say what he's probably thinking and what my mom, who has no filter to speak of, straight up said to me a week before the wedding: *Whirlwind romances are a wonderful thing, but sooner or later, reality bites you in the butt.*

"Just don't panic," he adds. "It's not like this is the rainbow flame."

I laugh as he invokes an inside joke that runs all the way back to the day our high school chemistry teacher accidentally set his entire desk ablaze while trying to inspire a roomful of bored sophomores to appreciate the mystical joys of atomic composition.

"Definitely not the rainbow flame." The knot in my gut loosens.

Another beat of silence. "Let me know if you want to get a beer after the Pinewell thing," he says. "Whether things are on fire or not."

"Thanks. I'll be on the call tomorrow, and I'll be ready for Monday. I'm not about to drop this ball."

"Good. Because we're gonna fucking cure cancer, my friend, and get bloody rich in the process."

"Yup." I'm surprised the weight on my shoulders hasn't capsized the damn ferry.

He hangs up. I glance at my inbox—thirty new messages. Not a good time for the CFO to take off midweek. Worst possible time, to tell the truth.

I shove the phone in my pocket, drink my beer, and wonder if I'm being a total idiot. Am I being strategic, or am I just flailing here?

I'm *not* panicking about my marriage. I'm simply unwilling to let things fester. That's what Caitlin and I did, always. I won't do that with Mina, even if it means pushing into her space a little. She's told me she wants that. Needs it, even.

I've finished my second beer and answered ten emails by the time we glide past the seawall, waves lapping against the giant concrete blocks, and into the Provincetown Harbor. Along with a few hundred sweating men, women, and children, I shuffle my way off the boat and swing my pack onto my back. I've kept some stuff at the cottage, but it's Mina's place, her sanctum, purchased with the success of a dozen Mina Richards romances, furnished with the royalties from half a dozen more.

She says it's ours now, but I know better.

As I cross the street to the florist shop, I'm hit with a suffocating wave of what-the-hell-have-I-gotten-myself-into. Not this trip, but my entire fucking life. In the last two years, I quit my stable-but-boring job and joined a risky startup run by my brilliant but incurably impulsive best friend, and I married a woman I'd known for only six months. I pause on the sidewalk and take a breath. *Uber-rational*, that's what Caitlin always called me, though it was never a compliment. Near the end of our marriage, she dropped the euphemism and just called me a cold, unfeeling bastard.

I enjoyed watching her jaw drop back in April when I told her I was getting married again. *I guess it's the new you*, she said.

At the time, I was smug about it. I'd toed the line my entire life, and there I was, making my own rules, embracing the risk, and finally living.

Now I'm wondering if the new me is merely the old me gone temporarily insane.

Fuck. My mom has gotten inside my head. *Honey*, she said to me when I told her I was engaged, *are you sure this isn't a midlife crisis?* But Mina was worth a leap into the great unknown. She's worth a thousand more after that.

I pick my way through the crowd of tourists queuing up for lobster rolls, window-shopping for everything from cheap T-shirts to local artists' paintings of Race Point and the towering Pilgrim Monument, and peering at their phones for directions to their Airbnb or the nearest bike rental shop. After edging past two guys arguing about whether they should go to Monkey Bar ("You only want to go because you were hot for that bartender!") or Purgatory ("I'm just not as into leather as you are, okay?") tonight, I duck into the florist's shop and pick up the bouquet I ordered. Roses, tulips, peonies, sweet peas. A middle-aged woman with thin lips gives me a wistful smile as I turn for the door.

The walk through the West End is slow-going, a clog of sandaled feet, beach bags, ice cream cones, leashed pooches, and no one in any particular rush. Cars inch along Commercial Street, patiently waiting for wandering pedestrians to realize they're in the way and move aside. Rainbow flags flap in the salty breeze as I trudge past the

Boatslip, the afternoon Tea Dance just getting started, upbeat rave music pumping. Now that I've escaped the center of town, the streets become residential, a mix of quaint homes and B&Bs, folks lounging in rocking chairs on their porches or in fenced-in front yards, sipping on beers and watching the constant flow of human traffic. Mina's cottage is a ten-minute stroll away, nestled in a warren of hundred-year-old homes between Commercial and the lapping waters of the bay. The gray shiplap siding always looks damp and drab to me, but Mina says it makes her as happy as a hobbit in a hobbit-hole. I'm thinking the million-dollar view has a lot to do with it.

As I draw within a block of the place, everything in me is wound tight. I don't want to screw this up. I didn't come all the way here to rehash our last fight or start a new one. I need to be understanding if she's in the middle of a scene or a chapter or even one of her reveries where she sits there, fingers resting lightly on her keyboard, expression blank, eyes unfocused. If she's into her work, I'm going to smile and tell her I love her and I'm sorry and we'll talk later, and then I'll head to the Governor Bradford for a drink, maybe find someone to play a game of chess on one of the boards they have set up by the front windows. I'm not going to make it a thing.

I pause in front of the cottage. The curtains are drawn. I look down at the bouquet in my hand and reach for my key.

I step into the cramped entryway populated by colorful umbrellas, a few pairs of rain boots, and a basket brimming with scarves and gloves and hats. A bottle of sunblock rests on a little wooden bench. "Mina?" I call out, not too loud, not wanting to startle her. "It's me."

I glance through the living room windows toward the alley next to the house. Her car is gone. I have time to pull myself together. If I'm emanating tension, she'll pick it up immediately.

I kick off my shoes, then carefully align them on the mat beneath the bench before heading to the kitchen. I wrestle the flowers into a vase and consider where to leave them for maximum romantic effect. The dining table? Bedside table? Her desk?

There's a corked, half-empty bottle of pinot on the counter and a wineglass in the sink, lipstick on its rim and deep purple dregs in the very bottom. After cleaning up the flower scraps, I grab a wineglass from the open dishwasher, which is only partially unloaded, like Mina got distracted halfway through. Maybe she got inspired. I pour myself a splash of wine, then a glug.

After taking my first sip, I carry the vase of flowers to the living room. I'll put them where she'll see them right away, as soon as she comes through the front door. She'll know I'm here to fix things, and probably she'll let me. Hopefully this ends with us upstairs, in bed. We've both got other things to do, but I can't think of anything I want more than to waste the rest of the day with my wife, preferably with a bottle of champagne on ice and her thighs wrapped around my hips.

Mina's writing desk sits facing the grassy boardwalk path to the ocean, offering her glimpses of shimmering water as she writes stories of fiery women and the alpha males they alternately fight and fuck. She puts out two or three romances a year, and her readers devour them despite the fact that they already know how each story will end. Or perhaps because of that. I skimmed a few while we were dating. I didn't even have to buy them—I swiped the paperbacks off my mom's bookshelf.

I don't know what was more awkward, knowing Mom had read all those sex scenes my girlfriend had written or, the very first time I introduced them, overhearing Mom ask Mina if she planned to base any of her future heroes on me.

Now that I think about it, definitely the latter.

I take a gulp of my drink and move toward Mina's desk. A legal pad sits atop her closed laptop, pages filled with looping scrawl; she always writes in longhand before typing out her scenes. I don't look too closely; Mina's sensitive about that. She likes her words to be perfect before they escape her control.

She could walk in at any moment, back from a late lunch or a quick trip to the grocery store, maybe planning a dinner for one after a solitary afternoon of writing. Hopefully feeling lonely. Hopefully missing her husband. Maybe regretting her flat refusal when I broached the topic of starting a family, wishing she hadn't shut me down and shut me out. I'll apologize, and she'll apologize, and then she'll hook her finger through one of my belt loops and tell me that she hopes I took my vitamins this morning, because she's in the mood to do a little "literary research."

It's a rough job, being the husband of a romance author.

This desk is the place to leave the flowers, the first place her gaze will travel when she gets home. As I shuffle aside a couple of credit card statements and a playbill for *The Laramie Project* at the Provincetown Theater, I uncover a little ceramic bowl, chipped and quaint and exactly the kind of whimsical, antiquated thing Mina likes.

The sight of its contents hits me like a punch in the gut.

There, glittering in the sunlight filtering through the window facing the sea, left behind with as much care as that abandoned wineglass in the sink, are my wife's wedding and engagement rings.

CHAPTER ONE

She hummed quietly as she watched the churning waves. It was a song with words she couldn't quite remember, though surely she had known them at some point—the tune came to her as easily as breathing. The ocean folded over on itself, again and again, and she felt the relentless movement inside her. She swayed, her bare feet embedded in the sand, while the salty wind whipped her hair across her face. Sandpipers sprinted by on their toothpick legs. A gull cried out as it swooped overhead.

She hummed a little louder. The tune had been looping through her mind ever since she'd gotten up this morning, but she couldn't dredge up the name of the song or recall who sang it. Annoyance pricked at her once, twice, then faded to a dull twinge as she let the sight of the waves lull her again.

She'd stay here all day if she could. Race Point was the very edge of Cape Cod, surrounded by infinite water and sky. From here, she could drift away on the wind. She turned her face to the sun, closing her eyes and spreading her arms. The tune had fallen silent in her throat; she was a wisp of smoke, a silky ribbon spiraling in the breeze.

Somewhere to her left, a man shouted. She spun around, arms winding instinctively over her middle before falling to her sides. Just two guys playing Frisbee. They didn't even seem aware of her. She turned back to the ocean and stared as a wave deposited a swath of foam a yard from where she stood. She could float away. She could fly. She was a song on the breeze. Her mind was empty. Empty.

As the waves spread themselves thin along the sand, she tried to reclaim the soaring freedom that had seemed within her grasp only moments before.

After a few minutes, she gave up.

Her hair had coiled around her throat; strands were caught in her eyelashes and had wormed their way between her lips. Her cheeks felt warm; she'd been so eager to get here that she hadn't bothered to slather on the sunblock. Her bare calves stung with the scrape of sand. Suddenly, she felt it all a little *too* much—her body, her skin, her hair. The tune she'd just been humming was gone, crowded out by tiny shocks of irritation.

She had no idea what time it was, and Lou had warned her about being late. His words scrolled through her mind: *Easy hire, easy fire. Under the table works both ways.*

She took a step backward, trying to shed the sight of the ocean, until finally it let her go like an egg white slipping free from its yolk. She felt her brain quivering in her skull, a delicate membrane holding everything in place. One prick and all her thoughts might come dribbling out her ears.

Her shift started at five. When had she left the boardinghouse? As she slogged through the shifting sand toward the parking lot, past the Frisbee boys, shovel-and-pail-wielding kids hunched over mounds of sand, and their exhausted parents floppy as seals in their loungers, she tried to remember the morning. It was like fishing through the grease trap at Haverman's, coming up with a few chicken bones and a lot of sludge. She recalled the musky scent of Esteban's skin as she crawled from the bed. Rough granules of sand sticking to the bottoms of her feet as she headed for the bathroom. Frigid spray from the shower hitting her shoulder blades. Hanging the towel on the wobbly hook behind the door. Buttoning her shorts, feeling them sag down to her hips. Sliding her feet into flip-flops, the strap between her toes. Blinking in the sun as she stepped outside into the already-sweltering day.

She fiddled with her bike lock, her fingers automatically poking the numbers into place. One-two-zero-four. She maneuvered the bike away from the crowded rack as more riders rolled off the trail and came toward the railing. One of them, a middle-aged man in blue spandex, halted his bike right next to her and reached for his helmet. His gold watch glinted in the sunlight.

"Excuse me," she said, and then she pressed her lips together, startled by the sound of her voice. Was that what she always sounded like? Was that her actual voice?

The man was looking at her, expecting something. What did he want? Oh.

She smiled. "Do you know what time it is?"

He checked. "About four thirty."

She swung her leg over the seat and steered the bike onto the trail. Can't. Be. Late. One word per heartbeat, thumping against the inside of her skull. She pedaled up the hills and leaned into the curves, weaving around families with wriggling toddlers, older women in wide-brimmed hats, and a few cyclists struggling to figure out the gears on their rented bikes.

She didn't have time to shower or change for her shift, but it didn't really matter. She would be spending the next eight or so hours in a steamy kitchen, loading and unloading the dishwasher, her hair curling along her temples and sticking to her face, trying to avoid Amber, who always made her uneasy. Amber's days off were her favorite days to work. Hopefully today would be one of them.

She nearly rolled through the red light on Route 6 as she pondered what day it was. She'd lost track again, maybe because she'd been working seven days a week lately, five to closing, five to closing, five to closing. The only thing she really had to keep track of was the five part, and she could barely manage that.

She picked up speed as she pedaled along Conwell, nearly got winged by a pickup as she hooked left onto Bradford, and swerved to miss a lady with a stroller as she bumped up onto the sidewalk on Commercial, right out front of Haverman's. The restaurant consisted of a covered beer garden patio snugged up against a narrow old house that used to belong to some fishing captain but was now taken up entirely by the kitchen, storage room, and Lou's upstairs office and apartment. The high-tops and bar seats were already full, and several folks were standing at the vine-covered arch marking the entrance to the patio, giving their names and numbers to Jenn, the hostess for tonight. As she chained her bike to the rack on the sidewalk, she gave Jenn a quick wave and was rewarded with a blank, stone-faced look.

She ducked her head as she went around the other side of the house and opened the employees only door in the alley. It might be hot and humid outside, but the climate inside was positively tropical. She closed her eyes as the familiar steamy funk enveloped her.

"Hey, Layla! I was just asking Jaliesa if you were working today!"

It wasn't one of Amber's days off.

Layla hung her bag on one of the hooks along the wall, noting the other purses and backpacks and registering who each belonged to. Purple pack—Jaliesa, the nice bartender. Pink hobo bag—Amber, the nosy waitress. Worn leather pack with the little hole that always tempted Layla to stick her finger in it—Arthur, the cute line cook. Her tongue itched as she considered his bag for the thousandth time. The material was so thin, so ragged, that it didn't stand a chance if she decided to jab her finger right through.

"Hey there, space cadet."

She flinched and turned her head. Amber was right next to her. Her mascara was smudged. Layla glanced at the wall clock above the hooks. "I'm not late," she said and smiled with relief. Her voice no longer sounded like that of a stranger.

Amber returned her smile, probably thinking it had been meant to be friendly. "We're short-staffed. Reese is out tonight. Lou wants you out front."

The words splashed over her like a bucket of ice water. "Whoa. No. I d-don't think—I mean, I'm not—" She looked down at her flip-flops, her too-loose shorts, her secondhand T-shirt with a whale surrounded by plastic bottles. There was a faded brown stain on the blue fabric, right over her left boob. She raked her fingers through her hair, but they got caught in the tangles.

Amber gave her an appraising once-over. "No worries. I got you." Amber grabbed her by the elbow and snagged the pink hobo bag as they sailed toward the employees' bathroom.

Layla's skin had gone goose bumpy. "I'm a dishwasher," she mumbled. "I wash dishes."

"Honey, it's Friday night, and you're about to make ten times more an hour than you ever could loading greasy plates into the monster machine."

"Why can't Arthur or Serge—?"

"Lou wanted another female server. Lesbians deserve eye candy, too, ya know." She whipped a T-shirt out of her bag, *Haverman's Helles House* emblazoned across the chest, and motioned for Layla to strip off her shirt.

She crossed her arms over her middle. "I'm not a waitress."

"You are now." Amber held up the shirt. "And if you're not, you can go tell Lou yourself."

She took off her shirt and yanked the other over her head. She wished she'd stopped to put on a bra this morning. Her eyes and nose burned. A droning buzz filled the space between her ears. Her vision flashed with blotches of red and black. She braced her palm against the wall.

Amber slapped lightly at her cheeks. "Hey. Hey. Layla. Stop having a panic attack. Jenn and Wanny and Oscar and me'll all be out there, and we'll look out for you. We need the help tonight."

Help. "Is—is Esteban—?"

"Your guard dog ain't here tonight, though I expect you know his schedule better than I do these days." Amber took her by the shoulders and gave her a brisk shake. "Come on. You're a big girl. Act like it."

Layla blinked. Amber had a sinewy neck and yellow hair with black roots. Amber had big dangly earrings that bobbled and swayed and clinked. Amber had a narrow nose and a triangle face and eyes that were murky green. Amber had a voice that sounded like barbecue and corn bread, not lobster and quahogs.

"If I screw up—" Layla began.

"Then don't."

Amber turned her around, and a moment later, Layla felt a brush run through her hair. She clasped her hands together and squeezed, fingernails digging into skin. She swore she could feel every single bristle slicing across her scalp, but somehow, with each stroke, she relaxed a little. The sensation was like a weight pressing down, down, down, submerging the words and thoughts that had been crowding to the surface a moment before. By the time Amber yanked Layla's hair back into a ponytail, her cold sweat had gone warm.

Amber handed her an apron. She pointed to the pocket. "Tablet's already in there. Just tap on the right table number, then the menu items. Keep an eye out for your table numbers at the counter and the bar so you can get stuff to the diners quickly. Lou hates it when stuff sits for longer than a minute, and I swear he times us. Check in on your tables just before they've got an empty glass, always offer another round, always offer dessert, and pretend like the sea scallop crudo has given you multiple orgasms. Lou wants us to push that one."

Layla cringed at the thought of putting scallops, or any other seafood for that matter, in her mouth. She couldn't imagine ever having liked it, but the nights she'd spent scraping the half-chewed and picked-over remainders off customers' plates had only deepened her aversion.

Amber scowled as she read Layla's expression. "I don't care if the slimy little things give you hives, for heaven's sake—*pretend*. It's all about selling, okay?"

Layla tied on the apron over her shorts and pulled out the tablet as Amber continued to rattle off instructions. Her mouth moved a lot as she spoke, but her eyes and cheeks and brow were completely still somehow. Layla stared until a clatter from the kitchen startled her back to attention. The tablet was in her hands. The one she would use to punch in the orders. This would be fine. Just fine.

"Of course it will," Amber said, making her realize she'd spoken aloud.

It was fine until it wasn't. The hours whooshed by as she concentrated on making it through each individual minute. She mixed up a few orders and spilled a drink at the bar, but the patrons were mostly sweet. It was better than dishwashing, because there were no blank times. Every second demanded her complete focus, and it was all she could think about. Nothing else. Nothing but pressing the right button, picking up the right glass, saying the right words, and smiling the proper smile, even as she handed over plates of raw oysters and scallop crudo that made her stomach turn.

She had no idea how many tables she had turned over, and the faces of the customers were all a blur. The air had gone cooler as the night progressed, as the lanterns drooping over the space came on, the sky beyond went dark, revelers strolled past, and drag queens stalked by, waving regally and pausing for photos with admiring patrons. She liked watching them—there was no telling what the face beneath all that makeup really looked like. It was as if they came out of nowhere and disappeared just as easily.

The crowd thinned out as midnight approached, and she paused at the bar to sip a glass of water Jaliesa had set there for her. Her shirt and shorts were damp with sweat, and her ponytail had slipped down to the base of her neck, where her hair stuck to her nape.

"Almost there, girl, and then it's time to count tips over a double G&T." Jaliesa shook a silver cocktail shaker in each hand while her ebony curls jiggled around her face. "My favorite part of the night."

Layla smiled into her water glass, enjoying the feel of ice on her tongue. Her mind was a quiet hum of white noise.

"Hey," said Jenn, tapping her on the shoulder. "I just seated three at six."

She took a final gulp of her water. "Okay." She tucked a stray lock of hair behind her ear. Table six was in the back corner of the narrow patio. Seated there were one woman and two guys who looked about Layla's age. One of the guys had his muscular, tattooed arm around the woman, whose curly black hair hung loose around her shoulders. The other guy, whose back was to her, had short red hair. They were dressed casually—shorts and T-shirts—not for clubbing.

She threaded her way across the patio and approached the table where the three of them were absorbed in conversation.

"—don't really want to go back until Saturday, but my parents leave for Paris on Thursday, and there's no way they're taking Mr. Drillby to a kennel," the redhead was telling his friends. He was talking fast, but his words were a little slurred, his voice a little loud.

"Hi there, and welcome to Haverman's. My name's Layla, and I'll be taking care of you tonight," she said to his companions, who had seen her standing there. "Can I start you guys off with something other than water?"

"I'll have the house margarita," said the woman.

"I'd love a Cape Cod *Blonde*," said her partner, grinning at Layla while his companion rolled her eyes.

As his friend spoke, the redhead turned his head and looked up at her. The loose smile he'd been wearing dropped away. "Maggie?"

"Nope. Can I—"

"Maggie Wallace," said the redhead. His eyes were bloodshot. He smelled like pot and whiskey. He grabbed her wrist.

The tablet in her hand clattered to the ground, and she let out a cry. She pulled her arm free of the guy's sweaty grasp. People's heads were turning. Eyes were on them. She scooped the tablet up, peering at the screen. It hadn't cracked, thank God. "A margarita and a Blonde," she said, breathless. "Anything else?"

The guy had turned back to his friends, who were giving him concerned looks. The tattooed guy had put his hand on the redhead's arm.

"I swear it's her," the redhead was saying. "I was telling you. Remember?"

"He'll stick with water," the woman said.

"I'll get those orders in right now," she replied, but her voice had gone weird again. Strange and unfamiliar. It made her wish she didn't have a mouth at all.

The redhead turned in his chair again. "You look exactly like her," he said. "My girlfriend was talking about you the other day. Come *on*. Reina Ramirez. You know her, right?"

She realized she'd been shaking her head vigorously. She stopped when the tattooed guy said, "Let it go, dude." He hadn't released his friend's arm. "Let the lady do her job."

Before the redhead could free himself, she headed for the kitchen. Jaliesa's mouth was moving as she walked by, but she couldn't hear what the bartender was saying. Inside her head, there was a low buzz and snatches of a song that seemed familiar yet impossible to place.

"Layla?" called out Amber, poking her head into the back as Layla reached for her bag. "Wait—you're *leaving*?" She pushed through the swinging door and dropped her tablet into the pocket of her apron. "What the hell happened?" She looked over her shoulder. "Did one of those guys grope you or something? Because—"

"No." She tugged the Haverman's shirt over her head, which was buzzing, buzzing, buzzing. She could make out Amber's words, but only barely. The shirt fell from her loose fingers, where it landed crumpled at their feet.

"You're kinda pale," the waitress said. "Are you sick?"

"Yeah," she replied. "I'm...done."

"Oh, honey." Amber sounded sympathetic as she watched Layla tug her stained blue shirt over her head. "I know it's been a long night." Amber sighed. "You really did great. We'll set aside your—"

But she was already out the door, down the alleyway, unlocking her bike—one-two-zero-four—and pedaling down the road. She didn't even know where she was going. All she knew was that she needed to get away.

WEDNESDAY, JULY 29, TO THURSDAY, JULY 30

The first time I saw Mina's face was on December 17 of last year, on a poster outside the Brookline Booksmith. *Join us for an evening with Mina Richards*, I think it said. That part I don't remember so well, because I was too busy staring at her photo. Her eyes invited mischief.

"Look," I said to Devon, who I'd just picked up from her mom's—a cordial enough exchange but one that always left me in the mood for a strong drink. "There's an author here tonight, signing her books. Kinda cool, huh?"

Bundled into her winter coat, a woolly scarf covering half her face, Devon said sternly, "You're not supposed to write in books!"

"If you *wrote* the book, I think it's allowed. Lots of people like to have an author sign a book for them. It makes it special."

Devon looked intrigued. "Will she sign a book for me?"

I peered at the poster, which displayed the cover of the book in question. A man's muscular bare chest featured prominently. "I don't think she writes the kind of thing you like to read."

"But she looks nice," my daughter said. I agreed. Then I suggested that we go inside, get warm, and find a new picture book to read that evening. Always the bookworm and already starting to read on her own, Devon jumped at the chance.

"I'm tired of *I Want My Hat Back*," she said. "But we can still read it sometimes," she offered when she saw my face fall. I'd memorized every word of that one, and so had she, and we had taken to doing different animal voices as we read the story of a bear in search of his beloved, missing hat. Every time, it made me feel like I was about to win a Dad of the Year award.

"I'm sure we'll find something just as good," I said, even though I doubted it.

Pulling my gloves off and tucking them into my jacket pockets, I glanced around the bookstore as Devon guided me to the children's section at the back. On one side of the space, the employees had a table set up with several stacks of books—all the same title—lined up along its front edge. Another copy of that poster with Mina's picture was on an easel next to the table. *Beyond the Threshold*, the book was called. Obviously a romance novel. My mom had read at least four a week for as long as I could remember. My dad had loved to gripe that one day, he'd open his front door and be killed by an avalanche of smut, and didn't she have anything better to do all day? After he died, my mom frequently joked that she was glad she didn't have to sneak them into the house anymore, but she looked like she was about to cry every time she said it.

"We're about to have our Mina Richards book signing," said a woman over the PA. "Purchase your books at the front, and Ms. Richards herself will be over there at the table, ready to personalize them for you!"

Four or five women were already lined up at the checkout, each with at least one copy of *Beyond the Threshold* in hand. "Do you want to go look at books while Daddy buys Grandma's Christmas present?" I asked Devon.

"Yes! You *always* rush me." She happily let go of my hand, and I watched my independent daughter skip back to the kiddie section.

A few minutes later, I was standing in a short line, watching the author herself. She looked a little different from her picture. Her hair was longer, brown waves that fell past her shoulders. Her face seemed a bit fuller, as if she'd put on a bit of weight, but it looked good on her. She was younger than I was by maybe ten years, I thought (it turned out to be twelve). But those eyes—those were the same as in the poster. An eerie light gray, flashing with a vibrant, wicked playfulness. She was friendly with each fan, asking them how they were doing, thanking them for being there. Each time, it sounded like she actually meant it. She spoke with each person for a minute or so as she signed, and then it was on to the next fan, who she seemed equally happy to see. I had to remind myself of that when I reached the front of the line and her eyes skimmed up my body to my face. She grinned and let out a laugh so warm that I nearly melted right there in front of her.

"You're my first guy," she said, arching an eyebrow as she accepted the book I offered.

"Well, hey, I'm honored to be your first," I said, then automatically recognized that what I'd said could be read as anything from charmlessly awkward to hideously creepy. "I mean—"

"I'm a romance author, mister," she said. "And that's *totally* the line I would have written." She winked at me, and right then, I *knew*. I had to know her.

"Are you on a book tour?" I asked.

She shook her head. "I actually live nearby, and these folks are kind enough to have me in for my new releases. Publishers rarely pony up for tours anymore, especially because a lot of my sales are ebooks." She pursed her lips. "That was probably more information than you actually wanted to know."

So, so wrong. "We're neighbors," I said. "I didn't realize there was a famous author living in the area."

"Oh, come on. There are at least twenty famous authors living in the area! This is Boston!"

I put up my hands in surrender. "I'm clearly not as hooked into the literary scene as I should be."

"Get right on that." She held up the copy I'd given her. "Who can I make this one out to?"

"Sherri." I spelled out her name. "My mom. She loves this kind of book."

"*This* kind of book. Hmm." She bowed her head as she scrawled something on the page, quick and sure, no hesitation at all. A moment later, she handed it back to me.

For Sherri, it read. *Your son says you have excellent literary taste.*

I laughed. "She's gonna love this." Then I handed her the second copy I'd purchased.

"And who is this one for?" she asked, waving her Sharpie. "Sister? Girlfriend? Wife?" She was so goddamn cute, eyes and cheeks, that smile. When her gaze flicked to my bare ring finger, it felt like a triumph.

"None of the above. This one's for me. Literary research." I glanced over my shoulder to find a line of women beaming at me, the novelty. "I've never read a romance novel, but right now, I'm feeling inspired."

"I see," Mina murmured. "Can I personalize it for you, then?"

"What?" My voice had gone hushed, too. I leaned forward, almost in her space. Her perfume smelled like lavender and vanilla. It temporarily scrambled me.

I know, because she told me later, that I was staring at her mouth.

"I meant, what's your *name?*" she asked after a few seconds, looking like she was about to laugh.

"Oh. Alex."

She hunched over the book, shielding the words with one hand. "You'll have to wait until later to read this, Alex. It's top secret literary research stuff." She closed the book and handed it back to me with a conspiratorial look. "Thanks for coming."

It took every brain cell I possessed to make it to the back of the store and find my daughter, whose existence I had all but forgotten for a moment there. Her scarf, coat, and mittens were strewn along an aisle, and she was squatting at the end, surrounded by at least a dozen picture books. I bought Devon five of them, hustled her out of the store, and took her out for sushi because, for some reason, that is my otherwise-picky five-year-old's favorite food.

Once we were safely seated, I had ordered a bottle of sake, and Devon had buried her nose in one of her latest literary acquisitions, I pulled out Mina's book and opened it up.

For Alex, it said. *I'm honored to be your first.*

And underneath that, she'd written her phone number.

In that moment, I knew I was already in love with her.

My fingertips brush over Mina's rings as I sink into her desk chair. I pick them up and hold them in my palm. I remember putting each one onto her finger, the first at Race Point, right on the frigid beach in March, with icy ocean water seeping into the fabric of my jeans as I knelt in the wet sand, with the waves pounding and the wind howling, with Mina's wild laughter and her mittened hands on either side of my face. Mina doesn't just smile when she's happy; she full out laughs, something that used to confuse me. But by the time she broke into uncontrollable giggles at the altar, right after I slid the wedding ring past her knuckle—with my mother watching, looking as baffled as the minister, and Mina's mother watching, looking as if she wanted to sink through the floor—I knew what it meant. As Mina doubled over, red-faced and out of breath and still bubbling with laughter, I thought I might explode with happiness and triumph.

And now here I am, and these two rings feel so heavy that I have to put them down again. They plink into the bowl, rattle, and go still.

Why would Mina take them off? Me, I take off my wedding ring when I work out, because I don't want the weights to bend it out of shape. I take it off to shower, too, and at night. The few times I've forgotten to wear it out, Mina has given me grief for it, and with an impish smile, she's insisted on placing it back on my finger herself.

But Mina never takes her rings off. She wears them all the time. Or at least I thought so.

It's another thing I'll have to be careful about when she gets back. We're not going to fight about something this stupid. It's not like taking off the rings means we're not married anymore. That's what I always say to her when I forget.

It shouldn't hurt like it does.

I help myself to another glass of wine, and then I wait. I read the opening pages of a book I find on the shelf—believe it or not, a thriller about a man whose wife goes missing. The police, of course, suspect he's killed her. After a chapter, I have to put it down.

By the time it gets to be six o'clock, I'm in a terrible mood, and predictably, that's when my mother calls. "I got an email from Drew asking me to invest another $200,000 in Biostar," she informs me. "I expect to hear that kind of thing directly from you."

What the hell? Drew is panicking—and he went around me. "I'm sorry I didn't tell you," I say. "I was going to call you tomorrow. After the board meeting." I have to smooth this over. She's my mom, but she's also an investor—one who talks to other investors.

"Is everything going okay?" she asks. "I thought the next step was getting venture capital money."

"It is. Drew just wants to make absolutely sure we're able to fund the trial that's set for spring. He doesn't want a delay."

"None of us want that. If my damn cancer comes back, CaX429 may be my only chance."

"Don't say that, Mom. You have lots of options."

She laughs. "And if Biostar goes down the tubes, I won't be able to pay for them!"

I grimace. I'm the one who convinced her to invest. Drew sold me on the idea. God, he's a great salesman. Immunotherapies for solid tumors are the holy grail right now, and he'd partnered with a guy who'd identified a certain ion channel as an ideal target, one that could be boosted to supercharge the cells that might attack the cancer. It just so happened to be promising as a treatment for the same type of cancer my mom had been fighting for the past year and a half—she was diagnosed with squamous cell carcinoma in her salivary glands right before my dad died abruptly from a goddamn aneurysm, a double gut punch that had left me reeling.

I'm no scientist, but CaX429 sounded like some kind of miracle, and there was my best friend, pushing me to be his financial guy in the company he'd founded to bring it to market. I left the accounting firm where I'd worked for ten years to help him make it happen.

I convinced a lot of people I knew to invest in our company so that we could run a pilot—Drew and I grew up in Weston, which is thick with people who have more money than they know what to do with.

Our angel investors are still waiting for their returns. Our pilot data were really promising—enough so that we thought every VC in Boston would jump on us in a hot minute. Hasn't turned out that way, but I'm not giving up yet. "Don't jump straight to the doomsday scenario, Mom. Biotech is expensive, and Drew is trying to cover all the bases. He's being cautious."

Impulsive and reckless is what he's being, but it'll hurt the company if I ever say that aloud.

"I didn't realize money was such a problem. Can't Caroline give Biostar some positive publicity or something? I keep hearing about these viral online things where people raise boatloads of cash. You only need the right push."

Caroline, Drew's wife, is an on-air reporter for the Boston NBC station. "That's kind of a conflict of interest for her, Mom. And start-ups don't really raise money that way, not the ones that need millions of dollars, anyway. Look, we're on top of this, I promise. I'm sorry if his email worried you."

"I want to hear news like this from my son," Mom says.

"You do understand that I'm the CFO, and that means a lot of this is on me? I've been kinda busy."

"Poor Mina," she says. "I hope she's not feeling neglected."

"Did you call just to make me feel shitty?"

As soon as the words are out, I regret them, especially when my mom says, very quietly, "I didn't mean to make things worse. The pressure must be crushing."

She's trying to make me feel better, but somehow, it's only making my heart beat faster. "I'm handling it okay," I tell her, softening my tone. "Sorry for snarling at you."

"The last thing you need is to feel guilty. You go ahead and snarl if you need to."

How is this only making me feel *guiltier*? "I'll call next week to explain the investment stuff to you, okay? I'm still working on the numbers and negotiating with potential VC partners, and I want to make sure I give all our investors, and especially you, the right information. Make sense?"

"I'm lucky to have a son like you," she says, sounding wistful.

"And I'm lucky to have you for a mom." I actually mean that. She's a pain in the ass, my mom, but she'd lie down in traffic for me without a moment's hesitation.

"Oh! Oh. Is Mina there?"

"What?"

"Is your *wife* with you, silly? I read her newest, and I wanted to talk to her about it. I tried calling her a few days ago, but she hasn't gotten back to me yet."

I sit up in my chair. "When did you call her, exactly?"

"Hmm? Oh, Tuesday morning, I think? Yes. It was before my hair appointment. Went straight to voicemail. She didn't mention that I called?"

I close my eyes. "Like I said, I've been busy. So has she."

"My book club is next week, and my girls and I are discussing *Bound for Life*. I promised them I'd have insights from the author!"

"Mina's not here right now," I say, feeling hollow. Part of me wants to tell my mom what's happening, but the rest of me knows that won't help at all. "I'll have her call you."

"Before Tuesday would be great. This is one of the perks of having a famous author for a daughter-in-law!"

"Sure thing. Love you." We hang up, and I lean back in Mina's chair. Mina's always seemed super eager to please my mom, so I'm surprised she hasn't called or texted her back. She actually worries what Mom thinks of her, no matter how many times I've assured her that my mom loves her. I think it's because Mina hardly ever speaks to her own parents, and the first and only time I met them was at the wedding. They seemed perfectly normal and pleasant to me, and they live right nearby—in Truro, only a couple of miles down the road from Provincetown. But whenever I've suggested inviting them over or visiting them, she changes the subject.

Same strategy she's used when I ask about starting a family, too, until I forced the issue on Sunday.

It feels like the walls are closing in on me. Launching myself out of the chair, I shove my feet into my shoes and head out the door. I end up at this beer garden on Commercial Street that Mina loves. Not just for the drinks—they've got great burgers and several vegetarian options, which is great because Mina absolutely despises all forms of seafood, an unfortunate characteristic for a native New Englander. We've been there at least four times this summer, and the last time, the grizzled Italian guy who owns the place even came out to tell her he'd made sure to stock this one brown ale from Jester just for her.

The serious-faced blond hostess tells me there's a spot at the bar, and I squeeze myself between two couples to peruse what's on tap. I watch one of the bartenders, his black hair slicked away from his tanned face, as he shakes a cocktail into a glass. I'm almost sure he's been behind the bar when Mina and I have eaten here before. When he notices me, I order a Night Shift IPA. As he hands me my drink,

I say, "My wife and I come in here all the time. She's a big fan of this place. Mina Richards?"

"Lots of people come in here, man. It's Provincetown in the summer."

"The owner here stocked a beer she really likes. The Feste."

"I know who you're talking about now! The writer, right? She orders Feste every time." He chuckles. "About the only one who does."

"When was the last time you saw her?" I blurt out.

The relaxed smile disappears, and his gaze slides to the other bartender, a black woman with a tangle of ringlets pulled into a loose bun, who has her back to him as she banters with customers. "Um," he says. "I'm not sure. Like I said, it's pretty busy." He focuses on rearranging little jars of cocktail condiments lined up along the edge of the bar.

"I was supposed to meet her here for lunch, but I missed her," I improvise. "I just thought—"

"Haven't seen her today," he says, keeping his eyes on the jars, probably thinking I'm some jealous abuser he needs to save her from. "She always seems to have her phone with her, though, so..."

"Text her. Yeah. I will. Thanks."

I down my beer in about three minutes flat, pay in cash, and slink out of there before he has a chance to slide the bills off the bar.

I wake up alone. I know it before I open my eyes. My fist clenches over the sheets. My thoughts are a scrum of worry and anger.

Why is she doing this to me? Punishing me for wanting to have a *kid*, for fuck's sake? It's not like I demanded that we try to get pregnant immediately. I just asked a question. And now my wife has fucking ghosted me.

Fuck this. I won't let her blow up more of my life than she already has; I have a company to save. I was up working on my financial model until two, in part because I had a hell of a time getting to sleep—I was too busy listening for her car pulling into the drive, her key turning in the lock. In that grinding, oppressive silence, I pulled the model apart and put it back together a thousand times. On Monday, when I go to meet with the Pinewell guys and show them the details, it's going to turn things around. Our first meeting with them was generalities, just the beating heart, but I've got the bones. And the brain.

I make myself coffee, rifling through the kitchen for the filters and the beans, which Mina never seems to leave in the same place twice. Then I call in to the board meeting, which goes surprisingly well. Drew is buttoned down. He explains his email to our angel investors, including my mom, as a strategy to entice them to up their ownership in the company because the opportunity is too good to miss. Since half of them sit on our board, they're intrigued by the chance, but they want to know who else is going to offer up the big funds—the fifty million we want to keep us running and completing studies all the way to FDA approval. It's not the right moment to hand Drew his ass for going behind my back. It won't matter too much if Monday goes well, anyway.

When the phone call ends, I hang up and face the day. It's late morning and already hot as hell outside. My anger has cooled, though. Mina is a lot of things—she can be flighty sometimes. She's left the stove on more than once, and she even left one of Devon's plastic cups sitting on a hot burner one time, not noticing until the smoke alarms began to blare and the condo filled with acrid smoke. She sometimes waits to tell me that she parked my car in the town lot until I'm late for a meeting, and twice we've shown up at a restaurant only to discover that she never actually made the reservation. And she can be a little focused on herself, sure. If she's got a deadline or an appointment with her therapist that day or even just a new idea or a political bug up her ass, then good luck holding her attention for more than thirty seconds straight.

But she's not cruel.

I try calling her. Straight to voicemail. "Mina, call me when you get this. I'm in Provincetown—I came early to surprise you..." I sigh. "Surprise! Anyway, I'm sorry for being a dick on Sunday. Whether you're still mad or not, give me a call or text to let me know you're safe, all right?" I'm connected to her by this thin electronic thread, and I don't want to cut it. "We can work this out," I finally say. "I know we can."

I force myself to end the call, and then I sit there, fighting the urge to hit her number all over again. Where the hell *is* she? Being away all day is one thing, but overnight? And she left her rings behind. It takes a fierce mental push to shove from my mind images of Mina fucking another man. Or woman. Not that it matters. She wouldn't do that to me. She couldn't do that.

I grab the legal pad she left behind and read the first page—it's a scene in which two characters are fighting, and the heroine is enraged but still feels inexplicably and irritatingly drawn to the guy she's arguing with, who I assume is the romantic hero. I turn the page and keep reading. Scrawled in the margin of the second page is a list:

Eggs
English muffins
Bacon
Cheese
Seltzer
Bills
Cash
Stef
Emily

I know Emily—that's Mina's therapist in Boston. But Stef? Is that one of her friends? She doesn't have many; she's told me she's always been an introvert, and she's not good at staying in touch with people. Her best friend lives in Boston—another writer named Willa Penson, which I think is her real name even though it's always sounded to me like a pseudonym. I know she has other writer friends, too, mostly on the internet, because they live all over the place, but I think she mostly chats with them online. Perhaps Stef is a friend here in Provincetown, or it could be someone from her publisher.

For all I know, it could be her dentist.

I wonder if I should know all these details of my wife's life. It seems like I should. Especially now. After glancing toward the front door and half expecting her to be standing there, glaring at her obnoxious husband holding her precious legal pad and sitting at her writing desk, I put the pad down and open her laptop.

It's a lock screen. I type in my own name as the password. Nope. I try a few other things: our anniversary date, her birthday, my birth-day, and the name of a dog she mentioned having when she was a kid. Byron, his name was. No joy.

I give up and retrieve my own laptop from the bedroom. I'm not a big social media person. Never have been. I don't understand the pull to share the mundane details of one's life with a bunch of people on the internet. I have a Facebook account, but I think I've posted a grand total of five times. The last time was when Mina and I got married. I changed my status and posted a picture of us together, and I was deluged with several dozen friend requests from people I didn't know.

They all turned out to be my new wife's fans.

Mina is active on Facebook. She's got almost five thousand friends, but the vast majority of them are people she's never met in person and doesn't know at all. To me, that's like inviting a bunch of strangers to peer into our bedroom window, but Mina claims it's not like that because she doesn't post a lot of personal stuff.

The last time she posted was Sunday morning. The day of our fight and the day before she came to Provincetown. It's a picture from the Caffè Nero in Washington Square, a selfie of Mina at a tiny wooden café table with her coffee and her legal pad. I stare greedily at the image, pulling up the photo and zooming in. She looks tired despite the usual bright smile. *Up late writing a new scene. Now, like all passionate affairs, we'll see if it survives the morning after*, she's written. I squint at the image of the legal pad and then grab the one from her desk and compare the general outline of the prose on the page. I think the picture shows the same pad I've got in my hand. I zoom in as close as I can—the list is there in the margins, but the bottom three items are missing. She must have written those—cash, Stef, Emily—later.

I read the comments beneath. One is from my mother, saying she'd be more than happy to read the scene for Mina and offer feedback, which makes me roll my eyes so hard that I think I strain a muscle. The rest are friendly comments from readers, questions about when her next book will come out and whether it's a sequel or a stand-alone, stuff like that. Her friend Willa left a heart emoji and a comment about how they should get together this week.

I instantly click on Willa's name. Even though I've only met her once in person—at the wedding—we're Facebook friends, too, and her dot is green. Hi, I type, then pause. What the hell am I supposed to say? Embarrassment paralyzes me for a solid minute, but then my worry sets me back in motion. **When was the last time you heard from Mina?**

Her response is slow, and it seems like she's typing a lot, but then it turns out to be only four words: **Why do you ask?**

Just wondering, I type.

...? That's her response, and I don't blame her. I consider myself a strategic thinker, but right now, I'm acting as impulsively as Drew. I don't want to admit that I don't know where Mina is. We've been married for only two months after knowing each other for only half a year, and there's already trouble in paradise. I'm imagining the *I told you so*'s coming in fast and furious, and I don't want to deal with that. This is between Mina and me, and the rest of the world can mind its own damn business.

Seems like the kind of thing you should ask her, not me, Willa adds, and that clinches it for me.

I will, I type and sign out.

But two hours later, after the silence of the cottage turns oppressive, after reading Mina's handwritten scene four more times, after Googling "Mina Richards Stef" and finding nothing, after finishing the bottle of red, and after reminding myself that Mina *loves* me—she wouldn't let me worry about her for this long—I pick up the phone and call the Provincetown Police Department.

"Hello," I say to the woman who answers. "I need to file a missing person report."

CHAPTER TWO

She stared at her knees. Both skinned up, pink and abraded, twin trickles of blood diluted by the steady, warm rain. Drops slid along her nose and cheeks as she rocked slowly, her fingers curled over her shins.

Her butt hurt. She shifted on the brick steps and winced. Her back hurt, too. Her fingernails were filthy, broken, and crusted with grime. Grit crunched between her teeth.

She raised her head as a memory came to her: teetering as her bike hit soft, loose sand. Her shoulder and hip hitting the ground. She lifted her left arm and hissed at the deep, dull ache.

In front of her was a narrow street, water carving its path through the silt at the edge of the asphalt. On either side of her were small cottages. Everything was gray. The buildings. The sky. Even her hands were tinged with it. She peered at them, wondering if she was actually alive or dead and in some weird in-between, a hazy, wet waiting place where she was all alone, the only soul in the world.

From behind her came a metallic squeak. She whipped around, ending up crouched at the bottom of the brick steps, looking up at a white-haired man wearing a blue robe and pajama pants who was leaning out the front door of his cottage, the stoop of which she'd apparently been sitting on. Number thirty-nine.

His eyebrows were raised. "Hi there," he said quietly. "Can I help you?"

She backed off the porch and stood up. Her tongue writhed inside her mouth like an earthworm in rain-soaked dirt.

A younger, shirtless man with pink hair and black roots leaned around the white-haired guy, laying a hand on the older man's arm. "Who—?" the younger guy began, then frowned when he caught sight of her. "Honey, is she okay?" he asked, looking up at his partner.

"*Are* you okay?" the white-haired man asked her, his gaze traveling from the top of her head down to her knees. He frowned. "Do you need anything, sweetheart? We have some croissants if you want something to eat."

"How long has she been here?" the younger man whispered, but she heard it loud and clear.

Her fingers dug into her biceps as she waited for the answer.

The older man shrugged. "Did someone hurt you, dear? Do you have a phone? Need us to call someone for you?"

She shuddered and took another step back. Wiped the rain from her eyes. Smoothed her hair from her face. "I'm sorry," she said, licking raindrops from her lips. "S-sorry to bother you."

She turned and jogged onto the road. The two men didn't chase after her. She heard the squeaky cottage door closing as she made it to an intersection. She was back on Commercial Street. The Pilgrim's Monument was off to her left, and the ocean was in front of her, which meant she was in the West End.

Haverman's was in the East End. When had she left work? Where had she left her bike?

She began to meander toward the center of town, pausing only to observe a lone pigeon, its purple-tinged neck puffed out with seeming determination, bobbing along the sidewalk as if it was setting out to see the world. The rain tapered to a sprinkle and then to a mist, and she breathed it in, imagining the tiny specks of water gathering on the inside of her nose, her throat, her chest. Filling up every space, every cell. She wrung out her soggy shirt. With every step, her heels exacted a sad, distressed squish from her saturated flip-flops.

She was not alone here. If she were dead, then these other people were, too, the ones out walking their dogs and carrying cups of coffee and folding up their umbrellas and squinting at the sky. She flinched as the ferry's horn sounded off, a deep bellow of warning before the vessel shoved off into the bay. Unless the 8:30 a.m. fast ferry to Boston was piloted by Charon himself, she probably wasn't dead.

But she was tired. Her pace slowed to a zombie shuffle, and she plopped down on the steps of a T-shirt store. Her hands found her face, sliding over the planes of her cheeks and forehead, over the dome of her skull and down to her scraggly, loose ponytail.

"Layla?"

A guy was standing in front of her, clutching a paper coffee cup and frowning. His name floated up to the surface of her thoughts, alone and unaccompanied. "Matt?"

Her voice was small and hoarse but hers.

"What are you doing?" Matt asked. He had curly brown hair that was thinning on top and a few days' worth of stubble. He wore a shirt with *Cory's Bike Rentals* emblazoned across the chest. He looked up and down the street. "Have you been out all night?"

"Yes." Better than telling him she wasn't sure.

"Doing what?" He glared at her skinned-up knees as he fished his phone from his pocket. "Jesus," he muttered.

She wanted to ask how they knew each other, but she understood instinctively that it would make things worse. "Who are you texting?"

His thumb marched over the screen of his phone. "Who do you think?"

She began to push herself up from the steps, but Matt's hand clamped over her shoulder. She yelped, and he drew his hand back as if she'd bitten him. Her butt hit the steps again. Matt shook his head. He said something she couldn't catch because the buzz between her ears was too loud.

"I'm going to go get you something to eat," he said, louder this time, pointing to the Portuguese bakery right across the street. "You want a muffin? Or one of those fried dough things?"

She put her hand on her stomach, then peered down at it. When she raised her head, he was gone, but then he was back, carrying a wax paper sack. He shoved it at her. "You can pay me back later." His look said he doubted she was good for it.

The smell of cinnamon reached her, and she pushed her nose into the bag. Then she was shoving chunks of sweet, chewy pastry into her mouth. She couldn't eat fast enough. She needed five more just like it. She needed a million of them.

"What the fuck."

This voice she recognized, but she was too busy chewing to name its owner.

"That cost me three fifty," Matt said to Esteban, who was now standing next to him, wearing worn-out boat shoes and khaki shorts and a Haverman's T-shirt. His black hair was wet-looking, slicked back.

"This is where you found her?" he asked Matt as he took her by the arm. He pulled her up and steadied her with a hand on the small of her back. The wax paper sack crumpled in her fist.

"Ask *her*, dude," Matt said. "I have to get to work." He tossed an exasperated, disapproving look over his shoulder as he headed up the street toward the East End.

"I was out looking for you until three," Esteban snapped, steering her up the sidewalk. "I called Jaliesa, and she said you took off before your shift was even over. Where the hell have you been?"

"I worked last night," she said. The memories were hazy but there, a relief and a worry at the same time.

Esteban sighed, but he didn't say more. He simply guided her along, and she didn't fight him. She even knew where they were going. The boardinghouse. Robin's egg blue, paint peeling from the wooden siding, narrow stairs. He unlocked the front door and pushed her upward, to the third floor, and then to the second room on the right, with a loose doorknob that he had to twist a few times to open. The place was hushed, though she could hear strains of Led Zeppelin coming through the door next to Esteban's.

The cramped room was taken up almost entirely by a double bed, its headboard a shuttered window, the walls tilting inward as if they were about to collapse on top of them. She was several inches shorter than Esteban, and still she wanted to duck her head. He pushed her onto the bed and removed her flip-flops, then her shirt, his movements brusque. He knelt by the bed and pulled a battered suitcase from underneath. "Do you want a shower or just dry clothes?"

When she didn't answer, he sighed again and pushed a red shirt at her chest. She put it on. It was huge, the hem hitting her midthigh.

She rose and unbuttoned her shorts. They slid down her legs, soggy and cold, and suddenly she was desperate to get them off, to get them away. She kicked them toward the door. Underwear, too, because it was soaked through. She sat down on the foot of the bed again.

Esteban slid the suitcase under the bed. "Are you okay?" he asked. "Matt said you were messed up. Did you party last night?" He rose and took her face in his hands, turning her head up so she was looking at the old glass light fixture on the ceiling. "Did you take something?"

She tried to shake her head, but his hands prevented much movement. "I need to sleep," she said. "I'm tired."

He let her go. "I have to be in at ten anyway." He worked days at Haverman's and the occasional double. "Did Lou pay you last night?"

Her gaze flicked to her shorts, in a heap by the door. "I don't think so."

"It's the end of the month, and I need to pay rent. It'd be nice if you chipped in."

"Oh. Okay."

He crossed his arms over his chest. "You've been here longer than I expected."

"Sure." She frowned. "You told me I could stay for as long as I wanted."

It was more of a question, a need for confirmation, but it was also the wrong thing to say. "I've done everything for you that I could, Layla! I stuck my neck out for you with Lou. I gave you a place to stay." He looked at her there, the edge of the red shirt barely covering her upper thighs. "I've been your friend."

Layla tugged the hem all the way down to her knees.

He let out an exasperated groan. "How long do you think you'll need a place?"

She shrugged, gaze focused on her own feet. Her knees were stinging. Her left arm ached. She had no idea where her bike was.

"Look," he said, then paused. "Okay, look. Do you *have* anywhere to go? Did your folks kick you out or something? Are you from the Cape? You got people who might come get you?"

He had asked her this before.

"Because you don't seem like you should be on your own," he continued. "I mean, look at you."

She raised her knees, tucking them under the shirt until it stretched over her legs like a tent, pulling at the raw skin underneath. The pain was warm. It connected her to her body. "I can go."

"I'm not asking you to go, dammit! I'm just trying to know you, okay? I figured you'd talk to me when you got comfortable, but you're... I don't know. I can't figure out what's up with you." He sank down on the bed next to her, shoulders slumped. "You can trust me. I've been looking out for you, haven't I?"

She nodded.

He made a pained face. "Oh, honey. Look. I'm sorry." He put his arm around her, pulled her to him. It hurt her shoulder and arm, but she didn't resist. Her gaze rested on the loose doorknob. It still worked, but not well. Like her, she supposed.

"I can give you some money," she said.

"Forget I mentioned it. It was just—it was a rough night. I was worried about you."

"Why?"

"I like you." He looked down at her. "I care about you. I wish you'd trust me enough to let me in. And I thought we were headed in the right direction, but then last night..."

"I'm sorry."

"Forget it. I'm glad you're okay. You really should have a phone, though. I can probably get you one if you want. For cheap. I know a guy." He smiled. His upper left canine was gray. He let her go and stood up again. "I'd better head out, though. Gotta sling the drinks and pay the bills."

He was still smiling, but she could tell he wasn't actually happy. She didn't move as he opened the door, as he stepped into the hall and then turned back to her. "I'm gonna see you tonight?" he asked. "We could go for a walk. Talk a little more?"

She smiled at him. He nodded and closed the door.

She fell back onto the bed and stared up at the light fixture. Assorted bug carcasses littered the glass bowl that covered the light bulb. She wondered if the heat had killed them. Or the light, flooding every inch of that space, magnified by the glass, too bright and confusing.

Esteban wanted to talk. Wanted to know her. Where she came from. What she was doing in Provincetown. Where she was headed next. He thought she didn't trust him, and that was why she'd kept to herself, hadn't told him a thing.

But that wasn't it.

She *couldn't* tell him about herself.

Because she honestly didn't know.

FRIDAY, JULY 31,
TO SATURDAY, AUGUST 1

I don't regret calling the police last night, even though I could practically hear the dispatcher's eye roll through the phone. She asked
if I knew whether Mina had even made it to Provincetown—maybe
she went somewhere else. Free country, right? She asked when I was
supposed to meet Mina, and when I confess it was today and that I
showed up early, it only seemed to confirm her skepticism. She told
me that I should call back if I had any new information, but that
right now, with so little to go on and the high likelihood that everything was a miscommunication between me and my wife, there's not
much the police can do.

I think about taking the ferry back to Boston, meeting with Drew
in person and having it out with him, but I'm not up for that. Instead,
I stay put, hoping that my wife will come through the doorway of
the cottage, carrying with her a completely logical and innocent
explanation of where she's been.

She doesn't.

Around noon, I try to track her iPhone, and I realize that Mina
has her privacy settings efficiently and thoroughly geared to prevent
those kinds of shenanigans. I don't know if they've always been that

way—the perils of celebrity—or if she only recently changed them (the perils of...me?).

I've never thought to track her before.

Perhaps I should have.

On Friday afternoon, I call the only hospital on the Cape and several along the South Shore, as well as every hospital in Boston. I'm not sure if I'm relieved or disappointed when it turns out she isn't at any of them, when there aren't even any Jane Does admitted since Monday.

I also check with her neighbors. The couple who lives next door on the right, a slender older man and his younger, buff, pink-haired partner, invite me inside and offer me a drink. Their home is an ode to P-town, maritime and quaint, the walls bedecked with local art and old photographs of the docks and supper clubs. The older guy, whose name is Chris, tells me that he's been spending summers here since the eighties, and his partner, Aaron, explains that they met at the A-House about five years ago and have been inseparable ever since. They tell me they bought this place three years ago and did a whole gut rehab, and that Mina showed up with cake and lemonade to welcome them when they finally moved in last year. Over martinis made with, they inform me, South Hollow's Dry Line gin, which is a favorite of Mina's, Aaron tells me that he saw her leave in her car, but he can't remember if it was Monday or Tuesday evening. And he doesn't know if she came back after that. Chris asks if it's possible that Mina and I crossed wires—perhaps she's returned to Boston? I'd love to believe that, but surely she'd have at least texted me by now if she were back in our Brookline condo.

The elderly widow who lives in the cottage to the left says she saw Mina loading a cake carrier into her car on Monday evening. She says

I'm lucky, that Mina is a wonderful baker, that my wife has dropped off a batch of cookies on more than one occasion—raspberry short-bread and lemon butter the last time, about two weeks ago. And I smile and agree, yes, Mina's an awesome baker, no shortcuts, no mixes, and I accept her invitation to come over for tea the next time Mina and I are in town for the weekend. It's all very nice, but as I turn away from her door, my heart is pounding.

Before I'm even back inside the cottage, I'm dialing the police again. I tell the dispatcher I have new information. This time, she puts me through to the detective, who answers with a gruff, "Correia here."

I introduce myself. I explain everything. I tell her that Mina was definitely in Provincetown on Monday and that several of her neighbors saw her. That puts the disappearance in their jurisdiction.

Detective Correia is relatively unimpressed. Adults are allowed to disappear if they want to, she tells me. Mina took her car, her wallet, and her phone, and she could be in Florida or California by now, which is totally within her rights. She takes down all the usual infor-mation, though. I give her Mina's vital stats and email her a picture of my wife, links to her website and social media, our addresses in Brookline and here in Provincetown, my phone number and hers, all of it. I give her the color and plate number of Mina's Prius. I describe the last time I saw Mina. When the officer asks if we were having "relationship issues," I say we weren't, because we weren't. One fight is not a "relationship issue." It's just a fight. Every couple fights. And besides, it was barely that.

What happened: I asked Mina a question about when we could get pregnant, and Mina refused to answer it, and then I lost it and accused her of having second thoughts about sharing a life with me.

She said, "That was a shitty thing to say," and I said, "That wasn't exactly a denial," and then she withdrew into her shell, not even making eye contact, while I sulked and drank Macallan and fell asleep on the couch, and the next morning, she left.

Is it a fight when only one person participates?

The detective asks if Mina has any family. When I tell her, she asks if I've checked in with Mina's parents, especially because they live nearby—maybe Mina simply went to visit them for a couple of days? The detective's tone gives me the sense that she doesn't think much of the efforts I've taken to contact Mina so far. As if I expected the police to do my work for me, to handle my personal life because I can't quite manage it. I have trouble blaming her for that.

She promises they'll put out a BOLO for Mina and inform Truro police to be on the lookout as well, then reminds me that it's the middle of the summer season, which means that they're dealing with ten times more disruptive drunks, tweaked-out partiers, sex assaults, thefts, and yes, people temporarily going missing, than at any other time of year. Then she gives me her full name—Detective Felicia Correia—and asks me to let her know if Mina turns up or if anything else comes to light. She assures me Mina will probably show up soon, as most people do, and she hangs up. Busy, busy, on to the next caller.

Shamed by Correia, I dial Mina's parents next, more out of obligation than confidence that they'll be helpful in telling me where she is. I've always been close with my parents, and I talk on the phone with my mom at least once a week now that Dad's gone. Mina marvels at that and has said on more than one occasion that she'd literally go nuts if she had to spend that much time speaking to her own mother. When I joked one time that my mom isn't exactly a boon for my sanity, Mina gave me what I can only describe as a patronizing smile. So I brace myself for tension and unpleasantness as Rose Harkin Richards answers the phone.

What I get is the opposite: Mina's mother sounds surprised when I say my name—she hasn't spoken to me often enough to know my voice—but when I tell her I'm in Provincetown, she immediately invites me out for a visit the next day. She seems truly excited and asks me whether I have any allergies or food sensitivities. Although it's the reason I called, I don't ask if she knows where Mina is or tell her that Mina is missing, her pleasant tone proving to me that she doesn't know anything's amiss. Then she tells me she really must go because she has to visit a friend who's in the hospital all the way down in Hyannis and visiting hours end at eight. I hang up without managing to wedge more than a few words into the conversation. Rose's bubbliness shunted me along like a fast-moving current, and I didn't end up anywhere near where I thought I would.

On Saturday morning, after another near-sleepless night spent waiting for my wife to show up, I get out of my Lyft and turn to the front door of my in-laws' house. I'm keenly aware of the strangeness; Mina never brought me out to meet them or visit, even though she owns a home only ten miles away. And now I'm about to tell these nice people that I have no idea where their daughter has run off to.

As my ride pulls away, I stand frozen in the drive, bleached white shells crunching beneath my shoes as I shift my weight from foot to foot. Scott and Rose live right on the border of the National Seashore lands, only half a mile off Route 6, in a charming old Cape house surrounded by wax myrtles and evergreens on all sides. You can't even see the house until you pull into the drive, so even though we're in the middle of high season and the population around here has quintupled, right here, you wouldn't think there was another soul around for miles.

The only car in the carport is a Cadillac that's at least ten years old, if not fifteen. There's a pickup parked at the side of the house, and an old brown Mercedes in the drive. Mina's Prius isn't anywhere to be seen, and I swallow back a sour pang of disappointment. It would have been so easy, so obvious, so nice if she had just been here.

"Hello?"

I turn to see a woman with shoulder-length silver hair coming out the front door, but it isn't Mina's mom. "Hi," I say.

Her eyes go wide. "I know who you are! Your picture's on the mantel." She jerks her thumb back toward the house and then comes toward me, her hand outstretched. A broad, flat, cloth-covered basket hangs from the crook of her other arm.

"I'm Sharon Rawlings. I live next door." She waves her fingers vaguely at the thick, scrubby wall of wax myrtles to my right, then gives my hand a quick squeeze. "Rose was just telling me that you were coming over. She showed me the wedding album, too. Such a lovely, lovely day it must have been."

"It's really nice to meet you," I say, wondering if we should have invited her to the wedding. Mina only had a few guests on her side, mostly friends from the Boston area.

Sharon holds up her basket as I glance down at it. "Rose is the sweetest lady." She flips up a corner of the flowered tea towel covering the basket's contents, revealing a large plate of scones, complete with crocks of what appear to be clotted cream and raspberry jam, garnished with little pink and yellow flowers. "These are our favorite," Sharon says. "Strawberry almond. She knew we needed the lift."

"Is everything okay?"

"Oh, my Phillip is under the weather. He'll be fine, but this week hasn't been easy."

"I'm so sorry."

"He should be out of the hospital by tomorrow night."

"Rose did say she had a friend who'd been hospitalized. I'm glad he's on the mend."

Sharon nods, looking fretful. "We were lucky. Terrible bout of food poisoning, if you can believe it."

"Seafood?"

"You'd think it, wouldn't you? Around here?" She covers the scones again. "I had told Rose he's hesitant to try solid foods just yet, and look what she did! He won't be able to help himself once he sees these."

"Mina told me that her mother's always baking something." It's one of the few concrete things she's actually said about her mom and the one thing Mina's been willing to admit they have in common.

"Oh, *always*." Sharon's smile almost looks like a grimace. "Rose is a tough lady to keep up with. Always has been." Then her expression turns mischievous. "One day I thought to myself, why even try? Especially when I can benefit from the fruits of my friend's labor?" She pats my arm. "She was telling me she hadn't gotten to spend much time with you before the wedding. It sounded like quite a whirlwind affair! I actually wondered if..."

"What?"

Sharon's cheeks have gotten a little pink. "A shotgun wedding? Not that Scott would ever—"

"No," I say. "That's not... No." I let out a burst of awkward laughter.

Sharon drops her face into her hands, looking like she wants to sink into the ground. "Oh, dear Lord. I always manage to put my foot in my mouth," she says, her voice muffled against her palms. "I'm so sorry."

"It's totally fine."

"Please don't tell Rose or Scott." She peeks up from her hands and glances toward the ruffled curtains that grace the windows at the front of the house. "I'm so embarrassed."

"I wouldn't be surprised if they wondered about it themselves, now that you mention it." I'd never even considered that people might think that about us. I don't think it would have occurred to any of our friends.

"They have some strong beliefs in that department. They were thrilled when you two decided to tie the knot before living together."

"They'd actually care about that? I don't really know them that well."

"Oh, honey." Her laughter is throaty this time. She shakes her head. "Rose Harkin Richards is a Southern belle, from skin to soul. Loves God, country, and a perfectly set table. And Scott, he loves Rose. Once you know that about them, the rest makes sense. I'd better get going." She gives my arm another pat and heads for the Mercedes, pausing to wave toward the front door as she gets in.

Rose emerges from the house as Sharon pulls out of the drive. Mina's mother is wearing a flowered sundress and pink cardigan. She's a formidable woman, much taller than her daughter. I'm six two, and Rose has got to be only an inch or two shorter than I am. Her shoulders are broad. Everything about her is broad, in fact, including her smile. She holds out her arms. "It's *so* good to see you again," she says warmly as she envelops me in her perfumy embrace and voluptuous accent. "Your visit is an answer to prayer. We were hoping to get to know our new son! You met Sharon?"

"She was telling me how much she appreciated the scones."

Rose releases me, shaking her head. "It was a close call, apparently. Closer than she's making it out to be. She's such a tough lady, and she doesn't like to make a big deal when things are troubling her. He's been in the hospital for days, though! I visited with him last night for a little while, and the poor man looked downright hollowed out. I'm hoping he'll be willing to choke down a few crumbs."

"She seemed to think the scones would bring him around. They looked great to me."

"Well, I've got something else for us." She releases me and holds the front door wide. "Scott's making drinks. Bloody Mary?"

"Sure." I follow her into the immaculate living room. Wooden floors, rattan area rug, a chipped antique coffee table painted sea green, squashy beige couch and chairs in front of the fireplace. One of our wedding pictures is on the mantelpiece, black-and-white with me and Mina in the center and her parents on either side of us. Right next to it is a poem about footprints in the sand, words printed over a beach scene, a cross Photoshopped into the corner of the image.

"Sit down, sit down. Are you hungry?"

I shake my head, and her smile sags a bit.

"I've made a giant batch of zucchini bread, and I just finished the blackberry compote," she informs me. "Picked the zucchinis and berries right out back this morning."

"Now that I think about it, I'm famished."

Rose looks delighted. She leaves me in the living room and disappears into the kitchen, where I hear her murmuring to Scott. A moment later, he emerges with a Bloody Mary, which he hands to me. "We're glad to have you here, Alex," he says quietly. "It's nice to see you again."

From what I can tell, Scott says everything quietly. At the wedding, Rose did the talking for both of them while he stared into his drink and let her tow him around. The only time he smiled was when he looked at Mina. Meanwhile, as far as I could tell, Rose and Mina barely interacted after we got through with the wedding pictures. While Mina and I danced and celebrated with our friends, Rose circulated, seeming to enjoy being the mother of the bride and determined to make friends with every single guest, including my mom, who didn't quite seem to know what to make of her.

Scott seems like the perfect match for his wife—he's as big as she is. Same height, same width. But in every other way, he's her opposite, as if he'd been built to complement her. He rarely makes a noise while she fills the room with the sound of her voice. His stillness is the inverse of her bustling energy. When she walks into the room carrying a tray laden with thick slices of bread beside a crock of butter and another of compote, Scott fetches a vase of flowers and brings it to the coffee table. When she sits down next to me and leans forward attentively, he stands behind her chair like a butler.

They bow their heads at the same time and mutter quietly for a moment. A prayer, I realize, too late to at least bow my head in respect. They clearly don't expect me to join in; maybe Mina told them I'm not religious. Mina describes herself as a recovering Protestant, but I think she's careful around her parents. After talking with Sharon, I can see why Mina insisted we have a minister perform the wedding.

Once Rose has served me a plate of bread, once I've taken a sip of my drink and been informed the mix was made from scratch with heirloom tomatoes from the garden, she fixes me with a look. She has the same pale-gray eyes as her daughter, the only physical similarity they share. "She didn't come with you," she says. Her tone is pleasant, as if she were simply commenting about the weather. "Did she send you over by yourself, or did you decide you needed to independently verify that we're exactly as monstrous as she's told you?"

I blink at her. "She hasn't—"

Rose's face breaks into a smile once more, and she lets out a laugh. "You poor thing. I'm joking!" She grins and shakes her head as she plucks crumbs from the coffee table and places them back on the scone plate, one by one. "I'm sorry. We finally have a chance to visit with you, and I'm already scaring you away!"

"No, it's all right," I say. "I was actually hoping to talk to you about Mina." Then I pause and glance up at Scott, who is once again looking into his drink.

"Scott," says Rose. "Why don't you go make those bouquets and get them into the fridge?" As her husband obeys, she turns back to me. "It's for one of the ladies in my Bible study. Her mother passed, and the wake is tonight. We're providing the flowers."

Startled by the change of subject, I stammer, "That's really kind of you." Rose is one of those church ladies, always whipping up a casserole for a funeral or a cake for a baby shower or meals to freeze for families with a loved one in the hospital. She's the one who coordinates the socials and the bake sales and the youth groups and the fund-raisers for missionaries. She's the one who drives the children of undocumented landscapers to their medical appointments and runs boot and coat drives for the poor in the winter. I know all this not because Mina told me or because I'm seeing it live and in person today. Rose friended me on Facebook just after the wedding, and I've seen post after post about her good deeds and how each blesses her just as much as those she serves. "I don't know how you find the time, but I'm sure it's really appreciated."

She pats my knee. Despite all her gardening and baking, her fingernails are perfect ovals, shimmering with a pearly white polish. I'm thinking Scott does most of the dirty work. "I do what I can to help people, but I'm not exactly saving the world from cancer like you are."

I take a bite of my zucchini bread. "This is delicious."

Rose is practically glowing with the compliment, and it makes my chest hurt, because now I have to tell her why I'm here. "Rose, have you heard from Mina this past week?"

"She didn't tell you? She came to dinner on Monday, right out of the blue! Such a treat, since we hadn't seen hide nor hair of her since the big day." She gives me a perplexed look. "She's not in Provincetown with you?"

When I don't immediately answer, she says, "I'm surprised you newlyweds are choosing to spend so much time apart!"

"She was here Monday?" I sit back in my chair. One of Mina's neighbors saw her putting a cake carrier into her car, and another saw her leaving on Monday or Tuesday night, and it could have been to visit her parents. "Did she say anything about her plans?"

"Plans?" Rose's glow has dimmed. "Why? Are you two having problems already?"

Now, this is awkward. I have no idea whether Mina told her parents anything about our fight or our marriage. I don't see why she would have, given her general pattern of parental avoidance, but then again, I wouldn't have predicted she'd choose to spend her Monday evening with them, either.

"No," I say. "I mean, we're both adjusting to married life, but nothing serious. It's just that..." I pause. There's no way to say this that sounds okay. No way to smooth it over or keep up appearances.

"Mina left Boston for Provincetown on Monday morning, Rose, and I haven't heard from her since." I say it all quickly, like ripping off the proverbial Band-Aid. "I took the ferry from Boston on Wednesday, but she wasn't at the cottage. She's not answering her phone. And I guess now I know that she visited you on Monday, but I'd sure like to know where she went after that and where she is now. Because I have no idea."

Scott appears in the doorway to the kitchen, but Rose doesn't seem to notice. Her hand has risen from her chest to her throat, and it seems like there's something caught there. "Do you think something happened to her?" she asks hoarsely.

"I don't know. Did she seem worried or upset on Monday?"

"She seemed perfectly fine, didn't she, Scott?"

Scott's nod is barely perceptible.

"When did she leave that night?" Rose asks him. "I didn't see her after the two of you went out to your workshop." She gestures at her husband and tells me, "This one is always working on a project, and he loves to show off for his daughter."

"She left around nine," Scott says, looking like a man who has never shown off for anyone ever.

"She seemed perfectly fine," Rose says again, and it makes me glad I didn't mention the fight. "Oh, do you think she's been in an accident?"

"I called all the hospitals in the area," I offer. "She wasn't at any of them. Not a Jane Doe, either."

Rose's fingers are worrying at her throat, and I realize she's rubbing a crucifix pendant on a thin gold chain. "We could call hospitals a little farther away," she says. "Just to make sure."

"Have you reported this to the police?" Scott asks.

I nod.

"Let me guess," Rose says bitterly, locking gazes with her husband. "They told you that she's an adult and has a right to disappear."

"How did you know?" I ask.

"Hmm?" Rose whips around to focus on me again. "Oh. I've seen every episode of *Law & Order* they ever made. The real ones, anyway. I don't count the ones after Lennie Briscoe died."

"I really hope this isn't headed in that direction," I say.

"My daughter is a free spirit," Rose says, jabbing at the ice in her glass with a stalk of celery. "You understand that. She's a creative person." She takes a long pull from her drink, looking like she needs the fortification.

"I do understand that," I say. "I've seen her get lost inside her own head sometimes, but never actually lost."

Rose lets out a choked little grunt before waving the noise away and setting her glass onto its marble coaster with a hard *clack*. "A bit of spice in my throat," she says hoarsely.

"I'm worried about her, Rose."

"And now we are, too. Sometimes I think she forgets that kind of thing," Rose murmurs. "How other people worry. How it affects us." Tears shine in her eyes. "None of her Boston friends have heard from her?"

"They might have. I'll check." Until now, I've been telling myself it was all going to be all right, but Rose's reaction is making this real. "And I'll call the police again. Maybe the Truro police?"

"Try the state police," says Rose. "Do you have any shared credit cards?" When I nod, she says, "Check to see if she's made any purchases. That could give you a hint as to where she's been." She looks at Scott again, but the man is still standing there like he's been carved out of ice.

"I'll do that," I promise Rose, feeling stupid for not having done it already. "I'll check the bank account to see if she pulled anything out, too."

Rose is nodding, pressing her lips together like she's trying not to cry. I feel like a dick for coming to her like this, without having made enough of an effort first. I want to explain that I was hoping Mina was here, but that sounds so lame that I'm sure it would make things worse.

"Her phone," Rose says. "What about her phone? Can't you track it?"

"We haven't changed that account yet. She's still got her own." And come to think of it, Mina has credit cards of her own, too, so if she's trying to avoid being found, it's unlikely she would have used the one we share. I'm still going to check it, but helplessness is already strangling me. "I'm sorry for worrying you two."

"It's our job to worry," says Rose. She lets out a weak chuckle. "We've been worrying about her for her entire life, whether she wants us to or not."

Scott is looking out the window now, to their lush garden plot, a riot of red and orange and purple and green. Then he walks to the double doors that lead out to the patio. "I'll be in my workshop," he says. "Nice seeing you, Alex."

He leaves, closing the doors gently. I watch him trudge across the patio toward a shed beyond the garden. It's painted to match the house, right down to the shutters.

"I'm sorry for my husband's rudeness," Rose says. "He's a good man. The most wonderful man. Always took care of us. Worked himself to the bone. He'd do anything to provide, especially for his daughter. But social graces..." She smiles. "Not in his DNA."

She offers me another slice of zucchini bread.

Again, it feels like the walls are closing in. I don't know why I thought Mina's parents might have the answers. Maybe because it was better than facing what's in front of me now—a missing wife, police who don't seem to give a shit, and not many places to look.

Rose is back to picking tiny crumbs from the coffee table. "I'm sure we'll find her," she says. "She's fine." She nods as if she's made a decision. "I know it might not be your thing, but will you pray with me, Alex? I wouldn't normally ask, but right now..." She looks like she's about to burst into tears. "It would mean a lot to me."

The next minutes are among the most uncomfortable I've ever endured. I hold hands with Mina's mother, bow my head, and listen to her beg the Lord Jesus to bring her baby home to her family and the husband who loves her.

Unbidden, I'm reminded of Mina's rings, left abandoned in her cottage.

What if Mina doesn't *want* to come home to me?

Anything could have happened to her. An accident. A kidnapping. But I also can't avoid a possibility that's both more plausible and probable: she chose this. She wanted to get away from me, and she decided to disappear. She's a writer. A creative person. Has a flare for the dramatic. Her mother literally just said as much. Maybe Mina figured this was the best way to punish me for being an asshole.

I never thought she would do something like this. But then again, I met her less than a year ago. How well do I know her, really?

After Rose says "amen" and releases my hand from her warm, strong grip, I make my excuses, offer my apologies, promise to keep her updated, and leave as quickly as my legs will carry me.

CHAPTER THREE

The sun had come out by the time she emerged from the boardinghouse. She'd showered and changed into a clean set of clothes that had been left folded on a shelf in the bathroom. She was pretty sure they were hers—they fit reasonably well, and the shirt said Haverman's on the front. Her flip-flops still squished with every step as she set out along the sidewalk, but the rest of her was dry. She enjoyed the warmth of the summer sun on her skin for a moment, and then she began to sweat. She tromped along Commercial back to the West End, looking for her bike—until she remembered that there was nothing that really set it apart from any other bike. Nothing except the combination on her lock. One-two-zero-four. That, she could remember. The rest of...everything...was like a murmured conversation coming from behind a closed door.

Sometimes that frightened her. It wasn't as if she didn't care at all. She knew she was supposed to have the answers to questions people asked her, like where and whether she was going to school or what had brought her to Provincetown. Sometimes she tried to remember, but that trying made her head throb and her teeth hurt. It made her heart pound and her skin tingle. She could only bear to do it for a few minutes at a time before giving up. And did it matter, really? She was here, and she was alive, and she had a place to stay, and she wasn't hungry, and nobody was hurting her, and she even had a job. That was more than a lot of people had.

She gave up searching for her bike and wandered for a while. The streets around the pier were packed with milling tourists, straight couples, gay couples, families with kids, groups of friends heading for the bars, and the drag queens with their impossibly high heels and big hair and impressive masks of makeup. They were like walking works of art, and she couldn't help but watch them and smile. The air was filled with the scent of fried things and saltwater taffy, and people walked by with ice cream cones stacked with fat scoops of colorful, melty gelato. She wasn't sure when she'd eaten last. She wished she had some money so she could buy something to eat.

Money.

She was pretty sure she was supposed to be at work. Her pace quickened as her thoughts jolted out of their sluggish drift, crystallizing into anxious splinters. The boardinghouse was a good place to stay. She didn't want to lose it. She wasn't sure where she'd go if Esteban kicked her out, and it seemed like he was thinking of it. She should get some money and give it to him, to help pay the rent. She looked down at the shirt. She worked at Haverman's, and Lou was supposed to pay her.

She marched up Commercial as the ferry horn sounded off. She knew the sound, almost knew the schedule, wondered what it was like to get on that boat and float away to Boston. Maybe she'd do it someday. She frowned—had she done it before? She pushed the question away and skipped up onto the sidewalk to allow a car to squeeze through the crowded street.

She paused in front of Haverman's, packed and bustling with

its weekend crowd. Esteban was behind the bar, apron on, mixing drinks and smiling at a customer as a rivulet of sweat made its way down his temple. Jaliesa was there, too. And Amber—

"Hey, kitty," said a gruff voice. She looked toward a screened window on the second floor of the Haverman's house. "Yeah, you. Get up here. We need to talk."

Lou. Well, she needed to talk to him, too. She made her way to the alley, through the kitchen, and up the stairs to the un-air-conditioned second floor. The stale air pressed against her like an overfriendly dog. Lou, a big man with black, squiggly chest hair poking up from the collar of his shirt, leaned out of his office. "You always turn up, like a stray."

She paused.

He rolled his eyes and beckoned her into his office. She stood on the threshold; the cramped, cluttered room—rickety chair, old wooden desk nearly buckling under the weight of stacks and stacks of ledgers, filing cabinets covering every inch of remaining wall— didn't seem able to accommodate another body. Lou sat on the edge of his desk, steadying a teetering pile dislodged by his butt. He folded his arms over his chest. "You walked off yesterday in the middle of table service, Layla girl. Give me one reason why I should let you come within twenty feet of my establishment again."

Suddenly, her mouth was filled with too much saliva, and she swallowed noisily. The sound filled her whole head. "I'm sorry," she said. "I...I felt sick."

"Amber said as much, but you left us scrambling." He chuckled. "And you don't even work here!"

"I..." Confusion pushed too many words into her throat at once, where they got caught in one big pileup. She remembered closing her eyes as steam wafted up from the dishes in the dishwasher, the plates and glasses ready to sear the fingertips off anyone stupid enough to grab them before they cooled. She remembered standing next to the ovens, watching the cheese melting and bubbling over pizzas and crocks of French onion soup.

"Oh, don't wet yourself. Officially, I meant." He muttered something about his heart being soft. "It's hard to find good bartenders. I needed to keep Esteban happy. But it looks like he's got buyer's remorse if you ask me."

"I want to give him some money for rent."

Lou's eyebrows shot up. "I figured you were working that off already. Amber told me you were shacking up with him."

Her heart was beating too quickly, and it made her short of breath. She shook her head.

"None of my business anyway." He opened a file drawer and pulled out an envelope, which he held out and shook. "For the last two weeks. You did pretty good. But if you ever disappear before a shift is over again, you better not come back."

She took the envelope and peeked inside. It contained a healthy stack of twenties. She had no idea how many, but it seemed like a lot of money. Enough to pay Esteban and have plenty left. Happiness warmed her chest, and she let out a laugh.

"What are you laughing at?" Lou said, scowling. "That's a fair wage right there."

"No, it's not that at all." Still giggling, she folded the envelope and stuffed it into the pocket of her shorts. "I appreciate it, that's all."

Lou grunted. "Speaking of not coming back, I got a busboy out. Another one bites the dust. You're up. Now get out of my sight."

"Okay. Thank you." Elation carried her down the hall. She had *money*. Maybe she could get herself a new bike. And a phone. Maybe a ferry ticket. She skipped down the stairs, all the way into the steamy kitchen. She grabbed an apron from the stack in the closet and headed for the outside, snagging an empty basin from next to the dishwasher as she went. The beer garden was so packed that the waitresses, including Amber, had to hold the trays high to avoid beaning the customers. People were clustered along the bar like barnacles, shoulders pressed together and drinks sweating in their hands.

She threw herself into her work, loading up dishes as soon as customers pushed their chairs back, shuttling full basins to the dishwasher, carrying fresh settings back out and laying the tables just as quickly. The work absorbed her, and she got lost in watching her own hands moving like bees over honeysuckle, almost as if they were someone else's and she was an observer, safe and swaddled behind her eyes.

A couple of hours later, she emerged from the bathroom, her hands still wet. Amber was standing there, blocking her path back to the kitchen. "I'm surprised Lou let you come back," she said, the sinewy lines of her neck moving with every word. "He was absolutely rippin' last night."

"I won't do it again."

"Good, because I had to clean the whole thing up." Amber made a gagging noise. "One of your customers puked all over the floor about two minutes after you took off. Jaliesa said he was giving you a hard time—the red-haired guy? Kind of cute but totally sloppy. What a mess."

Red-haired guy. She peered down at her own arm as the memory wrapped its fingers around her limb. She could picture his bloodshot eyes and feel the shaky strength of his grip. The skin of her left forearm went rough with goose bumps.

Amber poked her in the shoulder. "His friends said he mistook you for someone else."

She rubbed her forearm against her side, smoothing everything down. "Happens all the time."

"Really?"

"I must have a familiar face."

Amber's eyes narrowed. "I Googled you last night. Couldn't find a single Layla Watersley anywhere. No Facebook, no Twitter, no Instagram, no nothing."

"You probably didn't spell my name right."

She made to slide past Amber in the narrow hallway, but the woman barred her way with a skinny arm. "I want to help you, Layla! I'm trying to be your friend. Lots of people change their names or whatever—I'm not saying you did anything wrong. You seem...like you need a friend."

"Esteban is my friend."

Amber arched one eyebrow, and it wrinkled half her forehead. "Esteban wants a blond blow-up doll, doll. Been there, done that. Probably in the same place you did. You bump your head on the walls yet?"

There had been only one bed in his room. Suddenly, the blank spaces in her memory weren't a source of comfort. They were dark alleys where anything could happen.

"I need to get back to work," she said, and then her throat constricted. It sounded like someone else had said those words, someone she didn't like.

Amber moved her arm. "Don't say I didn't warn you," she muttered at Layla's back.

Sweat dampened her armpits as she plowed through the swinging door to the beer garden and was greeted by a "Whoa!" from the other side. Esteban stood there, holding the door. He gave her a smile. "You nearly broke my nose."

"Sorry," she said and winced. This voice.

He gave her a concerned look, then glanced over her shoulder. "What did you say to her?"

"Nothing but a little truth, *Tebi*," Amber said from behind her. *Her* voice had gone flinty. She edged past them, her face morphing from grimace to grin as she crossed the threshold. "Excuse me now."

Esteban gripped the door and shook his head. "Bitter as hell."

She looked back and forth from Esteban to Amber and back again. "I didn't know..."

He drew his head back. "I told you about her, soon as you came to work here. I was totally honest with you."

"Oh yeah." It made sense, didn't it? But suddenly, everyone around her looked like a stranger, including Esteban.

"She was telling me she tried looking you up earlier," he said. "I think she's just trying to stir shit up." But his eyes said something else. It was one more way to ask the same questions all over again.

"I need to get back to work. Lou is mad at me about last night."

His shoulders slumped. "I have to go to the basement for another case of Tito's. I'll talk to you later." He opened the door wider to let her by, then disappeared behind it.

Before he came back, as Layla cleared used cocktail glasses from the bar, Jaliesa leaned forward and spoke quietly. "He really does care about you."

Layla ignored her. She had no idea what she was supposed to say. Lou thought she and Esteban were sleeping together in exchange for rent money. Amber had accused her of being a blond blow-up doll.

And Jaliesa was making it sound like Esteban was just a nice guy. Layla had thought he was, but her own mind wouldn't give her the answers, and her stomach churned with the uncertainty.

"Hey, Maggie!"

She loaded the glasses into her brown plastic basin.

"Maggie Wallace!"

"Oh, here he is again," Amber said as she edged up to the bar. "Layla, look, it's your friend from last night." She and Jaliesa were staring out at the street, but Layla picked up her basin to head to the kitchen. She'd taken two steps in that direction when Esteban pushed his way through the swinging door with a box of Tito's bottles in his arms. He squinted toward the street as a man shouted "Maggie Wallace" yet again.

Amber tugged at Layla's arm. "You should go talk to him."

"Why me?" she asked, turning around to see a redheaded guy standing right at the half wall that ran between Haverman's and the sidewalk. "I don't know him."

"Who is that guy?" Esteban asked right as Amber said, "But *he* thinks he knows you." Right as Jaliesa said, "Lou's not gonna like this at *all*."

Several patrons sitting at the bar had gone quiet and watchful, an eager audience as the redhead shifted to the side, trying to get a view of Layla. Amber pulled her forward, and Esteban said, "Hey!"

"She says she's not who you're looking for," Jaliesa said, flicking her fingers at the guy. "Step off now."

Layla dug in her heels as Amber tugged on her. "I'm trying to work!"

"Why do you think she's Maggie?" Amber asked the redhead, but then she grunted as Esteban took hold of her arm.

"Lay off," he snapped, wrenching Amber's hand away from her and turning to the redhead guy. "What the fuck is your problem, man? Layla says she doesn't know you."

The redhead scanned the faces before him—Esteban, Jaliesa, the staring patrons. He seemed to be clenching his jaw. Then he pulled out his phone, held it up, and tapped at its screen.

Taking a picture.

"Fuck this guy." Esteban lunged for the arch.

The redhead took off running, shoving through a gaggle of men who had been admiring the paintings in the storefront of the gallery next door. Esteban charged after him, and both disappeared into the crowd.

"Well, that escalated quickly," Amber said. Her tone was as dry as cracked earth.

Layla's fingers were locked over the edges of her basin. Shock and confusion jittered along her spine, up into her skull, and along her limbs. Jenn was staring at Layla, questions in her eyes. Jaliesa, too. And Amber stood next to her, smirking.

"I have to get back to work," Layla said. She turned around and marched back to the kitchen with her load of dishes.

SUNDAY, AUGUST 2,
TO MONDAY, AUGUST 3

I return to Boston Sunday afternoon, across water so choppy that people are throwing up all over the damn ferry, not even able to make it to the bathrooms at the back. Me, I haven't eaten since the zucchini bread on Saturday, so I sit in my seat, filled with a queasiness that has nothing to do with seasickness.

Mina hasn't used our joint credit card, but she withdrew $400 in cash from our bank account on Monday at 10:36 a.m. from an ATM in Barnstable, probably on her way to the cottage. At some point, she drank a glass or two of wine and left it, empty and stained with her lipstick, in the sink. She took off her engagement and wedding rings. She loaded a cake carrier into her car, presumably after baking said cake and cleaning up the kitchen, because there wasn't a trace of mess to be found apart from that wineglass. And then, on Monday or Tuesday night, she drove off and disappeared into the ether.

When I get home to our condo in Brookline, I go through her office, starting with her calendar. She has a therapy appointment scheduled for Tuesday, August 4. With Emily, who Mina told me she'd been seeing for the past several years. When I'd asked why she was meeting with a shrink, especially for so long, she laughed it off. She told me everyone needs a therapist, and writers especially. She said that she was fine but felt like it was healthy to pay attention to one's mental well-being. She sounded so confident that I'd even wondered if I should go see a therapist, too.

I plan to call Emily, but I put it off. It's Sunday, and it's late, and tomorrow morning, I have the most important meeting of my life. If I'm not sharp, it's not just my job on the line.

I go to bed, trying to ignore the impotent fury clawing its way up from the pettiest corners of my mind. Did Mina have to pick this week to do this? She knew what I was going through. She knew the stress was stealing my sleep and appetite. She knew I was worried about my mom and my best friend and the company we're trying to keep afloat. I was already texting her an apology by early Monday afternoon, and I know she was okay then, baking that damn cake, heading over to her parents'. She had to have seen it and probably all the others I sent after that. And still, she never replied. Still, she left. Still, she's gone.

And it doesn't fucking matter. I've already put this meeting off once, and the Pinewell guys are our last chance. I go over my financial model one more time, down a slug of Macallan, then another, and tumble into sleep.

I wake up early, groggy and confused, but it all comes back quickly. Too quickly. I have no space to think about Mina right now. Biostar is all that matters this morning. I get ready on autopilot, tending to my body as if I'm on the outside of it, scrubbing and shaving and draping it with clothes. Double-checking my model, stowing the laptop, driving up Memorial to Kendall Square in Cambridge.

Pinewell is on the tenth floor of one of the gleaming glass buildings that line the street. As I ride up in the elevator, I silence my phone. If Mina hasn't called yet, she's unlikely to in the next hour.

When I step out into the Pinewell office, I am greeted with a nice view of the Charles sparkling in the summer sun and the partner Drew and I met with at the beginning of last week. Blake Pierce looks relaxed in his jeans and sports jacket, all smiles and well-trimmed beard. During our first meeting, he joked about how his Model S is smarter than he is, that he was considering making *it* a partner, but I've looked the guy up. He's an MD from Harvard, just one who doesn't whip it out and lay it on the table first chance he gets.

He gives my hand a vigorous double pump. "Feeling better today? Your assistant said you had an awful cold last week."

A nice, easy excuse, and far preferable to the truth. "Much better, thanks. Appreciate the reschedule on such short notice."

"Happy to accommodate. Now, don't take this the wrong way, but you look like a man in need of really good espresso." He gestures eagerly toward a coffee bar that takes up the back half of their reception area. On one side, atop the glazed concrete counter, sits a beer tap—Trillium, of course, a source of bragging rights in these here parts—and on the other end is a machine that looks a lot like an engine, slick and chrome with the word *Speedster* emblazoned on one end.

"They only make four hundred of these babies a year," he says as he snags a little ceramic cup from the cabinet. "Best rocket fuel on the planet."

"Can you make it a cappuccino?" Any more acid and it'll probably burn a hole right through my stomach.

"Can do, but I'm telling you, it's a shame to dilute it. Nectar of the gods." He's grinding beans to powder, packing it down into the little metal cup, slotting it into the machine.

"He always wants to show off the Speedster" comes a deep voice from behind us. I turn to see a middle-aged Indian guy, also casually dressed, also smiling. "If we cut back on our espresso budget, we could probably invest in one or two more companies this year."

"Nah. We'd all be asleep at our desks," Blake says as he steams the milk. "You have to be alert if you want to spot the real gems." He claps me on the shoulder. "Alex, this is Francis, our finance director. As I told Drew last week, if we're going to go forward, I figured it was best to make sure we're speaking the same language."

I pat my laptop bag. "Ready when you are."

Blake presses the cappuccino into my hand, laser focused. "*Now* you're ready. I have another meeting, but you two have fun. Francis, make the sausage." And then it's like someone's cut the string, and he's moved on to the next agenda item for his day. He strides down the hall, presumably toward his corner office.

I like him, but I also understand why Drew hates his guts. He's ten years younger than we are and already where Drew wants to go.

Francis leads me to a tidy office at the other end of the hall. The space is populated by orchid plants on every available flat surface. There's a Yankees pennant on the wall, and I wonder if he's a diehard fan or just likes to bait people. On the desk next to his laptop is a picture of him with what I assume is his family, solemn-looking wife, two smiling teenagers. He sees me looking and nods. "I've got one at Harvard and the other at Hopkins. I won't be retiring anytime soon. Do you have children?"

"A daughter. She's five."

"That's a fun age," Francis says, efficiently concluding the obligatory small-talk portion of the program as he moves us to a conference table across the office. "Let's set up here."

I fire up my laptop, pull up the model, and walk him through. Of all the Cambridge VCs we've met with, Pinewell is the only one we've gotten into the details with, mostly because Drew walked away from the others in search of a better deal. He thought they'd come crawling back to us with offers to sweeten the pot, but it's obvious—to me, at least—that these guys have plenty of options.

For Biostar, Pinewell is the only option we have left.

"So here you can see how I got to our valuation," I say after I run through the fundamentals. "We've got a risk-adjusted NPV of three fifty, and we estimate $80 million to get to market."

Francis has a pair of glasses perched on the tip of his nose as he peers at my screen. He sighs and sits back.

"I've been pretty conservative," I say quickly.

He shrugs. "Your modeling is solid. Your assumptions are rational."

"But."

"They do not take the true risk into account."

"I factored it in." I nod toward my screen. "Sixty percent chance of FDA approval. We understand that this isn't a sure thing, but if it pans out, it's really going to be something."

He chuckles. "Off the top of my head, I can name ten companies we've invested in that have cured cancer—in mice. Just like you did." He takes off his glasses, folds them, and slips them into the inside pocket of his jacket. "We have a graveyard in the basement for all those companies, with a slick logo on every tombstone. Every single one went under."

I decide that now is a good time to drink my cappuccino.

"Allow me to explain," he continues. "While it's truly wonderful to heal the ills of our furry little friends, mice are not people."

"I think I went to business school with a few rats." I'm smiling, but I'm also grinding my teeth.

"Yes," he says. "I looked you up. You have deep experience, Mr. Zarabian, but not in biotech. This business is all about risk."

"All business is about risk. Preferably calculated."

"Is that what you did when you made the leap into this industry? Took a calculated risk?"

I drain my cup while Francis chuckles.

"Forgive me," he says. "I am simply trying to impress upon you the unique nature of our business. Let's say, for argument's sake, this ion channel that Biostar has identified is the golden ticket. Okay? You've got yourself a treatment! You've gotten CaX429 through clinic! You've gotten FDA approval!" He's been waving his arms, grinning, but then the smile drops away. "Look out the window, my friend. Within one block of here, there are twenty other MIT startups, perhaps fifty. Immunotherapy is very hot right now. If even one comes up with a treatment for squamous cell carcinoma that's 10 percent more effective than Biostar's, please tell me the name of one doctor who will choose you over the competition."

I set my coffee cup on the table next to my laptop. "The pilot data were impressive. You have to admit that, at least. And the market potential is high."

He puts his hands up. "I don't make the decisions—I'm not a partner. Blake is intrigued, and that's why we offered $25 million, pre-money, in exchange for 50 percent. It was a good offer."

"But that's less than 10 percent of our valuation—"

"And fully half of *my* valuation."

"—in exchange for control of the company!" This is the point in every past meeting where Drew's head nearly exploded. Biostar is his baby, and he's gotten us this far. He's not about to hand over the keys.

Francis gives me a look that says he's had this conversation a dozen times at least. "Alex, my friend, we have invested in sixty-three companies so far, and nearly 70 percent have gone under within five years. Do you know what that means?" He aims a finger at the picture of his family. "If I want to get those little geniuses of mine through school, the remaining 30 percent of our investments had better fly. To grow wings, you need our help. We are the opposite of dumb money—we know how to get things to market. And by necessity, we're not in the business of handing out cash without being able to pull the levers. I can tell you right now that no other sophisticated VC will either. This is how the game is played."

"Drew isn't going to like this," I mutter, snapping my laptop shut.

Francis pushes his chair away from the table. "You can always go out and find that dumb money. But another $25 million will be difficult to come by unless you have best friends in Silicon Valley or Saudi Arabia." His eyes narrow. "And I've seen a list of your board members. It's *already* full of dumb money."

"Well, I wouldn't say *dumb*—"

"Friends and family, yes? You have a lot of people who believe in you, and that's wonderful."

He makes it sound like we're a couple of college kids with a garage band. "They believe in the data," I remind him. "They want to see this therapy get to the people who could benefit from it."

"Sherri Zarabian. Your mother by any chance?" When I nod, he says, "I thought so. Does she have a PhD in immunology? How many companies has she started?"

"Look, we'd be happy to have some guidance from Pinewell. Blake knows what he's doing, and he's got an awesome reputation. But even if I convince Drew to agree to this, when we go for Series B funding in a year or two, this is going to be a problem for him." Drew's not going to want to see his shares diluted like that.

Francis waves my concern away. "He won't be around for Series B. By then, Blake will have recruited someone with market experience."

I go still. "What?"

Perhaps seeing the unguarded shock on my face, he stands up and pushes his chair in. "I have said too much. But startup CEOs are merely that, Alex."

"And startup CFOs?"

He laughs. "Like I said, my friend, your modeling is solid. Once you understand the biotech terrain a bit better, you'll do beautifully. And don't worry about your CEO. He'll make enough money on this to buy a craft distillery if he needs to drown his sorrows. But without funding..."

Without funding, he'll have 50 percent of nothing. So will my mom. And all those stock options I took in lieu of meeting the salary at my old job, all in the hope that the risk would pay off? Garbage.

"I appreciate your candor."

He's already out in the hallway. "Explain the logic to your CEO. Most of them don't mind letting go once they understand that someone else will carry the ball into the end zone. There is tremendous risk here but also great potential. Biostar has promise, and we'd love to see it succeed."

I follow him out to the lobby. I shake his hand. I ask him to thank Blake and assure him that I'll be in touch after I go over the offer with Drew and our board. Once I'm on the elevator, shell-shocked and already dreading the next several hours, I check my phone.

Four new messages.

One text is from Drew. He wants to meet me to celebrate.

Confident and oblivious bastard that he is, he assumes that I've set Pinewell straight and walked away victorious.

Another is from my mom, complaining that Mina still hasn't gotten back to her and asking if I'll have her call tonight—the book club meeting is tomorrow.

I also have a text from Caitlin, asking whether I'll be picking up Devon or if Mina will be doing it. Apparently Devon has a surprise for Mina. Something she made at her day camp yesterday.

And I have a voicemail from Detective Felicia Correia, asking me to call her back as soon as I can. Still in the shadow of the Pinewell offices, I dial the detective's number, my hands trembling.

"Mr. Zarabian," she says when I get through. "Thank you for getting back to me so quickly."

"You found her," I say. I should probably sit down. I'm feeling light-headed.

"No," she replies. "We haven't found Mina. We found her car."

"Where?"

"Park ranger called it in from Beech Forest. The car was there overnight, maybe the past two nights. Your wife's wallet and keys were locked inside."

CHAPTER FOUR

Let's get out of here," Esteban said. "There's a place I want to take
you."

She jerked her head from the pillow. Esteban was dressed and
showered. She glanced at the empty expanse of bed next to her.

"I slept on Matt's couch last night," he said. "You seemed like you
needed space."

She sat up, holding the sheet to her chest. "You want to take me
somewhere?"

He held up a key. "Borrowed a set of wheels and everything. Come
on. Nice day for a Sunday drive."

She eyed the key and then Esteban himself. She remembered the
previous evening, Amber making her uncomfortable as usual, Jaliesa
being nice, and Esteban chasing that redheaded guy down the street.
By the end of her shift, her entire body had been drooping with
exhaustion, and the rest of the night was a fog. But it seemed like
Esteban had left her alone, and it eased the anxiety she'd felt upon
seeing his face. "Okay," she said. "I'll get ready."

"I'll be outside." He closed the bedroom door, and his footsteps
retreated down the hall.

She showered and dressed in the same clothes she'd worn the

previous night. They weren't the freshest; she would wash them in the sink when they got back. She slathered on some deodorant she found in the cabinet and headed downstairs. She tucked her hand into her pocket and pulled out an envelope full of twenties. It made her feel powerful. Smiling, she slid the money back into her shorts and found Esteban waiting in the street outside the guesthouse, leaning against an old silver Corolla with a crumpled back bumper.

"Where are we going again?"

"Can't it be a surprise?" He opened the passenger door for her. She eyed the seat, and he bowed and gestured grandly. "Your chariot awaits."

A warm breeze gusted around her, and a gull cried overhead. Fluffy clouds glided across the vibrant blue of the sky. "Are we going to the beach? Do I need my swimsuit?"

He looked startled for a moment. "Oh. No. We're going to a restaurant."

"Where?"

"Come on," he said. "Just get in." He cleared his throat and chuckled. "I already told you more than I meant to! Leave me some mystery. You like that, right? Mystery?"

She took a step back.

He groaned. "Layla, just go with this, okay? It's my treat."

She put her hand on her stomach. The sun was already high in the sky, and she was hungry. Really hungry. She slid into the car.

Esteban closed the door gently and plopped into the driver's seat a moment later. The car was filthy, the back seat cluttered with empty pizza boxes and grease-spotted paper bags, the floor littered with empty soda cans and a few beer cans, too. "Sorry about the mess," Esteban said as he pulled onto the road.

"There are a bunch of restaurants we could have walked to," she commented when he turned onto Route 6 a minute later.

"I thought it would be good to get out of Provincetown." He opened the center console, which was packed with CD cases. "Remember how we met?"

She nibbled at a hangnail on her thumb.

"You said you weren't from Provincetown, and I said I wasn't either? Remember that?"

"Of course I do," she said. Though she didn't, not clearly. Playing along was often easier than confessing, as most people would fill in enough gaps that she could pretend well enough.

"You remember the song that was playing, outside of Haverman's?"

"When?"

"When we *met*. Jesus, girl. Your memory is shit. Like someone hit you in the head." He slid a CD into the player and punched the button to move to a specific track. "I remember it like it was yesterday. You were sitting on the curb, right outside the restaurant, and Lou sent me out to get rid of you because we didn't need a homeless person scaring away customers. You remember the song that was playing?"

"You do?" she asked.

A song began to play, the first notes washing over her, the next couple catching like cogs. It was familiar, so familiar. It was the tune she'd been humming for...as long as she could remember. "Oh! Yeah. I know this one."

He grunted. "Not sure how you'd forget. You remember what you said to me?"

"When we met?"

"I didn't think you were high, but now I wonder."

Had she been high? That might explain a thing or two. "Let me listen," she said. It was a rock tune with soaring guitar, and the singer began to wail. She was greedy for the lyrics, as all she'd had was the melody. She tittered as she caught a few words—lonely, running, hiding... "Are you trying to tell me something?" Her voice had gone weird again.

He paused. "Are *you*?" He went quiet again just as the singer belted out, "Layla!"

Cold prickles spread across Layla's chest as the chorus went on and Esteban began to sing along with it. "Like a fool, I fell in love with you," he practically shouted, off-key. His grin sent a chill through her. It was too wide, too sharp.

She slapped her palm against the buttons on the dash, sending the tracks skipping forward before the sound cut off entirely.

"Now do you remember what you said?" he asked. "I asked you what your name was. And you said it was Layla. Right as the song was playing. I asked you if you were for real, but I knew you were just making it up."

"But that *is* my name." Her voice was thick with irritation.

"Uh-huh."

Layla watched the scenery go by; the dunes and cottages by the bay had disappeared, leaving scrubby forest on either side. "I want to go home."

"And where is that, exactly?"

"I want to go back!"

"Calm down. I didn't mean to upset you." He reached to pat her thigh but drew back, and she pressed herself against the passenger door. "Jeez." His thick fingers were white-knuckled as they gripped the steering wheel. "I should have asked more questions. Earlier," he said after several tense seconds.

"Why are you giving me such a hard time?"

"I'm trying to be your friend. Why can't you believe that?"

Her vision was hot with tears that she instinctively knew she wasn't supposed to shed. She turned in her seat. "Amber said you were just looking for a blow-up doll."

"Jesus Christ. Amber is a first-class bitch."

"But an honest one?"

"What the fuck?" He leaned his head back and bumped it against the headrest several times. "You're driving me crazy."

"Did we sleep together?" Her whole body had gone tense. She clutched the seat like it was about to jettison her.

He rolled his eyes and muttered a curse. "And now you're going to tell me you don't remember that either? That's fucking convenient."

"Is that a *yes*?" she asked, her voice little more than a squeak. There wasn't enough air in the car. She rolled down the window and let the wind yank at her hair. "I'm going to be sick."

"Breathe." He sounded so sad. "It's going to be okay."

"Just tell me what happened!"

"I thought you were into it, okay?" he said. "You seemed like you were cool with me. And sober. I mean, I don't take advantage of drunk girls. I'm not some frat boy rapist if that's what you're thinking."

There was a dead stinkbug, legs up, caught between the dash and the windshield. Only five legs.

"I stopped when I realized you were just...gone," he continued. "Okay? That's what happened. You stopped responding and just lay there like a corpse, and I don't take advantage of those either. I tried to talk to you about it, and you just gave me this blank, dead stare. I know something happened to you."

"Nothing happened to me!" shouted Layla, her voice filling the whole car, her whole head. She reached for the door handle.

His hand closed around her wrist as the car swerved. "You want to kill both of us?"

"Let me out!" She struggled against his grip, but he was using his whole arm to press her back into the seat. She tried to reach for the button to release her seat belt, but he jammed his elbow against her upper arm, making her shriek with pain.

"Calm down," he bellowed as he steadied the wheel. A car passed them on the other side, speeding up to get around them before the dotted yellow lines became solid once more. She caught a flash of wide eyes and white faces. The car was going over fifty miles an hour on this two-lane highway, scenery whipping by, wind gushing through the open car window.

She slumped in the seat, her muscles going slack, her eyes on that dead stinkbug.

"If I let go of you, are you gonna do something stupid?" he asked, breathing hard.

She shook her head.

"Good." He moved his arm. "I didn't want it to go like this."

"You thought we'd just go out on a date and then I'd hop into bed with you?"

"This wasn't how I wanted it to go." He almost sounded like he was pleading with her. "I'm trying to do the right thing here. Believe that."

She didn't believe a single word he said.

Ten minutes later, his gaze flicked to an orange rooftop up ahead. "It's right here." He slowed the car. Then he looked at his phone, where the lock screen displayed the time.

Everything inside her pulled tight. "It looks nice," she said, focusing on getting every word out the right way.

"Everything's gonna be fine," Esteban said as he turned off the road. The car's tires crunched over the white shells that graveled the lot of Moby Dick's Restaurant—*For a whale of a meal.*

Before he reached the parking area, she had unbuckled her seat belt and thrown the door open. As she leapt from the car, she stumbled but kept her footing, and then she was running and running and running, panic drumming in her ears and tears bursting loose.

"Layla, no," he shouted.

His footsteps sounded off behind her, and she screamed, terror exploding inside her, up from the lightless recesses of her mind, bringing with it a torrent of images and sounds and words and faces. Her feet pounded against the ground. One of her flip-flops was gone, but it didn't matter. All that mattered was getting away. Escaping. Outrunning the monster behind her, the one bellowing and roaring and snapping at her heels. She didn't know where she was going, but as long as it carried her farther from him, it was salvation. Confusion squeezed at her lungs and billowed inside her head.

How had she gotten here?

Where the hell was she?

She screamed again. The sound merged with that of other voices, all raised high and loud and yet not enough to penetrate the din of memories inside her head.

She didn't hear the skid or the horn. There was only a blast of pain, the whoosh of air, and then nothing at all.

MONDAY, AUGUST 3

Do you think someone abducted her?" I ask the detective. The sky is such a bright, heartbreaking blue, and it's making my chest hurt. For days, I've been thinking she probably did this on purpose, trying to punish me. Suddenly, in one devastating moment, I realize I was wrong. And I know she's in trouble.

"Mr. Zarabian, right now there's no way of knowing—"

"No way of *knowing*? Isn't that your job? Who leaves their wallet and keys locked in their car voluntarily?"

Detective Correia lets my question hang between us for a moment before asking, "Has your wife been under any stress lately? Has she been feeling depressed?"

"No, why?"

"She got any emotional problems? Was she taking any medication?"

"*Why?*"

Detective Correia sighs. "I have to cover these bases, sir. We're trying to figure out what's happened. Does she receive any mental health care? Has she been—"

"She's got a therapist, just to talk."

"Just to talk."

Irritation flashes hot across my skin. "Are you guys actually looking for her?"

"We've got Provincetown and Truro force here, along with National Park Service and State Police. We're combing the perimeter of the park. Have you been here? Pretty big pond right in the middle."

"I know," I say, remembering. "Mina took me on a walk there earlier this summer." There's a trail around the pond, and the whole thing is thick with trees and scrub right to the edge of the water. If you hold out handfuls of birdseed, a bunch of adorable little birds will come down and alight on your fingers. Mina said we'd get ticketed if we were caught, but she couldn't help herself. She called it magic. She couldn't stop laughing as those little birds pecked at her palms.

"So she's familiar with the place," Detective Correia says.

"What exactly do you think happened, Detective?"

"We're trying to suss that out, Mr. Zarabian."

"Have you gone through the car? Are there signs of a struggle?"

"None that we can see. Her wallet's there, cash and credit cards inside."

"Don't you guys have a forensic lab or something?"

"It's a little early for that."

"A little *early*? If someone has her, every minute counts!"

Another sigh. "Mr. Zarabian, have you considered the possibility that no one else is involved here?"

I stare out at the traffic. Watch an Uber pull up and spit out a guy in a suit and sunglasses.

"Are you in Provincetown, Mr. Zarabian? I think it would be good if we spoke in person."

"I can be there later today," I mumble. We arrange to meet at the cottage at six, then I listen to the call cut off.

I hadn't considered suicide. The thought hadn't even entered my mind. But now, as I once again wonder why Mina left her rings behind, there's yet another awful possibility.

But I've never met anyone so alive.

I drive to Caitlin's in a daze. My ex-wife is smiling when she answers the door, but the look fades soon as she sees me. "What's wrong?"

"Can you keep Devon tonight?"

"Daddy!" My little girl squirms past her mom and wraps her arms around my legs. "Sushi night!"

I look up at the eaves of the house where I used to live, on this quiet Brookline street where tragedy is a stranger and nobody disappears into thin air. Caitlin really needs to have the gutters cleaned. My hand is on Devon's head, and my throat is so tight. But I manage to say, "Something's come up, kiddo."

Devon starts to whine, but Caitlin already has her by the shoulders, gently prying her arms off my legs. "Daddy needs some space, Dev."

"I have to get Mina's present!" Devon whirls around and disappears back into the house.

I bow my head. It feels like I'm going to throw up. Caitlin touches my arm.

"It's Mina," I whisper.

"Oh my God, Alex. Is she—"

"She's missing. I have to go to Provincetown."

"Okay," she says. "Ryan and I were headed to Portland, but we can stay—"

"Don't tell Devon, okay? I don't want her to worry."

"*Should* she be worried?"

"Don't you think I'd tell you?" I snap.

"I didn't know your mom had cancer until you told me she'd started chemo," Caitlin murmurs. "I didn't know your dad was in the hospital until you told me he'd passed away."

"I don't need this." I take a step back. "Last thing I need."

She takes a quick look over her shoulder and moves onto the porch. She's got her chin up like she always does when she's royally pissed. She doesn't yell, though. She *hisses*. "I'm not trying to make this harder for you, Alex. I'm trying to take care of *our* little girl."

"Then take care of her. She doesn't need to know anything until there's something to know."

Our eyes meet, and I can't read Caitlin's face. Suddenly, I remember loving her, though. I remember when her arms were a refuge, when the sound of her voice smoothed my edges, and I don't know why, and I shouldn't be, but I'm wishing for that comfort now, when it's years past and long since dead.

She tilts her head. The chin is down now. "I don't know everything that's happening, and I don't need to," she says. "But you have to believe me—I hope Mina's okay. And I'm here if you want to talk."

She was always talking about magic, my wife. The first time she met Devon, Mina knelt down so they were at eye level, and she pointed to the book my daughter held cradled against her chest. "I haven't read that one," Mina said, then poked at the image on the cover. "That pigeon looks like he's up to no good, though."

Devon accepted Mina's request to read it with her, and a few hours later, after they'd become fast friends, after my daughter insisted Mina tuck her in, and after watching Mina do exactly that had filled my head with fantasies of our future children, we sat in the living room and shared a bottle of wine. "Devon is so much fun," Mina said. "She told me a whole story about this pigeon in her book, and how he wanted so badly to learn how to drive the bus so he could go visit his grandma in New York."

"Caitlin's parents live upstate," I told her. "I hope Devon isn't considering hijacking a vehicle to go visit them."

"I love that," she said. "I love that she lets herself live through this character, even though it's a pigeon."

"Have you spent a lot of time around kids?" I poured a little more wine for her as she turned to look at the fire I'd built. I knew we were both only children, and I wondered if growing up without siblings had done to her what it had done to me.

Mina gave me a bashful smile. "I never even babysat."

"You seem like a natural, though."

She sipped at her wine and turned the conversation back to the pigeon. "Where do you think he wanted to go, Alex?"

"I don't know—joyride? Never thought about it, honestly." I slid a fingertip along her shoulder. "What about you?"

Mina held up her glass and gazed into the ruby depths of her wine. "Maybe he wanted to step out of his old life and go find the magic in the world."

"Is his current life so bad?"

She shook her head. "And he knows he should stay put. But he always wonders what's out there."

"Are we still talking about the pigeon?"

She grinned. "I should slip him into the book I'm working on right now."

She's a master at the art of changing the subject, and I fall for it almost every time. I'm so clueless sometimes—I don't even realize until later that what we *didn't* talk about might have been more important than what we did.

I could take the ferry to Provincetown, but I want to have my car, so I drive south out of the city and along the South Shore. Even though it's midday on a Monday, the Cape traffic is still enough to make me sweat. On the way, antsy as hell, I call Emily, Mina's therapist, and I leave a message. She calls me back an hour or so later as I'm rolling along Route 6, past shops and restaurants with charming names like Lobster Shack and Moby Dick's. I explain to her what's happened, when I last saw Mina, how Mina apparently made a cake and took it to her parents' for dinner, how she disappeared into the night and no one has seen her since. How her car was found at Beech Forest, and how there's an ongoing search, and how they asked if Mina was depressed. "Was she?" I ask.

"You must be so incredibly worried," she says. "I'm worried, too."

"That's a great way of talking and saying absolutely nothing."

"I can understand your frustration, Alex. But I hope you can understand my obligation to Mina and her privacy."

"Her privacy?" The center line of the highway is solid, telling me not to pass. I swerve around a minivan that's going five under the speed limit. "What about her safety?"

"Alex, if I had information that Mina planned to hurt herself, I would have taken action already. I can promise you that."

I hate this woman, even though she sounds nice. My wife has been going to her almost every week since before we met, and she probably knows all the most private moments of our lives. Feeling stripped bare and surly, I blurt out, "The last time I saw Mina, she was walking out the door after we argued. About having kids."

"You blame yourself."

"No," I say, braking to avoid colliding with the back of yet another car that's moving too goddamn slow. "I just want to know where she went. And why. I thought she was leaving me, and now I'm afraid something's happened to her."

"Do you have anyone with you?" she asks. "It must be difficult to be alone with such stress and uncertainty."

I hang up on her. It seems better than shouting. I make it to the cottage with eight minutes to spare, but the detective is already out front, waiting by a squad car. She's a tall, slender woman, with cropped black hair and dark-brown eyes that size me up as I get out of my Lexus. We exchange terse greetings and head inside where she turns down water, tea, and coffee. I consider offering her a scotch because I'm badly in need of one myself, but then I wonder if she'll think I'm a drunk and start making assumptions.

We sit in the living room. I watch her scan the place and take in the wilted bouquet on Mina's desk. "We haven't found any trace of Mina yet," she tells me. "If there's nothing by tomorrow, we'll call in the dive team."

I'm glad my stomach is empty. "You think she's in the water?"

"We're doing all we can to find her."

"Including combing her car for clues?"

"Yes, but there's no sign of anything unusual in the car, Mr. Zarabian."

"She's been missing for a week, Detective. Plenty of time for someone to clean it out or something."

"Right," she says. "That's possible."

"Was everything still in her wallet? Cash? Credit cards?"

"You can give me a list of what you think should have been in there. I can tell you that there were a few credit cards. No cash."

"She took $400 cash out of our account late Monday morning."

The detective pulls out her phone and makes a note of it, but doesn't speculate. When she raises her head, I don't like the way she's looking at me. I get up and get myself a glass of water in the kitchen.

"Can you walk me through your understanding of where she might have been since you last saw her?" she asks when I return.

I do, including her going to her parents for dinner on Monday. "Did you find a cake carrier in the car?"

"Cake carrier?" She shakes her head. "Nothing in the cab or the trunk."

"She must have left it with her parents. Are you going to talk to them?"

Detective Correia leans her elbows on her knees. "I will. I've also filed for a search warrant for her cell phone and local cell towers. Her phone wasn't in the car, so wherever she is, the phone could be with her."

"It'll let you track her movements?"

She grimaces, almost apologetic. "This isn't Boston, cell tower on every block, practically. It may tell us if she's still in Provincetown or not, but that's about it."

"What about surveillance cameras in the area?" I feel like I'm always seeing viral videos of crazy incidents.

"Like I said, this isn't Boston. There's really nothing nearby."

"'Nearby'?" I roll my eyes. "How nearby are we talking? Which streets? Any businesses with cameras that might capture images of the road? Did you even try?"

She spends a full ten seconds watching me. "We can get a search warrant for the credit card records as well. Unless they're all joint?"

"No."

"You guys didn't share finances?"

I'm reconsidering the scotch. "We've only been married for a few months."

"How's married life been treating you?"

"We're fine," I tell her. "We're happy."

"It can be quite an adjustment, am I right?"

I recall reading somewhere that the husband is always a suspect when a wife disappears. "Of course." I open my mouth to say more, but any words are crushed by the realization of being here, in Mina's cottage, speaking to a detective while her car sits abandoned. While police are looking for her body in the woods. It's fucking obvious they don't expect to find her alive.

"Jesus." I stand up and head for the window, nausea churning in my gut. "This can't be happening."

"We're doing all we can."

"You keep saying that," I mutter from between clenched teeth.

"It would be helpful to understand anything that's been stressing her out lately."

She's looking for evidence that confirms her suicide theory. "Mina wasn't depressed. She wouldn't hurt herself. But she's a well-known romance author. How do you know some sick fan wasn't stalking her?"

I glance over and see Mina's wedding and engagement rings in the bowl. For all I know, she's run off with that fan. Our conversation about the damn bus-driving pigeon takes on a whole new, horrifying meaning.

"I've got someone combing her public social media for any threats," says the detective. "If you have access to her account, then I can—"

"I don't, okay? I don't have any of that." And I'm sweating now. Probably bright red in the face. "What about the news media? Are they on this?"

"I'm not sure you want a lot of public attention, Mr. Zarabian. If it's what we think—"

"And if it's not?" I know I shouldn't be raising my voice, but this is too much. "Are you guys hoping no one will pay attention while you do as little as possible to find her?"

The floor creaks as the detective shifts her weight. "I'll be going, Mr. Zarabian. I appreciate you talking to me, and we'll be in touch as soon as we know anything at all."

I turn to face her. "You've got to look at the car."

"I've requested a state mobile forensic unit. And if you happen to come across any of her passwords, in a file, maybe, or—"

"Sure thing." I see the detective to the door, and when she's gone, I barely make it to the couch before my legs give out. Mina's gone, the police think she's dead, and the whole world is humming along as if that doesn't matter.

I have no fucking idea what I'm supposed to do, but I have to do something. If I stay still for another minute, I'm going to go insane. I head back over to Mina's desk. Her laptop could hold the answers to everything, if I can figure out how to get past the lock screen.

I think back to all the times I've seen Mina type in her password to access the machine. It's not a long one—I'm almost sure it has six characters or less. I recall her fingers dancing over the keyboard, unlocking the device in the space of a second. I never asked her what it was. Why would I? It's always seemed very much *hers* and no one else's, and she's always got it with her. In fact, I remember teasing her recently when she mentioned that she'd let Devon use it to play a game... Holy shit.

My heart is rattling my entire body as I reach for the phone and call Caitlin. When she answers, she tells me that my daughter is right there, and they've gotten takeout sushi, and on a normal day, that would probably send a twinge through me because sushi is *my* thing with Devon, but today, I'm just glad to have reached them. "Can I talk to Devon?"

"She's in the middle of dinner—"

"Put her on the phone, Caitlin."

"If this is news about Mina, then you should tell me first," she says quietly.

She assumes the fucking worst of me, every time. "*If* I had news, I would tell you. Put my daughter on the phone."

"Daddy!"

My voice instantly morphs into the lilting and playful tone that only my little girl can pull from my mouth. "Hi, silly girl. You're eating sushi?"

"From Genki Ya! I got the salmon roll."

She always gets the salmon roll. "I wish Mina and I had been able to take you out."

"I made a drawing for Mina."

"Mommy told me. I bet she's going to love it." I consider for a moment, trying to figure out my approach. "Baby, you like to play with Mina, don't you?"

"We like to play games."

"What kind of games?"

"Lots of kinds. But not board games!"

"Oh, I know all about that." Mina refuses to play board games of any kind. And for some reason, she particularly hates chess, which happens to be my favorite. *Too much strategery for my poor brain*, she said, brushing me off with a laugh. *I can tell just by looking at the board.* "You play other games with her, though!"

"Plants vs. Zombies!" She sounds so adorably excited that it makes my eyes burn. "Mina thought it was scary, but I think it's funny!"

I can hear Caitlin muttering in the background and suddenly wonder if she's thinking Mina's a bad influence or something. "I love that game," I tell her. "You played it on Mina's computer?"

"Mm-hmm," my daughter says. Now she sounds distracted.

"Baby, I need your listening ears. Did Mina let you unlock her computer?"

"Unlock?"

"Did she let you type in her password?"

"Mm-hmm. I had to type in the magic word. I spelled it wrong, and then she told me the right way."

"The magic word," I say slowly. The fingers of my left hand tap on the keys of my wife's laptop. *P-L-E-A-S-E.* Nope. "What's the magic word, Devon?"

She giggles. "She said it was a secret. I'm not supposed to tell anyone."

I speak slowly, keeping my voice level. "Mina needs you to tell me her password, honey. It's important."

"Did she forget it?"

"Yes!" Out of the mouths of babes—the kid has given me an innocent explanation. "Yes. She forgot it, and she needs you to tell me what it is so that I can give it to her."

Devon seems to ponder this for a moment, and then she says, very solemnly, "She told me the password is magic, Daddy."

"I know, I know. Mina loves magic. So what is it? The magic word?"

"I have to go. Mommy wants me to take a bath."

"Devon," I snap. "I—" The call cuts out. My thumb jerks over my screen, about to jab the number and redial, when it hits me. Magic. Mina loves magic.

What the hell. I type it in. *M-A-G-I-C*.

And I'm in.

CHAPTER FIVE

The sky overhead was a cheerful and cloudless blue. She stared up at it while her ears throbbed and buzzed.

"Did someone call 911?" Sound returned, the shield of white noise pierced by a man's shouted plea. He hunched over her, blocking her view of the sky. "You ran right out in front of me!"

Her lips moved, but she couldn't get enough air to speak.

"Stay awake, okay? Don't pass out." The man jerked up to his knees. "Are any of you doctors?"

She slowly turned her head. She was lying next to a road, at the mouth of a parking lot. A large beige car was parked at a diagonal only feet away. Exhaust puffed from its tailpipe.

"Should I be letting her turn her head?" Beads of sweat sparkled on the dome of his bald head. It was almost pretty. "Should I keep her from moving?" His voice cracked with strain.

She turned her head to the other side and saw who the man was speaking to. A small crowd had gathered, coming out of what looked like a restaurant behind them. They were speaking urgently. Gesturing at her and then at something several feet away. She shifted her gaze, struggling against the balding man who was now trying to turn her face to the sky again. Just before he succeeded, she caught sight of two men on top of a third guy, a young man with black hair who was struggling and shouting. The two men holding him down—one in an apron and hairnet and the other with tattoos down both his muscular arms—looked tense and angry. The tattooed guy had his knee planted in the black-haired guy's back and was pressing the young man's anguished face to the gravel.

"The ambulance'll be here in a few minutes," said a man with a Spanish sort of accent. She couldn't turn her head to see who was speaking exactly. "Police, too. Can you guys keep hold of him?"

"No problem" came the gruff reply.

"I don't know what... I don't know..." she whispered. Confusion was smothering her; she could barely breathe. Her legs and arms were moving on their own, aimless but determined. Like they wanted to run away and leave her behind. Somewhere in the distance, sirens wailed. She was lost in it, lost in the noise and the pain and the light and the faces all around her, not a one of them familiar.

Another stranger leaned over her, this one in a uniform. EMT, she guessed. "Hey there. Keep still for me," the guy said as he braced her head and strapped rigid plastic around her neck, chin to shoulders. "What's your name?"

Her name. That was the one thing she did know. "Maggie," she whispered.

The EMT smiled. "You're gonna be fine, Maggie. I'm gonna make sure of it."

As the ambulance turned onto Route 6, the EMT sat next to her gurney. "Quite a day, huh?"

"Someone needs to call my mom," she said, her voice rasping. "She was expecting me."

"We'll do that as soon as we get to the hospital," he told her as he wiped an alcohol swab over the crook of her elbow. "What's your last name, sweetheart?"

"Wallace."

"And how old are you?"

"Twenty."

"Your birth date?"

"December 4."

"Great. Any medical problems we need to know about? You on any medications?"

"No."

"You know where you are right now?"

"In hell?" She glanced around the ambulance. "Sorry."

He chuckled. "No, that's great. Humor. Perfect. Where were you born?"

"Boston. My mom lives in Yarmouth."

"Nearby, then. That's great. And your dad?"

It felt like someone was strangling her. She closed her eyes and sucked in a tight, squeaky breath.

"Just relax. The IV pinches a little going in." He thought he understood. "You know what day it is?"

"No," she whispered. Then she thought about it. "Wednesday?"

"That's okay. No worries." But his brow was furrowed when she opened her eyes to look. "Do you know what happened to you?"

"Hit by a car?"

"The guy who hit you said you were running." He chewed at the inside of his cheek. "Because someone was chasing you. You remember that?"

Maggie blinked. "Who was chasing me?"

"You got a bump on the head," the EMT said as he hung the IV bag from its pole. "Probably a concussion. That can interfere with memory for sure. What's the last thing you remember before getting hit?"

Maggie searched the earnest lines of his face as if they held the answer. She shifted her gaze to the small back window of the ambulance, through which she could see a slice of blue sky. Then she pondered her bare feet poking out from under the thin blanket, wobbling with every bump in the road. "I remember...I remember getting in my car. In the parking lot."

"Which parking lot?"

"Student lot. A, I think."

"Okay," he said slowly. "And when was that?"

"After my last exam."

He tilted his head. "Where do you go to school?"

"UMass."

"Boston?"

"No, Amherst..." She paused when she saw the concern flicker in his eyes. "That's not where we are?"

"*When* was your exam, kiddo?" His voice was light, but there was something coiled inside each word, a snake preparing to strike. "You're in summer school?"

"No. Why?"

He smiled and patted her hand. "We'll be at the hospital soon. You're going to be fine, sweetheart. Just fine."

Maggie stared at the side of his face as he busied himself typing notes. He was an absolutely terrible liar.

———

They drew blood. They took X-rays. They called her mom. They took off the plastic collar, but then they put her in a noisy tube and told her to stay still so they could take pictures of her brain. They asked her question after question after question. The whole time, they were cheery and sweet and positive.

Maggie did as she was told, and she *didn't* ask questions. She took the pills, Tylenol or something, for the headache. She let them probe and prod everywhere. She put her feet in stirrups and closed her eyes and forced her mind away and away and away. Fatigue lay over her like a weighted blanket, and the things they did to her body couldn't lift it. Only the questions threatened to strip it off.

She remembered getting into her car. She remembered looking at the gas gauge and thinking she needed to fill up before she hit the road for the three-hour drive back to Yarmouth. And now she was in the hospital in Hyannis. She'd seen a sign as the ambulance pulled up—Cape Cod Hospital. Only a few miles from her mom's house. She'd ended up back on the Cape, but she had no idea how.

No worries, the nurses said. No worries, the technicians said. It'll all sort itself out. Mild concussion. Memory issues. Now she lay on the gurney in a little room, door closed, lights low, trying to sleep. They were going to admit her for overnight observation, and all she needed to do was wait until someone came to wheel her upstairs. The doctor would come and speak to her soon, to let her know the results of the MRI. No worries, no worries.

Her mom would be here soon. A familiar feeling gripped her, a jittery and uneasy mixture of dread and need, of craving and the desire to run fast and far. A squirmy feeling, but also comforting in a weird way.

It was familiar when nothing else was.

"Ms. Wallace?" She turned to see an Indian man in a lab coat come through the door, a friendly smile on his bespectacled face. "I'm Dr. Mehta." He reached her bedside and offered his hand. She shook it gingerly. "We're going to be transferring you up to another floor here in a minute, and your mom is going to meet you up there."

"You talked to her?"

"I told her that you're going to be fine and that you'll be able to talk to her yourself in a little bit."

She watched his face. "Was she mad?"

He looked a bit perplexed. "She's worried, like any mother would be." He pushed his glasses up the bridge of his nose. "You don't have any fractures or spinal injuries. And as far as we can tell, you don't have any neurological injuries. No brain damage."

"I know what neurological means."

He smiled. "You're a student at Amherst?"

"UMass Amherst. I just finished my sophomore year."

"Your MRI revealed no swelling, no hemorrhages. It's possible you have a mild concussion, and I've been told you're having some issues with memory."

"I don't know how I got to the Cape." She bit her lip. "And it's not May anymore, is it?"

He shook his head. "It's July 31."

A rushing sound filled her ears. "Two *months*?"

"Your mother said she expected you to arrive home from school in May, but you never did. She began a search and talked to some friends of yours, and I guess they told her you'd had a rough end of the year. Do you remember telling your roommate that you were dreading going home?"

"Mom thinks I ran away or something?" The rushing sound had

enveloped her in a kind of auditory fog, dimming the sound of his voice. "I think I did well on my finals. My grades are good. Everything was fine."

"You have no sense of where you've been all this time? Who you've been with?"

A shaky breath escaped her, though it couldn't quite expel the horror of her thoughts. "I was told someone was chasing me," she whispered. "In that parking lot where I got hit."

"There was a police officer here. He told us the suspect is being questioned."

"Do they think he abducted me? What...you think he's had me tied up in a basement somewhere? Why don't I remember?"

"I'm in no position to speculate right now, Ms. Wallace. But our consulting neurologist—you remember the lady who came in here and asked you all those questions? She and the radiologist took a look at your scans and confirmed that there's nothing physically wrong with your brain. So what I can tell you is that you're generally in very good health, though a bit undernourished. Your bloodwork seems to suggest that you're not under the influence of alcohol or opioids." He met her eyes. "And you don't have any obvious injuries apart from a few contusions. Your HIV status is negative. We're still waiting on other blood tests, though, just to make sure."

"Can you tell whether he... Did he..." Her voice faded away, strangled and small, too quiet to make any kind of difference, to ask the questions that might blow up her entire world. And maybe that was best. *Why open old wounds?* That's what her mother always, always said.

"I think the thing to do is to focus on helping you figure out what's happened, Ms. Wallace, and to give you the chance to talk to someone about it. Medically, you are fine. But I do have a piece of information that you need to know before you go speak with your mother. Although it may not be news to you at all."

She could barely hear him now; the rush had become a roar. "Okay." Her mother would be waiting upstairs. Maggie had been planning to live with her over the summer. She'd had a job lined up at Flour Child, the bakery on Main. She'd made sure to let them know that she wanted to work on Sundays and then told her mom that they'd demanded it. She'd felt so clever.

"Your blood test was positive for hCG."

This time, she didn't have a smart-ass response. "Is that a disease?"

Why was he looking at her like that? Not as if she was stupid—as if she might explode.

"It means, Ms. Wallace, that you're pregnant."

MONDAY, AUGUST 3,
TO WEDNESDAY, AUGUST 5

Ignoring about a dozen calls from Drew, I start with Mina's email. Luckily, the screen is the only thing that's locked, and everything else is pretty much logged in already. Her Gmail account contains some emails from her agent, Bridget Cameron, about a new three-book deal she's about to sign with Diva, the romance imprint of Granite Square. Apparently, they're pleased with the sales of her last several books and want to lock her in for more. It sits like cement in my stomach, reading my wife's words, especially when Bridget gushes about how gorgeous the wedding was, and Mina replies that she couldn't have written a better ending even if she tried.

I know what she means—a lot of romances end when the love story is just beginning. That has to be what she meant.

The final email exchange, which is from July 24, is about the publishing timeline being negotiated for the deal. It includes Mina telling Bridget that there has to be an understanding that she's not going to start another book until March—eight months from now. Mina writes about three books a year, and she didn't mention slowing down, so I expect surprise or pushback. But Bridget replies that she thinks they'll understand, given the circumstances. She suggests that Mina talk the timing over with Lauren, her editor at Diva.

What circumstances? After doing the mental math, I have a moment of simultaneous hope and fear, wondering if it has anything to do with us, with having kids. Could Mina *already* be pregnant? It took me and Caitlin a painful four years to conceive, and by the time Devon was born, our marriage was headed for the cliff. It lasted for another three years, but we were in no place to try for another baby, which only deepened my unhappiness. I'd always imagined two or three kids, filling our home with a joyful kind of chaos, so different from the smothering isolation and boredom I grew up with as an only child.

I didn't hide any of that from Mina. When we first started talking about a future together, I was honest about wanting more kids. And I thought she wanted the same thing, but now, as I think about it, I wonder if she kept changing the subject without me even realizing it.

I wonder what else I missed, all the conversational on-ramps we blew past without me even noticing.

So even though Mina's requested writing timeline instantly stands out, after I think about it for more than a second, I realize it probably has nothing to do with her being pregnant. Why would she be starting a new book right around the time she gave birth? After our fight, the first one in which I wouldn't let her change the subject, the one where I tried to pin her down, I wonder if having a baby with me was the last thing Mina wanted.

I love her anyway. I love her more than that fantasy.

Why didn't I say that to her when I had the chance?

As I continue to shuffle through her email, as the sky outside turns purple then black, I silently promise her that I'll tell her once I have her back.

Her email inbox contains little else useful that I can see, though

I give up after an hour and turn to her social media accounts. Her Twitter DMs are all interactions between her and her fans, mostly questions about release dates and sequels, along with lots of love for Garrett and Blain and Sly and Finn, all heroes of her most recent books. Nothing threatening or weird. Same with Instagram. All book stuff, nothing personal. And then there's Facebook.

Within seconds of pulling up the page, Willa Penson opens a chat.

Hey, lady! Where have you been? Did you finish it?

She thinks I'm Mina, of course. Why wouldn't she?

I shouldn't do this. I shouldn't. **Almost,** I reply. I instantly rethink it, though, because this isn't cool. I'm about to fess up when her next response comes through:

I need to tell you something. Your hubby chatted me up the other day. He wanted to know when I'd last spoken to you.

She's a fast typist, though I guess that's unsurprising, given her profession. **Seemed a shade controlling,** she continues. **I know you love that buttoned-up smolder he's got going, but I need to be honest—it gave me the chills. I've been thinking about it for the last couple days.**

Controlling? *Fuck you*, I almost type. **He just worries about me,** I type instead.

Have you told him yet?

"Tell me *what?*" The sound of my own voice startles me. My hands are shaking as I tap out a careful answer. **I can't quite figure out how to say it.**

Oh, come on. You're good at that.

I groan. **Not this time,** I try. **Any suggestions?**

Just be honest. And brave.

Jesus. My heart is beating so fucking hard. I know I'm digging the hole deeper, but I can't help it. **I don't want to hurt him.**

You're being true to yourself, she writes. *He's a grown-ass man, and he'll deal with it. Are you worried about how he'll take it after what I just told you?*

I want to say *No.* But I need an answer, and that doesn't seem like the way to get it. *How do you think I should frame it?*

LOL "frame it"?

I frown. *What's so funny?*

She goes silent, and I'm sweating again. Finally, she types, *Are you sure you're okay?*

Shit. That was probably some inside joke. *Yeah. Just tired.*

Me, too. I'm shutting down for the night. Chat soon?

I whisper a curse under my breath. *Sure. Good night.*

The green dot next to her name disappears. I don't know whether I dodged a bullet or got hit square between the eyes. Mina was going to tell me something. Whatever it was, it scared her, enough so that her friend thought it would take some courage to get it out. But I can't just chat Willa back and explain what's happened, because if she thought I was controlling before, now she's probably going to think I'm an utter psycho for impersonating my wife on Facebook. Hell, she'll probably think I *caused* Mina to disappear.

I go through the rest of Mina's recent messages. Most are incoming, in that someone wrote to her and she replied, usually a fan, like on Twitter. She initiates messages with a few people, Willa and other writers, all discussing their deadlines, agents, editors, and creative blocks. In one case, Mina advises an author who's thinking of leaving her agent and offers to put in a good word with Bridget. My vision blurs as I skim down the list of names. She gets so many messages. And then one sets in my brain like a hook.

It's a message that Mina sent two weeks or so ago. July 16. When I read my wife's words, my skin runs hot. It reads: Is that really you?

The response, sent almost immediately: Seems like I'm the one who should be asking that.

And then hers, instant: I need to see you. I have to talk to you. Please. Then she offers her cell number.

There's no correspondence between them before or after that.

The user who she's writing to: Stefan Silva.

Stef. I click on the name. He and Mina aren't Facebook friends, so I can only see what's public. There's not much in the profile; the pic is of a cocktail, amber and ice in a highball glass. The only public posts are about a place called the Mariner, which turns out to be a bar in Harwich on the lower Cape. There's no number in his basic information and no birthday.

He's not online right now.

I Google his name. This guy my wife just had to see. And wouldn't you know it, there are six Stefan Silvas in Massachusetts, but only one of them lives in Harwich, and he's thirty-four years old. I'm operating on pure impulse again as rage and suspicion tangle in my chest. She had to see him. *Please*, she said. *Please.*

"Fuck," I whisper. I should be calling Correia right now and telling her I've accessed Mina's account, but knowing she'll immediately see I've been impersonating my wife online, it would only be a distraction. I'll find another way to tell her about this asshole. But first I type in my credit card number and buy the full report on him.

Stefan G. Silva lives on Driftwood Lane in East Harwich, Massachusetts. He's married, too, to a woman named Melanie Silva, formerly Melanie Fogerly.

He's also an ex-con. He was arrested twelve years ago on suspicion of assault, ten years ago for DUI, and has a conviction for felony possession with intent to distribute. He sounds like a first-class loser, and yet Mina wanted to see him. Needed to see him.

Buzzing with the same jittery, dangerous energy that's kept me going ever since this morning, I dial his number.

"Silva," he answers, his voice low. There's a lot of noise in the background. Music. People talking.

"Hi," I say. "This is Alex Zarabian."

"Who? Hang on." After a moment, there's a snap, like the sound of a door closing sharply. The background noise fades. "Who did you say you are?"

"Alex Zarabian. Mina Richards's husband."

Five solid seconds of silence. "Um," he finally says. "Why are you calling me?"

"Mina's missing. The police are searching for her. If you know anything—"

"I don't have a fucking clue what you're talking about."

"You know Mina, right? I know she contacted you."

"She told you?"

"Does she have a reason to keep secrets?"

He *laughs*. "I really can't help you. Sorry."

Determined to get the words out before he cuts off the call, I say, "If you have any idea where she is or where she might have gone, the police—"

"I don't," he says. "I don't know her. Never really did. And I don't know you, and I don't have anything to do with your wife. Okay?"

"But you did," I guess. "At some point, you did."

"I can't help you. Sorry."

He ends the call. It's all I can do not to hurl my phone against the wall.

Instead, I'm up with keys in hand and a vague plan to go to the Mariner and see if I can hunt the asshole down. I pull onto Commercial and head for Route 6. Provincetown is home to upward of a hundred thousand in the summer, but it's a tiny place. Minutes later, I brake suddenly at Beech Forest, and I turn into the parking lot. I need to catch my breath. I need to *think*. I look around, expecting to find the whole place lit up, floodlights and search parties, but there's only one patrol car in the lot, parked next to a silver Prius. Mina's car.

As I get out of my Lexus and approach through the close, humid night air, the cop gets out of his cruiser. "Can I help you?" he asks.

"I heard you guys were conducting a search," I say. "Where is everyone?"

"The guys just left—rain's coming in. They'll pick it up first light tomorrow."

Rage pulls me tight, but I keep my voice light as I say, "Seems to me every minute counts."

He nods. "But we've covered every inch of terrain inside the trail and plenty outside, too. No trace, at least, not in the usual places."

"Usual places."

"We get at least a few of these a year." Then he seems to catch himself, and his eyes narrow. "You a reporter or something?"

"Why? Afraid of a little publicity?"

He gives me a baffled look.

"I'm her *husband*." And for all I know, my wife is off with some asshole in Harwich. Or she was, and he fucking killed her. Before I can say any of that, I slide my hand down my face and look away.

"I didn't mean any disrespect," he says quickly. "Like I said, dive team's gearing up for sunrise."

"What about the car?" I walk over to the Prius, but he heads me off.

"The vehicle has been sealed until it's processed, sir, so I'm going to have to ask you to step away." He touches the receiver at his shoulder. "I'll let Detective Correia know you're here."

"Do that. I need to talk to her anyway." I stalk back to my car, because the urge to punch someone is rising fast. I'm going to take this to the next level. I need a little sunlight, and I don't care what it reveals, as long as I find Mina.

My phone rings before I pull out of the lot again. "We just spoke to a detective about our daughter's disappearance," comes the rigid, prim reply when I answer. It's Rose.

"I'm glad she actually followed up with you."

"So you knew she would be contacting us. It would have been nice to have some advance notice before she simply showed up at our door."

"I'm sorry, Rose. It's been a rough day."

I hear the muffled sound of a sniffle. "I forgive you," she says. "But we're going through this as a family, and I want us to help each other through it until we find her."

I can hear the tears in her voice, and suddenly, I realize that *I'm* the asshole. "I'm here at Beech Forest, where they found her car. They're bringing a dive team in tomorrow."

"They won't find her there," she says fiercely. "That's a dead end. I'm sure of it."

"She wasn't suicidal. She wasn't depressed. Right?"

"I don't think she was. Really, I don't know!" She stifles a sob. "Try as I might, and believe me, I have, I've never understood her way of looking at the world. I don't want to mess this up and put her in danger."

Mess this up? "Wait—do you know something about where she is?"

She clears her throat. "She could be anywhere, so no, not really."

"Not *really*?"

I almost mention Stefan, but before I can, she says, "Come to the house tomorrow afternoon." Her tone goes bright as she dives back into her comfort zone with a force that nearly gives me whiplash. "I'm making scones and cookies for the search teams, and you can help me bring them over. It will be good to show the officers that we appreciate their efforts."

A thousand biting comments crowd my thoughts. This woman's daughter is missing, and it's obvious, to me at least, that Mina's in trouble. But Rose is babbling to me about various flavors of scone and jam as if she's preparing to go to a church picnic. I know this might just be the way she copes with extreme stress, but from where I sit, it also looks like she's laser-focused on being the perfect hostess, the perfect worried mom, the perfect, well-behaved, grateful victim-by-proxy. Something I don't give a shit about. I'll blow things up if it means we find Mina faster. So I have to wonder, is the hostess act just one more way to change the subject, just like Mina does? And if so, why would she want to at a time like this? What's Rose hiding beneath that perfect veneer?

In hopes of finding out, I agree to stop by the Richardses' house on Tuesday. I'm almost certain that there's something Rose isn't telling me, and a face-to-face might help her spit it out. But when she tells me she's praying for me, I tell her I've got another call.

Which is not a lie. "What the fuck, Alex? I've been trying to reach you for hours."

"Mina's missing, Drew. I had to take off."

"Caitlin told me there was something going on. And I'm here for you, but I've also got the entire board up my ass."

I give him the thirty-second rundown on my Pinewell meeting, but I don't mention that they're planning to oust him. I need my friend to be on my side. "So right now, they're wanting our okay, and I honestly don't think we're going to get a better deal. This is why the other shops didn't swing at our pitch, either, Drew. But they're offering to help us get CaX429 through the next steps, and without that, we're going to have trouble paying the rent after New Year's."

He curses. "I need you here. Do you have any idea where Mina's gone?"

I tell him what I know, including this mysterious Stefan. But as I get ready to tell Drew my plan to drive down to Harwich and confront him, I realize how idiotic it is and how idiotic I've already been. I have to be more strategic than that. "I'm going to tell the police all of it," I say. "But now I need a favor, because this situation is pretty much the definition of rainbow flame."

To his credit, Drew doesn't waste time asking me any more questions. He doesn't even hesitate. "Name it."

"I need to talk to Caroline."

If the cops aren't going to consider any other explanation for Mina's disappearance apart from suicide, I'm going to light a fucking rainbow flame under their asses. Caroline agrees that it's an important story, and though she doesn't feel comfortable covering it herself, she gets a colleague to work with me. She doesn't make any promises, but she says the attention might help.

Might, because there's always the possibility that Mina really did commit suicide. It doesn't sit right, though. Her emails with her agent more or less cinched it—she was planning for the future. New book deal and everything. And obviously, she had something big to tell me, and if she'd been about to kill herself, why bother? On top of that and even though I took an instant dislike to Mina's therapist, I believed Emily when she said she would have taken action if Mina were suicidal. Even if it was just to cover her ass.

So after leaving a message for Detective Correia about how she needs to check out Stefan Silva, I talk to a producer from the NBC station. She says they'll come out to Beech Forest tomorrow morning, early. And after a rough couple hours of sleep, I meet the news team in the muggy parking lot. True to their word, the police are already there, including the dive team. Apparently, they're using sonar and have a team of three sweeping the pond. Their flippers and heads break the surface every once in a while, and other groups search the woods again.

A mobile forensics unit comes and combs through the Prius. Detective Correia catches my eye and heads in my direction. No attitude, no friendliness. She's simply doing her job. Keeping her promises. Possibly keeping an eye on me. She tells me that she's gotten the search warrant for Mina's phone and expects to have some information no later than tomorrow. And then: "I got your message. Stefan Silva."

"Yeah. He lives in Harwich. I found a list in one of Mina's notepads, and his name is on it."

Detective Correia arches one black eyebrow. "A *list?*"

"It was a grocery list, eggs and English muffins and stuff, but there were two names on it. One was her therapist. And the other was this Stefan guy."

"Someone you know?"

I shake my head.

"But you know he lives in Harwich."

I put my hands up. Guilty. "I looked him up."

"So she had a list with this guy's name on it. A guy you don't know. And you looked him up. Anything else you want to tell me?"

"She added his name to the list at some point between Sunday and Tuesday."

"And you know this how?"

"Facebook post. There's a picture of the notepad on Sunday morning with no names. On Wednesday, I found the notepad in the cottage, names added. Last time the neighbors saw her was Monday or Tuesday."

"Fancy yourself a detective, Mr. Zarabian?"

"I fancy myself a husband who's worried sick."

Correia nods. "I checked with the neighbors. The couple across the street—the one guy, pink hair? He said he told you it might have been Tuesday, but he remembered that he was heading out to a boot camp class at Mussel Beach, which is a class that only happens on Monday. So he thinks it's Monday."

He thinks it's Monday. What she means is that's the last time anyone saw my wife. Eight fucking days ago. I shake my head. "You're going to check out this Stefan guy? What if he has her? He's got a criminal record."

I can't tell if Correia thinks I'm a jealous, murderous husband, a sane, concerned spouse, or something in between. This woman is inscrutable. She types a note into her phone and tucks the device into her pocket. "I'll give him a call. Let me know if you come upon anything else." Her dark eyes lock onto mine. "Like her passwords and such."

I don't blink. "Of course."

"I'm following every lead, Mr. Zarabian." Her voice is dead level. "You understand that, don't you?"

"Yeah," I say. "Keep it up, please."

With a tight nod, Correia heads back to the scrum of law enforcement at the pond's edge. I give a brief on-camera statement about how I believe Mina's out there somewhere, how I don't believe she's hurt herself. I say that I appreciate the dedicated work of the searchers and the police, but I hope they'll continue to investigate *every* possible lead, including any forensic evidence in her car and all her last-known contacts.

It occurs to me, as the camera lens glints and the lights shine down on me, that I sound robotic. Like I'm talking about a business deal. Next steps. Points of negotiation. Contract terms. I have the distant thought that people will expect me to cry and be emotional. But it all feels like it's happening outside me, like I'm watching along with everyone else. It reminds me of my dad's funeral, when I sat there numb while my mom sobbed against my chest. And the moment Caitlin announced she wanted a divorce. And the morning Mina walked out the door, and I let her.

That day, I failed her. Today, I have no time to indulge in a breakdown. She needs me.

It's on the news at noon, and that's when I start to get calls. The CBS station. ABC, too. Also, the one that used to call itself FOX but dropped the label because this is Massachusetts and it was killing their ratings. They're skeptical about this case being anything other than a suicide—I can tell. But they're interested because Mina's a reasonably well-known author, and hell, if that's what they need to latch onto, fine with me.

I'm so crushed with calls and interviews that I forget all about going over to the Richardses'. Rose shows up early Tuesday afternoon, chauffeured by Scott and dressed in her Sunday best, looking unsurprised at the presence of several news crews in addition to the police. My first thought is that she saw it all on television and decided to get out here for her close-up. But instead of basking in the spotlight, she gives a brief statement about wanting her daughter to come home safely, hands a few plates of treats to Correia, and then retreats back to her car, where Scott is waiting. By the time I extricate myself from yet another interview, they're gone. I suspect I've got some apologizing to do.

But only after I blow this thing up as big as it needs to be.

Unexpectedly, my mom helps. After getting yet another text about how Mina hasn't gotten back to her, I call her late Tuesday night to fill her in. Without giving me a heads-up, she hangs up and goes straight to her second home—Facebook—and makes an emotional post about her talented, beautiful, famous daughter-in-law. It earns her a viral moment. When I start getting calls on Wednesday morning from people at the *Boston Globe*, the *New York Times*, and the *Washington Post*, as well as CNN, the *Daily Beast*, *BuzzFeed*, and several other online sites, they all say they got my number from my mom.

It takes up all my time. All my energy. It keeps me from thinking about what I'm going to do if they find my wife in that pond. It keeps me from wondering if she really left me on purpose, because even if she did, even if she ran off to fuck this Stefan guy's brains out, I don't think she would have left everything—wallet, keys, car—behind. She's in trouble. She needs me. That's what I say over and over. I won't just accept suicide as an explanation and give up.

At some point during the afternoon, Detective Correia comes over to tell me that she's talked to Stefan Silva, and he has a solid alibi for Monday night through Tuesday morning, one that she's already checked out. Everything in her manner tells me she thinks that lead is dead. I question the timing—how is she so sure? I mention the guy's criminal record again—suspicion of assault. She tells me she'll let me know if she has any other pertinent information and reminds me to keep her informed as well.

She's holding me at arm's length. I don't know what that means.

By six, the reporters look bored, the cops look grim, my phone is almost dead, and I'm about to drop. Despite the news about Stefan, I feel a certain savage happiness that they've found absolutely no trace of Mina in the water or the park after three days of searching. But my hope that it will energize the detective to keep digging for other explanations dies when I overhear one officer tell another that it would have been easy for Mina to walk up the trail to the beach at Race Point and go into the water there. Into the ocean, where she'll never be found, where the current will carry her body for miles and where white sharks are increasingly common. So basically, they've found a way to write this off even if they don't find anything. Ocean, shark, done. I guess it saves them a lot of work.

Though I'm more queasy than hungry, I need to get something to eat and probably take a shower, so I head for my car. I connect the phone to its charger, noting that I've gotten eight missed calls in the last hour from an unknown number. Probably another reporter. I'm not really in the right headspace to give yet another interview, but when the phone rings again, I answer. I owe it to Mina.

"Mr. Zarabian? Is this Alexander Zarabian?"

"Yeah. Who's calling?"

She clears her throat. "My name is Hannah, Mr. Zarabian." She's quiet for so long that I have time to wonder if the call dropped. Then she says, "I work for Granite Square. And I just saw a report that Mina Richards is missing."

Granite Square is Mina's publisher, but her editor's name is Lauren, not Hannah. "Is this about one of her books? If she's got a deadline or something, that's going to have to—"

"No, that's...not why I'm calling. Can we meet?"

"I'm a little busy at the moment. Try calling her agent." There's another call waiting, probably that CNN reporter who's been trying to connect with me. "Look, I have to go."

"No!" She sounds almost panicked and also young, right out of Wellesley or something. "No, please. I need to meet with you. In person. As soon as possible."

"Aren't you in New York?"

"I can come up on the train."

"You're gonna need to tell me why, Hannah. I've got a lot going on, and I seriously have no time or patience for bullshit."

"I'm sorry," she says quietly. Her voice is shaking. "I'm not supposed to be doing this."

Now I'm curious. As gently as I can, I say, "I'm listening."

"Okay." She lets out a deep breath. "I think I might have information about what's happened to Mina."

CHAPTER SIX

She snapped back into awareness, looking back and forth between the doctor and a woman in scrubs at the foot of her bed.

"—to see you," the woman, probably a nurse, said. She was looking right at Maggie, eyebrows raised.

"What?"

Dr. Mehta moved toward the doorway. "We're transferring you up to the room now," he told Maggie. "Your mother will be able to come up to visit."

The sudden collision of what he'd just said and the news he'd dropped on her sent a shock through her body. "Does she know? Did you tell her?"

The sharpness of her demand led his eyes back to hers. "This is your news to tell," he said gently. "And it's your body. You have choices, and we won't make them for you. But I've notified our on-call psychiatrist that you may need some support tonight, all right?"

"I'm not crazy."

"Of course you're not," the nurse said. Her name tag said her name was Jamie. "You've been through a lot, though."

"But I'm fine," said Maggie, even as her breath came fast and uneven. Even as hot tears gathered in the corners of her eyes.

Dr. Mehta and Jamie gave each other a look, one that made Maggie cover her face with her hands. She heard the door to the room open and a clanking sound that shook the bed. Next, she was rolling, and the noises of the hospital grew louder, snatches of conversation, beeping monitors, metal rattling on metal, raising images of bloody instruments on trays. She felt laid open, her organs exposed, and she rolled onto her side and drew her knees up to her chest. It hurt. Every muscle and limb seemed scraped or bruised, and suddenly, every breath and movement stung and ached. They'd told her she didn't have any broken bones, but it felt like every single one was webbed with little cracks. Ready to shatter.

Behind her, Jamie murmured soft, supportive things. Sounds that didn't translate fully, because Maggie's heartbeat was too loud. Then a hand stroked over her head. "Your mother's here," the nurse said. "Are you ready to see her? Do you want me to stay?"

"I'm fine," Maggie mumbled against her palms. "I'm fine."

She peeked through her fingers at the sound of whispered conversation. Jamie was in the doorway—they were in a different room now, the door on a different side, the hallway outside a pale blue instead of creamy white—and she was talking to Maggie's mother. Ivy Wallace-Gainer nearly blocked out the light. Her blond, highlighted hair was styled in soft waves around her face. She wore a shimmery green shawl over her broad, sloped shoulders and was holding the fabric closed over her décolletage. She looked like she'd come from a social occasion. She probably had.

She was frowning, and the sight made Maggie's stomach pulse with nausea. Of course, that was the moment her mother noticed her looking. Her face transformed, caught between grimace and smile, tears and choked laughter, but all glowing with perfect concern and perfect highlighting along her cheekbones and brow. "Oh, my baby," she said, words tumbling over each other as she threw out her arms and rushed to Maggie's bedside, and then it was the overpowering scent of jasmine and orange and cedar, the smothering warmth of her soft but strong body, and the scratch of the sequins dotting her shawl.

Maggie squirmed as her mother enveloped her, as her ample arm slid beneath Maggie's shoulders and pulled her up to be pressed against that neck, the epicenter of the scent. She turned her head and breathed through her mouth. It wouldn't be good if she threw up.

Her mother released her. "She's too weak to even hug me back," she said to Jamie, who watched them from the doorway. "What did you give her? A sedative?"

Jamie glanced over at Maggie. She looked conflicted, and Maggie remembered what Dr. Mehta had said about all this being her story to tell.

"I'm fine, Mom," Maggie said quietly.

Her mother turned back to her and took her hand. She patted it. Ivy's fingernails were short but immaculate ovals, painted a tasteful, shimmery summer pink. "My poor lamb," she said, her voice tight. "You've been through so much. But I'm here now." She nodded toward Jamie. "Thank you for taking such good care of her. I want to speak with the attending as soon as possible about when I can take her home."

"I'll let Dr. Atkinson know." Jamie looked eager to escape the room. Her fingers were wrapped over the door handle.

"You're an angel," Ivy said to her. "I'm so thankful for you."

Jamie disappeared, leaving Maggie to heft the weight of her mother's complete attention. The face that swung back toward hers was no longer wreathed in a beatific smile. Lines bracketed her mother's mouth. "Where have you been?" The sharp whisper knifed into Maggie's ears, raising echoes of overlong church services and a firm hand clamped over her skinny thigh in warning.

Good girls are quiet girls.

Maggie flinched. "I don't remember."

Ivy shook her head. She pulled a chair over to the bed. Its feet shrieked and moaned along the floor, and Maggie almost looked to see if they had drawn blood from the linoleum. Maggie let out a breath as her mother sank into the chair. Her face was close, but at least she wasn't leaning over Maggie anymore.

"Do you have any idea what you've put me through the last few months?" Ivy asked, pulling a lacy handkerchief from her purse. She carefully dabbed at her eyes. The fabric came away flecked with mascara. "When you didn't arrive, I called the university and then the police. They found your car in a lot at Wachusett Mountain."

Wachusett. About an hour from the university and in the opposite direction of where she'd intended to go, north instead of south... happiness instead of dread. Cold wind and fluffy snow. Pure joy. Her feet dangling, skis clacking together, as the lift carried them upward, lights twinkling over a blanket of pristine white. Her hand enveloped in her father's warm grip.

"Your phone and keys and wallet were all inside the car," her mother continued, jarring Maggie out of the memory. "We thought you might have been kidnapped, but then I spoke with your roommate, and she told me what you said. About not wanting to come home."

"I never said that!"

"I just knew," Ivy said. "I knew you'd run away, and probably with some man. Sure enough, I was right."

"I had every intention of coming home for the summer! I don't know what happened." And now she was pregnant. *Jesus Christ.* At the thought, she tensed for a moment. It had been years, but she still felt the automatic kick of guilt at taking the Lord's name in vain, internalized and bone deep. "Did they tell you about the guy in the parking lot? How he was chasing me?"

"The Wellfleet police let him go. He said you'd been *living* with him."

"No. That... I don't know who he is." She remembered the guy they'd been holding down in the parking lot. Olive skin and dark hair. "I'd never seen him before in my life."

"Lying is a sin," her mother said quietly. "You're not just hurting me, and you're not just dishonoring your poor father. You're breaking your savior's heart."

Maggie looked out the window, wishing she could beam herself right through it, into the open air, over miles and miles until she was far from this place. "I'm not lying. I don't remember. And I don't know why."

"I heard them mention a psychiatrist." Ivy spat it out like a dirty word. "What on earth did you tell them?"

"Mom—"

"Because you don't have to lie, and you don't have to pretend." Her hands shook as she dabbed at her eyes again. "Haven't I always told you that forgiveness is a gift? Just tell the truth, and it's yours. We can pretend this never happened."

Maggie pressed her lips together.

"Whatever you've done and wherever you've been, whatever you've gotten into and whomever you've been with, I'll forgive you. We all will. Haven't we always, even when you were at your absolute worst? Claiming you don't remember only draws more attention to all this."

Maggie jerked her hand away from the bed rail as her mother reached for it.

Ivy's eyes narrowed. "You *want* attention," she snarled. "That's what this is all about, isn't it? Some sick little revenge? Haven't you punished me *enough*?"

Spit pooled under Maggie's tongue. "I'm going to throw up."

"I won't let you turn this around on me," Ivy was saying, her voice a quiet venom that no one in the hall would ever hear. "If you decided to live in sin with some man..."

Maggie wasn't listening anymore. She was too busy leaning over the other side of the bed rail, reaching for the kidney-shaped basin on the bedside table. She yanked it over beneath her chin and began to heave. The world turned black, and her body folded in on itself. She imagined the tiny creature inside her, pushing its way up through the coils of her organs, forcing itself along the tunnel of her throat, climbing from her mouth in all its malevolent and bloody glory. It was all noise and chaos and way too much light, and she had nothing to shield herself. Everything burned. Everything hurt.

And then, second by second, the pain receded. Her exhausted muscles went loose, and she sagged against the pillow. Jamie had reappeared and was holding the basin for her now. Her mother was stroking Maggie's stringy, greasy blond hair away from her face. Both were making sympathetic, comforting noises, and the mismatch between her mother's tone in this moment and the last few was so jarring that Maggie started to cry.

"My poor baby," whispered Ivy, still stroking. "My poor, poor baby."

Jamie offered a cup of water, poking its straw at Maggie's dry lips.

Maggie took a weak pull and let her head fall to the pillow again. "I'm tired."

"Of course," her mother said. "Of course you are. You've been through so much."

"I want to sleep."

"I've got my Bible study tonight anyway," her mother said. "I can come back afterward. Nurse, can you roll in one of those sleeper chairs for me?"

"We don't generally allow visitors to sleep—"

"I'm her *mother.*"

"Mom," Maggie rasped. "Go home. I'll be fine."

"We'll be watching over her tonight, Mrs. Gainer."

"Wallace-Gainer," her mother corrected. "I want you all to call me if there's any change. I'm all she's got."

Maggie put a hand on her belly. It felt hollow now. She glanced at the basin, which Jamie had set over on the counter near the sink. She'd been invaded, and it would take a lot more than a few heaves to have her body to herself again. She rolled on her side and pulled her legs to her chest. She wished she could ball up tiny enough to be invisible. She pressed her forehead to her knees. Tightened her arms around her thighs and calves. Wished herself unseen.

There were more murmurs and mutterings, but then the room went quiet save for distant beeps and shufflings and intercom messages filtering in from the hallway. She peeked over her shoulder. Her mother's chair was still there, vacant now. She'd gone off to commune with her church friends. Maggie wondered how Ivy would spin the situation, how she would sculpt and mold it for maximum sainthood and minimum embarrassment.

Maggie examined her hands, her fingers. Her nails were filthy and ragged. Her knuckles and the heels of her palms were all scraped up. She imagined herself trying to claw her way out of a dark, closed box. Or the dirt walls of a basement. She imagined herself handcuffed to a rusty old radiator or tied to a chair, a gag over her mouth. She tried on those images like dresses, checking to see if any fit, if any clung to the curves of her brain and the angles of reality.

The police had released the man who'd chased her. He'd convinced them she'd been living with him. What had he done to her? Why had she been running from him? She remembered the terror of those moments, when she'd crashed into awareness and onto the hood of some guy's car.

Would the man who'd chased her come here?

She gasped as the door opened and Jamie peeked in. "I know you said you wanted to sleep, but there's a friend here to see you. I thought it might cheer you up?"

Behind her, out in the hallway, stood Reina, petite with her brown hair in a pixie cut, hugging herself as if she was cold. Next to her was a redheaded guy Maggie recognized from pictures that had hung in their dorm room. Reina's boyfriend, Dan. The two of them had gone to high school together in Lowell, and Reina had frequently driven up to visit him at Dartmouth. Dan from Dartmouth, that was how Maggie had referred to him all year. She didn't like the way he was staring at her now. He turned to whisper something in Reina's ear. She raised her head and saw Maggie watching them.

"Okay," Maggie said to Jamie. "It's fine." It would be awkward to send them away now. It might cause a scene. They might talk and tell people that Maggie had been rude or weird. She didn't have the energy to deal with that.

Jamie ushered Reina and Dan into the room. Both of them were looking at her like Dr. Mehta had, as if she were about to detonate. "Hey," Reina said in a hushed voice. Like her mother's had, Reina's eyes were sparkling with tears. "How are you?"

"Fine," said Maggie. She pulled the thin blanket at the foot of her bed up over her body while Dan hovered near the doorway. "Hi, Dan."

He grinned. "You remember me now?" He came forward as if Maggie had issued an invitation to sit on her lap, but he paused when Reina clutched at his arm. He gave her a questioning look.

"He called me three nights ago," Reina said. "He claimed he'd seen you in Provincetown." She rolled her eyes. "But he was drunk off his ass, so I didn't believe him."

"So I went back the next day and took a picture of you, to prove it to her," he said, clearly pleased with himself. He had his phone out, and he turned its screen to show Maggie.

It was indeed a picture of her, in what looked like the patio of a restaurant. Standing next to a bar, holding a basin full of dishes, circles under her eyes, looking guarded and scraggly and lost. The black-haired guy who'd been facedown in the parking lot—he was next to her in the picture, scowling.

Maggie stared, nausea bubbling inside her once again. "That's in Provincetown? Two days ago?"

Dan nodded. "That guy—Esteban. He chased me down the street right after I took that. But when he caught up with me, he gave me a chance to explain, and I told him about you and how you'd been missing for months. He didn't seem all that surprised, actually. He agreed to help me get you back. He didn't think you'd just go with me if we told you all that."

"We said we'd meet him at the Moby Dick," said Reina. "We were ready to do a whole intervention. But either you were early or we were late, because by the time we got there, they were taking you away in an ambulance and him away in a police car."

"Because he was *chasing* me. I was trying to get away from him."

"Yeah, he said you freaked out," said Dan.

"Who is he?"

"To hear him tell it, he's the guy who's kept you safe for the last three weeks."

"Three weeks," said Maggie. "But I've been gone since mid-May."

"He said you just showed up about three weeks ago," Reina said. "You wouldn't say where you'd come from. He doesn't know how you got there. We hoped you might be able to explain what happened."

A noise came out of Maggie, part groan and part bitter laugh. "What the hell is happening to me?"

"You're okay," said Reina. "I'm so glad you're okay. I was so worried about you."

"She's been obsessing about it the whole summer," said Dan.

"I felt so guilty," Reina said. "I should have done more. You were acting so weird."

"What are you talking about?" asked Maggie. "When?"

"Before you took off. You were stressed about finals, and then that jackass decided it would be the perfect week to break up with you—"

"Wes," Maggie whispered. This, she remembered. They'd met in Romanesque and Gothic Art class last semester. She'd instantly spotted him, dark hair flopping over his forehead, intense blue eyes. They'd started going out in February, and she'd been convinced she was in love.

Then so many things had gone wrong. All her fault. And he'd broken up with her just before finals started. She'd been hurt, but...

"I was okay," she said. "I was fine."

Reina shrugged. "You seemed like it until the day before your last final. After that...it was weird, Maggie. You said you didn't want to go home, that everything was ruined. You were like this zombie girl, barely responding when I spoke to you. I was surprised you even made it to that final. You were like a different person."

"Did she call herself Layla?" asked Dan.

"Don't make fun of me," said Maggie. "That's shitty."

"I'm not making fun of you! You *told* me your name was Layla when I first saw you in Provincetown. You were waiting tables at the restaurant in the picture."

"Esteban said he knew it wasn't your real name," Reina explained. "He was pretty sure you stole it from that Eric Clapton song."

"I swear, I don't remember any of this," Maggie said. She couldn't quite catch her breath, and terror nibbled at the edges of her, raising goose bumps. "How do you know he's not lying?"

"I believe him," said Dan. "I told the cops as much."

"They called the owner of the restaurant where you guys worked," Reina said. "He vouched for Esteban, too. So did one of the waitresses. They both swore up and down that you were there of your own free will and that Esteban had only been looking out for you. And when we showed the police our texts about you and how Esteban was trying to get you back to your family, that was enough for them. They couldn't hold him."

Maggie's heels rubbed back and forth against the sheets, and she watched the movement, letting it hypnotize her. "I'm a nothing," she mumbled. "I feel sick."

Reina frowned. "Do you want me to call the nurse?"

She nodded, if only to make them leave. "I'm going to be sick." She grabbed the call button and pressed it.

Reina and Dan left a minute later, wishing her well, Reina saying they could get together once she was back home at her mom's. She mentioned registering for fall semester classes, which caused Maggie to lunge for the clean basin at her bedside. She hunched over it as her friends left, certain she was going to puke again. Several dry heaves later, she fell back onto her bed. Her breath came in desperate squeaks, and tears slipped from her eyes, running into her hair.

"Knock, knock," said a jaunty voice from the doorway. A woman stood there, with wiry, corkscrew-curly hair and a heart-shaped face. "Maggie?"

"Are you the nurse?"

The woman entered the room. "I'm Lori Schwartz. I'm the on-call psychiatrist, and Dr. Mehta let me know that you might need a little support tonight."

"I'm fine," Maggie said, putting the basin back on the table next to her bed.

"I took a peek at your chart," Lori said. "It must be so scary, not knowing where you've been or what happened."

"I hit my head. They said that could interfere with memory."

"It wouldn't quite explain what you're experiencing, though. Especially because your scans were completely unremarkable." Lori moved a little closer. She wasn't wearing a lab coat, just navy slacks and a floral shell with a light cardigan. Her ID badge hung from a lanyard around her neck. "Besides, a mild concussion might make sense if we were talking about a few hours of amnesia. But months?" She shook her head, making her curls jiggle around her face. "There's another reason."

"Maybe I was drugged," said Maggie. "I know they said that guy didn't kidnap me, but—"

"I heard about that. Dr. Mehta put a note in your chart after getting updated by the Wellfleet Police Department. Lots to figure out there. But if drugs were the culprit, I'd expect you to have some hazy recollections at least."

"I'm not lying," Maggie snapped.

Lori's eyes went wide. "Why would you say that?"

"Because it's obviously what everyone thinks. You don't believe the concussion explains it. You don't believe me when I say that guy might have drugged me—"

"But you just said that's what *everyone* thinks," Lori said. "Who are we talking about?"

"My mom," she whispered.

"Ah." Lori leaned forward. "Is there any reason why you'd lie to her?"

Maggie felt like an amber-eyed animal trapped in the beam of oncoming headlights. "No."

"I think we should talk about what you were dealing with. *Before* you walked away from your life."

"Because you think I'm only pretending to not remember?"

"I guess that's a possibility. And if that's true, I want to understand what happened to make you feel like you needed to go out of your way to tell this story. But also, I want to know if something happened that your mind *needed* to forget. Because that's another possibility."

Maggie thought back. She remembered walking toward her car in the student lot. She remembered hitting the button to unlock. Sliding into the seat, breathing in the hot air, turning on the AC. Checking the gas gauge, thinking she needed to fill up on the drive home. And that was it...until she found herself running through a completely different parking lot, riven with terror, over a hundred and fifty miles away. "There's literally nothing there. I sort of...

blacked out? But my roommate told me I was going by another name and waiting tables in a restaurant. They showed me a picture, and there I was. So suddenly I became this other person?"

Lori didn't look surprised. "It's more complicated than that, but it's also one of the possibilities here. We have more evaluation to do in order to confirm it."

She knew Lori was a psychiatrist and knew the last thing she should do was talk to one, but she needed to know as much as she needed to breathe. "Can you help me get my memory back so I can figure out what happened to me?"

"It depends on what caused you to lose it in the first place."

"Can you give me any actual answers? Something other than 'possibly' and 'it depends'? God, you're all alike."

"Who?"

Maggie rolled her eyes and kept her gaze rooted on her feet, shifting beneath the sheet and blanket. "Real doctors can do a blood test. A scan. An X-ray. They can tell you what's going on. All you do is sound smart without ever actually saying anything."

"You want a definitive answer."

"Duh?"

"Have you ever heard of dissociative fugue?"

"Isn't fugue a music term? Like a kind of music?"

"One definition of fugue is music related. But the other is psychological. Sometimes, a person just kind of forgets who they are, and they walk away from their life. Sometimes, they even adopt a new identity. A new name."

"That's actually a thing?"

Lori smiled. "Not a common thing, but yeah, definitely a thing."

"Why does it happen? Why would it happen to me?"

"I'm not saying it did, but I was hoping we could figure that out together. May I?" She gestured at the chair where Ivy had sat only an hour or so ago.

Maggie looked away, toward the window. "Go ahead."

"Maggie, I know this must be confusing. And frightening. Understanding will help, I think. You must feel so out of control."

"I'm fine," she whispered.

"You've said that twice now, and honestly, you're not convincing me." Her expression was kind when Maggie whipped around to glare at her. "Maggie, it wouldn't be *normal* to be fine after what happened to you today. It wouldn't be normal to feel fine after finding out that you've been missing for two months and have no idea where you've been. It would be normal to be completely freaked out."

"I'm just tired."

"That's fair. But I can tell you're also wondering. And you're worried."

"I'm pregnant," she whimpered.

"I know."

Maggie squeezed her eyes shut, her mouth shut, her knees together. Everything, closed up tight. But it didn't make her feel safer. She knew it was only a matter of time until she was pried open again.

Lori cleared her throat. "Do you know how it happened?"

Maggie shook her head.

"We'll work on figuring that out," said Lori. "And as we do, you can decide what to do about the pregnancy. But, Maggie, there's something you have to know about fugue, if that's what's going on here. It's going to be an important part of getting better and making sure it doesn't happen to you again."

"It could happen *again*?"

"It's possible," said Lori. "But it's unlikely if you're willing to take a good look at how it happened in the first place."

"I don't know how it happened!"

"With your permission, I can help. This type of event...it's often caused by some type of severe stress or trauma." Lori's gaze was unwavering. Unapologetic. Gentle and merciless at the same time. Her gaze was a scalpel, Maggie realized, cutting right into her mind.

She turned over to face the window. "I didn't go through a trauma," she said. "I was under some stress, and my boyfriend broke up with me, but it wasn't a trauma. I'm not crazy."

"Experiencing a trauma doesn't make a person crazy, Maggie. It means they've suffered an injury, one that needs some treatment to ensure recovery."

"Whatever."

"I think you might have suffered an injury, Maggie. I think it might be what drove you away from your life in May. If you'll work with me, I can—"

"Get out." She was curled into a ball again, shaking and doing her best not to cry. "Get out."

"I'll be on my way," said Lori. "I can see that you're tired. Would you like me to prescribe something to help you sleep tonight?"

"Yes," she murmured. "Please."

"I can do that. But you're probably going to be discharged tomorrow morning, and it may be difficult for you to adjust without some help." She pulled a business card from her pocket and set it on the folds of Maggie's blanket. "Please consider talking to me again, Maggie, or, if I'm not your cup of tea, letting me refer you to someone else who could help. You deserve that. You deserve the chance to puzzle through what happened to you, with support. And without judgment. Good night."

Maggie stared out the window until she heard the door close behind the shrink. There was no trauma. There never had been a trauma.

This is why she couldn't talk to a psychiatrist. They were just as crazy as the people they were trying to help.

She shifted her knees and flicked the business card off of her blanket like the rubbish it was.

WEDNESDAY, AUGUST 5

"Y ou know where she is?" I lean forward, my eyes wide, even though the only things I see through my rain-flecked windshield are the trees of Beech Forest.

"N-no," Hannah says. "Not exactly."

"Who did you say you were? Hannah who?"

"Please," she says, her voice breaking. "I'll get fired if anyone knows I'm talking to you. I-I just...I think I might be able to help."

"I know you're not her editor, so who are you?" The last thing I need right now is to buy the bullshit story of some attention-seeking nutjob. "Do you really work for Granite Square?"

"I already told you I did. I don't want to say anything else."

"The police are dredging the bottom of a goddamn pond for my wife's body, Hannah. If you've got any information that could help me find her, you *need* to help. And if you don't, you need to fuck off and leave me the hell alone." I pause, and then I realize what *she* might need. "Listen, if you've got something that can help me find Mina, there's no way I'm going to get you in trouble. We'll figure out a way to keep you out of it if possible."

"Will you meet me in Boston?"

It'll take her at least four hours to get from NYC to Boston by train, and it would take me nearly three to get to Boston myself. "Why can't you tell me whatever it is you know right now?"

"It's not something to tell. I need to show you."

"Show me *what?*"

Her breath rushes over the phone's speaker, a blast of white noise. "It's a manuscript."

"Something Mina wrote? Send it to me via email."

"I can't have any electronic trail that traces this back to me. Please, Mr. Zarabian—"

"Alex," I say wearily. "And my wife writes romances, Hannah. Fiction. She makes shit up for a living."

"This is different." For the first time, she sounds like an adult instead of a scared girl. "I wouldn't risk the job I've wanted my whole life if I thought this was nothing."

"I believe you," I say. "And I'll meet you halfway."

It might turn out to be nothing, but the hope that it's not keeps me moving. Helps me feel a shade less helpless. I've set the media monster rolling, but after countless interviews today, I'm not sure I have more to say, and knowing that the police have decided that Mina's dead even if they don't find her in Beech Forest makes me all the more determined to do as much as I can. Hannah and I agree to meet in New London, one of the stops on the Northeast Regional. I gas up the car and head out, though I stop at that Moby Dick place in Wellfleet and grab a lobster roll to go as I make my way off the Cape. I drive past signs for Harwich, grinding my teeth and drumming my fingers on the steering wheel. Half-tempted to head for the Mariner.

I'm not sure what this manuscript is actually going to change. I mean, Mina pens romance novels, and having read a couple, I can say that they're good and clever and, yeah, sexy. But they're not *The Da Vinci Code* or *Gone Girl*, mysteries or thrillers or suspense, nor are they anything even remotely resembling our life. I even asked Mina once, half-joking, half-apprehensive, if I was ever going to recognize myself in the pages of her books. We'd been dating for two months, and I was smitten to the point of obsession.

She laughed at my question, and because I didn't understand her quite yet, I took it the wrong way. We were lying in my bed, the Saturday morning of a weekend when I didn't have Devon, so it was just the two of us there with our champagne and coffee. And her laughter. "Jesus," I said. "I know I'm not exactly SEAL Team Six or whatever the hell alpha male you're writing about at the moment, but I didn't think it was a joke—"

Her smile died. "Alex, I'm never going to write about you. You'll never be in one of my books."

"Yeah," I said. "You want some more coffee?"

Her slender fingers grabbed my wrist. "You *don't* get it," she said. "There's no way I'm going to write about you, or us, because it's too precious to me." Her smile was like one of those blown-glass Christmas ornaments—exquisite but easily cracked. "You're this treasure I've found, and I don't want to share. I don't want to pull us apart and lay us on a table. I don't want to worry about pacing or plot structure or tension or twists. We're real. We're plain and ordinary and real, and yet still utterly magical. And that's everything to me."

I scooted closer to her as I saw tears shine in her eyes. "I'm sorry," I mumbled. "Sometimes I'm an ass."

"Yeah," she said. "You are. But you're also mine. You don't belong to some other heroine, even one I invent. When I'm with you, *I* want to be real. And present. I'm not always good at that, but with you, it's been easy. I don't want to distance myself from this relationship by caging it with words on a page." She set down her champagne flute and ran her hands along my shoulders as I moved next to her. "I want to feel this, not bind it up in a story. A happy ending is still an ending." Her lips brushed across my mouth. "And I don't want this to end."

I am driving down 95 South with fucking tears in my eyes, remembering that. How she looked, how her body felt beneath my hands, the lilt of her voice, it's all so real that I can barely breathe. We were too precious to her. We were too real. And she didn't want it to end.

Did that change? What was she afraid to tell me? Is this manuscript the answer to why she took off and left her rings behind? Or is this Hannah person bringing me something totally unrelated to our relationship? And should I have stopped in Harwich instead? Maybe what she was afraid of telling me had more to do with *him* than this damn manuscript.

I've committed to following this particular lead, so I drive, and I think about Mina. I have to keep pushing away the nagging fear that she really was depressed and really did hurt herself. It goes against everything I understood about her, but with every hour of her absence, I'm trusting that understanding a little less.

As I roll south through Rhode Island, needing to stay awake, I call Drew to check in about next steps with Pinewell. I'm hoping to hear that he's given in to the reality of our situation and is prepared to sign the deal, because I need at least one thing in my life to go smoothly right now. But he's focused on Mina's disappearance. He tells me that Caroline is suggesting that I talk to a PR person.

"Why?" I ask. "Am I coming across like a murderer?"

"Only about a dozen times." He chuckles, but it's tense and sad. "I've been flipping back and forth between the networks and reading every article as soon as it comes out. The police are telling a damn good story, and it makes sense."

"Jesus Christ, Drew."

"I'm just saying that if you want attention to stay focused on this, you're gonna have to be strategic. Otherwise..."

"Because our national attention span is all of a half second long."

"Unless there's something new that pops up, Caroline's saying they're going to move on quickly. A lot of other stuff to cover. Another shark attack today in Truro. Did you hear?"

"Are you fucking kidding me?"

"Well, that's not the only thing. There's always a new thing to freak out about. You know what I mean."

"Yeah." Because I'm not immune to it, either. In fact, a month ago, Mina and I agreed to keep our phones out of the bedroom so we weren't picking them up off the bedside table and getting lost in a screen every time the other person took a thirty-second trip to the bathroom. It was Mina's idea—*I'm learning to be content with my thoughts*, she told me. *I shouldn't be diving into that virtual world for entertainment and stimulation and comfort and outrage every time I'm left alone—and you shouldn't either.* She always seemed so healthy. Like she'd figured it all out.

Or maybe she was texting Stefan on the sly and didn't want me to see.

"I'm not trying to drag you down," Drew is saying, probably interpreting my silence as fury. "But that's why Caroline thinks you might need some help to keep the story front and center."

"If she's got a person to recommend, she can text me," I tell him. "I'll look into it."

"Are you driving back to Boston? We could—"

"I'm headed in the other direction, actually." I offer my CEO the executive summary of tonight's events.

"You really think this is going to pan out?" Skepticism bleeds from every word. "And it's worth driving halfway to New York to meet some potential nut instead of being here?"

"I'll be back later tonight," I snap. "And I'll call in tomorrow so we can talk about accepting Pinewell's offer."

I hang up before he can argue with me. And before I end up confessing that signing this deal with Pinewell will mean the end of his reign as CEO of his own company. Even though he'll make money, it'll kill him. He imagines he's going to be the one who finds some amazing cure for a deadly cancer, but the people who can actually make that happen don't deal in dreams or fantasies or feelings or egos. They just want to get shit done and make money.

I'm wondering whether the Pinewell guys ever watch cable news. Kinda hoping they don't.

As I pull up to the New London train station and learn that Hannah's train isn't due for another ten minutes, I discover someone else has been watching the news.

Did you do something to her?? It's Willa, chatting me up through the Facebook app.

NO, I reply.

Last week you asked me when I'd spoken to her, and now I find out she'd already been missing for a few days at that point. Except I messaged with her TWO DAYS AGO.

For a brief moment, my heart jolts to a stop. Then I remember—that wasn't Mina. I need to come clean.

Except Willa does it for me. That was you, wasn't it?

After a moment of hesitance, I admit it.

You're a fucking scary motherfucker, she replies, and I'm going to the police.

I roll my eyes. I didn't do anything to Mina, I type. And if you have ANY information about where she went, you'd better tell me. Or the police. I don't care.

As if I'd tell the guy who fucking catfished me!

"Give me a fucking break," I groan. She told you she had something important to tell me, and you told her to be brave. If that has anything to do with where she might have gone or something that's happening to her, hiding it makes you complicit.

I'm telling them you probably killed her, you controlling bastard.

I thought you were supposed to be creative.

You're shady as hell. And that's her final message. She disappears from chat, and when I search for her, I realize she's not only unfriended me, she's blocked me as well. I make a mental note to go ahead and give Detective Correia the news that I cracked into Mina's laptop. She'll see that I impersonated my wife, but she'll also have the confirmation that Stefan Silva is a guy to watch.

I snap out of my miserable churning as the train pulls into the station. I'm supposed to be on the platform, waiting for Hannah. As people trickle through the double doors of the old brick building, I leave my car in a tow zone and rush inside. A minute later, I smooth down my hair and check to make sure my fly is up, because I get some weird looks as I scan the exiting passengers. I have no idea what this Hannah person looks like, but I'm imagining a nervous, bookish girl, pale as a fish and kind of bohemian.

She's not that at all. I'm approached by a young woman in a colorful hijab, wearing bright red lipstick and skinny jeans. She's got a messenger bag slung across her chest and comes right up to me, offers her hand. "Alex?"

I shake. "Yeah. Hi."

"I recognized you from the news."

I guess that explains the funny looks. "Want to go grab a drink?"

We head across the street, but the first place we try, Oasis, is so loud inside that even on the sidewalk, I can't hear what she's saying. After I move my car, we walk up the road and end up at a good old-fashioned hole in the wall, the Dutch Tavern. Inside, I order a beer and she orders...water. "You hungry? Want a hamburger or something?"

She asks for fries. I gesture at a table in a corner. The place isn't crowded, but I still feel like I'm sitting in the middle of that train station, on display. "So, is Hannah your real name?"

"What, you think it should be Tahira or Fadiyah or something?" She tugs on her head scarf and arches an eyebrow. "Why does it matter?"

"Please convince me that I didn't drive three hours to meet a crank."

She has the good grace to smile, and it doesn't even seem hostile, which I probably deserve. "I met Mina last summer," she says, "though I didn't know it was her at the time."

She's known Mina longer than I have. "What do you mean, you didn't know it was her?"

"I work for Pleiades. I'm an assistant to one of the editors there. Her editor, actually."

"Pleiades?"

"It's an imprint at Granite Square."

"Mina writes for Diva."

Hannah strokes her finger through the condensation on her

slightly smudged water glass. "Mina Richards writes for Diva. But Quinn Garrison got a single book deal from Pleiades about a year ago, for her debut novel."

"Quinn Garrison?"

She's looking at me like I'm slow. "Did Mina tell you that she had a pseudonym?" When I shake my head, she doesn't seem surprised. "It was top secret. We all had to sign NDAs. She didn't want anyone to know it was her."

Including her husband, I guess. But I wonder if she told her friend Willa. I sip my beer and then nudge it aside. "It's not romance, I take it?"

"Far from it."

"That doesn't make it real, though. It's fiction, right?"

Her hand slips down and touches the messenger bag hanging on the back of her chair. "Supposedly." She opens the flap and pulls out a thick stack of paper. "I haven't read any of her romances, but this..."

It's all I can do not to snatch it out of her hands. "Is this something that's going to be published?"

"The pub date is set for February, and ARCs—advance review copies—are going out next week." Her brow furrows. "She said there was no way she'd do any appearances unless she could go in disguise. I thought she was joking at first."

"Did she give you any clue why she was so cloak and dagger about it?"

"You'll have to read it. When I asked Kyle—he's her editor and my boss—this afternoon if he thought this book had anything to do with Mina's disappearance..." She presses her lips together. "He totally shut me down. I don't think he wants to believe there's a connection. He's pretty beside himself."

"Over Mina's disappearance or because he's afraid this 'investment' is going to go down the tubes if she's..." I look away and give up. "He doesn't know you're here."

"He'd probably toss me out the window and enjoy watching me hit the pavement. And our offices are on the seventeenth floor." She slides the stack of paper across the table. "This is an older version of the manuscript, from revisions—it has Kyle's comments in the margins. It was my job to input them into the electronic file for her. When I heard she was missing this afternoon, it made me think of something he wrote." She pulls up the first half of the manuscript, revealing a dog-eared page near the middle. There, in the margins, Kyle has scrawled, *Didn't you say this is from your own experience? You're filtering the whole thing for the reader! Make me feel it! Push!*

I meet Hannah's eyes. "What's the book about?"

"A woman with a rare psychological issue. I don't know how much of it is real and how much is fiction. I never got to ask her."

Psychological *issue*. I accept the manuscript and look down at the cover page. *The Quiet Girl*, it's called. By Quinn Garrison. "When did she finish this?"

"She finished the draft last December," says Hannah, picking at her fries. "She was revising in the spring, and she's supposed to be doing copyedits now."

We met in December, when she'd already written the book, but I guess she's been tinkering with it for the last several months. "Did you ever talk to her about the story?"

"Only once. She came down to the city, and I took her out for lunch because Kyle had a family emergency. I thought Mina might be angry, having to go to lunch with a nobody, but she was really nice. She almost seemed nervous about the whole thing, which I didn't quite get. I told her how much I loved the book, and she said it was the most scarily honest thing she's ever written. She said she was absolutely terrified that people would find out it was her."

"Did she say why?"

Hannah glances at her phone. "I have to go."

"What? Already?"

"My train back to New York arrives in fifteen minutes."

I stand up as she does. "What do I—"

She puts her hand over mine. Her touch is warm and startling. "This is going to be hard for you," she says, "and I know this is already a hard time. I really hope it helps. But this is all I can do. I've told you everything I know, and now I need to step away from it. I don't want to lose my job. Please."

When I offer my thanks, she gives me a sad smile. "I hope you find her," she murmurs, and then she leaves me there. Disappears into the night, back to the train, back to New York. I sink back into my seat, manuscript in hand. *This is going to be hard.* I already feel that, but I'm braced for it. Nothing is worse than Mina being gone.

I read the first chapter.

The character doesn't even seem to have a name for the first few pages, and she walks around in a fog. Then I find out her name is Layla, and she doesn't seem anything like Mina. Not the Mina I know, at least.

Until the little similarities start to peek out. Just a few lines here and there, but they stand out to me like a clown at a funeral parlor. The main character laughs when she's happy, to the confusion of those around her. She hates seafood. Mina's real-life neighbors—there they are, Chris and Aaron, transplanted into the story—are kind to the lost, drifting girl. She even gave the damn, determined pigeon a cameo.

I keep reading, page after page, searching for more clues, devouring my wife's prose, hunched over the table as the tension rises. Before I know it, I'm several chapters in, almost halfway, deep enough for Layla to realize that her real name is Maggie and that she lost herself for two whole months.

And that she's pregnant.

She walked away from her life, including her car, her keys, her phone, and her wallet...and became someone else. No memory of her old life or of the people who loved her.

The psychiatrist in the story warns that it might happen again.

"Closing soon, buddy. Last call." The bartender taps at his watch.

I stand up and check my phone. It's nearly midnight. And I have to get back, because a new, terrible, weird, hopeful, horrible possibility has presented itself.

CHAPTER SEVEN

It was her room, but it wasn't. Years ago, before college and high school, before her father died and everything fell apart, back when she had laid her head on this pillow every night, she had been a different person. A little girl in another world. Her fingers tripped along the meticulous stitches in the square patches of the quilt bunched around her body. Did a square remain a square when it was pulled and twisted and distorted by every connecting stitch, every other square around it? Perhaps it became something else, but she didn't know what to call it.

This room. White walls, white curtains, white sheets that she was not supposed to stain. Washed every week with bleach. Polished wood floors, no shoes, only socks, and break that rule at your peril, a matching dresser and desk and bookcase, no drinks, no food, no crumbs, nothing sticky. Stuffed animals at the foot of the bed. Flower Flopears, the elephant. Wilbur Longfoot, the kangaroo. Sweetie Flufftail, the rabbit. She hadn't named them. And the person who had was gone.

With a brisk knock, her mother entered. Her nose wrinkled slightly. "When you're ready, darling, I can run a bath." She smiled. "I'll put bubbles in. The lavender kind."

Ivy was dressed for going out, someplace casual, some occasion that called for *effortless*. Linen slacks and a flowered shirt with an embroidered collar. Golden cross pendant dangling from a delicate chain, nestled into the hollow of her throat. Shell-pink nails and matching lip gloss.

"Bible study?" Maggie guessed.

"I've left supper for you in the refrigerator. Fried chicken and potato salad. And I made fresh rolls. Have one while they're still warm!" Ivy fluttered near the window, pulling the curtains wide to let in the harsh afternoon sun, running her fingertips along the blinds. "I haven't dusted these since May!" An accusation wrapped in gauzy self-blame.

"It's fine, Mom." Maggie turned her face into the pillow, fighting back a wave of nausea. "I just want to sleep."

"Lying around all the time won't help you feel better. I have a half hour before my group. If you want to get ready, maybe do your hair, you could come. The ladies would be so happy to see you looking pretty and well. They've been nonstop prayer warriors, and here you are."

So they could take credit for her return. Did they want to take credit for whatever had happened to her while she was gone, too? No, no. God only brought the good things, and the rest, well, that was what happened when people didn't behave according to His will.

All these things that could never be said aloud.

Maggie sensed her mother near the bed, raising the fine hairs along Maggie's exposed forearm. She pulled the sheet up to cover her shoulders. "They told me to take it easy. You heard the nurse."

"She didn't mean forever. People need to see that you're all right. It will make them feel better after so much worry."

"People."

"This isn't just about you." Her mother's voice was low and sweet and dangerous, a straight razor against soft skin. Even the tiniest diversion from its path would bring blood. "When you disappeared, it hurt a lot of people. While you were gone, doing whatever you were doing without letting anyone know you were even alive, the rest of us were worrying ourselves to an early grave." A blessed moment of silence, then the inevitable: "I bought a third plot at Woodside. I thought I might be laying you in the ground next to your father."

"Mom, please," she whispered. She couldn't be sick. Not now. She pulled her knees to her chest.

Her mother let out a delicate sniffle. Maggie stayed limp as she felt her mother's hand on her back. Rubbing. She gritted her teeth.

"What am I complaining for? I should just be grateful you're home safe," her mother murmured. "And we have this month to get you ready to go back to school. Your junior year! What a time in your life! That's a blessing, too."

A distant ringing from the landline in the living room. Ivy's steps receded, swift and silent, until she reached the creaky spot a foot beyond the threshold. Maggie's fingers clawed into her pillow at the sound.

The trill of her mother's perfect laughter filtered down the hall, followed by the lightest of everything-is-all-right tones. As her mother chatted away, Maggie's muscles unspooled slowly. Sunlight had turned the room a faint shade of gold, imposing its buttery stain on an empty white canvas. Her gaze darted to the plastic bag near the closet. She had to get that put away before Ivy did it for her; she never tolerated a mess. Untidiness was an insult to the Lord. A sign that you weren't grateful for what you'd been given.

Inside the bag were the clothes she'd been wearing when she'd been hit. The clothes she'd been wearing when she'd run for her life. Or maybe not, but it had felt like it at the time. Wincing at the pull of bruises and scratches, wounds not nearly serious enough to keep her safe, she sat up. Slid off the bed. Crawled toward the bag. Sat in front of it. Her belly hurt, a fierce pang. She didn't know if she needed to puke or to eat or both. Probably both.

Morning sickness. The realization raised another wave of queasiness, and her stomach became a fist. Swallowing hard, Maggie yanked the bag into her lap. She pulled out an oversized T-shirt. *Haverman's Helles House*, it said across the chest. She pressed the fabric to her nose. It smelled of stale smoke and sweat, a combination that made her throat tighten. She coughed and tossed the shirt toward the white ceramic trash can next to the desk. She pulled a pair of shorts from the bag next, intending it for the same destination, but one pocket seemed bulky and misshapen. She reached inside and pulled out a wad of bills, which she counted quickly. Three hundred and twenty dollars. With a quick glance toward the door, she pressed the money to her chest, then crawled over to her bed and tucked it under the mattress.

She smoothed the sheet over the side of the bed. Pulled up the quilt and did the same. Neat, neat. She felt a little more powerful— until she heard the creak outside the door. Her mother reentered the room without knocking this time, her blue eyes alighting on her daughter sitting on the floor next to the bed.

"Did you fall?" Ivy scanned the room, spotting the plastic bag, the shorts on the floor, the shirt in the garbage. "Oh, dear." She bustled toward the closet, scooped up the bag, the shorts, and the shirt. "I'll deal with these. I put the suitcase we found in your car inside the closet, so there are clothes in there, but for winter and spring. I'll buy you some nice, new summer clothes. I meant to tell you; the summer festival is this Sunday."

Maggie pulled herself back onto the bed and sat on the edge as her mind scrambled for the words she needed. She'd had this all figured out in May, but her plans...her plans had been ruined. "I might have to work," she tried. "The bakery. I have to see."

Her mother gave her a pitying look. "Oh, I spoke to Doris at Flour Child. She said she hopes you feel better. Next summer, I'm sure it will all work out."

Saliva filled Maggie's mouth, and then she was lumbering past her mom, desperate to make it to the bathroom in time. It would be bad in so many ways if she didn't. Her knees hit tile, and she lunged for the bowl while her mother cried out from the hallway. And then it was all dark and swirling and hands on her back and fingers scraping against her scalp, pulling at her hair. Then it was sour and hurting, acid seeping into well-worn grooves.

She opened her eyes when her mother pressed the rim of a cup to her mouth. "Will you be all right if I leave you?" Ivy was asking. "I can call to cancel—"

"No," Maggie said. "My stomach is just unsettled. Maybe some of the medication they gave me in the hospital. I'll be fine. I'm fine."

"Yes." Ivy straightened and washed her hands in the sink. After drying them, she pulled her blouse straight and examined her hair in the mirror. "You're fine. Eat something, though. It'll help get that stuff out of your system."

She helped Maggie off the floor, wiped her mouth with a damp washcloth, and led her back to her room. Ivy tucked her into the bed that had known a different girl. One who believed in magic. It had all made sense to that girl, and Maggie could remember the safety that came with such certainty. She'd been a baby bird nestled in a warm, divine palm more secure than any nest. She'd believed in all the things she couldn't see, the forces that pulled her toward good and bad, angels and demons and a God that heard her thoughts and had a plan for her, for her life, for everyone around her, for all time. And she was loved, and her soul would go on forever, as long as she followed the right path. It had been easy, once.

She couldn't quite remember when it had stopped making sense. Was that another month she'd forgotten? A whole year? Or just a thread of memory that had been pulled from the intricate netting of her mind? Not that it mattered. She had other things to worry about now.

Her mother called out her goodbyes as she left, and Maggie edged over to the window to watch the car pull out of the drive. Then, stepping over the creaky spot by habit, she padded down the hall to the living room and began the hunt. Her phone wasn't in her room, so it had to be out here somewhere. And sure enough, the charge cord snaked out of the front drawer of her mother's writing desk, leading her to the treasure. There were dozens of missed calls, dozens of voicemails.

She looked for one number, one name, the one that had mattered most, but didn't see it. Not even once. Wes hadn't even bothered to try to reach her, to check in, to say hi, to say he was worried. Did he even know she'd been missing?

She stifled a low, pathetic whine with a hand pressed over her mouth. Then she listened to the messages that had been left since she'd been found. Two days, two messages. One from Reina, to see how she was doing. One from Dr. Schwartz, also to see how she was doing. Inviting her to call and follow up. Couldn't take the hint. Couldn't help even if Maggie gave her the chance.

But Reina...that was different. She pressed her friend's number. She had to tell someone. As the phone rang, Maggie panicked. She hung up without leaving a voicemail.

Once she opened her mouth, it would be real. And she couldn't pluck the knowledge out of Reina's brain. Who knew who she would tell? Maybe even Ivy.

She froze as an idea occurred to her. There was one person who might be able to help if Reina and Dan had been telling the truth. She texted Reina: Hey. Sorry I missed you. Can you give me Esteban's number? I'd like to thank him for trying to help me.

She pondered for a solid few minutes before finally sending it. After that, she gave in to the hunger that had been clawing at her. Knowing her mother would likely be gone for at least three hours, she settled in at the kitchen table with the food laid out around her. Her hands tore at the cold fried chicken, letting the greasy strands of bird muscle slide across her fingers and her lips. She scooped the potato salad out with those same polluted fingers, shoved it between the same oily lips. If only Ivy could see her now, slouched over the table, elbows on wood, napkin nowhere in sight, let alone folded across her thighs, mayonnaise beneath her fingernails, smears of barbecue sauce on her cheeks, gobs of both in the lank strands of hair swinging like pendulums on either side of her face while she rocked back and forth, back to swallow and forth to gorge.

She staggered away from the carnage as her phone buzzed. Reina was pissed that she was more interested in getting Esteban's number than actually talking, she could tell. No pleasantries, no emojis. But she'd given Maggie what she wanted. Feeling reckless and drunken with the feast and the power of not being watched, she sent another text before she could consider whether or not it was sensible.

Hi. This is Maggie. Can we meet?

Oh, here came the debate. This was the guy who'd chased her through a parking lot, toward a road. She remembered the terror. It was the first thing, in fact, that she remembered since Student Lot A. Terror. And being chased. By Esteban.

But Dan and Reina had told her that was all a mistake. Esteban had been looking out for her. Trying to save her from herself. She—

I don't know if that's a good idea.

She let out a shaky breath. I'm sorry you got arrested.

It's ok, as long as you really believe I was only trying to help.

She wasn't sure if she believed that or not. Are you still willing to help? ??

She frowned. Bit her lip. Will you tell me what happened? I can't remember. It seemed the safest way.

I have to be at work at 7.

Can we meet halfway?

Maggie tensed against a lurch of anxiety. It needed to be someplace public but not enclosed. She needed to be able to run, to get away. She didn't want to be watched. Then she remembered just the place. How about the Salt Pond? There's a visitor center.

They agreed to meet in an hour.

Maggie looked in the mirror for the first time since she'd come back to herself. One glance was enough to have her in the shower. Not because she cared so much about how she looked but because she didn't want people noticing her, and a girl with circles under her eyes and congealed potato salad residue all over her face would probably earn some stares.

A half hour later, she had swiped her keys from her mother's desk, along with a twenty from Ivy's secret cash stash that she didn't think Maggie knew about.

Maggie had learned so many of her mother's tricks and games so long ago...but it hadn't ever been enough. She caught the front door handle, her hand suddenly trembling. Confusion washed over her. As if she'd just popped into this place and time, into this mind and these thoughts. But the feeling departed as quickly as it had arrived, and her desperation propelled her forward. Out to the drive. To the carport. To the Corolla she'd apparently left abandoned in a ski resort's parking lot miles from where she went to school, in the opposite direction of where she'd planned to go. She sat in the driver's seat, waiting to lose herself. Almost wishing it would happen, that she'd disappear, blink out, and when she awakened, her body would be her own again, and all would be well.

No such luck, either good or bad. Maggie examined the gas gauge and turned the key in the ignition and set herself in motion, keenly aware of every heartbeat and every second, keeping time for all the lives she carried inside her. She turned on the radio, Y101, and cranked it up until the relentless beat chased everything else away. He would be there at four, he'd said.

She made it to the parking lot of the visitor center with several minutes to spare. She parked her car and got out, skittered away from it like it was radioactive. As if someone might see the car, read the license plate, hunt her down. She strode along the sidewalk, momentarily focused on stepping on each and every crack, before pausing in front of the dry erase board that held the day's schedule of talks. She was missing "The Mysterious World of Eels," which had begun on the terrace about fifteen minutes earlier.

She sought out a spot along the split rail fence that separated the parking lot from the pond. Plenty of people around, bikers and walkers and families introducing their children to the history of Cape Cod as a respite from the packed, sweltering beaches. She'd been here before, seen it all. Several times. She rubbed her fingertips along the rough wood and watched the parking lot.

She could tell it was him not because she recognized him but because of the way he looked at her. Like he knew her. He drove a Corolla, too, only much more beaten up than hers. He closed the door gingerly, like he was patting the hand of an old lady, before coming toward her. Approaching like she was a wild animal. His lips formed a word, then changed their shape. "Maggie," he said. "Hi." He stopped about ten feet away. "You look better than the last time I saw you."

"I washed my hair."

He smiled. "You also look slightly less terrified. But only slightly." He looked around as if the police might tackle him at any moment.

"Everyone thought you were chasing me. I remember them holding you down in the parking lot."

"It's almost never a good idea to chase a screaming woman, right?" He shook his head. "I was scared you were going to run right into the road. You were so freaked out. Not that I blame you." He sighed. "And I did lie to you."

"Because you were taking me to Reina and Dan."

"I didn't think you'd come if I told you that."

She shrugged. She had no idea if she would have or not. "Do you want to walk, Esteban?"

His smile grew wide with surprise. He had a gray canine tooth. "You say my name differently. ESTehbahn."

"Is that not the right way?"

"People say it all kinds of ways. You just...you used to say EstAYbahn."

She watched him run his hand through his hair. Like he was nervous. "How do you want me to say it?"

"I don't know yet," he muttered, following her along the dirt trail lined with thick seagrass.

When they reached a wooden bridge, Maggie paused, and he stood next to her, his hands on the railing, eyes downcast. "I didn't think you'd ever want to see me again," he said. "I wasn't sure if I wanted to see you."

"I can't remember anything. I have to be honest about that. I don't know who I was or how I got there or what I did or said."

He nodded. "Reina told me as much. And that the doctors didn't have a good explanation. That's all she knew."

"What was I like?" she blurted out.

"Honestly? Kinda stoned. Like, all the time. Just foggy, but also like it didn't bother you too much." He moved his hands while he talked, fingers spread, as if he were asking the universe to have mercy.

She turned to him. "Were we friends?"

His eyes fell closed. "That's a weird question."

"Why?"

"It just is. I wanted to help you, and I knew you weren't any good on your own."

But she'd been on her own, *somewhere*, for weeks before she'd met him. Hadn't she? She wasn't going to focus on that, though. It wouldn't get her what she needed. "You must be a nice person." She touched his wrist and drew her hand back quickly. Careful not to push too hard too soon.

His hands were back on the railing, holding on for dear life. "I tried, Maggie."

"*Why?*"

"You seemed really lost, and it felt good to be there for you. I cared about you."

More or less what she expected—no actual reason, nothing to do with her and everything to do with his own issues. Which was enraging. And perfect. "Cared." Emphasis on that *d*. Grinding it in.

"I'm here, right? After the police tossed me into a cell and interrogated me like I was Whitey or something."

She watched his veins, blue under light brown, carrying oxygen-starved blood back to his beating heart. "I'm pregnant." And she watched his face.

His gaze rose, lofted by the news, up from the marsh and headed for the ocean beyond. "Okay..."

"Any ideas how I got that way?"

"No, not—" His Adam's apple shifted as he swallowed. "How far along are you?"

She had no idea. She was supposed to get an ultrasound but hadn't made the appointment. "Just a few weeks. Too soon to get an ultrasound, I guess. They did a blood test when I was in the hospital."

He cursed under his breath. "I'm...I'm not..."

She put her hand over his. "Did you mean it, that you care about me?"

He pulled his hand from beneath hers. "I..." Now his voice was shaking. "Okay. I wasn't prepared for this. I didn't think of it."

"Did we have sex, Esteban?"

He had nice brown eyes. Soft-looking, with long lashes, like a cow's. "I don't see how it could be mine."

"Because we didn't have sex?"

He looked away.

Something savage curled inside her, the tentacle of some long-buried thing. "We did, didn't we?" She kept her voice quiet, soft and silken, coaxing him closer. She'd learned a thing or two.

He shrugged.

She let out a breath of laughter. "Do we *both* have amnesia?"

"It's not that," he said. "It was only the one time. And...fuck, I told you this before, but you don't remember. And you were there! God." He turned his back to her, ran both hands through his hair. "I do *not* need this."

She opened her eyes wide, letting the sea breeze turn them shiny. "Me neither," she whispered. "I don't know what..." She let her voice waver and break, both things she was never supposed to do.

He turned to her, put his arms around her cautiously. She tensed but didn't step away. It felt foreign and wonderful and awful. "What are you going to do?" he asked.

She pressed her forehead to the ridge of his collarbone. He had showered before he'd come to meet her. He smelled like soap and cheap aftershave. It had mattered to him. "I don't know. My mom is super-religious. She's never going to help me get an abortion." She whispered the word as a couple walked by, flanking a giggling toddler. She squeezed her eyes shut and shuddered, hoping it would trigger the right response—the white knight, offering to help her get what she needed. He'd already shown he had it in him.

His arms tightened around her. "It's going to be okay."

She breathed him in again before delivering her closing line. "Does that mean you'll help me?"

His arms loosened a fraction. "Is there a way we could find out, you know, if it's mine?"

Panic stirred inside her. She pulled away from him quickly. "Got it. It might not be your mess to clean up. Okay. Thanks." She needed the words, the moves, the strategy, and all her clever gambits were flaking off her like dead skin. *Knight to h3, stupid, stupid, stupid.* Terror swirled, coalescing like a whirlpool, sucking her down. "I have to go," she choked out.

"Maggie, come on." Esteban trailed her as she stalked down the path toward the parking lot. "I just asked a question!" He lowered his voice to a fierce whisper as a nearby couple looked over at them. "It's kind of an important one, right?"

She walked faster. At some point, he stopped following. Either because he didn't want to or because he was afraid people would tackle him for chasing her again, and it didn't matter, she was running now, all the way back to her car. Short-circuited and shaking. One moment, she'd been in control, and now? She wanted to scream. She needed to. And once she was back on Route 6, speeding back toward Yarmouth, she did, letting it stream long and loud and frantic against the pumping music pouring from the radio. She had to figure this out on her own. Had to decide. Had to do something. Abortion. Or having a baby. Or drowning herself in the ocean. Cutting herself long and deep and jagged until she had nothing left inside.

There were too many things inside her.

When she walked into the house again, she knew it would be bad. Ivy stood in the living room, her eyes alight, her voice quiet. "Where have you been?"

"I went for a walk."

"In your car?"

"A drive, I meant. To a park. For a walk."

"I came home to *this*," Ivy hissed, gesturing toward the kitchen.

Maggie looked past her. Remembered. The chicken. Rolls and butter. And barbecue sauce. Stains on the white tablecloth. Dishes left out. Claw marks in the formerly smooth facade of the potato salad. Bird bones strewn across the table. "I forgot," she said, scratchy and weak.

Her mother seized the back of her neck and shoved her toward the mess. Maggie stumbled and caught herself against the doorframe. "Where were you?" Ivy shrieked. "Out doing drugs? Being a whore?" She shoved Maggie again.

Maggie grabbed the edge of the table to keep from ending up on the floor. "I'll clean it up!"

"Spotless," Ivy shouted. "My book group meets here tomorrow, and look what you did! Like an *animal*. I didn't raise an animal!"

Maggie clapped her hands over her ears and shut her eyes. "I'll clean it up," she screamed. "Leave me alone!"

"I'll leave you alone when you act like a civilized little girl," Ivy roared.

She slapped a wet rag across Maggie's left hand, still cupped over her ear, and the tip of it snapped against her forehead, hitting her like a hornet sting. Maggie fell to her knees and covered her head.

"Don't you cry," said Ivy. "You have no reason to cry. I made you this meal. Did you enjoy it?" Her voice was level again now. Flinty. Invincible.

Maggie didn't answer.

Something wet and heavy fell onto the back of her head.

The leftover potato salad. It plopped onto her hair and the back of her neck and her hands. "But you didn't finish," Ivy said. "Are you still hungry?"

Maggie shook her head. "No."

"No, what?"

"No, thank you." Lips against the tile. Wished she could sink through and disappear into the foundation.

"Make it spotless." The words slithered along the inside of Maggie's skull, up and back, arcing between the two halves of her brain, swan-diving toward the top of her spine.

When she opened her eyes, *pop* like an old camera flash, she was in the bathroom. Her knees on the soft pink rug, her elbows on the edge of the bathtub.

Scissors in her hand. Blond hair scattered across the white basin. Flecked with blood.

She lurched backward, her butt hitting the floor, her breath exploding from her body, the scissors bouncing and clattering across the tile. The door was closed. She covered her mouth. Blinked like it would change things. Looked down at her wrist. One short, neat slice. That was where the blood came from. Her hand scrabbled for toilet paper, pressed it to the wound.

"Maggie."

Her mother was right outside the door.

"Maggie." She knocked. "Are you sick, baby? Do you want some water?"

Maggie's fist clenched. "I'm fine."

"You've been in there for a while."

"I'm fine." She got to her feet. The mirror revealed more damage, a missing chunk of hair on the left side. Her gaze flicked to the scissors, then the tub. Confusion clenched its fist in her gut.

"You cleaned up beautifully, darling," her mother said through the door. "I'm so proud of you."

Maggie's eyes kept blinking, blinking, blinking, as if the world would right itself with enough resets. "Thanks," she murmured. "I need a minute, okay? I'm fine."

"Take your time. I wanted to make sure you didn't need anything. I'm worried that if I don't pay close attention, you might disappear again."

The laugh burst from her mouth before she could stifle it. *Me too.* "I'm fine, Mom!"

Ivy whispered her love through the door and finally padded away. Maggie could tell by the creaky planks, one four steps down the hall, the other nine steps. Then the closing of the master bedroom door. She knew the sound so well, both the going and the coming. One caused relief. The other...well.

Every strand of hair. Every drop of blood. Flushed down the toilet. Wiped up and rinsed down the drain. Not a trace left. She was good at cleaning up, so very good. Her hands were still shaking, but not enough to keep her from pulling hair over the missing hank. She spent a moment considering the scissors, then slid them into the waistband of her pants, enough to get her to the safety of her room. Her feet nimbly carried her over the creaking floorboards, a dance she'd learned long ago.

The number was in her phone. It was nearly seven. She'd probably have to leave a message.

Wrong.

"Hello?"

"Dr. Schwartz?"

"Yes. Maggie?"

Maggie swallowed. "Yeah," she whispered.

"I'm so glad you called. I've been thinking about you a lot this week. How are you doing?"

She squeezed her eyes shut. She could end the call, but what then? End up in the bathroom again. Or Wachusett, or Missouri. Who knew? *Please fix me*, she wanted to scream. *Please tell me what's happening to me.* Instead, she laughed.

"Maggie?"

"Sorry."

"Maggie, I'd really like it if you'd come and talk to me. Just to check in. Being back home after such a long time away can be an adjustment for anyone."

For anyone. Sure, this was normal. She was normal. It was difficult not to laugh again. Instead, she said, "Yeah. When are you available?"

THURSDAY, AUGUST 6

make it back to the cottage at three in the morning after a silent ride home, alone with frenzied thoughts alight in a rainbow flame. She always seemed so healthy. So incredibly healthy. Confident in herself, in her likes and loves, secure and unapologetic in her feelings. She explained things to *me*. She was teaching *me*. To be honest and real and open. That vulnerability isn't the same thing as weakness.

Maybe it was all therapy speak. Maybe she was parroting Emily the psychologist. Maybe it only ran an inch deep. Maybe it was all a lie.

If it *was* an act, Mina deserves a fucking Academy Award.

Yes, she drifted away in her thoughts. Often. But I could always get her back with a touch, and it was charming, not sick. Artistic, driven by all the characters and worlds churning in that brilliant mind of hers. This manuscript could easily be all that, just fiction. Mina, trying her hand at a new genre. Something darker and more twisted than she's ever written before. That alone could explain why she might want a pseudonym. It doesn't have to be because she's spilling the hideous, agonizing secrets of her actual life.

God, I hope she wasn't writing about her actual life.

I'd dismiss it—and Hannah—out of hand, except for a few hard realities. One, Mina's still gone, so I can't be dismissing anything. And two, I can see glimpses of Mina in the main character. Same likes and dislikes, same habit of stepping on each crack in the sidewalk—when I noticed and asked her about that during a Sunday stroll along Beacon Street a few weeks before the wedding, making a joke about that old saying, she gave me the most enigmatic smile and said, "It's just a superstition," before stomping on the next one with childlike relish. Now she's written the same quirk into the Maggie character. But there are larger similarities as well: both Mina and Maggie are from the Cape and went to school in the same town in Western Mass, though Mina went to the more exclusive Amherst College while her character went to the state university.

And then there are the similarities between Rose and Ivy, the fictional mother. They have the same body type, same meticulous appearance, and the same frenetic focus on hospitality. I can't picture the Rose I met turning into a monster who shoves her daughter and dumps potato salad on her head, but then again, Rose does seem intent on showing people her most perfect self. Who knows what she's like in the privacy of her own home? Mina never mentioned being treated poorly, but she also doesn't talk about her parents much at all. Is this why?

There are differences, too, though. In the book, the Maggie character's father is dead, so that doesn't match up, though Scott does seem to drift around like a ghost. Still, I find that departure from Mina's actual history reassuring. This isn't an autobiography.

It's something much more complicated.

So the question remains: What does this novel tell me about where Mina is now?

Perhaps I should ask her editor, as he seems to know her better than I do. So many little comments in the margins, pushing her. *Be raw! Be real! Be brave!* He urged her to bare all the truths she never bothered to tell me. I'm halfway through the fucking book, and he's constantly encouraging her to bare her soul. But Hannah could have misinterpreted the comments. Or overinterpreted.

Or she could be dead-on. Maybe Mina wrote about her past—and maybe history is repeating itself.

I call Correia. It goes straight to voicemail. I'm about to leave a message when I realize that nothing I say will help. How can I put it? Mina wrote a semi (maybe?) autobiographical (maybe?) book in which the main character forgets who she is and walks away from her life?

It would only confirm for the detective that my wife is crazy. What I need Correia to do is dig deeper on Stefan Silva. On Mina's missing phone. On the possibility that someone took her. Has her. Hurt her. Those are all realistic scenarios, given the way her car turned up. But there's now another: What if Mina's out there somewhere on her own, lost and confused and not herself?

What if something triggered her—and what if it was me? Our fight, my churlish, childish insistence that we talk about having kids, the way I implied that her resistance was a sign of her lack of commitment to our marriage. This could have been my fault.

I pour myself two fingers of Macallan 18 and sit on the couch— her desk is hers, still hers, always hers, and it hurts to sit where she did, because it only reminds me that she's not here—and I Google "fugue." Wikipedia tells me it's a rare psychiatric disorder. Can last for days or months. Associated with trauma, especially childhood sexual abuse. My hands fist as the internet tells me all the things I never would have suspected. The things I can't believe, the things it kills me to picture. Especially when Devon's little face fills my thoughts. If anyone ever did anything to my daughter...

It doesn't sit right, though. Mina was so open about sex. She claimed to love every second we spent connected, to want me as badly as I wanted her. Sometimes it was profound. Emotional. Tears in the eyes, her fingernails in my skin, her face pressed to my neck, her shaking arms around me, clinging like she would never let go. Sometimes it was free and easy, laughing and joking and playful. Joyful. Sometimes it was just fucking, intense and treading that knife's edge, and she professed to like that just as well.

What it never was: complicated or delicate. I've been with some women where I went into it fully aware that there were traps hidden in the dark, set by memories that only needed the wrong move or sensation to trigger a cascade of awfulness. I've been with women where it was a surprise, too, which was worse. So many women have these horrible things in their pasts, though, experiences that steal their joy and render sex an act of bravery instead of simple fun. Mina just...didn't seem like one of them.

Or maybe I'm an oblivious idiot.

Wikipedia tells me that once a fugue is over, it doesn't necessarily require treatment. The person might feel depressed or anxious in the aftermath, or even angry. But once it happens, it's not likely to happen again. Though there's always that possibility.

In the manuscript, Mina's character ends up pregnant.

In our life, she disappeared after I pressed her on when she might *get* pregnant.

Now that the link is forged in my brain, it's almost impossible to break.

I do more research, read some case studies that scare the shit out of me, and know I have to talk to her parents. I have to go back there and find out all the things they're not telling me about their daughter. It's obvious to me that Rose has a whole story to tell. But now that I've read about Ivy, I have to wonder if I'm walking into some sort of psychological tinderbox. If what Mina wrote veers close to her actual past, then Rose might have every motivation to hide what she knows, and she might even be part of why Mina's gone. Mina went to her parents' for dinner last Monday, and as far as I know, they're the last people who saw her. Did *they* trigger her somehow? I'm fully aware this might be my fault, but Rose might bear some responsibility as well.

After another glass of single malt, I head up to our bed as the time creeps past five, manuscript in hand, planning on reading another few chapters and digging deeper into the mystery. But I'm asleep almost as soon as my head hits the pillow, sinking into an oppressive dream in which I find Mina, but she looks nothing like herself. She's *not* herself. She knows me, but I don't know her, and as she reaches for me, I run. Behind me, I hear her chasing, hear her breathing, but the sound is animal and terrifying. I want to stop running, but I can't.

I wake up in a panic, my heart hammering, head feeling as if someone's using the inside of my skull as a bass drum. I'm still in my clothes, and I reek of sweat and fear. Hard beams of sunlight bisect the room. The pages of the manuscript lie scattered across the floor. Cursing, I drop to my knees and crawl around, trying to get them in the right order, not sure I want to read what lies ahead.

One of the editor's comments, in the margin of page 156, just says *I'm so sorry, honey.*

With a churning stomach, I take a shower, shave, run my fingers through my hair, avoid looking in the mirror. I can't bear to see my own face right now.

It's already past noon. I should check in with Drew and with my mom. I should watch the news or call Correia. Instead, I drive toward Truro, ready to clarify the line between truth and fiction. When I pull into the Richardses' driveway, psyched up for a difficult talk or even a confrontation, the space is jammed with vehicles. As soon as I open the car door, the scent of barbecue hits me.

Mina is missing, and her parents appear to be having a party. On a Thursday afternoon. And my first thought hits me with an icy chill: that's just what Ivy would do.

As I stand in the drive and listen to the faint lilt of country music filtering through the open windows, a black pickup truck pulls in behind my Lexus. The driver, barrel-chested, square-jawed, grizzled with white stubble, slides out of his ride. A woman with short, graying blond hair gets out the other side. She's holding a plastic cake carrier, one that looks cheap and sad compared to the antique tin carrier—pale blue with a floral pattern—that Mina used to transport a coconut cream cake when we went over to have dinner with a group of local artists in April.

The man gives me a wary look. "Here to read the meter?" His lip curls. "Or are you another damn reporter?"

The woman clucks her tongue at him. "That's her *husband*, Winn. His picture's on the mantel!"

Instantly, the man's face changes, morphing from cautious and vaguely hostile to friendly and vaguely distressed. "No offense," he says sheepishly. "Just hadn't seen you before is all." He holds out his hand. "Winn Dalrumple."

I shake. "Alex Zarabian."

"I'm Michelle," the woman says, offering a warm smile. "Did Rose and Scott let you know we were doing this?"

"I didn't mean to crash the party," I say. "I can come back later."

"That's silly," Michelle says. "They'll be so happy to see you." She and Winn march up to the front door, me trailing along in their wake.

I enter the living room and am greeted by the stares of several strangers and one friendly face—Sharon Rawlings. Her silver hair wags around her ears as she comes forward and hugs me. Not grinning this time, not cheerful. "I'm so sorry," she murmurs. "This must be so stressful."

I mumble a thank-you as she lets me go and turns to the rest of the people in the room. Her gaze settles on a stringy bald guy with a beard who is sitting near the fireplace, a cane leaning against his chair. "Phillip, this is *Alex*," Sharon says.

While the other people in the room make sympathetic welcoming noises at my arrival, the thin man's eyebrows rise in question, and then he glances back at the photo on the mantelpiece. "You don't say!" Phillip's face transforms with a smile as he swivels back in my direction and uses his cane to lever himself up.

I move forward to shake his hand, which trembles as he extends it. "Are you feeling better?"

"I told him you were in the hospital," Sharon says.

He rolls his eyes. "Did you tell *everyone* I was in the hospital?" He looks back at me in that fraternal kind of way that says *Women, am I right?*

"I happened to show up here last Saturday as Sharon was departing with scones for you."

"I've always had an incorrigible sweet tooth." His cheeks are flushed as if he's embarrassed. "Rose is very kind."

Sharon puts her hand on his forearm and squeezes. She stands so close to him, offering him some of her steadiness, and her smile is bright now, as if she can't suppress it for long. "Isn't she?"

"Are you back to normal?" I ask Phillip. "It sounded like you had a pretty nasty bout."

Phillip puts his shaking hand over Sharon's. "It's going to take me a while, but the doctor says I should be fine in the long run. I was lucky."

Sharon leans her head on his shoulder. "You were."

"You're lucky you didn't get sick, too," I said. "You never figured out what it was?"

Phillip shrugs. "We'd gone out for lunch. Might have been the crab salad."

Sharon makes a face. "Mayonnaise."

"God is good," announces Rose as she bustles into the room, wearing a frilly apron and carrying a tiered tray, tea sandwiches on the bottom, cookies in the middle, chocolates on top. She sets it on the coffee table while several of the ladies flap their hands in dismay.

"Rose," a petite, bespectacled woman says. "We're taking care of you this time, remember? When you brought the flowers for Mother, I didn't go out and pluck my own garden clean in response!"

Rose leans over and envelops the smaller woman in an embrace. "I can't help myself, Julie. I go into hostess mode! My mother was the same." As she turns to the room, she finally catches sight of me. "Alex!" She blinks in surprise and looks around. "Where did you come from?"

"You had said—"

"Yes! Yes, I'm so glad to see you!" She rushes over to envelop me. "Do you have news?" she asks quietly in my ear.

The genuine dread and worry in her voice makes me question

how much of Ivy is actually real. I'm realizing I have a lot more pages to read when I get home. It's possible I've gotten this wrong, and either way, Mina's mother deserves the benefit of the doubt. "Not really," I tell her. "But I'm—"

"You must be starving, in that cottage all alone," says Rose. She gestures to the people milling around us, helping themselves to the tea sandwiches and bonbons. "Our friends have really come together for us. Everyone brought a dish, and we're setting up in the backyard! Rob and Coral Blackstone brought us some homemade sausages"— she wriggles her fingers toward a middle-aged couple standing near the front windows—"and Andy brought clams!" She gestures toward the backyard, where I assume Andy is lurking. "He's the shellfish constable for Truro. And the Tindalls brought burgers. Scott's by his grill, which means he's the happiest man alive."

I shift to one side and peer through the kitchen window, where I see Mina's father solemnly prodding burgers and sausages as a tall, burly guy with curly hair chats him up. "Yeah," I say. "He looks absolutely giddy."

Winn laughs. "He actually does, by Scott standards."

Sharon gives him a light slap on the arm. "He keeps his feelings close to the vest." She turns to Rose. "You've always been able to draw them out, though, haven't you?" Then she pokes her elbow at her husband, causing him to sway. "Hasn't she? Rose has a gift."

Phillip's cheeks are red again. "I need to sit down."

Sharon instantly puts her arm around him. "We shouldn't have let you get up in the first place." She guides him back to his chair.

Rose offers the room a closed-mouth smile. Her lips are a bright pink. "I'm going to get myself a drink. Can I offer anyone else a sweet tea?"

A couple of people raise their hands, and a few others—all women—offer to help, but Rose waves them off, clearly more comfortable with being in charge than being served. I follow her as she flits back into the kitchen. "Sorry I didn't come by earlier this week," I say. "I was going to, but—"

"Don't say another word about it," Rose says as she pulls a pitcher of tawny liquid from the refrigerator.

"I think we should talk, though. Over the phone, you had said—"

"Oh, I've been a mess lately. I don't even know what I said." Rose breezes past me and sets the pitcher on the counter, then pulls several glasses bedecked with sunflowers from the cabinet. She's not looking at me. It's as if she's talking to herself.

"Rose." I move closer, standing between her and a plate of lemon wedges on the kitchen island. I wait until she turns to retrieve it. Our eyes meet. "You know something about what might have happened to Mina." She shakes her head and starts to move past me, but I sidestep and block her path. I decide to take a risk, to jump into that unknown space opened up by the story Mina decided to tell strangers but not her husband. "Mina's disappeared before, hasn't she?" I ask quietly.

She pivots and walks around the island, reaching the lemons before I can grab the plate. "Can't you see I have people here?" she whispers, her gaze sliding toward the living room. Beyond the door, I see curious faces—Michelle, Julie, and Sharon, who gives me a smile when she sees me looking.

"I understand, Rose, but if you know anything—"

"I don't know anything!" She's still whispering, but it's shrill. Almost desperate. "This is *not* the time." Another sidelong glance at the little crowd in the living room.

"Your daughter is missing," I snap. "She's been gone for a week and a half. She could be anywhere! If you—"

"*Stop it!*" Rose sets the plate of lemons down so hard that there's a sudden crack. It's broken in two. She blinks down at it, looks back at the guests in the living room to see if anyone noticed (Phillip is staring at us, and so is Julie), and immediately gathers the mess and dumps it into the trash before heading for the fruit bowl to pluck two lemons from the pile. She does all this in the space of a second or two while my heart pounds and my brain tries to catch up. She pulls a cutting board from a cupboard and a knife from the block. Standing there, blade in hand, she finally makes eye contact with me again.

"I apologize for my outburst," she says in her usual genteel voice. "That was entirely ungracious." Her eyes are shiny, but there are no tears there, only a fierce kind of desperation. "All I'm saying is that this isn't the time to get into it right now, with all these *guests* here." She turns her focus to slicing the lemons, wielding the knife with a smooth, practiced expertise.

That benefit of the doubt I was trying to extend? It's gone. I'm inching closer to believing that Rose, beneath the gracious hostess mask, is exactly the monster that Ivy appears to be, at least according to what I've read so far. I peer out the window to see Scott looking back at me. I don't know how he possibly could have heard what just transpired, as almost nobody in the living room seemed to. Maybe he sensed the waves of distress rolling off his wife. "I didn't mean to upset you," I say, hoping to bring her back to a more cooperative frame of mind. "I'm trying to find your daughter."

"Of course you are," Rose said. "And so are the police. The detective seemed very determined."

"Did you talk to her about Mina's past?"

"Detective Correia was very focused on the present. Besides, my daughter is thirty-two years old. Which part of the past do you think we should be dredging up, exactly?"

"The part where she disappeared," I say, careful to keep my voice quiet and level. No inflection, no question.

Rose finishes cutting the lemons and goes to the fridge to retrieve the ice basin. "Alex, this isn't a good time."

"When *is* a good time to talk about your missing daughter, whose abandoned car was just found in Beech Forest with her keys and wallet inside?"

She clamps her eyes shut and presses her hand over her mouth for a moment before saying, "The phone has been ringing nonstop. This morning, a reporter showed up at the door. Asking all sorts of questions. I'm just trying to protect her privacy. Can't you understand that?"

"Not even a little. Unless you know where she is."

Our eyes meet. "I don't," she says. "I have no idea. But it's the police who are going to find her, not some nosy reporter who's in it for the ratings and would love to use all the sordid details of my daughter's life to make a name for himself."

Of *course* she's worried about that. "What are the sordid details, Rose? What happened to Mina?" My jaw clenches, and I lean forward. I can't keep the derision out of my voice as I snap, "Are you afraid it'll reflect poorly on you, maybe damage your social standing?"

Rose watches me for a moment, and then she tilts her head. Her eyes narrow. Her voice, when it comes, is sickly sweet. "I'm wondering how comfortable she was with you, Alex. Is it possible my daughter was afraid to talk to you? I tried to raise her to make the right choices, but even good women end up with controlling, violent men." She pauses, letting her words sink in as I think of Willa Penson, instructing Mina to be brave as she prepared to tell me whatever it was she'd been hiding.

"Well," Rose continues with a hint of a victorious smile, seeing that her bullet struck home, "I've been trying to give you the benefit of the doubt. I've asked Scott to do the same. And while I *am* willing to discuss some details of Mina's early life with you, I hope you'll show us some courtesy and allow that conversation to wait until a more mutually convenient time."

"She's done this before, hasn't she?"

Rose once again glances toward the living room. "No one outside the family knows," she hisses. "And if you press me on this now, you will regret it. The detective was very interested in your relationship with my daughter, Alex, and whether it was troubled. I don't want to have to call her and confess my newfound fears."

The threat sails right past me. All I hear is the confirmation— Mina *has* disappeared before. I don't know for how long or where or if it was this dissociative fugue thing or something else, but I know what Mina wrote isn't just a story. She told her editor the truth; the book is based on her past. Now I need to find out what it can tell me about her present.

"We'll talk later, then," I say. "When you're not entertaining."

I'm not backing down because I'm intimidated by Rose. This is a strategic retreat. Rose gave me something just now, and she's willing to give me more. But I'm not going to get it now because Rose is playing hostess. It's so utterly fucked up, but I'm getting the feeling that the fucked-upness is more of a feature than a bug. It makes my chest hurt.

"Thank you for understanding," she says as she finishes scooping ice into the glasses, which she has placed on a handled tray. She pours tea into each glass and garnishes each with a lemon. "Please stay and have some lunch. There's plenty of food!"

She picks up the tray and heads for the living room, entering with another pronouncement that God is good.

I suppress the urge to shout *WHAT THE FUCK* and head out to the backyard. If Rose won't talk to me, there are other ways I can gather information. I snag a beer from the cooler and introduce myself to a man who turns out to be Andy Poole, the shellfish constable. He looks the part of a guy who has spent most of his adult life at sea, with skin weathered by the elements and eyes a washed-out, watery blue. When he hears who I am, he mutters something sympathetic and asks me how I'm holding up.

I think about that. "Honestly, it's weird, being in Provincetown. I've lived in Massachusetts my whole life, but it feels like her place. I'd never been here until Mina first brought me." It was in February, of all times, winds howling and sleet pelting the windows of the cottage. We spent most of the weekend in bed, rising only to make eggs and retrieve a bottle of champagne from the fridge. And now I'm there alone.

Andy laughs, raspy and low. "So you're a tourist."

"Do I get any credit for marrying a native?"

He shrugs. "Mina never seemed like much of a native to me. Rose moved here with Scott about twenty years ago when he inherited the house." He waves a broad, spotted hand at the Cape house. His fingernails are black with grime. "Mina was already headed for middle school—she and my Amy were pals for a while. But she left for school only a few years later. Barely saw her after that."

"For college, you mean?"

He shakes his head. "Rose had to send her to some fancy boarding school in Connecticut. Pomfret, I think it was. As if this wasn't
good enough." He snorts. "Surprised Rose didn't ship her off to some
debutante finishing school in Georgia." He tosses a furtive look at Scott
and clears his throat. "I mean, I know she wanted the best for her."

Mina went to boarding school? Yet another thing she never bothered
to tell me. Rose's comment about Mina not feeling comfortable talking
to me sinks its claws into my heart. "Scott was okay with that?"

Andy grunts. "Tough to tell."

"You have a daughter the same age as Mina," I prompt.

His face opens as if he's waking from a reverie. "Oh, yeah, they
were fast friends. Inseparable for a while. My wife, God rest her soul,
she was so thrilled, because Amy was always a shy one. Still is. She's a
librarian over in Brewster now."

"Did she and Mina stay in touch once she left for school?" Mina
didn't invite her to the wedding.

He chuckles. "Oh, I think Mina moved on long before that. Like
she already knew she was too good for my girl. Amy moped around
for weeks. A rough summer, that was." He makes this damning
pronouncement so calmly. Then he once again seems to realize where
he is and calls out, "Hey, Scott, you want me to do the clams now?"

He's already headed over there, walking away from me. Scott is
shoveling burgers and sausages onto serving plates. Three picnic
tables have been set up near the back of the yard, paper table cover-
ings flapping in the summer breeze, yet another couple laying out
foil-covered dishes of various shapes and sizes. I swipe at my sweaty
forehead and take a swig of my beer as I try to piece together a
timetable of my wife's early life. Mina moved here when she was
ten. Left a few years later for boarding school. She went to Amherst

College, a small private school in the same town as the state university her character Maggie attends. Mina's not like me, in one place most of her life. Drew and I have been friends since our mothers put us in the same preschool, where we apparently terrorized the rookie teacher so badly that she changed professions. Mina never mentioned friends from her youth, only writing friends or those she met in Provincetown, all in the last decade or so. I work over my memories of all the things we told each other late at night, naked in bed, two people getting to know each other story by story. She had so many stories, and she told them so well. Well enough that I didn't realize I only had half the chapters. She didn't lie, I don't think. She let me assume. Somehow, I never noticed the gaps, because I filled them in with my own assumptions.

Suddenly, she's a stranger to me, this woman I love so much. She's a black box, and maybe she always was. I thought I knew her so well. I've memorized every freckle and mole, the pucker of the dimple on her left cheek when she smiles just so, the ice-gray color of her eyes, the languid motion of her hands as she talks about her imaginary worlds, her wild laugh, the curve of her spine, the feel of her hair, the scent of her skin, the way she always bites the inside of her cheek when she's trying to concentrate.

I look up at the clear blue sky as my throat goes tight. This is all so wrong. She should be here. I don't want to do this without her.

"Alex?" It's Scott. He's standing nearby with tongs in his hands. When I turn his way, he's looking at my feet instead of my face. "Burger or sausage?"

"Burger, please." I can't believe I'm here, eating with her parents and their friends as if everything is okay.

But I am, and I do. I bow my head as Rose says grace. I end up being seated at the middle of the three picnic tables, with Sharon and Phillip across from me, Julie Leicester on my left, and Michelle Dalrumple on my right. They ask me all about myself, and I tell them about the company and our hope to bring a new cancer treatment to market. Michelle tells the story of her mother's cancer treatment, and Julie whispers that Andy's wife died of cancer not even a year ago, poor man. For a moment, there's a pall over our little group, and then Michelle says, "Alex, what do you do when you're *not* working?"

I hem and haw; work is the thing I'm most comfortable sharing about. I could tell them about Devon, but I don't feel like answering questions about my daughter and my previous marriage. "I work out," I say, then realize that makes me sound like a complete drone. "I play chess sometimes. Mostly online these days, though."

Phillip tilts his head. "You any good?"

"Used to be. I don't play as much anymore. I tried to get Mina to play with me, but she has no interest in learning."

"Really?" says Michelle. "I could swear that she used to play." She looks around at the others as if for confirmation. "Wasn't she in the chess club at the middle school? I remember that Mina beat all the boys, including Bobby!"

Heat spreads slowly from my chest to my cheeks, creeping up like an infection. Everyone at the table is nodding and chuckling as I frantically dig through my memory, wondering if I somehow misunderstood. Did she tell me she simply didn't *like* chess?

No. We were at the Governor Bradford on a Sunday in April, sharing the space with a bunch of locals gathered to watch the Red Sox play the Diamondbacks, and I tried to drag her over to one of the tables by the windows that's already set up for chess play. She tugged her hand out of mine and told me there was no way she'd be able to wrap her head around all the pieces, all the different moves. I promised I'd teach her, promised it would be fun. She said it would only be fun for me, and even though it was delivered with a smile, it was obvious she wasn't kidding. So I gave up, ordered a beer, and watched Boston lose 15–8. Then we walked home through a flurry of late-winter flakes, and she whispered that she knew exactly how to raise my spirits...and a few other things.

It's not a hazy memory at all.

So forget leaving stuff out—she *did* lie. But why lie about something so trivial?

On Michelle's other side, Winn laughs. "Well, our Bobby's good at a lot of things, but chess was never one of them. I think he might have only been in that club because he had a crush on Mina. I don't think he minded when she whipped him."

"She was a very pretty little girl," Julie tells me. "Always so pretty and well-behaved. She seemed much older than she actually was."

Michelle nods and glances at the far table, where Mina's mother is holding court. "I didn't blame Rose for wanting to send her away to school."

Winn rolls his eyes. "Nauset wasn't good enough?" he mutters. He and Andy are obviously on the same page.

"Well, you can hardly blame her," says Phillip. "Middle school's in P-town, not a bad drive. But Nauset's in Eastham. Kids from Provincetown"—he nods at the Tindalls—"Wellfleet"—he gestures at Julie—"Orleans"—this time, it's another couple I haven't met yet, who are sitting next to Rose at the table to my right—"and Brewster all bus to Nauset. It can be a hassle."

Michelle sniffs. "I never thought it was that bad."

"Truro's too small to have its own middle and high school," Sharon tells me. "Most people come here to retire. Not a lot of natives."

"My family's been here for six generations," says Winn with a proud jerk of his chin. "Phil here, at least that long. Right?"

Phillip nods as he lifts a glass of sweet tea to his mouth. He's still a little shaky, and Sharon's watching him like a hawk. "Seven, I think," she says as he sips. "Me, I'm from the Berkshires!"

"Scott's family, the Wallaces, they go all the way back to the pilgrims," says Julie.

"Wow." Mina had told me this about her dad's family. She said that when Rose met Scott at Gordon, a Christian college on the North Shore, she thought he was a wealthy, pedigreed Yankee, just the kind her parents had sent her to New England to meet. She only found out later that Scott's dad was an alcoholic lobsterman already drinking his way to an early grave and that his mom had long since left and married a car salesman over in Plainville. I wonder if Rose ever regretted marrying a guy who ended up as a fishery inspector.

"Rose is an exotic bird around here," says Sharon, tucking silver hair behind her ear and glancing admiringly at Mina's mom, who is up and making the rounds with a basket of what appear to be fresh-baked corn muffins. "What do they call them, ladies from the South? Hothouse flowers?"

"I don't think that's a nice term," says Phillip. "Mean's someone's fragile."

Right now, Phillip looks like a hothouse flower.

"College boy here," says Winn.

Phillip pats his wife's hand and takes a bite of a cookie he must have brought from inside.

"I certainly meant no offense," Sharon murmurs as Rose reaches our table.

Mina's mother smiles down at me as she tilts the basket in my direction. "Having a good time?"

I decline the muffin. "All things considered."

"I've realized I have an appointment this afternoon. Scott is driving me. And aren't you heading to Boston tonight to see your little one soon? She must miss you a lot."

I feel all the eyes at the table laser over to me, but I don't care. Rose is trying to get rid of me. "How about lunch tomorrow? I can take you and Scott out. We'll have a chance to talk."

She hesitates, then gives me a bright smile. "That would be lovely!"

"Perfect," I say, looking hard in her eyes. Mina's eyes. "I'll pick you two up at noon."

CHAPTER EIGHT

She told Ivy that she was meeting a friend. Beth Dover. They'd gone to middle school together, until Maggie had gone away to Lexington Christian Academy. Far away, not far enough.

It was a risk; she hadn't talked to Beth in years. But she remembered—Beth was Jewish. She wasn't part of the church; her parents weren't part of the church.

Dr. Schwartz's office was in a suite, but there was no receptionist. Just a waiting room with one other person sitting in a chair near the window. He gazed out at the parking lot as if he were willing himself alone again. Maggie sat close to the door as if willing herself to accommodate. She was pondering making a run for it when a door opened, disgorging a middle-aged woman who walked swiftly out of the suite, a tissue peeking from between her clenched fingers.

Dr. Schwartz poked her head out not three seconds later. Their eyes met. "Hey," she said with a smile. "Come on in."

Maggie got up and headed toward the door. The office was larger than she expected. A bookcase lined one wall. A couch, a coffee table, a chair, a fluffy area rug, a throw blanket.

And a chess set. Of course.

"Do you play?" asked Dr. Schwartz.

Maggie tore her eyes from it. She smiled blandly. "No, never."

"I could teach you."

Maggie put a hand on her stomach as if her palm could smooth the nausea down, shove it back where it belonged. She shook her head.

Dr. Schwartz watched her. Looked back and forth from Maggie to the board, its knights and pawns and bishops and queens waiting for an opening gambit. Maggie shuddered.

Dr. Schwartz gestured at the couch. "Would you like to sit down? Can I get you some water?"

"I'm fine." She took one slow breath, then another, and sank into the couch. Pulled a pillow to her middle. Dr. Schwartz sat in the chair facing her, a notepad in her lap. Maggie examined the area rug.

"I wasn't sure you'd call me back," Dr. Schwartz said. "I'm so glad you did."

Maggie nodded. "I figured, why not?"

Dr. Schwartz appeared to know the value of strategic silence. "It's been five days since you were discharged," she said after a solid minute of quiet. "How are you doing?"

About to shake herself apart in midair, shedding engines and propellers, flaps and wings. "Mostly okay."

"I'm glad. Are you planning to go back to school in September?"

"Why wouldn't I?"

"You've been through something, Maggie."

"But I can't remember it." She looked over at the doctor. "Can you help me remember, Dr. Schwartz?"

"You can call me Lori if you like. And I have to be honest with you: I'm not sure."

"Why?"

"Our brains are amazing contraptions, Maggie. Sometimes the

brain seals off parts of memory. It's a protective mechanism. Meant to keep you functioning. Does that make sense?"

"Sure. But can't you, you know, hypnotize me or something?"

Lori's smile was gentle. "Would you like me to?"

"You can?" Maggie laughed. "I thought that was something that only happened on TV."

"Nope. We can decide together if that's something we should do."

"And that could help me remember?"

"No promises. It might be better as a way to help us figure out how your fugue happened in the first place."

"That's a gross word. Like mucus or something."

Still smiling. "Would you like to call it something different?"

Maggie shrugged. "I just don't want it to happen again. And I want to go back to normal."

"What's normal to you?"

She rolled her eyes. "That's such a shrink question."

"Have you been to a shrink before?"

"Why would I?"

More silence. Maggie picked at a frayed thread sticking out of the pillow.

"Tell me about earlier this year. The spring semester."

"I'm majoring in art history."

"History. What about it appeals to you?"

"It's already happened."

Lori's eyebrows rose. "And you like that. Understanding the past."

"I guess."

"What about your own past?"

"Can't you just tell me what you'd like me to say?"

"Is that what you need from me?"

"Do you answer every question with a question?"

Lori seemed to have an advanced degree in smiling. A smile for every statement, challenging or pleading, friendly or barbed. "I'd love to know more about your life in college. You were a sophomore last year. Did you have a roommate?"

"Reina. We met in freshman year."

"And you're friends?"

Maggie nodded. "I'm kind of an introvert, though."

"Do you keep in touch with friends from high school?"

"Nope."

"Any romantic involvements?"

Maggie clutched the pillow tighter to her middle. "Are you kidding? I'm pregnant."

"I don't draw any conclusions from that," Lori said quietly. "It's just something that's often important to people."

"My boyfriend and I broke up before finals."

"It was mutual?"

Maggie let out a shaky sigh. "All right, he broke up with me. Happy?"

"Why would I be happy about that, Maggie? It obviously hurt you. How long had you been together?"

"Three months? Not a big deal."

"Ah. Not serious?"

"Define serious."

"I'd rather you define it."

"Can we talk about something else? Wes was fine. He was nice. I wasn't. He figured it out and got away from me as fast as he could. I don't blame him."

"You're being awfully hard on yourself."

"I'm being honest. Would you rather I lie?"

Lori shook her head. "But I'm wondering why you think about yourself like that. Have you always been hard on yourself? Were your parents hard on you?"

"My parents were fine."

"But not anymore?"

"My dad's dead," Maggie snapped. "So no, not anymore."

"I'm sorry," Lori murmured. "When did he pass away?"

"I was nine. Pancreatic cancer."

"Any siblings?"

Maggie shook her head.

"So it was just you and your mother."

"She remarried a month later, so no."

"Oh." For the first time, Lori really sounded surprised.

Maggie laughed, an ugly sound. The nausea was a living thing in her belly.

She had a living thing in her belly. "I think I'm going to be sick," she whispered.

Lori stood up. "Bathroom's over here." She walked to another door and pushed it open.

Maggie shot across the room, lunging for the toilet in the small half bath. Dry heaved. She hadn't eaten since the day before.

Lori set a glass of water on the counter by the sink and stood just outside. When Maggie emerged, smoothing down the sprigs of recently chopped hair trying to poke through the curtain of long strands she'd meticulously brushed over them that morning, Lori asked, "Can you continue our meeting?"

Maggie nodded, if only because she didn't feel steady enough to drive away quite yet. She spread herself on the couch like soft butter, then pulled her knees to her chest. Then realized that was inappropriate and began to sit up.

"You can lie down," Lori said. "It's okay."

Maggie went limp. "Sorry. Morning sickness, I guess."

"Physical and emotional upheaval are so closely entwined."

"Are you saying it's all in my head?"

"Not at all. But you had been talking about something intensely painful to you."

"My dad died a long time ago. I've had a while to get used to it."

"And your stepfather?"

"They separated a few years ago, I guess. I was in school."

"Already in college?"

"No, high school. I went to boarding school."

"Your choice?"

Maggie studied Lori's feet. She wore sensible flats, brown, rounded toe. "It was a good school."

"Was it difficult, to be away from home?"

"No." It was a tight lump of a sound.

"Was it good, to be away from home?"

Maggie glanced at the chessboard like her eyes had been yanked there, a fish on a hook. Sickness curdled in her gut yet again. She pressed her hands over her face.

"It's not easy, being home," Lori said.

"It's fine."

"Maggie, tell me about your mom."

"Such a shrink."

"That's why they pay me the big bucks."

Maggie's eyes popped open beneath her palms. She sat up straight. "Oh God. You probably charge a thousand dollars an hour. I—"

"You know what? Let's worry about that another time. We can do a sliding scale. We'll make this work for you."

"I can't use my mom's insurance."

"We'll make sure this is confidential. And I'd really like to know about your mom. You have the same eyes, but you seemed really different otherwise. Apart from your mutual suspicion of people in my profession."

"You met her."

"Briefly, at the hospital. I introduced myself as part of the team. She made it clear that my services were unnecessary. And I take it she doesn't know you're here."

Maggie shook her head and let her hands fall from her face. "My mom's fine. She's just really religious. Thinks anything can be fixed with the power of prayer."

"You don't agree."

"I think it's bullshit."

"Does that cause tension?"

Maggie scoffed. "I'd never tell her that. It's not worth it."

"Not worth it to tell her you don't share her beliefs."

"They're important to her."

"Aren't you important to her?"

"She's my mom, so...obviously?"

Lori shrugged one shoulder. "Did you get along with your stepfather?"

That fucking chessboard. Maggie winced and pulled her gaze away yet again. "It was fine. We're not close."

"Did you know him before your father died?"

"Church," Maggie muttered. "He went to our church."

"What's his name?"

Saliva pooled in her mouth. "Lawrence."

"You said they divorced."

"No, I said they were separated."

"Was there a lot of conflict in your house?"

She shrugged. "It doesn't matter. It's over."

"So you don't talk to him anymore."

"Did you hear me say we weren't close?" She cleared her throat as the sound of her own voice reached her ears. "Sorry. God, I'm such a bitch sometimes."

"I did hear you say that," Lori said. "But you also said he went to your family's church. And though you don't believe anymore, you told me your mother doesn't know that, so it seemed plausible that you might still attend services with her."

She sounded so reasonable, so logical. "I try not to be home on Sundays."

"Does your mother question that?"

"She's always inviting me to some Bible study or another. The church is the center of her life."

"At what point did you decide it was bullshit?"

"If there is a God, he's a sick and twisted fuck," Maggie said. "Easier to believe there isn't one." One piece was overturned. The black pawn at g7. A white pawn sat naked and oblivious at e4. She clutched at her knees, pulling them closer. *Black allows white to occupy the center.*

"Maggie, how can I support you today? You're dealing with so much."

The note of concern struck and vibrated inside Maggie, bringing her up, her feet to the floor, her hands to her lap. A nice young lady. One who didn't cause trouble. She'd been acting like an idiot child.

"I'm fine. Really. I just..." She laughed, realizing tears were gathering at the corners of her eyes. Her fingers darted toward the coffee table, snagged a tissue. She remembered the middle-aged lady who'd come out of this office before her, leaving with a tissue of her own. A parting souvenir. She dabbed at her eyes and snickered at herself, at this whole stupid situation. She shouldn't have come.

She'd needed to come. She'd wanted Lori to fix her. "I'm so stupid," she whispered.

"It's quite obvious to me that you're not," Lori said. "And I'm pretty good at assessing intelligence. In fact, I think your intelligence is making this even harder for you. You feel like you should be able to control your own mind."

"If I can't, isn't that the definition of crazy?" Her phone vibrated in her purse. She looked down. Esteban. She'd have to unlock the screen to see what he had to say.

"None of us has complete control. Is that what you want?"

"I don't want to black out and come to weeks later, if that's what you're asking."

"Then we should figure out what triggered this episode," Lori said. "It might be painful, but digging deep and understanding it could help you. In a lot of ways."

Digging deep. Maggie stood up, her thoughts breaking apart and reconfiguring second by second, each time a different, ghastly shape. She glanced at the chessboard again. That fucking pawn. Who had knocked it over? She marched over to the board and righted it. Moved it to g6. *The Modern Defense.*

She swept every piece from the board. The sound of them hitting the wall sent a chill through her, made her gasp. She froze, her eyes bouncing from the fallen white queen to the startled-looking woman standing nearby, surrounded by black pawns, the white knight resting against the toe of her right shoe. "I'm so sorry," Maggie muttered, dropping to her knees and raking at the pieces. "God, I'm so sorry."

Lori knelt down and began to pick up the pieces, too. "You have nothing to apologize for, Maggie. It's okay. Let me do this."

Maggie rose to her feet, her eyes burning. "I should go."

"You don't have to. This is really okay."

Her shoulder hit the closed door. The escape hatch. "I didn't mean—"

Lori stood up and placed a handful of pieces on the board. "I have this time available next week, but I also have a slot open on Friday. I think it might make sense—"

"I have to go." Maggie shoved the door open, surfacing into the overly air-conditioned hallway, jogging through the waiting room.

Clutching her souvenir tissue between clenched fingers.

When she made it to the parking lot, she looked at her phone again. Read the text from Esteban.

And knew what she needed to do.

THURSDAY, AUGUST 6

I leave Mina's parents' house by three and head for Boston, still reeling from the sheer weirdness of what's happening. Whatever Rose's motives, she was right that I should go and see Devon. I was supposed to have her for a few days this week as well as the weekend, and she must be wondering where the hell her dad has gone.

I can't help but make a little detour, though. Brewster has only one library, and it's open. I slide along Route 6, past traffic crawling in the other direction, people in search of sunsets and waves. I roll into Brewster looking for something more fundamental, more desperate. The library is adorable in the way so many things in this part of New England are. It's maroon with yellow trim, quaint and welcoming. Not a lot of cars in the parking lot; it's a great day for the beach.

I walk into the hushed, cool interior and find the reference desk. "Hi. Is Amy around?"

The librarian, with horn-rimmed glasses and almost-buzzed silver hair, looks me up and down. Her eyebrows rise. "And you are?"

"My name is Alex. Her dad told me I could find her here."

"Oh," says the lady. I can see the debate behind her eyes as her gaze slides over me yet again. Stalker? Suitor? Good or bad news?

She smiles. "I think she's in back. Hang on." She rises and heads through a doorway behind her.

I spend my waiting time reading a wall display about the history of the library, started by twelve Brewster ladies in the mid-1800s. It reminds me of Scott and his pilgrim roots. Rose and her Southern heritage. All these deep ties, and yet as I think of Mina, I can't pin her down anywhere.

"Can I help you?"

I spin around to see a short, mousy woman with frizzy brown hair pulled back in a tight ponytail. She's wearing a long skirt and a loose, short-sleeved shirt. She has the same blue eyes as her father, the same forlorn yet defiant look in them. "Amy," I say. "I'm Alex Zarabian." I offer my hand, and she shakes it.

"I saw you on the news last night," she says. "You know my dad?"

"I just came from the Richardses'."

She nods, unsurprised. "I'm glad he has that community. They all support each other, no matter what."

"Do you have some time to talk?"

"About Mina."

It's not a question. I nod.

"I can't tell you much," she says.

"Anything might be helpful. I'm just trying to understand... everything."

She gives me a strange smile, with the corners of her mouth angled down. "There's a little reading lounge."

I follow her into a sitting area next to a bay window looking out on a patch of woods. She sits in a rocking chair, and I sink onto a worn leather couch. "Your dad told me that you and Mina were friends."

"That was a long time ago." She's watching me with an almost amused curiosity. "Surely she's made new friends since middle school."

I shrug. "The Cape has always meant a lot to her. I mean, we live in Boston, but she escapes to Provincetown whenever she can."

"Weird how people do that." She continues when she sees my confusion. "I thought she'd leave and never come back."

"Because she thought she was too good for it?" That's what Amy's dad said. Winn Dalrumple, too.

So I'm surprised to see the genuine puzzlement on Amy's face. "Why would you say that? I never said that. No, I just thought...she wasn't happy here."

"She told you that?"

Amy looks out the window. "She never told me much. I didn't understand it then, okay? We rode the bus to P-town every morning, only twenty kids or so from Truro, and we sat together every day. Lunch, too. In class, she was always the teacher's pet. Always with a stack of books. I was, too, so we fit." This time, her smile is right side up. "We'd make up stories—she was good at it, even then. I'd draw the pictures, and she'd write a few pages to go with them. At the time, I thought that was what we'd do when we grew up. Write books together."

"Did you have a falling out?"

"It wasn't like that. She...pulled away, I guess. Lost interest? One day, she didn't want to do it, and I thought she'd change her mind, but she didn't. She wasn't mean, though. She seemed like she was somewhere else. I wasn't the only one who noticed. She quit all her activities, one by one."

"Including chess?"

She nods. "She was the best player, too. Tournaments and everything."

I still don't get that. "Did something happen to her? How old were you?"

"We were in eighth grade. I remember because it was our last year at the school—high school's in a different town. We had to go on a tour of the school, and Mina stayed home that day. My parents told me she was going away for school."

"You didn't know why?"

"Not at the time. But a few months later, I overheard something one night. My parents talking. It was unseasonably hot, and the windows were open. Their bedroom was next to mine, so it happened sometimes." She looks over at me and sees me there, leaning forward and desperate for answers. "It might not have had anything to do with it."

"It was about Mina."

She shakes her head. "Dad told Mom that the Richardses were having trouble."

"I'm surprised either of Mina's parents would share that kind of thing." Rose is all about appearances, and even Scott's friends seem to think he's a mystery.

"Scott had asked my dad about renting one of his properties. My dad has a couple of cottages near the bay side. Wanted a month-to-month lease. And my mom said that Rose hadn't been herself lately, and my dad wondered if they were having problems. I guess it was temporary, though. I mean, they're still together."

I sit back, somewhat disappointed. Doesn't every marriage hit a rough patch at some point? But it might also make a weird kind of sense, matched up with Mina's manuscript. In the book, Maggie's father, someone she has happy memories with, is dead and gone. And there's a stepdad, with whom she isn't close, who's separated from Maggie's mom. In Mina's life, could these two characters be the same man? The engaged, fun-loving father who transformed into the stoic man I know today? "You think that's why Mina got so withdrawn? Her parents were fighting and Scott had moved out?"

"Honestly, I don't know. She left for sleepaway camp that summer, and then she was off at school. I got the address from my mom and wrote her, but she never wrote back." She doesn't sound sad, merely relating old facts no longer stitched to the pain they once caused. "I ran into her once or twice after that. Truro's a tiny place, only a few restaurants. She was friendly, but her life was somewhere else."

"Did you ever hear anything about her disappearing?"

She ponders the question for a second. "I guess she sort of did? Or at least I heard things, but I never thought of it like that."

So many questions crowd my mind that I can't get them out fast enough. Rose said no one outside the family knew, but maybe that was a lie, to keep me from asking their friends about it? "What happened? When was it? Did you talk to her? I—"

She holds up her hands as if trying to stem the flow. "I was in school. My freshman year at URI. I just remember my mom told me that Mina wasn't starting college until the spring, and she'd been away all summer. My mom hinted that she wasn't doing well. She said Rose was taking care of her. I figured she'd had a nervous breakdown or something. It happens, right? But I saw her at Christmas services that year with her parents, and she seemed fine, mostly? She'd gained a little weight, and her hair was really short, but she told me she was headed to Amherst in January. And she did, and I haven't seen her since. Congratulations, by the way." Her gaze is on my ring finger. She sighs. "And I'm sorry."

———

I leave the library with more questions than answers, glad I have the manuscript tucked into my bag. I skim over what I've read so far to confirm what matches and what doesn't. Amy didn't seem to know much about Mina disappearing, but what she described—Mina being away for the summer, then being home with her mom and out of school for a semester—sounds like the aftermath of the fugue she writes about in the book. Only she was younger than the character she's created—only eighteen or so instead of twenty. Why would she age the character up? And I'm still puzzling over the whole stepfather-father thing. If so much of this is true to her life, and Rose and Ivy line up right down to the flower names, where's Scott in the book? The father, the stepfather, or both? And was she really pregnant, or is that fiction, too, to spice up the drama and tension of the novel? Amy described Mina as having gained some weight when she saw her that Christmas, but that isn't definitive in the slightest.

I want to keep reading, but Mina's manuscript isn't the only lead I have. And I need to get back to Brookline, but it's rush hour, so I make yet another detour, this one even more uncertain but less than a twenty-minute drive from Brewster. It would be a waste if I didn't even try.

I make it to Harwich by half past four and pull up in front of the Mariner. It's a standard gray clapboard structure on Main Street, across from a bakery. The interior is dark and plain and smells like yeast and grease. There are people at the bar, but it's not crowded this early.

The bartender has his back to me and is drying a set of pint glasses. When he turns to speak to a patron, I see him in profile, and my insides clench. It's Stefan Silva. Has to be. I edge onto a barstool and wait for him to spot his new customer. During the few minutes it takes, I watch him. He's built. Looks like he works out. Broad, sloped shoulders. Tats up the arms. Olive skin, black hair slicked back into a ponytail, beard. The ex-con that Mina had to see, had to speak to. This man from her past.

The one she put in her book. Subtract a few years, and this is Esteban, straight out of the novel.

"What can I get you?" asks Stefan as he turns to me, smiling, revealing a dead gray canine tooth that isn't even a surprise. His eyes narrow. "Oh."

"Saw me on TV?"

His nostrils flare. "What can I get you?"

I glance at what's on tap even as my thoughts churn at the eerie similarity between the man in front of me and the character from Mina's book. This, at least, is a near-exact match. "The Mayflower IPA."

He fills a pint and slides it over to me. "I'm working," he says quietly.

"You're not that busy." When he starts to turn away, I lean forward. "Please."

Maybe the urgency in my voice turns him around. "I have no idea where she is," he says. "The detective already called me. I was working the night she disappeared. Right here the whole time. Then straight home to my *wife*."

"I'm trying to figure out where she might have gone, all right? And I know she was trying to contact you."

He shakes his head and wipes at the bar with a black rag. "She reached out to *me*. Right? A few weeks ago. Doesn't mean I know where she is."

"What did she want?"

"Aren't you the one she's married to?"

"Did you sleep with her?" Is that why she left her wedding ring behind? She was headed off to have an affair? Or just one night, to exorcise old feelings?

Very quietly, he says, "With all due respect, fuck you." His jaw clenches, his gaze on the Employees Only door beyond the bar. "Sorry. No. We didn't sleep together. I mean—"

"Not this year?"

He turns away to dry another glass.

I take a different tack. "What did she call herself, when you knew her?"

He goes still, then looks over his shoulder. "What did she tell you?"

"Plenty." I'm bluffing, but I've always been good at poker. "I know you were her friend when she needed one."

He gives me a wary look. "Lisa. That's what she told me her name was. And I don't think she was lying. She really believed it."

Lisa. Layla. Mina. Maggie. It hits me like a solid punch in the chest. This really happened to my wife. Just like in her book. "How old was she?"

The wariness seems to deepen. "What did she tell you exactly? You sure it was the truth?"

No. "She forgot who she was for a while. And you helped get her back to her family."

He scoffs. "Okaaay."

I plow forward. "And when she came back to herself, she couldn't remember where she'd been." Our eyes meet. "But she was pregnant."

He runs his tongue over his teeth. "Was she." Neither question nor confirmation. This guy is probably pretty good at poker, too.

"She reached out to you after she was back home."

A shrug. "I kept up my end of the deal."

"Deal."

"She didn't tell you about Daddy Dearest." He chuckles, an edgy, sad sound.

In this moment, it is almost impossible to keep my face where it is, to not let my mouth drop open or my eyes go wide. "Scott paid you off?"

"One way to put it. I guess silence is golden to people like them."

"Mina knew?"

"How the fuck would I know what she knew?"

"Scott Richards—he wanted you to stay quiet about what happened?"

"Didn't want me anywhere near his precious daughter."

"But you helped get her back home, didn't you?"

"It was a long time ago, man. Different time, different place."

Not really that different—Provincetown and Harwich are only forty miles apart. And for all I know, she was never in Provincetown to begin with—she's changed a few of the locations in her book, with Yarmouth standing in for Truro as her hometown, for example. She might have ended up here during her actual fugue instead of the tip of Cape Cod for all I know. "But she found you again," I say. "She wanted to see you." *Why?* I want to shout.

He glances around the bar like he hopes another customer needs him. "I can't be wrapped up in this, okay?" he tells me, his mouth barely moving. "I never asked for this."

"Asked for what?"

"I have to go get some stock from the back." He grabs a shot glass, sets it on the bar, and pours out a measure of Jack Daniel's. "On the house. I'm sorry for your troubles. Wish I could help."

I wait a long time for him to come back. Finally, a different guy comes out from the back, bald and blank. He eyes me up and starts to wait on customers. When I give up and leave at half past five, Stefan still hasn't reappeared.

I drive back to Brookline, wondering if I'm chasing my tail. Knowing I need to read the rest of Mina's manuscript, knowing it might lead exactly nowhere.

But it's still there, the knowledge that Mina wanted to talk to him. To see him. After over a decade, she reached out. And she kept it a secret—from me, at least.

I call Drew on the way home and let him know I'll be in on Friday morning. He sounds relieved but stunned. "You sure you're up for it?"

"I'm in town anyway. I need to spend a little time with Devon. I'm taking her out to dinner." I've already texted Caitlin, who made it easy, thank God. Didn't give me a hard time about keeping Devon up late or anything like that.

"I could use the backup," Drew says. "I'm going to turn down the Pinewell offer, and I need you with me."

I almost have to pull the fucking car over. "Drew. No."

"I'm talking to some people. We could pull funds from different places."

"I'll be in the office tomorrow. Nine?"

"I'll see you then."

"Drew, don't do anything before we meet. I know I've been out of pocket—"

"With good reason, Alex. I get it."

"—but I'm in this. Just wait, okay?"

"Will do."

And that's it. Jesus. One more thing. My wife is gone, and my best friend seems to be doing his damnedest to tank his career, my career, and our entire fucking company.

These risks I took, shocking everyone who knew me from before—conservative Alex who followed a set path, who stuck to what he knew—they don't look so smart or calculated anymore. Suddenly, dropping off the face of the earth, forgetting who I am, what I need to do, what I might lose...it seems pretty tempting. Was that what happened to Mina? Was it all too much, and she just had to walk away? What happened to push her that far? What was so bad that she couldn't even remain herself?

Caitlin always hated what she called my "walls." She always felt shut out. But really, sometimes stuff has to be kept at bay if you want to keep functioning. Go to school. Do your job. Deal with your parents. Your wife. Your kid. Your boss. Everything in its box, safe and sound. Why should one thing bleed into another? That I understand. But I can't imagine it ever being so bad that I'd forget any of it, let alone all of it.

But walls can be useful. Now I shove everything—Drew, Rose, Scott, fucking Stefan, the detective, and even Mina—behind those barriers. And I take my little girl out to dinner.

Devon is exactly what I need tonight. She chatters about her camp and how she can swim underwater now, how she wants to be princess of the dolphins when she grows up. She asks me when Mina will let her play *Plants vs. Zombies* again.

I tell her that Mina is off on a trip. I don't falter or pause. I lie and try to believe it.

Caitlin invites me in when I bring Devon back. After she lets me tuck our daughter in, I accept her offer of a drink. She asks me about the search for Mina, tells me it's been all over the news. I can tell she wants me to talk about it, but she's also unsurprised when I deflect. She knows me too well. What would have turned into a nasty fight three years ago just shifts to a conversation about our daughter, safe territory. For a while, it's nice to share this one wonderful thing with her, uncomplicated and glowing and happy. Devon is perfect and whole and sweet, and she reminds me why I could never, ever disappear, no matter what happens. It makes me think of Mina at this age and Scott as her father and why she constructed an otherwise fairly accurate story with this one big departure from real life. Of course, it might not be the only one, but right now, it's glaring.

Caitlin must sense I'm not fully in the conversation; she gently suggests I go home and get some rest. As I leave, we share a long hug that's half-alien and half-familiar, holding between us all the things we've lost and the one thing we still have.

"I'm here if you need me," she whispers before she closes the door. I'm sure she wants it to be true.

When I finally get home, it's almost eleven. With heavy limbs, I head up the stairs and enter the condo, half expecting Mina to come out of her office, happy to have me home at last. I am greeted by nothing but silence.

I pour myself a generous tumbler of Macallan and pull the manuscript from my bag, but then my mom calls, demanding to know why I haven't returned any of her calls. My penance is allowing her to talk my ear off for over an hour about all the things she's doing to try to help me find Mina. I know she's mostly trying to make me feel better, but in her usual way, she's only making me feel worse, reminding me that despite all these good intentions, all these efforts, the woman I love is still missing.

When Mom tells me that Drew called her personally to ask her to invest more funds, I tell her I have to go. Before I tumble into a restless sleep, I set the alarm for six so I can plow through the rest of the manuscript before my meeting. I jerk awake what feels like ten minutes later, and it's twenty past seven. I've apparently been pushing snooze without even waking up. Fast as I can, I get ready for the day, and then I sit down at the kitchen table where I've shared coffee and breakfast with Mina so many times. I read two more chapters of her book.

When I finally have to force myself to stop because I'm about to be late to my meeting with Drew, chills of horror are rippling through me, waves on a fast-eroding shore. And two things are obvious to me: Scott has some serious explaining to do, and I didn't ask Stefan Silva the right questions.

CHAPTER NINE

Esteban got a ride to Yarmouth, and they met at the park. They took Maggie's car, but she accepted his offer to drive. Maggie brought the cash that had been in the pocket of her shorts, along with another $200 from her bank account.

Esteban brought the rest. Over $300. She had no idea how he'd scraped it together, but she sensed it wasn't easy.

At first, she'd felt powerful. He was willing to go with her, willing to lay down hard-earned cash for her. Something about him seemed so malleable, like she could squeeze him to nothing, like she could make him do anything. Part of her wanted to. The part that made her teeth clench and her fingers twitch and her muscles tense. But that sense of control sloughed off as they reached the city, exposing a new, raw layer that stiffened as it hit the air, drying and hardening like a chrysalis around her.

They didn't talk much. The radio filled the silence. Maggie gazed out the window, wondering if they'd done this before.

"Almost there," he said as he exited the turnpike at Cambridge/ Brighton and took the right at the fork. Cambridge Street. Soldiers Field Road. University, then Commonwealth. Maggie mouthed the street names, watching the time.

Her appointment was at eleven. She'd told her mother she'd be hanging out with Beth again today, that she'd be home by dinner. Ivy was making cassoulet. A tribute to her French roots. She liked to remind anyone who would listen that she had French roots.

Maggie had French roots, too, that meant. So did this baby inside her.

Her throat tightened, and she rubbed at it, wincing. She hated cassoulet.

But it was his favorite.

She clutched at her seat belt as fog and static crackled at the edges of her vision.

"Where the fuck am I supposed to park?" Esteban muttered, slowing the car to roll past the building. Cars lined the busy street. There didn't seem to be any protesters out front, waving pictures of aborted fetuses, blood and tissue and shame. Thank God.

"Want me to just drop you off?"

"Sure."

"I'll meet you in the waiting room."

"Okay." She hopped out when he stopped the car and walked the half block. Planned Parenthood. Ivy would have a heart attack if she knew. Thank heaven for Jewish Beth.

Maggie walked through the doors, down the hall, into a plain, sterile waiting room, posters all around, all supportive, all welcoming, all nonthreatening. She didn't meet the eyes of the other ladies waiting around, some very pregnant, one with a toddler, another clinging to her man. She knew she shouldn't judge.

"Hi," she said as she reached the attendant behind glass. She wondered if it was bulletproof. "I have an appointment at eleven."

"Name?" The lady's jaw worked at a piece of gum.

Maggie leaned forward as if it mattered whether the people in the waiting room heard her name, as if any of them cared. "Wallace," she said quietly.

The woman nodded. "Have a seat. There's water if you need it."

If you need it. In the next two hours, that phrase was uttered so many times, by so many kind people. She was told it would be all right. She was told she would be fine.

She was already fine, and she had said it aloud, over and over. *I'm fine, I'm fine, I'm fine.* A brief flash of memory—Lori telling her she wasn't convincing. But no one here questioned her. It wasn't their job to question or to judge, and they didn't. Not at all.

The nurse ushering her through the process asked her when her last period was, and she said she couldn't remember. She nodded—Maggie had told them this over the phone. She did an ultrasound to determine just how pregnant Maggie was. Important. Less than ten weeks meant she could take a pill, ride out what came next.

But she was twelve weeks along at least.

Esteban would never know. He'd asked if a pill could have done it. She'd brushed him off. He wasn't the curious type. Apparently didn't do research.

This baby inside her, it had taken root at least three months ago. It wasn't his. And as she lay there, wand in her body, lights dimmed, soft hand on her belly, soft voice telling her it would be okay as if she were a skittish horse, as if she didn't know better, she remembered a little.

Walking into the CVS. Looking away from the cashier. No, she didn't have a CVS card. Drifting out, eyes averted, everything is fine here. Nothing to see.

Peeing on the stick in the stall of the cavernous dorm bathroom. Plus sign.

Everything is fine here. She was going to hell even though it didn't exist. *Everything is fine.*

She wouldn't tell anyone, not even Wes. Especially not Wes. He'd given her a nervous smile and headed in the other direction when she'd run into him at the library that morning, not that she could blame him for running. She'd turned into a crazy bitch; that was how he put it. She couldn't blame him at all. And she had a final to study for anyway. Another A, another A. Perfection. The opposite of a waste of time.

After the final, she might go take a swim in the Quabbin Reservoir. Maybe never resurface. She'd read the other day that there were whole towns submerged in the depths, sacrificed in the name of drinking water for thirsty Bostonians. Paved roads that once led to town commons ran straight from the shore to the depths. Everything is fine, and nothing hurts.

That was all she remembered. Nothing after that, nothing coherent or whole or right, until the parking lot and the running and the hard kiss of a bumper.

"Is it a boy or a girl?" she blurted out.

The nurse looked startled, then uncomfortable, then blandly clinical once again. "That's not something we could know for several more weeks. And—"

"Right." Maggie stared at a poster of female anatomy hanging on the opposite side of the room. "Of course. It doesn't matter."

"Would you like to talk to our counselor? She's really—"

"Definitely not." Maggie's hand slid off the table to cover her belly. A few months would make it round with the tiny creature inside her, one that would be entirely dependent on her. Hers to protect. Hers to doom in any one of a million possible ways. "I made up my mind."

Would it love her? She knew it would, the helpless, needy, adoring love of a child for a parent. Linked by body and heart, so tightly that nothing could sever it. Even if you wanted to.

The nurse watched Maggie's fingers curling into the spare flesh of her abdomen. "It's okay to change it. This is an important decision, and it's entirely yours. No one here wants to pressure you. We only want to help."

Maggie clenched her fist and lowered her hand to her side. "I want to get this over with." Her heart was beating so fast. Her throat was so tight. "I'm in school. I'm not with anyone. I don't have a job. And—" *Something is very wrong with me.*

"You don't have to explain. Like I said, entirely your choice. But if you need some support—"

"I have a friend in the waiting room. I'm fine. But we have to get back to the Cape, so..."

The nurse cleared her throat. "Okay," she said. "We'll get everything set up."

She walked back into the waiting room, hollow. Esteban jumped to his feet when he saw her, and the concern in his eyes made her want to fly at him and tear at his hair, scratch his face, punch that dead gray tooth right out of his mouth.

Instead, she laughed, light and high. "I'm fine," she said. "It was quick. Let's go."

"Great," he said. "I won't have to feed the meter again."

She followed him out to her car, cramps gnawing away at her. Like they'd removed the baby and replaced it with a small demon, punishment for her sins.

"You hungry?" Esteban asked as he headed for the highway.

He almost seemed to be floating with happiness, the dead weight removed.

Or live weight, as it were.

When she didn't answer, he said, "There's a McDonald's up ahead."

"Whatever you want," said Maggie, and then when he pulled to the drive-thru window, she told him she wasn't hungry. He ordered himself a Big Mac and fries and a Coke. She flattened her palm against the warm window as he pulled back onto the road.

Teeth on edge, she listened to him eating, inhaled the greasy scent. A Taylor Swift song played as he drove up the highway, headed back to the Cape.

"You okay?" he asked after several miles. "Need anything?"

She glanced over at him. Considered grabbing the wheel and giving it a yank, wondered if they could make it through the concrete barrier and into the Neponset River, or bounce off and veer into the semi passing them on the right. Either way could be fine, enough to mash flesh and bone and brain.

She wondered when fetuses began to feel pain. Wondered what it felt like when it was clear something had gone horribly amiss, when everything went from darkened safety to agony to nothing. Wondered how long it lasted. She tried to remember being on the table but couldn't quite manage it. But the little thing had been so small, right? Maybe the right nerves hadn't connected yet. Probably it had all been over in a blink.

Her phone buzzed, and she pulled it out of her pocket and looked down at it. Ivy. It was almost two. She ignored it, pressed the phone facedown against her thigh.

"You want to get that?"

She shook her head. "Are you working tonight or do you have it off?"

"I forgot that you don't know my schedule anymore. I work almost every night in the summer, and plenty of days. It's busy, and the tips are good. I've had a couple thousand-dollar shifts."

"That's a lot." Maybe it hadn't been so difficult for him to find the $300.

"Not always, after you pool it. Lou always wants to make sure the busboys get their share." He shrugged. "Off-season can be pretty dead."

"You live in Provincetown year-round?"

"I'm from New Bedford, originally. My dad's there. Sometimes I stay with him in the cold months to save money—and make some. I help him with his plowing gigs, and there's a tavern there that'll let me pick up shifts."

"What's it called?"

A grin. "It's actually just called the Tavern. Right off Union."

"How old are you?"

"Lots of questions." He looked pleased, like it meant she was interested in his life. "Twenty-four."

She considered smashing her head against the window, wondered which would break first, her skull or the glass. How many blows would it take to find out? She clawed at the bare skin of her arms as another cramp twisted inside her.

"You in pain? Did they give you anything?"

He deserved better than this. "Just some Motrin."

"Doesn't look like it's enough."

She forced herself to lay her fingers flat against her inner arms. Her phone was ringing again. It had slid between her legs and was clutched between her thighs. She spread them slightly, enough to see that Ivy hadn't given up.

"You need to get that?"

"It's my mom. She thinks I'm with a friend." She looked over at him in time to see his smile fade. "I guess I am, though, right?" she added.

The smile returned. It was touching and pathetic, and she wanted to smack him and throw herself on him and beg him to hold her. All at the same time. She could hurt him. She could use him. She could do both simultaneously. She clenched her teeth over a scream and turned the music up. She sang along, loudly and badly and long enough to convince him she was being silly instead of trying to keep herself from going utterly crazy. It almost drowned out the ringing phone. Esteban added his voice to the mix as if they were on a road trip, as if this were the normal side of happy.

When they reached the rotary that could shunt them toward Yarmouth, a wave of nausea rolled through her, and she clutched at his shoulder. "Keep going. Please."

"Um. Where?"

Her phone rang, the sixth time. Maggie jabbed the music silent and lifted the phone to her ear. "Hi."

"*Hello*, Maggie," her mother said. "When can I expect you?"

"I'll be home later."

"Later? Could you be more specific, please? I'm making cassoulet and a—"

"Apple and fennel salad. With figs for dessert. You told me. I might not be home for dinner. Probably won't."

Esteban gave her a confused look. He took another turn around the rotary.

"This is a special dinner," said Ivy. "I thought we could have some time together, just the three of us."

"Three." There was a demon inside her for sure, dragging its claws along her walls. Cassoulet was his favorite.

Ivy sighed. "I was going to talk to you about this."

"But you said—"

"I needed support when you disappeared," Ivy snapped. "Did you think even for a minute about how hard it would be for me? I was alone, and you know why."

Maggie's mouth opened and closed over one aborted sentence, then another.

Ivy's voice had gone low, heavy with the shame of it all. "Maggie," she said. "Margaret. You are being incredibly selfish."

Esteban had pulled over. He watched Maggie from the driver's seat.

She faced the window, lips stiff, legs stiff. "I'll be out tonight," she finally said. Her heart wasn't stiff. It was galloping. She couldn't believe what she'd just said. It was exhilarating. Terrifying. "I won't be home until late."

"You will come home right now and get ready for dinner," her mother said shrilly. "He'll be here at six, and you will have your face on and be nice!"

"No," Maggie whispered.

"Do you realize who's paying for your education? Where do you think that money came from? You've been willing enough to take it, and you wouldn't have this chance if not for Lawrence!"

"Mom..." Her voice was as small as that baby inside her had been. And just as powerless.

"After all that mess, he forgave you. He supported you." Her mother's voice was like Maggie's uterus had been—nurturing, closing around her like a fist, dark, and never, never safe. "I forgave you, too, with the Lord's help. Neither of us is holding a grudge! You were so young. You didn't know what you were doing."

"I—"

"If you ruin this for me, for all of us, I'll—"

Maggie ended the call, though it took several taps of her thumb. She kept missing the button. She threw the phone down. It bounced off the top of her foot.

Esteban patted her shoulder, reminding her of his presence. "Hi. What's up?"

Maggie shook her head.

"You're shaking."

She was shaking.

"You don't want to go home?"

More shaking.

"It's going to be okay, Layl—Maggie." He leaned over, slid his arm across her shoulders.

For a second, a bare, infinite second, she let it happen. But then the monster rose up in her, fangs and claws and rage. "Don't fucking touch me," she screamed, slicing her fingernails across his cheek.

Esteban grunted and cursed as she grabbed a handful of his hair and yanked. His fingers closed over her hand and squeezed until she felt the bones rolling against each other.

"You bitch," he shouted. As soon as she let go of his hair, he shoved her. The force of it sent her head cracking against the window, but it didn't stop her. She leapt at him again, but this time, he was ready. He grabbed her wrists and shook her. She tried to bite him, but he jerked to the side. His elbow slammed into her cheek. The momentum sent her head crashing into the dash, blood on her tongue and pain riding down her spine. By the time she managed to right herself, he was out of the car, pulling his phone from his pocket.

She jumped out after him. He didn't see her coming. She snatched his phone and ran.

"What the fuck, Maggie?" Helpless and confused. She hated the sound of his weakness.

She threw the phone in a ditch at the side of the road. With a splash, it disappeared into the scummy green depths. She watched it sink with savage satisfaction.

"What the *fuck*!" roared Esteban.

Insane. Monster. Wrong and wrong and wrong, and this will never, ever be right. She ran as he chased her back to the car. Terror and fury and confusion gripped her, twisted her, shook her like a rat in the teeth of a hound.

"What the fuck, Maggie," Esteban yelled again.

She whirled around as she reached her car, her cheek hot and tight where he'd hit her, her lip stinging, her head pounding. "I did it, Est*AY*bahn." Bearing her teeth. A vicious grin. "I *killed* it. It's *dead*. Are you happy now? Back to normal? Did those fries taste good? No! Get away from me," she shrieked as he reached for her.

His eyes were wild, his face a dusky pink, three red welts across his cheek and jaw. Her back hit the window as he inched toward her, arms up and hands out. To contain her. To hold her down and keep her still and quiet like a good girl must always be. A tiny drop of blood shimmered and welled on his cheekbone. *First blood, first blood, first blood, it means you're a good girl.* She screamed and clapped her hands to the sides of her face. Dropped to her knees, let her elbows hit the ground. "Go away," she sobbed.

Look at all those nice things he'd done. Taken care of her. Paid his share.

He deserved better.

"Everything okay here?" This was a new voice. A man's voice. Maggie jerked up, panting. She scraped her hair out of her eyes.

A guy in his twenties, elbow hanging out the driver's side window of his pickup, backward baseball cap, messy blond hair peeking out, concerned eyes. Girlfriend in the passenger seat holding her phone up and ready.

"Yeah, we just—" Esteban said between breaths.

"He tried to hurt me," Maggie wailed. "He's going to kill me."

"What the—" Esteban spun on her, but the blond guy had thrown his truck into Park and the door wide open.

I am a monster.

"Keep him away from me!"

"She attacked *me*!" shouted Esteban as the blond guy, broad shoulders and at least a few inches taller, gave him a shove. "She's fucking crazy!"

"Give her some space," said the guy. "She's got a phone in there, okay?" He pointed at his girlfriend, tucked away in the truck and her world, safe and sane and sound. "We can call the police if we need to."

"Fuck this." Esteban shrugged off the guy and stalked toward the ditch where Maggie had thrown his phone.

The guy extended his hand. "You okay?"

Shaking, she took it, let him pull her from the ground. Couldn't look at Esteban. Couldn't look at the guy. "I need to go home." She inclined her head toward the Corolla. "This is my car."

"You okay to drive?" asked the guy. "We can give you a ride if you need."

"I need to get home," she whispered, touching her trembling fingertips to the tender spot on her cheek. Concealer. Foundation. Blush.

"Did he hit you?" the guy asked quietly.

Maggie could sense him shifting his stance, ready to rescue her, ready to slay the dragon. He just didn't know where it really was. He couldn't see it there, right next to him. She almost laughed, though it wasn't funny. Another nice guy. Another nice guy who shouldn't be allowed near someone as poisonous and broken as Maggie Wallace. Margaret Juliette Wallace. Layla...what had her name been? Had she been as vicious and venomous in that form? Not that it mattered now. Layla was gone.

"You want us to call the police?" asked the guy. "You guys live together?"

She shook her head. "I'll be fine. I just need to go home." She glanced through the window. The keys were still in the ignition. She rounded the car. Esteban was trying to fish his phone out of the murk, arm submerged to the shoulder. "Thank you for stopping," she said to the guy without looking at him.

She got in the car. Closed the door. Shifted the Corolla into Drive, put both hands on the wheel, stared straight ahead. Drove slowly past Esteban, his jaw set, his eyes narrowed with a new, violent hatred. Like he wanted to wrap his hands around her throat and choke the life out of her.

She turned the radio up and headed for home.

FRIDAY, AUGUST 7

Before I leave for my meeting with Drew, I tap out a quick message to Willa, who blocked my account but didn't bother to block Mina's. It's Alex. I know about her past with Stefan Silva, I write. And I'm worried that he did something to Mina. If you know anything, please let the detective know. I leave my phone number, too, hoping she sees that I'm trying to find Mina, not cover up a crime.

It's a leap. Mina was nervous about telling me something, and it could have been as simple as having this secret book deal. But based on what Hannah said and the editor's comments, the book is about a past Mina decided to reawaken. She reached out to Stefan, maybe to heal old wounds...or to reignite an old flame. Sure, based on what I've read, he has every reason to hate her guts. But the vicious fight Maggie and Esteban had, how much of that was real, and how much was drama to keep readers turning the pages? And if it was real, and if the baby wasn't Stefan's, then why would she seek him out at all? Why did she *need* to see him?

What if she just glossed over Esteban's paternity in the book? I'm thinking that's more likely than not—given what Stefan said about Scott paying him off—and that the manuscript still has more to tell me about Mina's past with Stefan Silva. As much as I try to push it from my mind, I picture my wife taking off her wedding rings, eating dinner with her parents, then driving down to Harwich for a dangerous romp with a legitimate bad boy. One who she may have hurt in the past.

Maybe it all went wrong.

The detective thinks he has an alibi, but judging by the way he disappeared when I showed up at the bar, he's got people willing to cover for him.

But he's not the only one I'm wondering about. This stepfather character who keeps being mentioned. Who the hell is that? Is it Scott or someone else? It's obvious that something's awful and wrong about that character's relationship with Maggie, and it leaves a sour lump of dread in the pit of my stomach.

Sitting behind the wheel of my car, I leave a message for Detective Correia. Just checking in. Still wondering about Stefan Silva. I think they have some kind of past. He might have had reason to hurt her.

It's one of the more awkward messages I've ever left, but I don't think it matters. The goal is to get her to call me back and to look at the manuscript. To at least consider the possibility that Stefan or Scott might be involved somehow. Both of them are, to use Willa's phrase, shady as hell. Then again, so is Rose. Threatening to feed the detective some nasty insinuation about my relationship with Mina, just to get me to stop asking questions. Who is she protecting? Scott? Herself? Is she just trying to keep up appearances, or are Mina's parents responsible for what's happened here?

They might have triggered another fugue.

Or they might have done something even worse.

And Mina isn't off the hook here, either. Taking off her wedding rings. Arranging clandestine meetings with an ex, ex-boyfriend or ex-con, whatever. Keeping some big secret from me, even though she knows I love her. Knows I'd never hurt her.

Once again, anger at her snakes around my heart, a poisonous vine. Maybe she's lost or she's hiding. Or she got herself in over her head. Either way, she was lying to me. About her past and about her present. Maybe about the future. I thought we were building it together. It's possible she had other plans.

As I drive out to Waltham, headquarters of the company that might not live to see the next fiscal year, I wall off the shit show that is my feelings right now. Drenched with worry and shot through with rage—at damn near everyone—I'll be no good as I try stop my best friend from making a terrible mistake.

I pause in the parking lot. We rented out the suite in this office park to save money. Drew wanted to be in Cambridge, at the heart of things, but I insisted we hold off. Cambridge is expensive, and I wanted us to use any capital we had to push the pilot study and extend our runway. From the very beginning, I've been the one anchoring us to reality. I feel like an anchor right now, sinking fast and deep.

"Morning, Raj," I say as I pass our assistant's cubicle.

He jerks around, his eyes wide. On his computer screen, CNN's website flashes red and black. There's a picture of Mina at the top, beneath the headline *Author missing, police searching for clues.* "Alex. Hi. I-I didn't think—"

"Don't worry about it," I mumble. I force myself to tear my eyes from my wife's face, her pale-gray eyes, her gorgeous mouth. I incline my head toward the door on my right, the only actual office in the suite. "Is Drew ready for me?" I know he's in; his Jaguar's in the parking lot.

"Yes, but he was on the phone with—"

I barge straight into his office. He shouldn't be talking to anyone except me. When I open the door, Drew has the receiver in his hand and is punching buttons. He pauses as I enter.

"You look like shit," he says to me.

"Put the phone down." I wait for him to obey. "You're calling our angel funders behind my back again. What the fuck, Drew? Did you think I wouldn't—"

"You've been a little preoccupied. Meanwhile, I'm trying to save our asses." He rubs his hands over his face, sits back in his chair, gestures for me to have a seat. "Sorry. I'm an asshole. I know my week doesn't hold a candle to yours."

"You are an asshole." I close the office door and sit down across from him. "I know this has been rough, Drew. I know we hoped for more, but Pinewell would give us enough to move forward. They want CaX429 to succeed, and they believe it might. Otherwise, they wouldn't bother with us."

"It'll succeed with or without them," he snaps. "You know our results."

"In mice."

"You sound like fucking Blake Pierce." Drew's initial dislike of the Pinewell partner has obviously crystallized.

"Fucking Blake Pierce is a fucking douchebag," I say. "Okay. But sometimes you have to deal with douchebags if you want to achieve your goal, right? I mean, you deal with me every day."

He gives me a grudging smile. "You're more of a dick than a douchebag. Anything new on Mina?"

I let my head fall back and let out a shaky breath. "I'm not sure."

"Listen," he says quietly. "You're sure she didn't...hurt herself?"

"I'm not sure of anything. Except that if she did, it wasn't last Monday. Her car didn't show up at Beech Forest until Saturday or Sunday. So where the fuck was she? Where *is* she?"

"No ideas?"

The manuscript swims in my memory. "There are things she didn't tell me." I lower my head and look at him. "Things she was hiding."

"Fuck," he says. "Was she cheating?"

I shrug. "No clue. Maybe."

He chuckles. "How can you sound so calm? If it were me—"

"You'd be throwing furniture. Kind of like you're doing with this Pinewell thing."

His eyes narrow. "Fuck you. We have thirty employees and five board members and—"

"I know the balance sheet better than you do. I also know that without Series A, we're done. You're scraping the bottom of a dry well with individual investors, Drew. We need more than a few million."

"Pinewell's trying to control us."

"Of course they are! They're not a charity!"

"They're fucking leeches!"

"They don't exist to feed your feelings," I say.

"You're such a cold bastard."

"You sound like my ex-wife."

"Which one?" When he sees the look on my face, he waves his hand. "Sorry. That was a dick move."

I arch one eyebrow. "You think you're in any state to negotiate when the stakes are this high? You're name-calling like an eight-year-old and lashing out like a wounded bear. This isn't personal. It's business. And it doesn't just affect *you*."

Drew's face is flushed. "I never said it did. I'm looking out for Biostar."

"Are you? CaX429 needs to be in clinic in the spring. We want results by the ASCO conference. To do that, we have to *exist* for that long."

"We wouldn't exist at all if it weren't for me."

I nod. "And that counts for a lot. But your goal then, and I assume now, was to establish CaX429 and bring it to market so that people who needed this treatment could get it. Pinewell is the only road available to us right now."

"I bet they're gonna oust me," he says. "That's how they roll. I did a little research on the last few companies they brought to IPO."

His eyes meet mine, and I know what he wants, because I've known him all my life. He wants me to tell him that his girlfriend didn't send a nude selfie to a mutual acquaintance of ours, that she'd never do a thing like that. He wants me to tell him that he's good enough to play lacrosse at Brown, that I believe he'll get the scholarship. In the past, that's what I've done.

Today, I can't. And he sees that.

"You knew," he says slowly. "You *fucking* bastard. You went off behind my back."

"It wasn't like that at all."

"Jesus Christ. Get out of my office."

"Drew."

"I don't blame Mina for taking off," he sneers. "It's amazing she stuck it out as long as she did."

I rise from my chair. Unhurried. Steady. "As CFO of this company, I strongly advise you to take the Pinewell offer," I say to him. My voice is dead level. "You will not get a better one. Nor can you raise enough capital without them. In the absence of a significant cash infusion,

Biostar will be financially swamped by January. But I'm going to give you a little more runway, a few more thousand to work with. Enough to throw a nice pity party for yourself." I turn toward the door. "You'll have my letter of resignation on your desk by the end of the day."

"Alex..."

I don't slam the door as I walk out. I close it softly. Raj's eyes are saucers as I walk past him and out the door. Drew was right.

I am a cold bastard.

I am a cold, unemployed bastard.

I am a cold, unemployed bastard whose wife has disappeared.

I stand in the parking lot and laugh. I completely sank the last two years of my life into this company. For Drew, for my mom. And yeah, for myself. I left my stable job and walked this high wire, took this leap. I should have known better.

Maybe I should have known better with Mina, too.

I am on Commonwealth, headed back to Brookline, when Willa calls me. Her voice pipes through the car's speakers, loud enough to make me wince. "How did you find out?" she asks me.

I lean my head on the headrest. "Hello, Willa. Nice to hear from you," I say wearily.

"She was so afraid you wouldn't take it well."

So that was it, and my bluff paid off. Stefan is the secret that Mina was so terrified to share. And connected to him—the fugue. The pregnancy. Maybe even the manuscript in my bag.

I just want to keep driving. Veer onto 95 South, head for Florida. The Keys. The ocean beyond it. "Because I'm obviously a monster, right? Controlling and abusive?"

She groans. "I overreacted. I'm worried about her."

I clench my teeth to keep from shouting at Willa. *She's* worried about Mina? Jesus fucking Christ. "Apology accepted," I say dryly.

"Do you have time to grab coffee?" she asks. "If we put our heads together, I bet we could figure out a lead or two. I've been frustrated as hell by what I've seen on the news. There's no way she committed suicide. No way."

"Surprised you haven't decided that I killed her."

"Did you?"

"Hanging up now." And I do. But she calls back a second later.

"I guess we'll be meeting in a public place," she says.

"Right. So you have nothing to fear."

"How can you be so calm?"

"Just tell me where you want to meet, Willa. I have to get back to the Cape." I'm supposed to be meeting with Mina's parents for lunch, but it's clear I'm going to have to push it to dinner.

We agree to meet at the Caffè Nero in Washington Square. The place from which Mina made her last Facebook post. Drew calls me three times on the drive there, but I don't answer. He needs time to marinate before we get somewhere productive.

Besides, I'm about to get confirmation of all my suspicions. I bluffed my way into this, and there's no reason to believe it won't carry me all the way.

Willa breezes into the coffeehouse and joins me in line. She's got her hair in a messy topknot and looks like a bespectacled vagrant. "Sorry," she says, tugging at her baggy T-shirt. "I'm on deadline."

"What are you having?"

She softens as I offer to pay for her drink, recites all her preferences, and goes off to find us a table. Five minutes later, I bring her large cortado—almond milk and stevia, slight dusting of chocolate powder—over to the booth she's staked out. I slide in across from her with my espresso. "How long have you known about Stefan?" I ask.

She tastes her drink and makes a face. "They used soy instead of almond. Ugh." She glances up at me. "Sorry. They do this all the time. I know you probably ordered it right."

Of course I did. I take a sip of my espresso and don't break eye contact.

She blinks. "She told me about him a year or so ago."

"When she was writing her book."

"I didn't think she told you about that. She said she was going to wait."

"Have you read it?"

"I was her beta reader. That's why she told me about Stefan." She takes off her glasses and rubs at her eyes. "God. I couldn't believe any one woman had been through that much."

More confirmation. So much of the manuscript is true, even with the details she changed. Too much of it is real. And I didn't know or suspect a single damn thing. Deep in my chest, I feel it, beneath layers of permafrost. Like magma, the pressure building. "Maybe she told me more than you thought."

"I'm glad. She was so scared you'd...I don't know." She's wearing a rueful smile as she blots at her eyes with a napkin. "She didn't want to mess things up with you."

Instead, she hid so many things that I'm not even sure what's real anymore or who I was actually married to. "Did she tell you she contacted Stefan?"

She nods. "She felt like she had to. And you know what? She was right. She needed to. She owed it to him."

"Because of their past."

"Duh?" She wipes her hand over her mouth. "I mean, yeah, obviously. But she was definitely afraid of how he would react."

I pause. This doesn't sound like she was having an affair, but if that's the case, then why did she leave her rings behind? "Do you think he did something to her, Willa?"

"I don't know, but I called the Provincetown detective and told her."

"When?"

"Two days ago."

So the detective knew about this, and she didn't keep me in the loop. "Did she take it seriously?"

"I couldn't tell. But it seems to me like a motive, you know? If he was angry enough?"

"It all happened a long time ago, though." This is what's been nagging at me. I get why Stefan would have been angry; if Mina acted like her character Maggie did, if she physically attacked him and destroyed his phone and nearly got him arrested *again* just for trying to help her, then hell yeah, I'd be pissed off, too. I'm betting his arrest all those years ago on suspicion of assault had everything to do with Mina. But it's been years. "It's not easy to stay enraged for that long, right?"

Willa is looking at me as if I'm slow. "I would think the more years, the *more* rage when he finally found out."

This time, I'm the one who blinks.

She sits back like I've kicked her. "Oh God. You don't actually know."

I put my hands up. "I know enough. I found the manuscript. I've read most of it."

"And you think that's what actually happened."

"I know she changed some of the details. Her age when it happened. Her hometown. The college she went to. Her dad being dead and this stepdad character—"

"You don't know all of it," she murmurs. "I mean, I'm not even sure I know. Some things I didn't ask. And she assured me it wasn't *all* true. I mean, how could it be? Especially that ending, right? But..." She gives me a helpless, pitying look that sets my teeth on edge.

"I know she went through a dissociative fugue. And she came out of it pregnant, right?"

Willa nods warily.

"And Stefan helped her get an abortion. She let him think he was the father."

Willa's mouth drops open. "Alex," she whispers. "I'm certain he *was*."

"Okay, fine. Another detail she changed in the story." And a confirmation of the reality I suspected. The intense heat inside my chest is shifting things. Cracking them. "So why did she need to talk to him now? Why did she search him out? Just to apologize before the book got published? It's not even under her name. He might never have known she'd written about him. He doesn't exactly seem like a bookworm." I might never have known either if not for Hannah.

Willa has her face in her hands. She's shaking her head. "I'm so sorry, Alex. I'm so sorry. She knew you wanted to have babies. She knew you didn't understand how difficult that would be..."

"Because she had an abortion? That doesn't make it hard to conceive again, does it?" Unless she ended up with complications. I haven't read far enough to know, but the way Willa's looking at me guarantees that I'm not going to ask her about it. There's something volcanic inside me, bubbling up from the deep. "Stop looking at me like that," I bark. Loud enough to turn heads.

Willa reaches out. Puts her hand on mine. "She should have told you. You shouldn't be hearing this from me."

I look down at her fingers, stubby, bitten fingernails, no rings. The tip of her index finger slides over my wedding ring. I withdraw my hand into my lap. "About the abortion? Why would I judge her for that? Why would she even hide it? It's not a big deal in the scheme of things."

"Alex," Willa says. "Mina never had an abortion."

CHAPTER TEN

S he helped Ivy set the table, country proper, casual but neat, dinner plate, salad plate on top, no bread plate this time; cassoulet was always served without accompaniments. It stood on its own. Except for the wine, and apparently Lawrence was bringing that. Maggie set the glasses, one for him, one for Ivy.

Maggie wouldn't be twenty-one until December, so she didn't set one for herself. She knew how all this went; they'd danced this waltz before. She could already taste the wine, acid-sour, secondhand, but that wouldn't be until later, when Ivy wasn't looking.

Her mother was in fine form, bustling about with determined efficiency, pretending as if she hadn't screamed at Maggie a few hours ago. Ivy Wallace-Gainer was so good at pretending. Maggie could only aspire. While Ivy infused honey with rose water and rinsed the fresh figs, humming the tune for "Great Is Thy Faithfulness," Maggie had crept into the house, into the shower, the demon in her abdomen gnawing away, the demon in her mind purring and dancing. It rubbed up relentlessly against the walls of her skull, a cat with barbed fur, loosening all the connections.

She thought she'd done a pretty good job covering the bruise on her cheek, and she wore a long-sleeved shirt to conceal the bruises on her wrists and arms, each in the shape of his fingers, encircling her with all that rage. He hated her now, and it felt good.

It made outside match inside. It made sense in a way that would make sense to no one else.

She was sweating in the kitchen; the thick scent of confit duck legs and garlic sausage worked her stomach like a butter churn. The windows were open, but the warm evening breeze did little to dissipate the heat. Seriously, who served cassoulet in August?

Maggie didn't bother to ask, though. She already knew: a woman determined to lure back the man she depended on. The man who could do no wrong.

"Maggie, a bouquet would be lovely for the table," Ivy said from her position at the cutting board, figs lined up for the slaughter. "Some peonies and a foxglove, the beach roses, and a few of those yellow tea roses, along with some of the fern fronds. Can you please bring them to me?"

"Yes, Mother," Maggie replied.

Ivy paused, knife in hand hanging guillotine-like over a helpless fig. "Tone," she said quietly. She opened the utility drawer and drew out a pair of shears.

Maggie cleared her throat and took the shears from her mother's outstretched hand. "I'll be right back."

She was in the backyard, decapitating a pink peony, when she heard the doorbell ring. Her mouth filled with the taste of metal. She leaned over and spat in the hedge.

"Maggie," her mother trilled. "Finish up and come inside! Guess who's here!"

She owed this to them, didn't she? After all she had done. "Coming," she called, tone perfect. She reentered the kitchen with an armful of flowers and greenery and a smile that sent hot shocks of pain along her jaw and temple.

Lawrence released Ivy from an embrace and turned to his stepdaughter, already grinning. "Welcome home," he said, coming toward her with his arms open. "I don't need to tell you how worried I've been, do I?" When he saw Maggie hesitate, he tilted his head. "I'm not angry, sweetheart. Not even a little."

She put down the flowers and stood there as his arms closed around her, demons dancing through her insides. His hand stroked along the length of her hair. She put her arms around him and squeezed.

He hissed. Tensed. "You're stronger than you look!" he said with a chuckle.

"Are you okay?"

"Ah, just some back trouble. I threw it out in May, and I guess... well." He smoothed his hand over his thinning brown hair. "When you're old like me, even small things can trigger a cascade of other problems."

"I think that can happen when you're young, too," she murmured as she pulled away from him. He smelled of salt and whisky, hard work and the reward that came after. "Are you okay?"

"Sciatica and three smashed discs. I take the pills, but..." He sighed and turned to Ivy. "Want to open that Marcillac? I splurged."

She smiled and nodded. "Would you like to sit down? I thought we could eat inside, fewer bugs, but if you prefer the patio—"

He waved his hand. "You've set a beautiful table, Ivy."

Her smile grew. Then her eyes fell on Maggie, and the happiness faded fast. "The flowers are already wilting."

Maggie pulled herself into action again, wishing the buzzing between her ears would fade. She assembled a bouquet, passable but of course not quite what her mother could have done. Apparently, there was only one thing she could do that her mother couldn't manage quite as well.

She figured that was why Ivy hated her.

She knew it was why she hated herself.

Chills rolled through her as they sat down for dinner. As Ivy presented the salad, pomegranate seeds tumbling and sparkling like blood cells, Lawrence turned to Maggie and took her hand. "Ivy updated me on how you came back to us," he said. "But she also said she received your grades in the mail."

Maggie's head swiveled to look at her mother.

Ivy nodded. "I opened it while you were away. Straight As again!"

"Really impressive, sweetheart," said Lawrence. He squeezed her hand. "You stayed focused, just like I told you."

Maggie pulled her hand away as Ivy's gaze lasered over to it. "Thanks."

"I'd love to come visit you on campus again. Wasn't that fun?" Lawrence turned to Ivy. "We had a lovely walk on some of the trails near the Quabbin. And then a nice dinner at—what was that place?"

"30Boltwood," Maggie mumbled. And then he'd taken her for a drive.

"You didn't tell me," Ivy said. Her lips barely moved, like she was practicing to be a ventriloquist. She glared at Maggie as if she wanted her to be the dummy.

There was no way Maggie's stomach was going to tolerate this salad. Or the cassoulet. Or the figs. But there was no good escape path, so she stayed where she was, hands in her lap as her mother plated the meal.

Lawrence focused on Ivy for much of the dinner, catching up like they were old friends instead of separated spouses. He asked about her church group, her friends, her book club, her flower club, her walking club, her charity work. He listened attentively as she gushed.

Maggie pushed food around her plate and willed herself invisible.

"Margaret," said Ivy perhaps ten minutes after she'd ladled a large serving of cassoulet onto each plate. "Eat your dinner."

Maggie stared down at the hunks of meat, the beans, the crumbled duck skin, and clumps of fat-soaked bread crumbs. "I don't feel good."

Ivy sighed and rolled her eyes. "How convenient. An hour or so ago, you were ready to stay out all evening with who knows who, doing who knows what, after being out all day. I called Beth Dover's mother, by the way. Did you know she's joined my walking club? Beth didn't even come home this summer. She stayed in Worcester so she could work for a professor in the psychology department at Clark."

Maggie started to push away from the table.

"Don't you dare," Ivy said in a low, deadly voice.

"Ivy," said Lawrence, chuckling. "Go easy. She's young! We can forgive her for wanting to spend more time with friends than us, and she's also an adult." He looked over at her, his blue eyes sad. "Not a little girl anymore."

Maggie shivered as her mother and stepfather watched.

"I've got an idea," he said. "Ivy, this cassoulet is the best you've ever made, and I've just scraped clean my second bowl of it. Would you mind pushing dessert back and letting me finish my wine?"

"Of course, Lawrence!" Ivy was practically glowing as she began to clear his plate.

He took a sip of his wine and rewarded her with a smile. "Perfect." He turned to Maggie. "How about you and I set up the chessboard, sweetheart?"

Maggie shot to her feet. "I'm not really—"

"That's such a wonderful idea," said Ivy. She'd been reaching over to clear Maggie's plate but grabbed her arm instead and squeezed. "She would love—"

Maggie cried out as her mother's fingers compressed the bruised skin beneath her sleeve.

Ivy and Lawrence both looked alarmed as Maggie pulled her arm out of her mother's grasp.

"I barely put any pressure," Ivy said breathlessly, giving Lawrence a pleading look.

He'd gotten to his feet and was looking at Maggie closely. He tilted his head in that way he had. No escaping that look. He could figure anything out. He knew everything in her head and always had. She froze, a rabbit in the beam of a flashlight. "Your face," he said quietly. "What happened?"

"What?" Ivy peered at her daughter.

"It's swollen. Her left cheek. Look." He reached out to touch Maggie, but she backed up quickly. His hand fell to his side.

"Margaret?" Ivy took a step toward her. "What's happened?"

"Nothing. I'm tired. I'm going to go to bed." *And I'm going to be up all night, listening. I'll run this time. I'll slide out the window and run and run.*

She already knew she wouldn't. She already knew.

Lawrence shook his head, disbelieving. "Someone hurt you." He grimaced. "Someone put their hands on you. Who was it?"

Maggie put her hands up, but this time, he moved in close and pulled her into a hug. "I'm fine," she whispered against his shoulder. "I'm fine."

"Who did this to you?" he murmured. "A boy?"

"It's fine," said Maggie. "I'm *fine*." She flinched as he shifted and her cheek hit his collarbone.

He must have felt her tense. "It was a boy."

"She's been lying about where she's been," said Ivy.

"Definitely a boy, then," said Lawrence.

It was as if Maggie wasn't even there.

Ivy pulled Maggie away from Lawrence and turned her so they were face-to-face. Maggie the dummy. Ivy the ventriloquist. "It was *that* boy, wasn't it?"

"What boy?" asked Lawrence.

She shook until Maggie whimpered, then let her go. "The one who she was living with!"

"*Living* with?"

"I didn't want to tell you." Ivy's face was contorted with pain. "It was too awful. I thought that once she was home, if I could get her back to the church—"

"The church?" Lawrence scoffed. "Your solution to everything."

Ivy put her hand on her chest, but her eyes held a flash of defiance. "I simply thought, *given her history*, she might need some help sticking to the straight and narrow."

Lawrence cleared his throat. His cheeks had gone ruddy. But his eyes were on Maggie. "We're not judging you, sweetheart. But we need to know who hurt you. Was it this person you lived with? What was his name?" This last question was directed at Ivy.

"Esteban Perreira," Ivy said. Her voice dripped with disgust. "He was arrested for suspicion of assault, but for some reason, they let him go."

"What the hell?" Lawrence said. "Why didn't you tell me any of this?"

"I didn't want to worry you!" quavered Ivy. "Who knows what he did to her? She claims she doesn't remember, but come on! If she's too ashamed to even tell us, it was bad, I know!"

"I'm fine," mumbled Maggie. She was pretty sure she was going to throw up soon.

"Esteban Perreira," Lawrence said, annunciating each syllable. "Lives in Yarmouth?"

"Provincetown," said Ivy.

"I'm fine," Maggie said loudly, even as her stomach clenched. "And Esteban... I'm not going to see him ever again." Her throat tightened.

"I'm going to kill him," Lawrence said.

"Lawrence!" Ivy's voice had gone shrill.

"Then I'll just have his legs broken. He hurt our little girl." He grabbed Maggie's hand and shoved up her sleeve.

Ivy cried out when she saw the bruises. Maggie pulled away and yanked the sleeve down to her wrist again. "I'm *fine!*" shrieked Maggie. "I'm fine, I'm fine, I'm fine!" Her hands clapped over her ears, her eyes slammed shut, her mind a jumble of red and black.

Lawrence's arms came around her again. "Shh," he whispered as she struggled. "Shh."

Maggie fought. She fought even though she knew it was all over. There were so many paths, but the outcome was certain. There had never been any escape.

"Ivy, run her a warm bath."

Ivy hesitated, looking back and forth between them.

"Ivy," Lawrence barked. "*Now.*"

Ivy's expression turned stony, but she walked down the hall and entered the bathroom.

Maggie sobbed. Lawrence held on tight, tensing as Maggie went limp. Probably his back hurt. But he was a big man, and he was still strong enough.

Slowly, his arms around her, he guided her down the hall.

———

She blinked. All the lights were on in her bedroom. She was on her knees in the middle of the rug. Blond hair lay scattered all around her.

In her right hand, she held a pair of scissors.

With her other hand, she reached up. Touched her hair, or what was left of it.

Dropped the scissors. Ran both hands over her head, came away with bloody palms. She winced. Whimpered.

Good girls are quiet girls. She clamped her hand over her mouth to stifle the sound.

Her breaths punctuated the silence as she wavered to her feet, leaning on the bed, the desk. She stood very still, listening. She ran her hands over her body. She was wearing a nightgown. It was too big. It must have been Ivy's. With shaking hands, she shed the gauzy garment and lunged for the suitcase in her closet. Her clothes from school, from before. She rifled through them, grabbed a T-shirt, jeans, a bra, socks.

And underwear.

She dressed quickly, wishing her heart would slow. But it beat between her ears, the demon playing the drum. She imagined its bloody grin. She glanced at the scissors. Considered using them to silence the monster.

Instead, she grabbed her keys. Slid her feet into a pair of flip-flops. She watched her hands unlatch the window, slide it upward, push at the screen. She marveled as her body heaved itself onto the desk, onto the sill. She gasped in surprise as one leg slid into the humid night air. She clamped her mouth shut as both feet hit the soft dirt of the front flower bed.

She glanced along the house, toward the master bedroom. The lights were off.

She turned and ran for her car, steps light, barely a sound. She turned the radio all the way down as soon as she started the engine. She drove up the driveway, paused at the street. She'd forgotten her phone.

But she couldn't bear to go back. If she did, she'd never leave. She'd let the scissors do what scissors liked to do.

Her foot pressed the gas, and the car jumped onto the road and cruised down the street. Every second put several feet between her and them. This couldn't be real. The clock on the dash told her it was three in the morning. This was insane.

But that was the problem. She didn't want to be insane anymore. She needed all this to stop, one way or the other.

She drove on instinct, on desperation. She rode behind her eyes while her body did the work. Somehow, though she hadn't been there more than once, she still knew the way.

She pulled into the parking lot. There was no way they'd find her here. Ivy didn't even know she'd come. Lawrence knew less than Ivy. And they couldn't use her phone to track her, either. It was good she'd left it behind.

She stared at the door of the darkened building. Her stomach growled. She laughed. Hunger. Somehow, her body kept going. It demanded what it needed, unapologetically. Why couldn't her mind be the same?

Her gaze remained riveted on the doors until her eyes drooped. In her dreams, everything made sense.

She jerked awake as someone banged on her window and brought the confusion back. As beams of sunlight stabbed at her eyeballs and a muffled voice called to her, terror washed over her. No. *No.* She'd gotten away. She remembered driving away! She reached for the keys in the ignition, ready to twist.

"Maggie?" Lori had both hands against the window and was peering into the car, her eyes alight with concern. "Maggie, are you all right?"

Maggie opened the door slowly, letting Lori step back. "I was waiting for you," Maggie said quietly.

Lori looked like she might cry as she looked Maggie over. "What happened?"

Maggie reached up to touch her head again. "Oh." She'd forgotten. "I must look..." She glanced at the rearview mirror. "Oh." This time, it was the sound of a balloon deflating.

"Did someone do this to you?"

"Sort of." She touched her aching cheek. "Some I did myself."

"Maggie..."

"I know." She forced herself to look at Lori. "Do you have time this morning?"

Lori nodded. "I came in early to catch up on notes. I don't have a client until ten."

This was why she had come. This was *why*. And yet somehow, she had to wrestle each word out of her mouth. "Something bad happened to me." She paused. So many years of silence, ended with only five muttered words. Now the only way forward was through, even though the thought made her feel sick. "It's...bad. And I think I need to talk about it."

FRIDAY, AUGUST 7

Detective Correia calls me as I'm driving back to Truro, caught in a snarl of relentless traffic and staring murderously at the SUV in front of me, kayak strapped to the top and bikes clamped to the back. "I got your messages," she tells me. "I wanted to update you."

"I appreciate that. I've learned a little more about Stefan Silva, and I—"

"Yeah," she says. "I'm aware that you've contacted him. I'm going to advise you not to further interfere with my investigation."

"It was my understanding that you'd already ruled him out as a suspect, and anyway, aren't you the one pushing suicide? You're convinced she killed herself, right?"

She meets the acid in my tone with complete blandness. "As I've told you, Mr. Zarabian, I'm pursuing every lead, no matter where it points. I'm not invested in any particular outcome except the one that makes it more likely Mina will come home safely."

"You believe she's still alive?"

The naked hope in my voice is the first and only thing that draws a human response from the detective. Her tone softens. "I hope so. I really hope so. But we have to be braced for any outcome. All I'm asking from you is that you let me do my job."

My fingers grind into the steering wheel. "You called just to tell me to sit back and do nothing."

"No. I'm calling to tell you that Mina's phone has been found. I'm driving out to pick it up."

"Where?"

"It's at a Verizon store. Brought in this morning by a good Samaritan who found it over in Hawksnest State Park. Verizon worker plugged it in to charge and recognized the picture on the lock screen. Gave us a call."

Mina's lock screen shows a picture of us together during a weekend at Wachusett Mountain in February, our faces pressed together, our eyes bright, our cheeks flushed with cold. She loves it there, and apparently so does her character Maggie. Mina told me Scott used to take her skiing there when she was little. She said he stopped once they moved to the Cape.

"Are you guys going to search that park?" I ask. "Do you think she—"

"No, this isn't like Beech Forest. The lady was out walking her dog on the trail. She saw the phone get left behind."

"She *saw* Mina?"

"No. She found the phone on a bench, and she said there had been a guy sitting there a minute before. She assumed it was his and tried to find him in the parking lot. He was nowhere to be found."

"So you have no idea who left it there, really."

"The woman was able to give us a description, Mr. Zarabian." Her tone is grim. Like a warning.

"I've been in Boston since last night."

"Mr. Zarabian. Hawksnest is in Harwich."

"Harwich," I murmur, my heart speeding. "And the guy who left Mina's phone in the park?"

"Matches the description of Stefan Silva. He's now officially a person of interest in her disappearance."

"Oh God," I whisper.

"Mr. Zarabian, there is something you can do. The password for her phone—"

"Magic." I swallow. "Try 'magic.' Have you told her parents?"

"I called them just before I called you."

She promises to keep me posted, and I keep driving toward Truro, hoping Mina's parents will offer me the truth their daughter never got around to telling me.

When I arrive at the Richardses', it's clear we're not going out to dinner. The smell of garlic and basil hits me as soon as Scott opens the door. He solemnly invites me in and offers me a drink. "Rose is finishing the salad," he says.

"The detective told me she called you."

He nods. From the kitchen, Rose says, "Scott, did you offer him a drink?"

"I'll just have water," I say.

Scott disappears into the kitchen and comes out a moment later carrying a tall glass of ice water complete with mint leaves and a lemon wedge. "We can sit on the patio." He leads me to the back door and gestures at a small table, beautifully set for three. It reminds me of the dinner Maggie has with her mother and stepfather, the perfect surface hiding something terrifyingly rotten beneath. It pretty much kills what little appetite I had. "We'll bring the dinner out here," Scott informs me.

It's like nothing's happened at all. Like everything's normal, like

Stefan Silva hasn't just shot his level of suspiciousness into the stratosphere. Like Mina's going to walk through the door at any minute to join the party. Rose flits around for several minutes, making sure I have a bit of everything—fresh tomato salad, couscous with raisins and pine nuts, roasted chicken with lemon and olives, homemade focaccia still warm from the oven—on my plate. I accept her offerings even though I feel sick to my stomach.

Stefan had Mina's phone. Tried to drop it in the park. He probably hoped someone would steal it or that people would assume Mina herself had lost it there. He pretended he had no clue where she was, then tried to trash the evidence the day after I went to talk to him. Chills ride over my skin despite the humid summer evening air.

But Scott and Rose? You'd think this was any other evening for them. Rose is perhaps a touch more frantic than her usual, but Scott is flat as a manhole cover, totally subdued.

"I spoke with Stefan Silva yesterday," I say as soon as they raise their heads from their premeal prayer.

Scott looks away, and Rose looks startled. "You...know him?"

"I do now. I went to see him at the bar he works at in Harwich."

Rose's cheek twitches. "You tracked him down. Somehow, you tracked him down."

"How do you know Mina didn't tell me about him?"

"Why should she?" Rose slices through a piece of chicken on her plate. "She'd left it behind. All in the past."

Scott is very focused on his couscous, using his knife to move a precise amount onto his fork, sliding it off, easing it back on again. When he sees me watching him, he spears a raisin and eats it.

"He hinted that you'd paid him to stay away from her," I say, and Rose sets down her silverware. Hard.

"Oh, is that what he said? What class," she says bitterly. "I'm surprised he didn't brag about it all over town."

"I take it he was telling the truth."

Scott raises his head. "We did what we thought was best for Mina."

Rose twists her napkin in her lap. "You didn't know her then. She was lost."

"Literally, right?" I run a finger down the length of my sweating water glass. "I know about the fugue."

"The what?" asks Scott.

"The fugue. She was triggered by something." The question is, triggered by what? Untangling history from fiction is twisting me up. As Rose mutters under her breath and her cheeks flush, I plow forward. "She forgot who she was and dropped out of her life. Stefan was with her during that time. He helped her get home."

Rose scoffs. "Is that what she told you?" She shakes her head. "She never took responsibility. She never confessed or repented."

"Rose," Scott murmurs, reaching over to put his hand over his wife's. She pulls it away and wrings her napkin again.

"She had *every* opportunity!" Rose clenches a fist over the poor napkin. "It wasn't easy, but we sent her to that private school. And then she turns eighteen and poof! Disappears for almost five months! It was ungrateful."

"Wait," I say. "*Five* months?" Maggie was gone for only about ten weeks.

"Oh," says Rose. "She didn't tell you everything, hmm? I knew she wouldn't."

"*Rose*," says Scott.

She gives her husband a sharp look. "And where were *you*?" she snaps. Then she covers her mouth and looks away.

Scott clears his throat. "I'm going to have another drink. Alex?"

"Did I see some Glenfiddich in there?" I ask weakly.

"I'll be right back." He gets up from the table, leaving me there with Rose, who is taking heavy breaths through her nose.

"Those were difficult years," she says quietly. "What I meant is that Scott had a lot of sea days, with all those fisheries to be inspected. He wasn't home very much. He was working hard for his family."

Or he had a month-to-month lease at one of Andy Poole's rental cottages.

"I spoke to Amy Poole yesterday."

Rose blinks. "Why would you do that?"

"Andy told me that she and Mina were friends in middle school."

"I doubt my daughter was the kind of friend that girl deserved." She apparently sees the naked what-the-fuck in my expression and changes course. "What I mean is that Mina was very...focused on herself." Her nostrils flare, and then she apparently can't help herself. "Selfish, if you want my honest opinion."

"Amy told me that Mina seemed unhappy. That she withdrew. Quit all her activities." And I can't help bringing it up, because it seems like such a weird lie for Mina to have told. "Like chess."

"And I suppose that's my fault?"

Huh? "No one's saying that. I'm trying to understand Mina a little better."

She begins to tidy up the table, covering her half-eaten plate of food with her napkin, picking up a grain of couscous and depositing it on the edge of Scott's plate. "Understand, then, that she made her own decisions. I raised her to behave, to consider others' needs before her own. But I also tried to support her. I did my *best*."

Another chill rides down my spine. I know what I read in the pages of my wife's novel. Maggie was raised to behave. To be *quiet*. To keep secrets. And now I know Mina kept a boatload of them, maybe because her mother trained her to do exactly that, but the pain it must have caused her...it bleeds from those pages. It's like she's screaming for someone to help her, and I haven't yet figured out how. I want to push, but now Rose is acting like she's about to clam up, so I move on to keep her talking. "So Mina, when she was eighteen, she disappeared for a while. When I first told you she was missing, that was what you were thinking about. You've been through this before."

"She *ran* away that time," says Rose, her hands fluttering over the glasses and dishes, straightening and adjusting. "For months. Do you think she's run away from you, Alex?"

I already know this tactic of hers, and I'm not letting her throw me off track. "Did you know where she was, Rose?"

She shakes her head. "I think she wanted to hurt me."

"Why would she want to do that?"

"Don't all young ladies need to be tough on their mothers?" Her voice is breezy until it breaks.

"Most young ladies don't take it that far," I say. "You really think this was a decision she made and not a mental health issue?"

"It was a convenient excuse. She was eighteen. An adult, the police told me. But I knew my daughter. So willful. I suspected she was easy prey for temptation and had probably followed a sinful path. I almost expected it." She rubs at her temples, fingernails glinting in the fading daylight. "And then she showed up all of a sudden as if nothing had happened, with five months gone by and an elaborate lie that fooled no one." Rose glances back at the house. "In the end, though, it strengthened our family. Brought us closer. God works in mysterious ways."

"She was pregnant."

Rose turns as Scott emerges from the house with two drinks. "Will you make me one, too?"

Scott sets one drink in front of me and the other in front of his wife before heading back inside.

Rose takes a sip and meets my gaze. "I tried to raise her right. She pushed against me at every turn. I love my daughter, but she seemed determined to flout her upbringing every chance she got. She wouldn't listen."

"Is that why you sent her away to boarding school?"

Rose flinches. "Is that what you think of me? Perhaps I shouldn't be surprised, if you're getting your information from my daughter. I've always done what was best for her."

I gulp down half my drink in one toss of my head, fortifying myself. It burns all the way down. "So when she was pregnant..."

"I took care of her," she says in a shrill voice. "Every single day. I made sure she had everything she needed so that she and that precious little life inside her were as healthy as possible."

God. "She has a child."

"We made sure he went to a good home."

He... Mina gave birth to a son. And if she was eighteen when she had him, this kid would have just hit adolescence. I sit back. Push my chair away from the table. That volcanic feeling is simmering again, the pressure growing. "Did she *want* to have a child?"

"She made that decision when she decided to have *intercourse* outside of the sanctity of marriage," Rose hisses.

"Rose!" It's Scott. He has emerged from the house, drink in hand. Then his gaze rests on me. "This is a very stressful time for all of us."

"You have a grandson."

Scott's lips press together. Rose bows her head. "She wasn't ready to be a mother," she says. "She was in no condition to take care of a baby. She couldn't even take care of herself. And we...we all thought it was best."

"Did she agree to any of it?" I ask. There might be seismic activity inside me, but my voice is steady.

"She came around," says Rose.

I don't know how much Mina is actually like Maggie. I don't know if she suffered like her character so obviously suffered and if the effects were as apparent, because I didn't know her then. But somehow, Mina wrote those pages. She tapped into the emotions. She knew what that felt like.

I'm guessing it was so painful that she had to change the story. In her novel, her character is older and gone for a shorter period of time, so she's barely twelve weeks pregnant when she sneaks off and has an abortion. In real life, eighteen-year-old Mina was gone for five months and carried her pregnancy to term, and then she gave the baby up.

Then she married a clueless asshole who blundered his way into the most agonizing chapter of her life without even sensing the pain hidden behind that beautiful face, that wild and carefree laugh.

"And you all pretend it never happened," I say. If this part of her life hurt her so much that she couldn't include it in the book, what else did she change or leave out? And what does that say about what's left? That's the *less* painful part? The stuff she could bear? "Jesus," I whisper.

"Sometimes it's best to let things lie," Rose says primly. "Why open old wounds?"

I have to work to draw air in my lungs. I *know* that phrase. It's in Mina's book. Maggie recalls being told that by her character's twisted, evil mother. And I'm sitting here with Mina's actual mother, and I wonder just how evil she is. "Old wounds," I murmur.

Rose nods. "Right. How can they heal if you keep poking at them?"

"Did Stefan know?" I ask, trying to sound normal instead of full of disgust for the woman in front of me. Especially because I don't *really* know how similar Rose and Ivy are. I don't know exactly what old wounds we're talking about and which Rose inflicted.

Scott looks down at his drink. "He was not the right type for her. Not able to support a child."

"He's the *father*," I snap. I wish I could spit this bitter taste right out of my mouth.

"He had absolutely nothing to do with us." Rose sniffs. "And weren't we right about all of it?" She leans forward, peering at me. "Look at all she accomplished after that. We got her back on track, into a good school. She moved on and made a living and found you."

While Rose and Scott got to pretend that their eighteen-year-old daughter hadn't had a baby out of wedlock. "Does Mina have any relationship with the child?" I ask.

"We felt that a closed adoption would be best for her."

"The decision wasn't yours to make."

"She signed the papers," Rose says.

I'm imagining Mina, my Mina, eighteen, messed up after whatever she went through, scared, and under the thumb of her judgmental and rigid parents. Of course she signed. She was totally at their mercy.

What if she changed her mind?

We're all there, stewing in tense silence, when Sharon Rawlings emerges from a concealed path at the back of the property, carrying a basket. "Oh," she says as she sees us there. "Hello, hello! I'm so sorry to disrupt your dinner. You said I could help myself to your raspberries?" She gestures at the brambles that bound the woods at the back of the property.

Rose's face transforms, aglow with pride and charity. "Help yourself, and then come join us for dessert! I made a berry crumble myself this afternoon."

Sharon gives me a rueful look, like I'm in on a private joke. "Of course you did," she says. "And it will be at least twice as good as the one I'm making for Phillip."

Rose waves the comment away. "Please. I'm probably using a recipe you gave me."

"Wouldn't that be ironic?" Sharon's eyes narrow as she looks us over again. "Is everything okay? Any word about Mina?"

"The police are doing a very thorough job," says Rose. "Pursuing every lead." She obviously doesn't want to talk about Stefan Silva right now. I wonder how many of the Richardses' friends know that Mina was even pregnant, let alone that she had a child.

"Does Phillip need any help on the property?" Scott asks Sharon. "You shouldn't have to shoulder all of it while he recovers. I can come over tomorrow."

"I can come by and clean your house for you!" offers Rose.

"We're *fine*!" says Sharon with a laugh. "Phillip was telling me this morning that he wants to get back to his garden. You can't keep that man down. But Winn and Andy have also offered to come around and do the mowing and mulching. We have plenty of help."

Scott nods. "Call if you need me." He raises his gaze from his glass. "I'll be in my workshop, Rose. Leave the dishes for me."

Rose glances between her husband and his almost-untouched

plate, and I see the calculation. She probably thinks he's being rude in front of guests but calling him out will only draw more attention to it. "A wonderful night for tinkering," she says with a smile. "I'll do the dishes."

He holds her eyes for a long moment, and I don't know either of them well enough to guess what's held inside that connection. Love? Resentment? Shared secrets, certainly. Ones I'll never get with Sharon right here, smiling and making small talk. Rose is deep inside her hostess role, playing it for all she's worth.

She and Scott are hiding things. It's possible that Stefan did something to Mina. I'm betting she met with him to tell him that they have a child together. It makes sense; she said she had to talk to him. She was worried he wouldn't take it well. Maybe he lost it when he found out that he had a teenage son he never got to meet, that he never had the choice to raise. Or he was still simmering with rage. What if, instead of paying Stefan off, Scott really did hire someone to try to break the guy's legs, just like the Lawrence character threatens? Or perhaps Stefan wanted more money to keep the whole thing secret and Mina wouldn't give in? Who knows? He's now a person of interest, so it's the detective's job to figure it out. She's already warned me off it.

But as I sit here in this lovely backyard, my senses filled with the scent of summer flowers and an uneaten meal, the trilling laughter of Mina's mother, and the pale gray flash of eyes that are way too familiar, I can't help but think that Mina's parents had something to do with her disappearance. Mina visited them the day she vanished. They haven't had an easy relationship. And Rose, at least, is desperate to keep up appearances.

Was Mina about to drop a grenade on their picture-perfect facade?

Suspicion is brewing inside me, but none of it quite fits. It's difficult to see why any of them, Stefan included, would go this far. It's hard to understand why Mina would take off her rings and just disappear. All I know is that when I get home, I need to read the rest of Mina's book.

Sure, not all of it is history. That's obvious now—some of it is fiction. But although it's shattering my heart to admit it, I have a feeling the desperate, dark heart of it is truth.

CHAPTER ELEVEN

Are you comfortable? Do you want something to eat? I think I have some crackers..." Lori moved a stack of folders from the floor to her desk, making way for her to sit across from Maggie, who was curled up on the couch.

She'd been hungry. She could remember that feeling in the depths of the morning as she sat in her car, waiting. Now, though, things were different. "I'm fine," she said, then shook her head. "God, I always say that."

"Why, do you think?"

"Maybe I always want it to be true." She paused. "Or I just want people to stop asking me how I am because I can't cover it up forever."

Lori glanced at Maggie's face, then her wrists. "I imagine that some times are easier than others. To pretend, I mean."

Maggie tugged at her sleeves, then realized the bruises on her arms were the least attention-grabbing thing about her appearance. Her hair, her face, the way she was lying on her side, knees pulled to her chest—everything about her positively screamed *Something is very wrong.* "It's never been that easy."

Lori waited.

"Ask me questions," said Maggie. "I don't know how to do this." *And I don't want to.*

As if that were obvious, Lori asked, "What made you come here this morning? I can tell it's not easy."

"Something happened to me last night, and it really scared me."

"More than having a three-month gap in your memory?"

Maggie snorted. "Maybe not. But this... Is there just another person inside me, one who comes out sometimes?" *If so, I think she's trying to hurt me.*

"I can't give you an easy answer. I need to have a better understanding of what's going on for you." The corner of Lori's mouth twitched. "Right. Questions. Can you walk me through your day yesterday?"

"It didn't happen until last night."

"Let's work up to that."

"I got an abortion yesterday morning."

"That's a hell of a way to start your day." Lori pressed her lips together. "I'm not being flippant, Maggie. I'm just—"

"Don't worry about it. I guess that probably was a part of everything. I wanted it to be no big deal, you know?"

"You chose the path that was best for you, but that doesn't mean it's a simple one. There can be short-term emotional fallout, depending on the person and their circumstances."

"I was further along than I wanted to be," Maggie murmured. "I was hoping..." She was hoping it had been Esteban's. "Part of me wanted a baby, you know? But—" A shudder cut her words short.

"Take your time."

"There was a man. He took care of me when I was—well, when I was someone else. I think he liked me. And I got him to help me. I manipulated him. I let him believe he was the father." She checked Lori's face for judgment and saw none. "And I kind of lost it afterward, on the way home. It got physical."

Lori leaned forward. "He assaulted you?"

"I started it."

"Maggie—"

"No, I did."

Lori sat back. "Is that how you got the bruises?"

"He probably has some bruises, too. I scratched him. I threw his phone in a ditch and left him stranded. Not sure how I could have been a bigger bitch, even if I'd tried."

"You have a right to defend yourself. And I imagine you were pretty emotionally vulnerable."

"I'm a monster," Maggie whispered. "I think I've always been one."

"Why would you say that?"

Maggie's throat constricted. "I've messed up so many people. Sometimes I think I do it on purpose."

"Why?"

"I can't help it. I'm so messed up."

"How did you get messed up?" Their eyes met. Very softly, Lori asked, "Who hurt you?"

Maggie touched her hair, her fingertips skimming over a crusted scab that sent shocks of pain along her scalp. "Besides me, you mean?"

"I see that more as a scream for help—and my question stands."

Maggie glanced at the chessboard and pressed her face to the pillow. "My dad used to love to play chess. He was a pretty good player. We used to play after dinner each night. I was in the chess club. I was playing with the middle schoolers when I was still in elementary school."

"Did your parents take pride in that?"

"I guess so. After my dad died, my mom made sure I kept playing." Maggie ran her fingers along the velvety couch fabric. "She got the middle school chess club coordinator to give me lessons."

"Did you want to keep playing?"

"She said my dad would want me to. That I could honor him by doing it." Maggie stared at a catch in the fabric, one thread pulled loose from the rest. She wished she had those scissors again.

"You didn't answer my question."

"I don't think it matters anymore, whether I wanted to keep playing or not."

"Why do your preferences not matter?"

Maggie sighed in exasperation. "This isn't working," she snapped.

"How can we make it work better?"

She shoved herself up to sitting. "Aren't you the doctor? Aren't you supposed to know that?" She was being rude. Her fingers curled over couch cushions, ready for blowback.

But Lori simply smiled. "I *am* the doctor. But you're the expert, Maggie. You're the only one who can tell me what feels good and bad."

Maggie jolted to her feet, laughing. "I have no fucking idea," she shouted.

"I believe you," Lori said. "Sometimes, things get really mixed up, and it's not easy to tell them apart. Good and bad. Love and abuse. I think that's what's happened to you."

"That I got mixed up? No shit, lady."

"Maggie, please stay," Lori said as Maggie turned for the door. "You can sit, you can stand, you can lie on the floor, hop on one foot, stand on your head, but please stay."

"You can't help me. Nobody can."

"False," Lori said firmly. "I can help you. But only if you give me permission."

Maggie began to pace, her body unable to contain the rage crackling along her limbs. "I've let people do all sorts of things to me, Lori," she snapped. "You'd just be one of many."

"Who else is on that list, Maggie?"

Maggie shook her head, clutched at it, rubbed until there was blood. When she looked up, Lori was standing there with a first-aid kit in hand. "For now, we'll deal with it this way," she said to Maggie. "Have a seat."

Maggie sat like her legs had been cut out from under her. Her eyes burned as Lori dabbed her wounds with antiseptic and pressed bandages to her shorn hair. Shame and fury bred and bloomed, filling her lungs and making it hard to breathe. Finally, when Lori stood behind her, when her hands lifted their weight from her skull, Maggie said, "He wanted to play. He wanted to teach me how to do things properly. He always said that. Every time."

"The chess tutor?"

Maggie nodded.

"But you're not talking about chess."

"It was, at first. I mean, it was and it wasn't. I know that now."

"It's called grooming."

Maggie flinched. "I was so stupid. I *liked* him."

"How long did it go on?"

Spit filled her mouth. She shook her head.

"Okay. But it didn't stop with chess lessons. He took it further. Crossed a line. Inched across it, I'm guessing."

"He told me I was special," she muttered.

"Did you tell anyone? Your mother?"

"I couldn't."

"Why?"

"Because, Lori," Maggie said, "she had already decided to marry him."

"Maggie..." Lori moved to her chair again and sat down. "You've been talking about your stepfather."

"I actually thought he'd leave me alone after they got married. And he did, for a while."

"You were nine? Ten?"

"I believed he had stopped forever. I even forgot about it for a long time." Maggie shrugged. "I was in middle school when he started up again." Ninth step, fourth step, right outside the door. *Creak, creak, creak,* a slice of light from the hall, a shadow blocking it out, signaling there was no escape. "He'd come into my room. He told my mom it was nightmares. He was a light sleeper. She wasn't."

"Oh, Maggie." Lori's voice was so sad.

Maggie couldn't bear to look at her. She was afraid that if she saw the pity, she'd run. Or attack. "When I was in eighth grade, she did wake up. She caught us."

"'Caught...*us*'?"

"She walked in. She saw us."

"Can you tell me what she saw?"

The whine sounded like it came from someone else, somewhere else. Ventriloquist's dummy. Maggie covered her face with her hands.

"It's okay if you don't want to. I know it's painful. You're being so brave, Maggie."

"What do you think she saw?" Maggie snapped, dropping her hands. "Just guess."

"A grown man abusing an innocent girl."

Maggie laughed, sharp as those scissors. "Oh no, that's not what *she* saw. No, Ivy Wallace-Gainer saw her whore daughter seducing her innocent husband. She saw the man she loved led into temptation by a tool of the devil. She saw a lot, but not a grown man abusing an innocent girl."

Lori had been listening, her whole body taut with attention, but the more Maggie spoke, the more Lori's face changed, transforming from queasiness to a rigid clench.

"You told me you wouldn't judge," Maggie said. "But I can see it. You can't help yourself, can you?"

"If you think for one moment that I'm judging *you*, I'm going to have to examine your reality testing." Lori shook her head. "The one person you should have been able to count on completely failed."

"Did she? She wanted me to be a good young lady. She wanted me to be quiet, to be polite, to be proper and obedient and attentive to everyone else's fucking feelings. She wanted me to be pretty and to get good grades and to have perfect manners and to make people around me feel good, all the time. And I did, right?" A sob pushed its way out of her, another far away, foreign sound. "I was really good at it. Still am when I want to be."

"You're a survivor is what you are."

"That's bullshit. I don't need that."

"You're here. You're still standing after everything. But it's taken a toll."

"She sent me away to boarding school," said Maggie. "She said she hoped they would succeed where she had failed."

"It might have been the best thing she could do for you—getting you away from that situation."

"Should I have written a thank-you note? How rude of me."

"I wasn't saying you owed her a single damn thing," said Lori. "She failed you, Maggie."

"I guess she'd probably agree with you at this point. You can't look at me and claim any kind of success."

"I wouldn't be so sure, because here you are." Lori held up her hands. "All I'm saying is that you could have done a lot of things last night, Maggie. The damage could have been to more than your hair. But instead, you chose the absolute healthiest thing—you came looking for help."

"She wants to get back together with him. I thought they were going to get divorced. He moved out after everything."

"When was that?"

"After I left for school."

"Have you had any contact with him?"

Maggie grimaced. "I guess she doesn't believe in divorce. And apparently neither does he. He paid for my education. He says he'll always be my dad. He says he'll always take care of me."

Lori watched her for what felt like a long time. "He didn't stop," she murmured. "The distance didn't protect you."

Maggie slowly sank to the floor. Her knees hit the soft rug, then her elbows, then her forehead. "He wanted me to show my gratitude," she mumbled.

"Maggie," Lori said, "when was the last time he visited you at school?"

"April," she whispered, rocking forward and back, forward and back.

"Of this *year*?"

"He came and took me out to the nicest restaurant in Amherst. He met my boyfriend." She shuddered. "He didn't like him. He said I wasn't focusing on my studies. He said he didn't want to pay for my education if I was going to waste my time."

"He wanted to keep you to himself." Lori sounded sick.

But Maggie had gone numb. Her whole body tingled with a heavy kind of nothing. "I guess he made his first mistake then, didn't he?"

"I'm not sure I follow. It sounds to me like he hasn't done *anything* right. Not one thing."

"But this..." Maggie began to laugh again, her fingers clawing at the rug, leaving little divots.

"This is what triggered your fugue," Lori said slowly.

"It wasn't the first time," Maggie said, curling into a ball, vaguely aware of how pathetic she was but unable to care. "He'd done it before."

"I know, Maggie. But this time, you got pregnant."

It was like a dam breaking. Maggie's body convulsed, and she began to sob.

Everything that came after was a blur. Lori said some words. Maggie heard "safety." She heard "hospital."

She heard herself say "Yes. Please."

She didn't fight when the ambulance came. She let Lori hold her hand. She nodded when Lori told her she was brave, when she said it was the beginning of her journey out of the darkness.

Maggie wasn't fooled, though. She was too tired to argue or fight or to say a single word, but she knew the truth. She knew where the darkness lay.

And no amount of talking could light that space.

SATURDAY, AUGUST 8

I finish reading Mina's book in a breathless rush on Friday night, and on Saturday morning, I have to read it again to make sure what I remember isn't the product of a drunken fever dream. But it's still there, all laid out, Mina's story of her past.

What. The. Fuck?

There's no way that actually happened in real life, in *her* life.

No. I've read the editor's comments, too, or lack thereof. There aren't many in the final chapters. If he believed that was all the truth, he would have said something, wouldn't he?

Maybe he didn't want to put any of his thoughts in writing. Or maybe there are some questions best left unasked and some answers left unknown, too dark and horrific to be seen in the light.

The only thing I really do know is that between the details, the heartbreaking, gut-wrenching threads she wove together, there is a reality I have to understand if I ever want to find her. I've been telling myself that it couldn't be Mina, that Maggie is a foreign creature from her imagination. But in Maggie, I see the shadow of my wife. I hear the echo of her voice. I understand that she was raised to please others, and even when she escaped her parents, that training was there, along with that skill. She knew how to make other people feel good. She made *me* feel good. And I hope to God it was because she actually wanted to. I wonder how she could have held all this inside her. The violation, the pain, the confusion, the rage. I wonder how any one soul could bear it.

I don't see how the manuscript can tell me where she went and what she's done unless I understand her actual past a hell of a lot better than I do now.

After yesterday, I know that her parents aren't going to help me. And Stefan is off-limits, given Correia's warning and the active case against him. Mina's therapist might know, but she's not going to tell me a damn thing.

I call Hannah. It goes straight to voicemail. Either her phone is off or she's blocked my number. I ask her to call me back, but I won't be holding my breath. So I search for Kyle, the editor who Hannah mentioned. Kyle Wu has been a senior editor at Pleiades Books for the last six years. I look up his number, but it's Saturday, so no one answers. Even if I reach him, I'm not sure he'll tell me anything. I leave a brief message asking for a call back and decide I need to stick closer to home to get the answers I need.

I look up Sharon Rawlings. She and Phillip have lived next door to the Richardses for years. If anyone knows them, it's her. She answers immediately and agrees to meet me for lunch at Montano's. When I arrive, her brown Mercedes is already in the gravel lot, and she's waiting at a table inside with an empty cocktail in front of her. She greets me with a hug. "I wondered if I might get a call from you, actually."

"Really? Why?"

"I saw the look on your face yesterday as Rose and Scott did their dance."

The waitress comes over and clears the empty glass. I order a beer, and so does Sharon, but only after asking after the young woman's parents, who are apparently friends of hers and Phillip's.

"I don't usually partake this early in the day," she says with a glint in her eye. "But I had the feeling this conversation would call for a drink."

"I'm getting the sense there's a lot that Scott and Rose don't want to tell me."

She chuckles. "They do give that impression, don't they?"

"I'm just trying to understand what happened to Mina."

Her face goes serious. "I've been thinking about you a lot. Almost hoping you'd reach out."

I watch her for a moment. "You've been hinting." There's been a weird intensity to all her pleasant, oh-so-complimentary comments about Rose.

A shrug as our drinks arrive. She takes a long sip of hers. "I don't like to overstep. I mean, sometimes I do, right? Sometimes I'm hopeless." She shakes her head. "Shotgun wedding."

"It's fine. But...did you ask me about that because of Mina's past?"

She sits back. Takes another drink. "I guess you know more than I thought."

"What I want to know is the truth." Because I know what I read, and it's disturbing as hell.

"How much truth?" she asks before taking another gulp of her beer. Her cheeks are getting pink. "Dig deep enough in the past and you might hit an artery."

I'm rapidly losing my appetite, but I order a sandwich. Sharon orders crab cakes. I make a bad joke about food poisoning, and she gives me a questioning look and then waves it away. "Different restaurant, thank God," she replies. And after another draft—emptying her glass—she looks me in the eye. "I never thought I'd talk about any of this. I've spent so many years pretending it never happened."

"You were more involved than you let on."

"Not by choice." She flags the waitress and orders another beer. "I love my husband," she says as the waitress walks away. She leans forward and speaks quietly. "But he's not perfect."

"No one is." I have no idea where she's headed with this, but my heart is beating too fast.

"I just want you to understand where I'm coming from."

"Okay..."

She hangs her head back. "I'm sorry, Alex. I wanted to make this easier, and I'm doing the opposite."

We sit in silence for a moment. I drink my beer and look around. The place is packed with families, and I'm guessing almost all of them are tourists, wearing their sunburns like uniforms.

Finally, Sharon says, "When Scott and Rose and Mina moved in next door, I was so happy. She was such a cute little girl. Phillip and I..." She presses her lips together. "We had a son. Robbie."

"Had..."

"Leukemia. He was four." Her face crumples. "He would have been Mina's age."

"I'm so sorry, Sharon."

She sniffles and looks toward the window as the waitress returns with her second beer. I thank the woman in order to give Sharon a second to pull herself back together, thinking the whole time about how it would feel to lose Devon that way. My chest is aching as Sharon looks back at me.

"I loved Mina from the start," she says in a husky voice. "From the very start."

"Did you have a sense of what she was going through?" Because I'm afraid I do. "Like, why they sent her off to boarding school? I talked to Amy Poole, and she said Mina was pretty withdrawn before she left."

"Oh, I can't blame her at all." She meets my eyes with an apologetic tilt of her head. "Out with it, right? I'm dancing around all this like a dog in need of a fire hydrant."

"Take your time." That's what I say. I'm no therapist, but I'm a fair negotiator, and I understand the benefit of letting people stew for a bit. It's why I still haven't answered Drew's calls from yesterday.

"At first, we were great friends," she says. "I mean, we don't go to that New Life church. People in Truro aren't usually that religious. Most of the people you met are their church folks, but only the Pooles live in Truro, too. Right up the road from us. But Rose was always all about the church and the community. Scott...he was always all about Rose."

"I don't know what to make of Scott," I tell her. And what I've read...I don't know how to translate it. In Mina's book, the dad is dead, and he's replaced by this nightmare stepdad who abuses her. Was that Mina's way of protecting herself from having to write about Scott doing all that to her? Yet another thing too painful to include in the story?

"He's a tough nut to crack," Sharon acknowledges. "Still waters run deep."

And are often cold as hell. "You described Rose as an exotic bird."

She smiles. "Well, she's obviously not from New England, now, is she? You know how it is."

"I'm not sure she's so out of place here. She's pretty good at keeping things close to the vest."

"More like she distracts from them with all her flouncing around." Sharon covers her mouth. "That wasn't nice," she mutters. Her second beer is half-empty.

"You don't like her."

"That's complicated." Her eyes narrow. "Because I loved her, Alex. I really did. I loved her and Scott and Mina like they were family. But then..." A shuddering sigh. "I don't know if it was because she was lonely or that she and Scott were having problems or because she couldn't stand not to be the center of attention. I'll never know."

Oh boy. "Are you saying..."

"That she slept with my husband? Yes. That's what I'm saying."

Now I'm the one gulping my beer. "I can see why you'd be mad at both of them."

"You have no idea. And poor Scott..."

"Amy told me that she overheard her parents talking about how Scott had asked Andy about renting one of his cottages way back when."

"Can't hardly blame him, can you? I mean, I don't know what he knew and when, but it knocked all of us off-kilter. Not least of all poor little Mina. I think that whole thing did lasting damage to her," she says with a slow shake of her head.

My brain is doing cartwheels, trying to link everything up. But no part of me is a gymnast. "So when people describe Mina as withdrawn, this was why? Because her parents were having problems?" Could this really be the cause of all Mina's distress, or were Scott and Rose having problems for another reason? Maybe one closer to the chilling explanation outlined in the chapters of her book.

Sharon dabs at her eyes with her napkin. "It was terrible. You see,

Mina's the one who caught them. And Rose...well. She's determined to keep up appearances, isn't she?"

"Jesus," I whisper. Now my beer is empty. The waitress brings over our food, and I order another one. "So she walked in on Rose and Phillip. Did she tell Scott?"

She shakes her head. "She didn't tell anyone. It was Phillip who told *me*. He confessed. He was just wrecked over it. And even then, he knew Rose well enough to know...well. That it would be difficult for Mina. Rose is that iron fist in a velvet glove." She snorts. "Or maybe one of those rhinos that stamps out forest fires. Don't they do that? She suffocates any little secret that might reveal that she's not quite as saintly as she tries to look."

I already know I'm not going to be able to take a single bite of my food. "So Phillip told you he'd had the affair after Mina caught them. But if Mina didn't tell anyone, did Rose tell Scott about it?"

"I'm almost certain she didn't." She swallows a bite of her crab cake. "And I didn't either." She looks around and lowers her voice. "To be honest, I was afraid he would kill my husband. Or Rose. They made a mistake. I didn't want... I was worried about everyone."

"But Scott must have found out, right? Why else would he be wanting to rent out a cottage for himself?"

Sharon looks out the window. "There were rumors...about Scott. He might have been out there at that cottage before the affair. I mean, Rose *was* lonely. And those cottages are all empty in the winter. Most of them aren't even fit to inhabit in the cold months, but some have woodstoves."

"It's a private place, in other words."

"A place one can go without being watched. This is such a small town. Everyone in everyone else's business. *Especially* in the cold months."

"You think he was having an affair, too?"

She shrugs. "He was doing something. I don't judge. Mina once told me the place just had a bed and a table. She said it was freezing inside and the mattress smelled funny. She didn't like it."

A chill runs through me. "He took her there."

"Well, sure, he was living there, for a time. He was so quiet about his comings and goings, but it's hard not to notice. Rose...she was beside herself. She wanted so badly to put it in the past, to pretend nothing had happened. And there was Mina, a reminder of her guilt. Phillip and I certainly decided never to mention any of it for that reason. She was over at our place a lot. We wanted to protect her. Maybe Scott was protecting Mina, too."

Or doing something else entirely. "Sharon, does Scott play chess?"

"Hmm? Oh. Yes! He used to play with Mina all the time, and he and Phillip would even play sometimes, before Scott became more distant." She clucks her tongue. "Rose never really thought her daughter needed to play chess. I remember she thought it was just a way to get attention from the boys. But then Mina lost interest, of course."

I push my plate away and welcome the arrival of my second beer by ordering a shot of Macallan, which the waitress informs me they don't have. I ask her to bring me whatever single malt they happen to stock. She comes back with Johnny Walker a second later, and I don't complain. "They really messed her up, didn't they? Both of them."

Sharon sighs. "I can't tell you exactly. Mina changed, though. She went from being a happy, outgoing little girl to a sad, sullen thing. Phillip dealt with a lot of guilt after that."

"You stayed married to him."

She's quiet for a long moment, during which she twists the rings on her fingers. Finally, she says, "We'd both been through a lot, losing a child. And I'm not perfect either. I guess, sometimes, it's worth it to forgive and forget." She winces. "Or I tried, at least."

I think of Mina and her book and Maggie. "Maybe some things are unforgivable."

Sharon looks into her empty glass. "I certainly agree with that," she murmurs.

"You never forgave Rose."

"She's been trying to convince me to for years, hasn't she? All those cakes and pies, all those invitations and favors. She'd tie herself into a knot if she thought it could make me forget. She doesn't understand how every single thing only reminds me."

"But you and Phillip are still friends with them."

"You know what they say about keeping your enemies close," she says. "I cared about Mina most of all. It would have felt like abandoning her if we had made a big deal out of all of it. And you know what? I'm glad I didn't. Because when she came home after being gone for so long, when none of us knew where she'd been..."

I sit forward. The waitress comes by and asks me if my food tastes all right. I reassure her that I'm just not hungry and ask her to box it up, knowing I'm going to toss it as soon as I get back to the cottage. "I was wondering about this."

"You know she was..."

"Pregnant."

Sharon squeezes her eyes shut. "I found out by accident. Just like I did the other night, I wandered over in search of raspberries, and there was Mina in the backyard, hair chopped up to a mess, obvious bun in the oven. I did what I could for her. Rose didn't want anyone to know. She kept Mina under lock and key. I'm almost sure she didn't tell anyone at the church. Or the Pooles. Scott asked me to keep it quiet for Mina's sake, and I most certainly did."

"Did you talk to Mina? Was she...okay? Was she making her own decisions?"

"Like I said, I did what I could."

"And Scott?"

"He wasn't home much during that time."

The memory hits me—last night, Rose snapping *And where were you?*

"It was almost as if he couldn't stand the sight of her," Sharon continues. "I felt so bad for her."

I wonder if he felt guilty. "I don't see how it was healthy for Mina to be in that house." If even half of what Mina wrote is true, I don't know how she survived.

"I would have offered my own house," Sharon says. "Rose wouldn't hear of it. And Mina was so vulnerable. She...she tried to kill herself at least once. We all just wanted to get her through it alive."

"Did she say who the father was?"

Sharon's cheeks go ruddy. "Rose had some ideas. And I didn't ask Mina. It didn't seem appropriate. I assumed it was some boy from her school."

But it was Esteban. Or Scott. I doubt Rose will ever tell me. "She did survive, though. She had the baby and gave it up."

Sharon bows her head. "That was the hardest thing of all. Phillip and I offered to take the child, to adopt him and raise him as our own. But Rose...she laughed in my face. She said it was the most ridiculous idea she'd ever heard."

"Why?"

Sharon blinks away tears. By the way she's eyeing my beer, I can tell she's thinking of ordering a third. "She didn't want any reminder of her daughter's shame." Then she rubs her hands over her face. Her rings clack together on her skinny fingers. "She told me I was being selfish. She said he wouldn't replace Robbie. As if I didn't know that."

"What did Mina say to the idea?"

She pauses as if considering, then says. "Mina was under Rose's thumb. She just repeated the lines her mother gave her." Then she scoffs. "Rose dropped her penitent little act, let me see who she really was underneath. I don't think she ever felt bad for what she did with Phillip. She just didn't want to lose what she had. She was desperate to hold on to Scott, to her life, her standing, her clubs, all that admiration she feeds off." Sharon's voice has taken on an edge. "She doesn't care about anyone but herself."

"What about Scott?" I ask. "What did he think about you adopting the baby?"

"Believe it or not, he backed up his wife." Sharon's lips twist as if she's gotten a mouthful of something bitter. "I don't think he wanted the reminder, either. Wanted to forget it ever happened, just like Rose. Just like Mina. And they all succeeded, didn't they? The child was sent away to who knows where, for some other family to raise."

"Sharon," I say. "What do you think happened to Mina? Not back then. Now."

"No idea. But if I were you, I'd take another look at those two."

I pay the check and give Sharon a hug in the parking lot.

"I'm so sorry for all this," she says to me. "I probably said too much."

I drive back to the cottage, trying to line up all those things she did say with Mina's book. The rental cottage, the chess, the baby, and the heartlessness of my wife's parents. Although all the details might not match, there's enough there to know that what Mina wrote is true enough. Real enough. They nearly destroyed her.

And as I think about how Mina ended her book, yet another horrifying thought occurs to me. One that gives new credence to the creeping feeling I got last night as I watched Scott and Rose together, the looks that passed between them.

When Mina wrote her book last year, maybe the ending just hadn't happened *yet*.

CHAPTER TWELVE

Happy birthday," Lori said as she welcomed Maggie into her office. "Cute haircut, by the way."

Maggie touched her hair. The stylist really had done a nice job. Now it was a pixie cut. It looked intentional rather than insane. "It finally grew out enough." Enough to cover the scars on her scalp.

"Time is often a remarkable salve," Lori said. "It doesn't heal all wounds, but it gives you a space..." She chuckled. "I've said that to you before."

"Only about a thousand times." Maggie paused. "So. Graduation day."

"I'm not pushing you out. If you want to—"

"No. I meant what I said a few weeks ago. I think this is good. Like a test run."

"I'm always a call away. You know that."

She nodded. "I might take you up on it."

"It's not a failure to struggle sometimes," Lori said as they sat down, her in her usual chair, Maggie on her usual couch. "For anyone and especially someone who endured what you did. You've come so far, Maggie. And fast. You tackled this with such strength and determination."

"It was that or go completely crazy." She'd stayed in the hospital for a full week after Lori admitted her. She'd asked that her mother and Lawrence not be allowed to visit. She'd learned to breathe again.

She'd learned to dwell inside her own mind. And day by passing day, the knowledge of what she needed to do had grown like an amaryllis flower, the naked bulb shooting up a thick, green stalk, the bud appearing, pushing its way into the light. Now it hovered at the edge of every thought, red and undeniable. Beautiful but terrifying.

"They're going to miss you at the resort, I'll bet. Have you given your notice?"

"What? Oh. My last day is December 31. That's when they close for the season. I leave for Amherst on the first."

"You're moving on the holiday?"

Maggie shrugged. "My lease is up at the end of the month." She would miss the tiny cottage on the bayside of Truro, far enough from Yarmouth to keep her from worrying about running into *them*, furnished but empty in the low season, cheap rent courtesy of an acquaintance of one of Lori's colleagues, and the first space she'd ever occupied that had been entirely her own.

"Working right up until the last second, huh?"

"It's good for me to be busy, *especially* during the holiday. And I need the money."

"You made arrangements with the school for your tuition? Can you get financial aid?"

Maggie sighed. "It's complicated. You can't just tell them that your parents are unsupportive."

"If they understood that your parents abused you..."

"I did the research like we talked about. I might be able to get what they call a 'dependency override' if I can prove it, but there's no record of any of it. And I'm not sure I want to get into it, you know?" They'd already decided that there would be no legal involvement. Maggie had insisted, and she was an adult. She got to decide. She could tell Lori didn't like it, but this time, Maggie was calling the shots.

She had her reasons.

"I'm more than happy to write a letter," Lori said.

"Which would only be what I've told you. For all you know, I'm a lying liar who lies."

Lori's gaze was steady on her. "I believe every word you've said."

Maggie looked away. "I know."

Sometimes she hated Lori's belief in her because it confirmed that this was all real, that it had happened, and that it had been exactly as horrifying as it had felt.

Sometimes she hated Lori's belief in her because she really was lying.

Not about everything. Just some things. To protect the innocent.

"Maggie, have you talked to either Ivy or Lawrence about confirming in writing that you're independent from them? I know I said you shouldn't see them or talk to them right now, but—"

"I can take out unsubsidized loans."

"Do you need to get yourself a lawyer? I know some people who do pro bono work."

"I'm going to work it out," Maggie said firmly. "Being in Amherst will help. I'll get a job. It's not so expensive there, especially in the summer."

"You should be in school," Lori said. "You deserve to be in school."

"I will, eventually. I'll figure it out."

"That's something I don't doubt for even a minute. And I can refer you to a therapist there should you need some support."

"Maybe." She met her therapist's eyes. "I'm not in denial, okay? I just want to do things on my own for a while."

"I think that makes complete sense. Sometimes you need a little space to let things settle and gel. The road to recovery and acceptance is a long one."

Maggie didn't argue. "What about forgiveness?" She needed some but probably didn't deserve it.

"That one's up to you. What I'd love to see you reach is peace."

"Me, too," Maggie murmured. "I'm working on it."

"So," said Lori, clasping her hands. "Last session. What would you like to do to celebrate?"

Maggie smiled and looked across the room. "How about a game of chess?"

She arrived in New Bedford around six, though it felt much later because it had gotten dark just after four. It was a Wednesday night, and the street wasn't too crowded. The Tavern was only a block up from the whaling museum apparently. She trudged up the street through an icy mist, pulling her jacket closer around her while her heart beat double time.

Probably, this was a huge mistake. But she had to try.

She had called earlier to make sure he was working that day. She'd said she was a friend who wanted to surprise him. She'd been flirtatious enough in those moments that the guy on the other end of the line had told her what she needed to know. She'd hung up and rocked in place until the nausea faded.

Now it was back in spades as she pushed through the front door and into the dimly lit, musty-smelling place, with a few people at the bar and one or two couples at high tops along the wall. Not a big space. Narrow but deep. Esteban was typing something into a screen that lit the side of his face with blue light, washing out his olive skin.

She remembered the look he'd given her as she drove away in August. Eyes narrowed, jaw set. When he turned and saw her, she could tell he didn't recognize her at first, because the look he gave her was so friendly. Open and relaxed. She approached the bar.

But as she sat on the stool, he blinked. Looked her up and down, his gaze lingering on her hair. And there it was, the tightening around his eyes, his mouth.

"Hi," she said. "How are you?"

He gave her a cold look. "What can I get you tonight?"

"What's on tap?"

He arched one eyebrow. "Let's see some ID. And I'll know if it's fake."

She grinned. "Today's my twenty-first birthday." She fished her license from her purse and handed it to him. In it, her younger self flashed an identical smile at the camera, only with bright eyes and long blond hair. "It's me, I promise."

"I know exactly who you are," he muttered as he handed the ID back to her. "I'm at work, Maggie."

"You're not busy," she said quietly. "I needed to see you."

"Why, so you can do your best to fuck me over again?" He glanced down the bar like he hoped no one else could hear him.

Whether they could or not, not one of them gave any signal that they cared.

"No, so I could apologize for being the biggest bitch who ever walked the planet." She leaned forward. "I really am sorry."

"What can I get you?" he asked again as if she were any other customer. She couldn't tell if it was a clean slate or a brush-off.

"I'll have a beer," she said.

He rolled his eyes. "Can you be more specific?"

She peered at the tap handles and chuckled. "Clown Shoes?"

"The Zen Garden. It's an IPA."

"Sure. Sounds good."

"Not the lightest choice. I've never seen you drink before."

"Doesn't mean I haven't. Thanks," she said as he filled a pint and slid it toward her. She took a sip and rolled the lush-then-bitter liquid over her tongue. "I figured I'd celebrate by asking your forgiveness."

"What, are you in some kind of twelve-step program or something?"

"Lots of therapy. Like, loads of it." After the hospital and the three-week partial program, it had been twice a week, every week, even the week of Thanksgiving.

His shoulders lost their rigid, hostile shape, as if he'd decided she wasn't about to leap over the bar and attack him. "Did it help?"

"Talking about stuff that's happened to me turns out to be only slightly less awful than when it actually happened."

"So, no?"

"Actually, yeah. It was helpful. But painful, too, you know? Like a really intense workout, except for my head instead of my body." After those sessions, so many times, it had been hours before she'd felt strong enough to face the world again. "It helped me sort some things out. Like what's my fault and what's not my fault. How I got the way I am. How to be different and stronger in the future." She stared at the cloudy yellow ale in her glass. "What I can live with and what I can't."

"I'm really glad to hear that."

She sighed. "There was a lot I never told you. About my family situation."

"I've thought a lot about that last day we were together. You..." He fiddled with the ties on his apron. "I know it was a rough day. I was stupid to think you were fine. But when your mom started to call—"

"She was abusive. In so many ways. And for a long time." Maggie took another cautious sip of her beer. "I never thought of her that way before, you know? She never hit me."

"There are lots of ways to hurt a person that don't involve hitting," he said quietly. Sympathetically.

She couldn't believe it. Could it really be that easy?

"I guess it took a professional to help me realize that."

"Do you remember now? Those weeks you were in Provincetown."

"No. And I don't think I ever will, which is weird and frustrating and scary. I mean, I know I was with you for a few weeks, but I was gone for over two months. I could have been anywhere, doing anything."

"You could have killed someone."

Her heart thudded against her sternum. *Knock, knock. Who's there?* "I guess I could have. I must have been pretty smart about it, to get away with it."

A smile pulled at his lips. "Are you sure this isn't all just an elaborate cover? Are you actually a CIA operative?"

She held up her beer in salute. "You've finally figured me out."

They were laughing together. Holy shit.

"I'd make a joke here about being your handler," he said, "but I'm afraid it's too soon. You might kick my ass again."

She watched his face for signals. He was still smiling. Gray canine on display. But there was a fear in his eyes. He worried he'd gone too far. And he was still a little bit mad about what had happened. "I think I was AWOL with that whole episode," she said, looking sheepish. "If you tell my boss, I'll probably be fired."

"Ah, no harm done. I mean, my phone…"

"Uh…it had been bugged by a hostile foreign power. I was secretly saving your life." She examined the dried foam crusted along the side of her glass. "Seriously, though, I brought money with me. To pay for it."

His eyes widened. "Maggie, honestly…yeah?"

She opened her purse and tilted it toward him. Bills stacked inside. She'd been working her ass off at the resort restaurant in Chatham, taking every available shift *including* Thanksgiving, knowing they'd close for the season come New Year's. She'd brought more than enough to pay for his crappy phone.

Because there was something else she wanted to buy. "How much was it?"

"Wasn't worth much." He waved it away, then glanced at her open purse again. "Okay. A hundred? A hundred and we're even."

She pulled one hundred and sixty out and handed it to him. She should probably have paid him back for the abortion, too, but the revelation that it hadn't been his would only complicate matters. So she simply said, "I owe you more than that. More than I could ever pay." Now she had to figure out how to pay for what she needed. "When are you off?"

He glanced at the wall clock over the bar. "As soon as Tommy comes out from the back, actually. I've been on since we opened at eleven." He walked over to a door on the other side of the bar and poked his head inside. Maggie could hear him chatting with someone, and a moment later, a middle-aged guy with black, curly hair and a healthy beer belly came out, turning sideways to edge behind the bar.

Esteban took off his apron, and Maggie paid for her beer. She'd drunk only a third of it but left it on the bar as Esteban raised his eyebrows and gestured toward the door. "Want to go for a walk?"

She zipped up her jacket and followed him out of the bar and onto the sidewalk where they were greeted by icy rain. She winced and backed under the building's awning. "Where's your car?"

"Don't have one. I take the bus usually."

"Mine's just up the block. Can I offer you a ride home?"

He paused, perhaps considering what had happened the last time they'd been in a car together.

She put her hand on his arm and looked him in the eye. "I am so sorry about what I did to you. I know you were trying to help, and I was so, so messed up. I've worked really hard to drag myself out of that place." She grinned. "You want my therapist's number? Her name is Lori. She could vouch for me."

He snorted. "That's all right." But he looked more relaxed now, and he trotted along next to her when she jogged for her car.

She wouldn't hurt him this time, she promised herself. She just needed this one thing, and he was the only person she knew who might know how to get it. "You said you live with your dad?" she asked when they were safely ensconced in her car, with her in the driver's seat this time.

He groaned. "I'm trying to save money."

"For what?"

A shy look. "I want to go back to school."

"For what?" she asked again.

"Not sure. Maybe nursing?"

"Really?"

"What? You think I'm stupid or something?"

"No! No. I actually think you'd make a great nurse. You're kind and gentle. Just the type of person I'd want taking care of me if I were sick." She put her hand on his arm again. "I mean, you did kind of do that already."

He looked down at her hand. "What do you want, Maggie?"

She pulled her hand back. "Nothing."

"Yeah, right. First time, you just needed help. Second time, an abortion. So what is it this time?"

"Didn't I already tell you? Forgiveness?"

"Well, you have that."

She put both hands on the steering wheel. "My stepfather molested me when I was little. Raped me. A bunch of times."

"Fuuuck," Esteban whispered.

"I'm only just trying to come to terms with it. For a long time, my brain pushed it into a dark corner, you know? Pretended it wasn't happening, that it hadn't happened."

"Maggie...God. I'm so sorry."

"I'm just telling you so you understand. Why I acted the way I did. Why I was so messed up." She gripped the steering wheel and stared out the windshield. She'd turned the key in the ignition, but they weren't moving. "I'm trying to figure out the best way to deal with it."

"How about calling the fucking *police*?"

"Honestly, I don't know if I have the energy to go through that. My word against his. I never told a single person." Another lie, but really, it wasn't like Ivy would ever back her up by admitting the truth. Not in a million years. Instead, she'd spew hatred and blame and denial. "I just...I know that's pathetic, but..."

"It's your choice. You don't think he's doing that to other girls?"

She squeezed her eyes shut and folded her arms around her body. "I don't think so. But I honestly don't know." She was afraid that he might. That was the thought that kept her up nights these days. Not what he'd done. What he *could* do. "I don't sleep well."

"Nightmares?"

Yes. "No. Just up, thinking. Driving myself crazy. Or craz*ier*, I guess. You ever take anything to help you get to sleep?"

"You mean besides a shot and a joint?" He winked at her.

She grinned. "You know how to get ahold of pot?"

He gave her a patronizing look. "It's not that hard."

"What about other stuff?"

His gaze darkened. "You really think that's a good idea?"

"I've tried pot," she lied. "It doesn't help me. I just want something to take away the pain. And help me sleep. I just wish I could sleep."

She could feel him staring at the side of her face. "Maggie," he said, "are you sure that's what you want it for?"

Startled, she turned to him. Her heart was pounding again. "Why? What else would I want it for? And what's *it*, by the way?"

He shrugged. "I don't know. I guess if you want to sleep and get rid of pain, Oxy or something."

"You could get that for me?"

"Whoa." He put his hands up. "Whoa. I never said I would do anything for you."

Frustration zinged around the inside of her head like a pinball. Moves. What was her next move? "I don't expect you to do anything," she said slowly. "I don't expect anything from you at all."

"Hold up." He was frowning now. "Are you here, apologizing and stuff, as a way of cleaning things up before you—I don't know—hurt yourself? Is that why you want something heavy-duty? Why come back and find me now, on your birthday? Why are you *alone* on your birthday?"

He was so much more perceptive than she'd thought. So much smarter. If she'd had a different life and if she were a different girl, she could have liked him. She could have offered him what he deserved. "I guess I'm more of a loser than you'd ever imagined," she said. "Or maybe you're more important to me than you thought."

For a solid minute, they looked at each other. Maggie barely breathed. Finally, Esteban said, "Maggie, just tell me what you want, and I might help you get it." He sounded so sad. "And then I think we need to go our separate ways. For good."

It stung, that he'd figured her out, but it also made her like him more. For a wild, twisted second, she thought about offering him sex as a kind of payment, a kind of penance. Then she snapped back into sanity, pulled there by countless sessions in which she and Lori had dissected her responses and impulses, the why of every crazy, damaging move she'd pulled.

She was about to pull another, but this one wasn't crazy at all. It felt like the sanest thing Maggie had ever done, would ever do. Something she needed to do, in fact, even if it was utterly terrifying. Even if anyone she told—Lori, Esteban—would tell her no, no, *don't* do it. She had to. She knew that now. It had been brewing inside her for weeks, months, through wakeful, solitary nights and long, monotonous days. The debate was over. It had been over for a long time. She was going to go through with it. Confront this fear. Her only chance for achieving any real peace.

And Esteban would only help if she told another lie.

A lie to protect the innocent.

"Fair enough. I get it, after everything." She shifted the car into gear and pulled away from the curb. "Can you direct me?" she asked, her thoughts spinning out like a spider's web. "I'll tell you on the way."

SATURDAY, AUGUST 8, TO SUNDAY, AUGUST 9

Detective Correia calls me up late Saturday afternoon when I've just gotten back to the cottage. "I've got a bit of news," she says to me. "I'm not sure if it changes the timeline or not."

"I'm all ears," I say, already pouring myself a tumbler of Macallan. I'm still reeling from my lunch with Sharon and fortifying myself for my next confrontation with Drew. We've scheduled a call for seven.

"It looks like the phone never left Harwich," Correia says. "She traveled from Brookline to Harwich on the morning of Monday, July 27, but the phone pings off that Harwich tower for the next three days before going dark."

"We know she was in Provincetown on Monday afternoon," I remind her. "And we also know she had dinner with her parents in Truro on Monday evening. They said she left at nine."

"Well, Mr. Silva claims that she forgot the phone at his place."

"He's admitting he saw her."

"Mm-hmm. Her phone does contain records of phone calls to a number listed under his name."

"The access code worked."

"Yes. Thank you." Her tone is flat. I can't tell if she's being sincere.

"So if there were calls between them, and if she went to Harwich and somehow he ended up with her phone, why did Stefan lie before? He told me he hadn't seen her."

"Well, Mr. Zarabian, with all due respect, you're the husband."

"Are you saying they had an affair?"

"I'm saying that Mr. Silva seems to have something to hide. He left her phone in the park. He's not saying why."

"Because he's an idiot who thought he could pin all this on someone else? Why didn't he just destroy it?"

"He didn't want to be linked to it, but he didn't want to impede the investigation. That's what he's saying. He told me he thinks it's possible that she killed herself."

"Did he say why?"

"He's not saying much. We've released him—we can't hold him without charging him with a hell of a lot more than obstruction of justice. I'm calling because I want to make sure you understand to keep your distance. Don't muddy these waters, Mr. Zarabian."

"They have a kid together," I blurt out. "Did he tell you that?"

"No," says the detective. "But her parents did."

"I'm surprised they admitted it."

"They are as desperate to find her as you are, sir. They also told me that you hadn't previously known about the child. Her friend Willa Penson said Mina was fairly nervous about telling you. I imagine finding out must have been a shock. How did that happen, by the way?"

"I figured it out. I didn't hear it from Mina, if that's what you're asking. And Stefan didn't tell me either."

"All right."

"You really think I would have done something to her just because she had a kid thirteen years before we met?"

"I'm not drawing any conclusions right now, Mr. Zarabian."

"Can't you focus on people who might actually have hurt her? What if she left her parents' house that night and drove back to Harwich to get her phone? What if something went bad between them? What if she told *him* about the kid that night? Are you sure he knew about it before then? Maybe her car ended up in Harwich, but he got worried after a few days and drove it up to dump in Provincetown."

"Why not put her phone in the car if that's what happened?"

"You're the detective."

"We should have results for the car early next week. And I'll be subpoenaing phones. Would you consider offering me a look at yours without one?"

"You're really doing this. Making me a suspect."

"Mr. Zarabian, I told you I was going to pursue all available leads."

"And despite the fact that I have a rock solid alibi for Monday through Wednesday—"

"We still have a lot to figure out about Mina Richards's where-abouts after she left her parents' house on Monday."

"What if she never did? You can't really tell me that you think those two are normal." I almost tell her about the affair Rose had with the neighbor, but I stop short. It doesn't seem like my story to tell, and it also doesn't seem directly relevant to where Mina might be right now—but something else does. "I'm concerned Rose and Scott might have abused her."

"On what basis?"

On the basis of a fictional book written by Mina... I groan. "Aren't you looking *any* closer at them? They were supposedly the last ones to see her before she disappeared! Do *they* have an alibi? What if she was about to disclose some secret that would ruin their lives?" I can't say what I suspect. Without evidence, it sounds utterly batshit. But the more I think about it, the more I'm worrying that they really did do something to her.

Detective Correia is quiet for moment. "Mr. Zarabian, I just wanted to update you on the case. Should I take it that you're not willing to surrender your phone?"

"You can have my damn phone whenever you want. I just want my wife back." I'm dead quiet again, dead level, dead tired. A cold bastard. If I'm anything else, I'm going to fall apart. "Just let me know when you want it."

"You can drop it by the station tomorrow if that's convenient."

"Sure. Fine."

"Have a good night, Mr. Zarabian."

I hang up the phone and drink my Macallan in one long, desperate gulp.

After yet another rough night, the only kind a guy can have when his wife has been missing for almost two weeks, I rise and do some research. Today, I'm going to figure some things out. I'm going to put the pieces together.

I'm going to look in the places the detective won't.

I check my phone. I texted Drew last night postponing the call until tonight. His response: I get it, but we need to talk before Monday.

He doesn't mention my letter of resignation. I whipped it off in a quick email on Friday night, but it's still marked as unopened. It's just another step in this dance we're doing, this game of chicken. Normally, I'd be plotting all the moves of this negotiation, but today, I've got something else on my mind.

After rolling my conversation with the detective through my head about a hundred times, I'm wondering if she's moved me up the list of suspects because of the revelation about this secret kid Mina had when she was eighteen. Willa told me that Stefan was the father, but what if she was only assuming? Mina had that way of letting people fill in the blanks she left. I know she did it with me.

But what if Stefan isn't the father? Though it kills me to even consider it, what if it was Scott? It would explain more of Scott and Rose's desperation to get the child out of their lives as rapidly as possible. It would explain why Rose laughed in Sharon's face when Sharon suggested that she and Phillip adopt the child so he could be part of Mina's life. I wonder if Mina's parents relayed the story to the detective in a certain kind of way, to aim the suspicion at me or Stefan. Either way, it was probably a move fueled by some sort of desperation. It was so obvious they wanted the secret to stay buried. If Mina was about to blow it wide open by telling Stefan and me, that would be something, though I'm not sure it's enough to make them want to silence her.

What if, though...what if she told them about the *book*?

My stomach clenches, and my hand skims over the first page of the dog-eared manuscript laid out next to me on the couch. Hannah said Mina was terrified of what would happen if people she knew were aware of the book, but what if Mina worked up the courage to let her parents know that she was about to lay out their sordid life for the *entire* reading public? I'm not sure why she would do that, but maybe she still felt some sort of obligation to warn them.

What if the book itself is the reason she's gone?

In the story, Esteban isn't the father of Maggie's baby. The father is the man who abused her for *years*. What if this part of the story is straight-up history—one only Mina's parents knew about and were desperate to keep hidden?

Mina might have underestimated them. Or possibly the end of her book isn't as fictional as I'd assumed. That thought scares the shit out of me, and it also doesn't explain where Mina herself is. The key to that has to be somewhere in their house.

Sharon said Scott and Rose went to the New Life church, so I look it up. The only church on the cape with that name is in Orleans, and the Sunday service started half an hour ago. They're certain to be there...which means they're not at home. I grab my keys and head out the door before allowing myself to think of all the reasons why I should stay where I am.

I pull right into their driveway. Like so many other homes on this street, the Richardses' drive and house are completely hidden from the road by thick walls of wax myrtles. If they're home, I'll just say I've come for a visit. But when I arrive, there's only one car in the drive—the pickup. The old Cadillac is gone.

I knock on the front door, then ring the doorbell. I wait. The warm, briny breeze ruffles my hair as I listen for any sounds from inside.

I test the door. Locked. I go around to the back, which is locked as well. My hope that they feel safe enough in their quiet enclave to leave their doors unlocked is dashed. Next I try the windows, hoping one is open, and end up cursing the fact that the Richardses have central air. Hoping to find something to help me pick the lock or pry open a window, I tromp back to Scott's workshop. The door is closed, but the padlock is open, hanging from the hasp.

Inside, the air is stifling and smells of sawdust and sweat. The shed is about ten by ten, and tools of all kinds hang from every spot on the wall—wrenches and chisels of various sizes, screwdrivers, a T bevel, a claw hammer—with little chalk outlines around them. Like at a crime scene.

Along one wall is a large, sturdy utility table. A jigsaw is set up on one side. Vises cling to the table's edge. There's a stool under the table, a pair of safety goggles hanging from one of those vises, and utility gloves stacked on the window ledge.

In the center of the table is a stack of paper. In the light streaming through the smudged glass pane and the half-open door, I move forward, the hairs on the back of my neck rising.

It's a copy of Mina's manuscript.

My thoughts lock up like someone just poured sugar in my tank.

This is Mina's book. The one that tells the story of her fugue and the reason for it. The one that tells the story of the pregnancy...and the reason for it. It's like an indictment, sitting right there, and I have no idea how long Scott has had this, how long he's known about it.

I only know he's been lying.

Slowly, my brain sputters into motion again. Correia needs to know this. I haven't gotten into the existence of the book with her, because she was already thinking Mina was unstable, and the book... it's not exactly reassuring in that regard. It's chilling and worrisome, and the more of it that's true, the more worrisome it is. But now it's time to break the glass, because Mina's parents know, and they've done something terrible.

I turn toward the door as a bulky shadow blocks out the light.

Our eyes meet. "You know about the book," I say.

"I do."

CHAPTER THIRTEEN

She'd gone over and over what to make, but in the end, she settled on a cake. She considered a boxed mix, but it seemed more appropriate to go all out and make it from scratch. There was no reason to skimp. It had to be made with all the love inside her.

She had to buy pans, a mixing bowl, a cake spatula, a spice grinder, measuring spoons and cups. Flour, sugar, eggs, butter, vanilla, food coloring. Powdered sugar, of course. She thought about buying a mixer, but it felt like a waste of money, and she didn't have much left. No icing bags or tips, either, but she could improvise. She could mix everything by hand. She had time. She'd talked Greta into taking a shift for her at the restaurant.

Baking was meditative, she realized as she carefully measured out the ingredients. Cleansing. Healing. She wondered if Ivy thought so or if her baking mind was always filled with fantasies of rising to the pinnacle of social standing on a staircase made of royal icing. All Maggie thought about as she mixed sugar and butter and milk and flour was *this had better be delicious.*

She poured the batter into its pans, watching its liquid tendrils spiral and settle. Then she put them into the cottage's tiny oven and went to work on the icing. Butter. Vanilla. And all the white powder, which sent a sweet cloud up from the bowl when she dumped it in. She leaned back and tossed the bag in the trash, then went to work mixing everything together. She regretted not splurging on a cheap hand mixer, but after a good ten minutes of work, she had a respectable buttercream.

When the cakes were golden brown, she pulled them from the oven and let them cool for a good hour. She filled the waiting time with cleaning, leaving not even a speck on the floors or the counters, the bowls, the spoons, the spice grinder. Even Ivy would have been proud. As soon as the thought came, she spotted a dusting of powder near the tiny table at which she'd eaten so many bowls of oatmeal over the past four months. She grabbed a rag and cleaned it up before her brain awakened the specter of that hand clamping onto the back of her neck, that voice growling *make it spotless.*

She made it spotless. Perfect. She could be perfect.

You have to give yourself permission to be imperfect, Lori had said to her. *You have to let things be messy sometimes.*

Maggie knew that. She believed it. But today, she had to stick to what she knew, with one difference.

This time, we play a different game.

She sliced the overbrowned dome off the top of the second cake slab; both layers needed to be level. She was not about to serve a lopsided cake. It would never convey all her good intentions, all the things she'd learned.

She sank to her haunches, wrapped her arms around her knees, and rocked, breathing deep and telling herself this was okay. She didn't want to do this, but that was because she was scared, not because it wasn't the thing that had to be done.

When the spots had cleared from her vision, she divided the buttercream into three bowls and colored two, pink and blue.

Pink for a girl, blue for a boy.

Pink for guilt, blue for innocence.

Pink for love, blue for cyanosis.

"Just kidding," she whispered. But she wasn't crazy. No one could hear her thoughts.

She'd been raised to believe such things. She was glad she didn't believe them anymore.

Maggie layered pink in the middle, thick and lush, because really, what other color would be just right? She sculpted the outside of the confection with painstaking effort: first the crumb coat and then the top layer, luxurious and dense with promise and temptation. She scooped a glob of blue icing into a ziplock bag, then cut a tiny hole in one corner. Not exactly a star tip, but she decided the effect could be charming with the right amount of conscientiousness. She carefully piped a swag pattern around the top of the cake, the garland drooping sensually from its anchor points. Next, she piped pink beads along the bottom and a cute pattern in the center in the shape of a heart. Simple but sincere.

A childlike hope had begun to speed her hands, her heart. This was really happening.

A half hour later, the cake was as close to perfect as she could make it without the benefit of specialized tools. She hoped that would count in her favor.

She put the plastic dome over the cake plate and snapped it into place.

She spent the next hour decorating herself. Preparing the foundation—scrubbing her skin, applying a nice lotion. Then the icing—concealer and foundation, a soft blush, a nude lip. This was about being real, not sultry. She styled her hair and dressed in jeans and a nice sweater she'd found in a consignment shop in Brewster.

She allowed herself a long, quiet moment to gaze into the spotty mirror over the sink. "Just be yourself," she murmured before letting out a shuddery breath. Then she leaned forward, touching her forehead to the glass, seeking solace from her reflection. "I know who you are," she whispered. "And I won't forget ever again."

She put on her shoes and grabbed her keys. Then she carried the cake to the car and positioned it carefully on the seat.

The drive down the Cape took a solid forty-five minutes, during which time she sang along with the radio and kept a respectful distance from other cars, not wanting to brake suddenly and ruin her masterpiece.

When she pulled into the driveway, she felt a swell of relief. A car in the drive, but only one. She tugged at her sweater and smoothed down her hair. Perfect, perfect, or as close to perfect as she could be. She got out, lifted the cake out of the passenger seat, and marched to the front door with her heart nearly exploding. Her cheeks were probably flushed, but that was okay.

She rang the doorbell with her elbow and positioned herself on the welcome mat.

Was this a sign of health, what she was doing? Or was it just the same sickness?

The door opened. She held up the cake and smiled. "I made this for you. I know it's just a small thing, but I was hoping it would be the first step in getting you to forgive me."

SUNDAY, AUGUST 9

S he gave it to me," Scott says as he steps into his workshop and closes the door behind him. He flips a switch next to the door-frame, and a utility lamp blazes to life directly over my head. The sensation of heat is instant, and I step aside to escape it.

"It was my understanding that she wanted it to stay a secret." I'm suddenly keenly aware of all the metal around me, the murderous potential of every single tool. Bludgeoning. Slicing. There are lots of options dangling from hooks, outlined in chalk.

Even a nail gun. It's a big cordless framing nailer, like a drill but with the nail cartridge attached to its short barrel. Hanging just to the left of the window.

Scott watches my gaze roaming over his arsenal. "I guess she changed her mind."

"You're not asking me why I'm in your workshop."

"Saw your car in the drive. Heard you at the door."

He's been here the whole time.

"You didn't go to church this morning."

"I haven't gone in years," he says. "Rose goes alone."

Just like Lawrence in Mina's book. He met Ivy at church but shows contempt for it later. "Crisis of faith?"

"You could say that."

"Where's Mina, Scott?"

His look is stony. "I was hoping you could tell me."

"You actually think I hurt her?"

"There are only a few people in this world who might want to hurt my daughter, the way I see it. And you're one of them."

"And you?"

His eyebrows rise. "Why would I ever hurt her?"

"Have you actually read the book?"

A flash of panic crosses his features before sinking into the thick planes of his face once more, leaving it heavy with resignation. "She knew this about me. She wanted me to read it, but she knows. I'm no good with books. The words and letters get mixed up for me. But I've spent every hour I can reading it. I'm almost halfway." His cheeks have turned ruddy. "I'm trying to understand it."

I don't know if I believe this dyslexic act or not, but a determination to keep trying to get through it might explain why he keeps disappearing into his workshop whenever I show up. "What did she tell you guys?"

"She told *me*. Not Rose. When she came out for dinner that evening, she asked to talk to me out here. In private. She gave me the book and asked me to read it. She said she knew it would take a while, but that she'd talk to me about it when I was done. She said it would help me understand."

That doesn't sound like the plan of someone who intended to kill herself. "Rose doesn't know about the book."

"Only Rose can tell you what she knows." There's an edge in his voice. Not exactly the worshipful attitude Sharon described. "She's an excellent liar. Took me a long damn time to realize it, though, so maybe I'm just an idiot."

I look around again, consider which tool I'll grab if Scott lunges for me. There's a heavy wrench within arm's reach, long enough to connect with his head, big enough to send him to the ground. "Did you abuse your daughter, Scott?"

"You're a sick bastard." His fists clench.

"It's not like I came up with the idea out of thin air." I jerk my thumb at the manuscript on the table. "She told the whole story."

"Mina *said* that?" He shakes his head. The rage dissolves as I watch, softening into what appears to be genuine confusion.

"All that and more. Your daughter went through hell, and she dared to tell the tale—until someone tried to silence her."

"You want to check my basement? See if I've got her tied up down there?" He looks disgusted. "You've been thinking that all this time? That I'm some kind of..."

"You both practically held her captive while she was pregnant, didn't you?" Again, I almost mention Sharon, but I don't want to get her in trouble. "Did you decide she needed to be 'taken care of' again?"

His jaw is working like there's something stuck in his throat. His meaty fists release and clench, release and clench. "Mina was *never* abused. It didn't happen. If that's what she said in her story, it's a lie."

"In that case, why would she give you the book to read?" Maybe she wanted to punish him. Maybe he punished her first.

He shakes his head. "She said this one was different. She asked me to read it and then to call her." He grimaces. "I've been trying," he says hoarsely. "I've been trying so hard to get through it." He shoves his knuckles against his eyes and curses. "I'm so *stupid*."

"You didn't tell Rose you had it. You didn't ask her for help."

He slides his hands down his face. "Mina asked me not to. And then, when she disappeared... I don't know."

I think back to what I read. All the viciousness. The cruelty. From Lawrence. From Ivy. I don't trust Scott any further than I could throw him, but I think I'm starting to believe he's been in the dark. "What if Rose knows something about what happened to Mina?"

He goes still. Looks over his shoulder. "She's here."

"Then how about we go ask her?" Our eyes meet. "I'm not going away. No more secrets."

"All right." He turns and heads out of the workshop.

I follow at a cautious distance. Braced for him to turn on me.

Rose is bustling around the kitchen when we enter from the porch. She's wearing an apron over a flowered dress. She turns to face us, and I pause.

She's holding a carving knife.

"Rose," Scott says quietly.

She looks back and forth between us. "I saw your car in the drive, Alex." Her face transforms with a bright smile, teeth bared. "I was about to pull the ham out of the oven." The knife blade glints in her hand. "Will you stay for Sunday dinner?"

"We have to talk about Mina," says Scott.

"What else is there to say, dear?" she asks. "I don't want to tell poor Alex any more tales out of school."

"Mina has been missing for almost two weeks," I say quietly. "I think it's time to put all the cards on the table." I look around, realizing I've never actually been in their basement. I don't even know how to get there. I know Scott joked about it, but...

Rose opens her mouth, and I can almost read the words of dismissal scrawled on her tongue. But she freezes when she sees the way Scott is looking at her. "It's ancient history," she whispers.

"It wasn't for Mina," Scott says. "She wrote a book."

Rose laughs. "She wrote dozens of books, you silly man. It's a good thing that you can barely read. You've been spared the embarrassment. Smut. All of it."

"This wasn't a romance novel," I say. "This time, she wrote about her life. Her past. And you."

The derisive smile is frozen on Rose's face. Only her eyes change. "She lied," she says. "She lied all the time. Even as a child."

Scott's face is still ruddy. His fists are still clenched. His words, when they come, are slow but steady: "Maybe she learned it from her mother."

"Scott," Rose says. "You can't possibly believe—" Her grip on the knife is white-knuckled. "I should have known. After not speaking to us since the wedding, she showed up at the door that night, expecting a free meal—"

"She brought you a *cake*," I say. It's not only in the book—the neighbor saw her load it into the car. And the carrier wasn't in the car when it was found. "Nicely decorated? Was it up to your standards, Rose? Did you not eat it because it wasn't perfect? Did you save the carrier?" I glance around the kitchen with a new curiosity. "It was pretty, wasn't it?"

Rose blinks at me, her mouth half-open.

Scott clears his throat. "Alex," he says. "What cake?"

CHAPTER FOURTEEN

awrence paused on the threshold, looking her up and down. "Maggie," he said quietly. His gaze rested on her head. "Your beautiful hair." He looked so sad to find it gone, like a child might mourn a broken toy.

She still wore her smile. "Can I come in?"

"What? Oh, of course. Of course." He pulled the door wide.

She stepped inside. It was a small place, his home away from Ivy, a little bungalow nestled into the surrounding woods on a quiet road. A woodstove hulked in the corner. Next to it was a small table, and on it was a chessboard, pieces in position.

He cleared his throat. "I know it's not much."

"It's cute. Can I put this down somewhere?"

He directed her around the corner to the kitchen. The counters were cluttered by bottles of Jack Daniel's and several magnums of red wine. "Can I offer you a completely legal drink? I thought about you all day on your birthday."

He moved a few bottles aside, and she set the cake on the counter. "I hate that it's been so weird between us." She sighed. "I know I kind of freaked out."

"When we found your hair all over the floor of your room, and the blood..." He blinked. His eyes were shiny. "I was so worried. But here you are. And you look beautiful."

"You weren't mad?"

He shook his head. "I don't pretend to understand what you've been through. I mean, Esteban Perreira." His nostrils flared. "When I think of him touching you..."

"He's not important," she said. "He never was."

"Yes, well. As long as you're not seeing him anymore. He was nothing but trouble from the sound of it. Trash."

Her hands rested on top of the carrier. They were steady. "I've been working through all of it. You know, like twelve steps?" She looked him right in the eye. "Admit you're powerless. Ask God to help you. Make a list of people you hurt. Make amends. Doesn't it go like that?"

He chuckled. "I'm not completely sure." His gaze danced over the counter. "Maybe I should find out. You struggle with the bottle, too?"

"No," said Maggie. "Lying is my issue. Hasn't it always been, Lawrence?"

He nodded. "I forgive you."

She went to him. Hugged him gently. "Thank you. Can I offer you a piece of cake?"

"Absolutely. Drink?"

"Absolutely."

She cut him a thick slice and laid it on a saucer she pulled from the cabinet. He poured her a half tumbler of wine and a full one for himself. "I'm not supposed to drink with the pills. My doc says I have to lay off. But this is a special occasion."

"Can I use your bathroom?" she asked.

"Right down the hall." He waved her in the right direction as he accepted the cake and snagged a fork from a drawer.

She padded down the hall and ducked into the bathroom. Opened the medicine cabinet and surveyed the contents. Smiled with relief. With triumph. Closed it carefully, quietly. Flushed the toilet and washed her hands.

By the time she emerged, he'd already taken a bite. "This is wonderful, Maggie. It's like we're celebrating your birthday, just a bit belated."

"Exactly," Maggie replied. "How's your back been? Do the pills help?"

He gave her a rueful look and rubbed at it. "Some days I can barely get out of bed. Today's not a bad day, though." He took another large bite of cake. "Getting better by the moment."

She picked up her tumbler of wine and held it up. "To good days."

He clinked his glass with hers. "And good company. Are you going to have some?" He looked down at the cake.

"If you had any idea how much frosting I ate as I made it this afternoon..." She rolled her eyes and rubbed her stomach. "I'm kind of regretting it now."

"I might not be able to keep myself from having another piece," he said as he carried the cake and his wine over to the little table by the woodstove.

She sat down across from him. The chess set lay between them.

"It's been a long time since we played," he commented.

"I'd be up for a match if you want."

His face brightened. He'd finished the cake and scraped one last bit of frosting from the plate. "Black or white?"

"You go ahead." She nodded at the white pieces arrayed in front of him. "It's your board."

They began. She nudged each piece with the back of a fingernail; inch by inch, they slid into position.

Lawrence touched her knee under the table. "You remember how we used to play?" he asked after taking a long sip of his wine.

She kept her leg still. She kept her hands still. *Good girls are quiet girls.* "You think I'd forget? If you win, we play a different game."

He gave her a silly smile. He probably meant it to be flirtatious. "I'm so glad you're here." His fingers squeezed.

She smiled back and moved a piece.

He grunted. "You sure you want to let me have the center like that?" He raised his eyebrows and grinned. "Do you *want* me to win?"

"The opening was the Modern Defense," she murmured as she began her attack, already too late for him to counter effectively. How many games had she played on her phone since August? How many times had she done this?

"You laid yourself a trap," he said.

It was a trap. But not for her. "I'm not a beginner anymore."

And ten moves later, he sat back. He shook his head, looking baffled. "I had the center. I had the advantage," he said, slurring. "How did you do that?"

"Do what?" She made her penultimate move. "Check. You've lost a step."

He rolled his eyes and knocked over his king. "Down he goes." He winced and put his hand on his stomach. His skin had shed its color.

"Down he goes," she murmured as she began to nudge the pieces back into position. "Another game?"

"I...don't know."

"Oh, come on. You always want another game if I win."

He squinted at the clock over the table like he couldn't quite get his eyes to focus. "Should've eaten dinner before having all that cake and wine."

"It wouldn't have helped," Maggie said.

He was breathing quickly now. Panting. Sweat glistened on his pale forehead.

"Do you want another slice?" she asked.

He swallowed like he still had a mouthful. "Don't feel good."

"Oh," she said. "That's because I ground up an entire bottle of OxyContin and put it in the frosting."

For a moment, they stared across the little table at each other. His face drew up like a stage curtain, the corners of his lips rising to show his teeth. "You bitch," he rasped.

Hands clawed, he lunged across the table at her.

SUNDAY, AUGUST 9

Rose sits on the couch with dry eyes and a slack mouth. Scott presses a drink into her hand. She swallows down the amber liquid and shudders. "I just wanted all of it to be in the past. That was all I wanted. For all of us to move forward and stick together."

"I've always stood by you," says Scott. "Sometimes when I shouldn't have."

Her brow furrows. "I might have made mistakes, but—"

"In her book, Mina says she was abused," says Scott.

Rose twitches. She looks out the window. "It was all in the past," she whispers.

"Rose," Scott says, horror breaking across his features like a sunrise. "Was she telling the truth?"

"Of course she wasn't!" She shoots to her feet and sways. "She was always good at lying. She made up stories even as a child."

"You sound so offended," I say. "Is that because *you* always tell the truth?"

Her head rocks back as if I've punched her.

"If the truth is so important," Scott says, "you shouldn't have slept with another man and lied to your husband about it. For *years*."

She blinks at him in apparent shock. "Scott, I—"

"You think I never knew it, Rose? You think that little of me?"

"You can't really believe—"

"That you're a liar and a whore?" shouts Scott.

The glass shatters against the wall before I register that Rose has thrown it. Now she looks as startled as the rest of us. She smooths her hair. "You aren't completely innocent," she says to her husband.

"I never cheated on you."

"You might as well have! You were never home! I was always alone."

"And Mina caught you in the act of having an affair," I say.

Both of them turn to me, eyes questioning. "No," Rose says, grimacing. "He...he threatened to tell Scott. Phillip said he would keep it all a secret if I gave him what he wanted."

What he wanted. The words land in my head like grenades.

"Can't you understand that?" she asks, focused on me. "Can't you understand that he was going to destroy my family if I didn't—"

"He wanted Mina," I say in a hollow voice. "That's it, isn't it?" Because now it makes sense. Dead father. Nightmare stepfather. Details changed to protect the guilty. In Mina's mind, Scott *was* dead. He wasn't at home, wasn't there to protect her when she needed him most.

"Phillip just wanted to play chess," she says, pleading. "It was just chess. Lessons for her. She'd shown so much promise!"

"You sent your daughter over there to protect yourself," I say, my voice rising. Phillip is Lawrence. *Phillip is Lawrence.* "Don't pretend like you didn't know!"

All the blood has drained from Scott's face. "*Did* you know, Rose?"

"No!" she howls. She holds up her hands as he takes a step toward her. "It was only chess!"

"She quit chess," I say.

"She told me she didn't want to play anymore," Scott says. "And that was why, wasn't it?"

Rose has her hands in her hair, mussing her perfect hairdo. "That can't be right," she says with a moan. "She said she wanted to stop the lessons. She had such a tantrum over it, but she had so many in those days. She'd gone from being a sweet, obedient girl to a moody, sullen child I could barely abide. I was happy to have her out of the house for a few hours each day! And Phillip..."

"He threatened to tell Scott if you stopped the lessons," I guess. "So you didn't listen to your own daughter. And then you sent her away to boarding school."

"That was her idea!" shrieks Rose. "She got the brochures, she applied for the scholarship, she pushed the whole thing!"

Probably because she was so determined to escape. It feels like someone is repeatedly stabbing me in the heart. "You didn't ask why?"

"I thought it would be good for her," says Rose, her voice breaking. "Her grades were dropping. She didn't want to do her activities anymore. She thought a new school would help, and I supported her!" She looks over at me. "She really wrote about it? Are you sure it was the truth?"

"I believe it," snaps Scott.

"But he's lived next to us all these years," she says weakly. "All these years. And I believed him. It was just chess."

"Rose," I say. Somehow, my voice is steady despite the truth I see in her eyes. She had a sense of what was happening to Mina but was too afraid of having her affair exposed to do anything about it. "The pregnancy. When she was eighteen."

"It was that boy's," says Scott. "Stefan Silva. That's what you told me." He's looking at Rose, almost begging her to agree. "That's why we got him to sign the papers and give up his rights to it."

"Of course it was that boy's," says Rose.

"Are you sure?" I ask.

"Why, because she wrote about it in one of her smutty books?" Rose's hair is mussed. Her mascara is smudged. But she looks defiant right now. Daring me to tell her that Mina's words are truth.

"She went through more than you're willing to admit." I'm not about to desert Mina now. I'm her voice here, and I trust the story she wrote. Though I can barely breathe for the dread that's rising inside me, I believe she's leading us straight to the truth. "Because some of those awful things, you put her through. And part of you *knows* that you failed her. You handed her over to a pedophile."

Rose looks at Scott, probably hoping for a defense of some kind. Instead, he looks like someone's shot him in the gut. "Phillip went to pick her up from school for the break," he says weakly. "Her senior year. Remember? You had a church picnic, and I was working. He drove out to Connecticut to get Mina. I even paid him for the gas."

"No," whispers Rose. "No."

"She wasn't the same when she came back. You even noticed it. And then she disappeared a week or so later. This was why."

"No!"

"This is why!" roars Scott, the words exploding out of him with the heat of decades of repressed agony.

Rose bows her head. Her shoulders shake.

With a strangled, animal cry, Scott throws open the back door and begins to run.

And when I see where he's headed, I'm right behind him.

CHAPTER FIFTEEN

She hadn't expected this kind of attack, and she wasn't quite ready. When his weight hit her, she fell backward. The back of her head slammed into the woodstove. White and red bloomed in her vision. Her bones rattled as she hit the floor with him on top of her, all his weight.

All his weight.

His body on hers.

Every cell in her body understood what happened next. Every shred of muscle locked, a paralysis of helplessness.

There is fight and there is flight. But there is also freeze.

That's what Lori had taught her. That her mind wasn't so different from a possum's in some ways. She hadn't let these things happen to her—she hadn't been willing. Instead, her body had learned to play dead to keep her alive. The circuits in her mind had all linked up to dig those pathways deep, to make the response reflexive, requiring no thought or planning. A survival mechanism. A way to live through what was happening to her. Her brain had taught itself to detach, to float away, to build another world while her body was in use.

Her eyes burned. Her lungs burned. Somewhere, deep inside her mind, was one faint thought: *Move. Please. Move.*

After all her planning and all that work, his body was on hers again.

His hips grinding into hers. His acid breath in her face.

Move.

His chest crushing hers.

Move.

She opened her eyes. His scarlet face hovered over hers. Grimacing. Terror exploded inside her. Forbidden tears blurred her vision. It should have been enough. Why hadn't it been enough? She'd measured everything out. Powdered it all in that spice grinder. Calculated the relative deadliness of each fucking slice.

But now his hands were around her throat. She couldn't pull any air into her tortured lungs. Her hands closed over his thick wrists. He was so strong. He'd always been too strong.

Her ears filled with a droning, heavy buzz. Her skull swam with a scrum of random thoughts and memories. The waves at Race Point. The sun over the sea. Clouds in a heartbreakingly blue sky. Skis clacking together as she rode in the chair lift, a warm hand enveloping hers. The last time she'd felt truly safe.

A tear slipped from her eye.

Move, part of her whispered. *Please.*

Don't move, whispered another part, the part that knew all the history and maybe the part that knew the future, too. *This will all be over soon.*

SUNDAY, AUGUST 9

By the time I reach the workshop, Scott's already emerging with his nail gun, slamming a butane cartridge into its chamber. "I'm going to kill him."

"He might still have her," I say as we head for the back of the yard, the path that connects the two properties. Scott pushes ahead of me, and I put my hands up to keep from getting blinded by the thin branches that whip into my face as I jog behind him. My head is full of Mina and what she might have done.

That cake wasn't meant for her parents. It was meant for Phillip.

That episode of food poisoning that landed him in the hospital—now I'm sure it was something else.

Except he's still alive.

After several yards, we emerge into a backyard lined with woods and brambles all around. There's a large garden plot full of sunflowers, tomatoes, beans, and peppers, and next to it is a compost pile nearly as tall as I am. A pitchfork sticks up out of the middle. The house is a Cape, just like the Richardses', only painted maroon. To the left is an empty carport. Maybe they're out.

Maybe that's best.

"Phillip," roars Scott as he lumbers by the garden and clomps up a set of wooden stairs leading to a back door. He rips open the screen door and pounds on the back door, then tries the knob.

It's unlocked. We enter the kitchen to find Phillip standing at the stove next to the kettle, his face white. "Scott," he says. "And...Alex?"

"Where is she?" I ask.

"Wh-who?"

"Mina," Scott shouts. "What did you do to my daughter, you bastard?"

Phillip puts his hands up, a tremulous smile wavering on his face. "I don't know what you're talking about."

As they're arguing, my gaze sweeps the kitchen until it reaches the top of the fridge. My stomach drops. "She was here, Scott," I say, alarm bells clanging in my head as I point to the cake carrier, pale blue with red flowers all over it, made of tin with metal handles. It's right there. In plain sight.

Phillip looks up at the cake carrier. "Oh," he says. The blood drains from his face. "It's Sharon's..."

I'm already in motion. "Where's the basement?"

Scott points to the door right next to me, just across from the back door in the small entryway. "I'll be upstairs."

"You have no right," Phillip is saying as I descend the stairs and pull a thin chain to get the lights on. Dank, humid air settles on my skin as I reach the bottom. It's not finished, and it's mostly empty. Just a cement floor, a water heater and large heating oil tank, a shelf with stacks and stacks of board games, a table holding a boxed-up chess set, a single bed covered in a green blanket, and absolutely no sign of Mina.

It hits me hard, the now-dead hope that I would find her down here alive. Sure, maybe bound and scared and hurt, but *alive*. A part of me is glad—finding nothing is still better than finding her body. There's still hope. Scott's searching other parts of the house.

When I come back up the stairs, though, I realize the search is over. Scott stands at the entrance to the living room, and Phillip is now hovering next to a utility closet.

He has a handgun pointed at Scott.

"We shouldn't have left him alone," Scott mutters.

"Alex," Phillip says. "Stand where I can see you."

I gauge the distance from me to Phillip and the fact that there's a kitchen island between us. I might have a physical advantage here, but there's no way I can get to him before he shoots. His finger is on the trigger.

Scott stares at Phillip with a cold, bleak kind of hatred in his eyes. "Where is she?"

"I want you to get the hell out of my house."

Scott's hand is still wrapped around that nail gun. "You have her cake carrier."

Phillip opens his mouth, possibly to make some excuse, but I say, "Mina was seen two Mondays ago, loading a cake carrier into her car." I jab my finger at it. "*That* cake carrier." There's no mistaking it. It's not some plastic, dime-a-dozen thing. It's an antique, and she loves it. She wouldn't have left it behind.

Especially if it contained incriminating evidence.

"Did you eat the cake, Phillip?" I ask. "I know you have a sweet tooth." For a second, I have to marvel at the diabolical plan Mina must have had. The way she'd finally decided to eliminate the man who hurt her so much, so many times. "Must have been a rude awakening when you realized."

Phillip's mask of innocence falls away. "She *poisoned* me!"

Scott starts to raise the nail gun, but Phillip takes a step closer to him, the gun aimed squarely at Scott's chest. "She came here to kill me," Phillip tells him, glancing over at me every few seconds. "She nearly succeeded."

"Why?" Scott asks. "Why would she do that?"

I can see in his eyes that he knows exactly why.

"She was crazy," Phillip snaps.

Was. Oh God. "What did you do to her?" I ask, remembering the book, Lawrence's hands around Maggie's throat, her despair in those moments. The sickness and rage coil inside me.

"I didn't do anything," Phillip shouts, his wiry frame emanating an agitated tension that I hope doesn't extend to his trigger finger. "I didn't lay a hand on her!"

"You have the cake carrier," I say. "And you moved her car, right? You dumped it in Beech Forest. You knew people might think it was a suicide. You killed her. You fucking killed her." It's the first time I say it aloud, and those words hit me like a heavy dose of poison, turning everything black. "You killed my wife."

"No! I never hurt her, and I never moved the car!"

I take a step closer to the kitchen island.

Phillip points at me while keeping the gun aimed at Scott. "Another step and I'll kill him. Don't make me do this!"

"You're already a murderer," Scott snarls. The nail gun twitches in his hand.

"No," shouts Phillip. His hands are shaking, but his finger is now tight on that trigger. "I swear I didn't kill her!"

"Liar," Scott roars, his face crimson, his eyes wild. "You killed my daughter!"

"No," says Sharon, her silhouette framed in the open back door. "I did."

CHAPTER SIXTEEN

Like that amaryllis reaching for sunlight, Maggie's thoughts stretched up and out of the despair. Up and out of the years and years keeping her where she was. It wasn't like that anymore. She wouldn't let it be.

If I win, we play a different *game.*

Her hands tightened around Lawrence's wrists. She pulled. She saw the look of fear in his eyes. She'd never fought back. She'd always frozen, always yielded, always been a good, good, perfect, quiet girl.

This is a different game.

She breathed. One tortured, racked breath. His fingers loosened in a trembling spasm. His weight was going slack all around her.

The poison, doing its work.

With a grunt, she shifted her hips and bucked him off her. He slid off her body in a sickening parody of the way it had happened in the past. Sated and spent, her purpose served. Herself no threat at all.

She shuddered and shoved him, sucking oxygen through a bruised throat, adrenaline billowing through her veins. She scrambled away and crouched near the overturned table, watching him like the snake he was.

Lawrence lay on his back, panting. His effort to snuff the life out of her had exhausted him. He stared up at the wooden ceiling as if it held all his answers.

She crawled toward him. A whole bottle. Thirty pills, all a powder in the spice grinder. Three was supposed to be enough, and she'd given him a huge slice of that cake. He'd scraped the icing off the plate. What if he had a tolerance, though? She'd seen the bottle in the medicine cabinet.

But probably he had taken some today already. That would help, not hurt.

His mouth was moving as she leaned over him. Soundless words. She surveyed his face, the sun spots, the gray stubble, the loose skin, the folds and wrinkles. This was her monster. This was the terror of her dreams. How had she ever allowed such a pathetic creature to control her?

Lori had reminded her that a predator's methods were insidious. And that the mind's focus was on survival, not truth. Put the two together, and evil men could get away with evil things.

"Did you think I would let you get away with all of it forever, though?" she murmured. "Had you just decided I would always be weak?"

He blinked up at the ceiling as his chest trembled. Up and down. She could see the vein fluttering in his neck. Pumping all that irresistible heaviness along his bones, his muscles, pushing it deeper. Into capillaries and cells. A slow-rolling takeover.

"Call 911," he rasped.

"That kind of defeats the purpose here."

"Maggie." He took a swipe at her, uncoordinated and weak.

"Lawrence," she said. "You aren't expecting company are you?"

She saw the moment he understood, and she almost smiled at the terror in his eyes. By the time he managed to nod, a frantic little jerk of his head, she knew it was yet another lie.

"Good," she said. "That would have been unfortunate." She felt like a spider now, watching her prey struggling in the web. "I can't figure out if you thought what you were doing to me was okay, if you were really that sick, or if you knew you were a fucking pedophile and just thought you could gaslight your way to getting away with it." She offered him a pretty smile. "I've been to therapy. I know either is possible."

I'm sorry, he mouthed. His eyes on her. Pleading. "Sorry."

"Don't worry about it." She leaned closer. "Your words don't matter anymore."

"Help," he coughed out, trying to roll toward the door. "Help!"

She stroked his chest. Touched his face. Moved into position. "Shh," she said. Pushing her face right over his. Smelling his scent and gritting her teeth. "Shh, Lawrence. Listen to me." She made sure he was looking up at her. Put both hands on his cheeks. Registered the horror in his eyes and understood it as justice.

"Good boys are quiet boys," she whispered.

Then she covered his mouth with her palm and pinched his nostrils shut.

SUNDAY, AUGUST 9

G et the nail gun from him," Phillip orders as his wife enters the kitchen.

Sharon approaches Scott from the side, careful not to step into Phillip's line of fire. "Hand it over, Scott," she says. "You shouldn't have come over here with that." She sounds like she's scolding a stubborn teenager.

Scott gives her a look that could burn a normal person to the ground, but he hands over the nail gun. She takes it, steps well to his left, unclicks the safety with a practiced nonchalance, and aims it at me. "I didn't want this to happen," she said. "I feel sorry for you most of all."

"Why?" That's the only word I can choke out. It's the only thought I can think in this moment. *Why?*

It covers the maelstrom deeper inside me. Mina is dead. My love is dead. My lungs lock up with the truth. My heart won't beat properly. Disbelief and despair are a tangle in my mind.

Please let this be a lie. A joke. Yet another nightmare. Anything but reality. Please.

"Sometimes you have to fight for what's yours," Sharon is saying. "And my husband is *mine*."

"Sharon has a book group on Monday nights," Phillip says, keeping his eyes on Scott. "I'm guessing Mina knew that. Rose probably told her. But Sharon came home just in time."

"He'd eaten a big ol' piece of cake," says Sharon. "The fruit of the poisoned tree." She shakes her head, and her silver hair flaps by her ears. She's not a big woman, but she holds the nail gun steady. I wonder how much damage she could do to me before I get it away from her. I'm guessing her husband would shoot me before I find out.

"I walked in on them," she continues. "I was standing right by the stove, right where you are now."

"You said you loved her," I say. "You went on and on about what she meant to you."

"You don't understand," she replies. "You don't understand what it's like, losing him over and over." She casts a narrow-eyed look at her husband before returning her attention to me. "After all the love I gave her, she decided to steal from me. *Again.* You married a little whore."

I take a step toward her, my hands rising from my sides.

She fires the nail gun. I flinch and look down at myself.

"Cabinet," says Scott, his mouth barely moving. I look over to see a three-inch framing nail embedded halfway in the cabinet door less than a foot from my head.

"Stay still, Alex," she says. "You have to understand it was all in self-defense. She was in my house. And she threatened me."

"You're a fucking liar." I stay where I am this time, though. My hands are at my sides again, but my phone is in my pocket. If I were alone, I'd run for it and hit Detective Correia's number as soon as I was in the yard, but Scott is right in Phillip's sights. And as weedy as the guy is, Phillip looks like he knows what he's doing with that weapon. "Whatever you did," I say to his wife, "you did it in cold blood."

"I didn't," Sharon says, her voice going shrill. "What I saw was that woman in my kitchen, seducing my husband *again*!" Her cheeks are stained crimson. Her eyes have gone glassy. "Can't you understand that? I swallowed all that humiliation for *years*. I tried to be the bigger person, and what did that get me?" She stomps her foot. "First Rose got him, then, as *soon* as Mina turned eighteen, she went after him, too. Like mother, like daughter. Two bitches in heat, I guess. And apparently Phillip can't control himself around them."

I'm trying to wrap my head around what she's saying, but it's so twisted that I only manage to gape at her. "You don't actually believe—"

"I don't have to believe," she shouts. "I *know*. I know that Rose stole him away. He admitted it! And a few years later, Mina did the same! I knew that baby was his, and she didn't even have the decency to let us raise him!"

"Are you fucking serious?" I ask. "He *raped* her. And you're surprised she wouldn't let you raise the baby?"

Sharon scoffs. "Rape? What a crock. Do you have any idea how it felt to see her last week, up to her old tricks?"

"You could have kicked her out of your house," Scott says. "You could have—"

"I did what I should have done all those years ago!" Sharon shrieks. "I grabbed my frying pan and gave her what she deserved!"

My stomach turns, imagining it. "Sharon—"

"I didn't mean for her to die," she wails. Then she draws in a shuddering breath. "When I realized she'd poisoned him, though, oh, I was glad I got her. An eye for an eye and a tooth for a tooth." She glances over her shoulder. "Isn't that what you and Rose believe, Scott?"

He stares at her, his eyes glittering with tears. "Where is my daughter, Sharon?"

"Phillip," she says, ignoring Scott. "We have to figure out what to do with them."

"You're not going to be able to hide this," I tell her. "If you do anything to us, that's it. Rose knows we're here."

"I've been waiting for something like this," Sharon tells me. "I'll figure it out."

"They're in our house. They brought a weapon," says Phillip. "We have a right to defend ourselves. We can say that they tried to frame us, too. For the whole thing."

For Mina's murder, he means. I scan the room. "Sharon," I say. "You're really willing to go to prison for the rest of your life for this guy?"

"I forgave him for cheating," she snaps. "He's weak, but he's a good husband."

"He's a fucking pedophile."

Confusion flits across her face, followed by rage. She aims the nail gun square at my face and moves a little closer to me but still too far for me to get to her before she fires. "Do you write fiction, too?" she asks, her lip curling in contempt. "How dare you—"

"It's true," says Scott. "We know it's true. He abused Mina for years."

"He had an *affair* with Mina," Sharon says. "She was eighteen. An adult. She knew what she was doing."

"He started molesting her right after the affair with Rose," I say. "When she was twelve at the most. He threatened Rose. He made her send Mina over here in exchange for keeping Scott in the dark. For all we know, he was trying to get to Mina all along."

"Don't believe them, Sharon," says Phillip. "They're lying."

"He was trying to *protect* Mina," Sharon says, rattling the nail gun in a way that makes me take a step back. "Trying to give her time away from that nightmare of a family she had."

"Chess. Lessons," I say, annunciating every syllable. "You mentioned Phillip played, and I saw the table downstairs, with the chess set." I look over at him. "Except that wasn't really what you were doing, was it? I saw the bed down there, too."

When you win, we play a different game.

"It's a lie, honey," says Phillip. He looks nervous, though, his twitchy gaze shifting from Scott to Sharon to me and back. "I sleep down there sometimes, when my snoring gets to be too much for her. Ask her."

Sharon nods, but she looks troubled, like a seed of doubt is germinating.

"You know what I'm saying is true, Sharon," I tell her. "You know what he did to her. And he lied to you for years."

"He would never do that," she says hoarsely, looking over at him. "He admitted when he made mistakes..."

"Why would Mina try to poison him?" I ask. "She'd never tried to hurt another person in her whole life."

"She hurt me," Sharon says.

"Phillip did that when he raped Mina," I shout. "Starting when she was a *little girl*. Up until the day he got her pregnant. And you wonder why she tried to kill herself."

"She seduced him!" But I can see the doubt in Sharon's eyes.

"She was a *child*," Scott reminds her. "I should have protected her, but I failed. Rose failed, too. He got away with it. He raped my daughter."

Sharon cringes. "No," she murmurs. "He wouldn't."

"He had too much control over her," I tell her. "Because he started when she was young. He probably told her no one would believe her if she told. Or he told her they'd both get in trouble. That's what pedophiles do, Sharon. Mina *begged* her mother not to have to come over here!"

"Lies," Phillip yells, swinging his weapon toward me. "Nothing but lies!"

Sharon pivots toward him. "You told me not to come downstairs while you were giving lessons. That's what you always said."

"It was for concentration," he says. "Chess requires focus."

"You always closed the door." Her voice is drifty now as she recalls. "Why would you need to close the door?"

"To let us concentrate!" Phillip's voice cracks, and his face is mottled. "I was trying to teach her the game!"

"You did it, didn't you?" she shrieks. "Did you abuse that little girl?"

"They're liars," Phillip says. "They're just looking for someone to blame for what she did to me. You *saw* what she did to me, honey. You saved my life that night. And now I can save you—save *us*—from these two."

I don't know if it's the twitch in his cheek or the way he can't quite meet her eyes, but something cinches it for Sharon. "I did save you," she says, sounding sick and weary. "That night, I did." Then she lowers the nail gun—taking aim at her husband's groin.

I dive for the floor as I hear the unmistakable percussive clicks of the nail gun and then the sharp crack of a gunshot. A gasp. A thump. A moan. After a beat of silence, I cautiously raise my head.

Phillip is still holding the gun. He looks down at himself in horror. Three nails have embedded themselves in his body, one in his belly and two in his right thigh.

Scott has taken shelter in the living room. He stands just out of Phillip's line of fire, staring at the kitchen floor. "Alex," he says. "I think she's dead."

I lean over. Sharon Rawlings has been shot in the head. Her face is covered with blood. She's not moving. The nail gun lies cradled in the crook of her right arm. Her finger is still hooked in the trigger. I pull out my phone to call 911.

Phillip swings the gun toward me. "Drop it," he says through clenched teeth.

I put the phone on the counter and raise my hands. "Phillip, let's think this through."

He gives me a pained smile. "Too late for that, I think."

Not even close. "You acted in self-defense," I say. "Scott and I can both vouch for that. Not to mention your injuries."

Scott has moved into the doorway of the kitchen again. He's looking down at his nail gun, maybe wondering if he can scoop it up.

Phillip must see that, too. "Step into the kitchen," he says, aiming at Scott.

Scott obeys. He's got his hands up.

"Phillip," I say, glancing around again to make sure I understand the layout of the place. "You didn't kill Mina. We both heard what Sharon said. We'll testify to that."

"If you think—" Scott begins, his face warped with rage.

I hold up my hand to stop him. "Scott. It's the truth."

Phillip keeps the gun aimed at Scott but looks at me. "She poisoned me," he says, panting as his gaze flits down to his wounds. "I almost died. I would have died."

"I know," I say. "You didn't ask for this."

"*What?*" shouts Scott.

I point my finger at him and fix him with a cold, fierce look. "Shut. Up."

He looks like he wishes he could fire a nail square between my eyes.

I focus on Phillip again. "Come on," I say. "I'll take you to the hospital. We'll call the police and have them come for Sharon."

"I won't go to prison," Phillip says with a groan, grimacing as one finger hovers near the nailhead poking out of his belly. A patch of blood is slowly spreading out from the epicenter of the wound, staining his T-shirt. Similar splotches decorate his shorts.

"You won't," I assure him. "Your wife killed Mina, and she attacked you when you found out the truth. You didn't know anything." I cast a warning look at Scott, who glares at me but stays quiet.

"You have every reason to hate me," Phillip says. The gun is still up, but it's aimed between me and Scott now, like he wants to be ready for either of us.

"I know," I say. "But I also understand that my wife came here to kill you."

"Alex," Scott barks.

I ignore him. Things have gone too far to do anything else. Not ten feet from me, there's a dead woman on the floor. Maybe right where Mina lay all those days ago.

"I would have died if Sharon hadn't gotten me to the hospital in time," Phillip says. He looks down at his wife's body and squeezes his eyes shut. A soft, keening noise snakes between his lips. "Sharon." His chest convulses with a sob.

"I know," I say, my fists clenched but my face neutral. Calm. "I get it. Put the gun down, Phillip. We can't help you while you're threatening us, and we're unarmed. Come on."

He opens his eyes and gives me a desolate look. "Okay," he says. "Okay." He puts the gun on the counter.

Scott jerks forward, hand outstretched, jaw set.

"Don't," I shout. I'm halfway over the counter in a fraction of a second, hand on his chest, shoving him backward before he ruins everything.

Phillip snatches the weapon from the counter. "Self-defense," he screeches, fumbling to get his finger on the trigger again.

"Phillip," I say, my voice level as I get both feet back on the floor. "Phillip, he's unarmed. Right now, you're off the hook, man. We can explain everything that's happened as long as you don't fire another shot."

"You'll accuse me of being a pedophile," he says, eyes red. "I know what you'll say."

"Mina never told anyone." It feels like I've taken one of those nails straight in my damn heart. My beautiful Mina, with all those words in her head, was never able to utter the ones that might have saved her. Because of this man in front of me. "She never told a single soul. Not her parents, not her friends. It would be her word against yours." I suck in a breath. "And she's dead. So there's nothing we can do." It's killing me, but nothing I'm saying is actually a lie.

"You're a cold bastard," Scott says. He spits on the floor. His eyes slide to the nail gun.

"Don't fucking touch it," I snap. "Or I will *let* Phillip shoot you."

"Cold. Bastard."

I know. I know I am.

"Take the clip out," I instruct Phillip. "If you need to keep the gun, just take out the bullets. I'm going to help you, but I don't want to get shot for my trouble. Okay?"

It might be my demeanor, calm and icy smooth. Or the fact that Scott so obviously wants to murder me. Or it could be the shock of killing Sharon or the agony of those nails driven deep into his flesh. Maybe it's all those things. With shaking hands, Phillip removes the clip from the weapon and pockets it. Then he shoves the gun into his belt.

I take a slow step forward. "The keys to the car?"

"She leaves them in the ignition," he says, letting out a strained chuckle. "Because it's so safe here."

I smile at him. "Perfect. Scott will call the police, but I want to get you some medical attention as quickly as possible. We'll sort everything out."

He looks at me in disbelief. "You're really going to help me."

"I don't have much choice in the matter. I need to do what's right." I reach his side. I'm a few inches taller, but I offer my hand and swing his arm over my shoulder. "And I think this'll be faster than an ambulance."

"You could shoot me," he mumbles.

"I know." I pivot us and support his weight until we're in the entryway, between the open basement doorway and the back door. "But that would be foolish."

He looks up at me.

"When I win, we play a different game," I explain.

Then I shove him down the basement stairs.

CHAPTER SEVENTEEN

She focused on the clock hanging over the table. Watched the second hand go around four times. Four minutes. Wasn't that what she'd read?

He'd stopped moving at two, but she wanted to be sure.

She let go of his mouth and put a hand on his still chest. Not even the faintest flutter of life.

She stood up and looked around. Tried to see this as someone else would.

Lawrence looked small in death. Frail and pathetic. His eyes were half-open. Glazed and unfocused. She resisted the urge to do more to him. Like kick that stupid, awful, slack-mouthed expression right off his face.

With a choked sob, she turned away and set to work. Took her wineglass and the cake plate and fork to the sink. She washed them thoroughly with soap, dried them with a dishrag, and put them away. She wiped the drawer and cabinet pulls with the rag, too. Then she wiped down all the chess pieces, the chair, the woodstove, the floor where she'd fallen. Just in case.

She went to the bathroom and took his pills from the medicine cabinet. She opened the bottle and removed several pills, then left it open on the counter.

She packed up the cake, wiped everything down a second time, not a crumb left to signal she'd been there, and left the house.

She drove home, washed all the remnants of the cake down the sink, and then put all the lovely things she'd purchased—the pans, the cake spatula, the flour, the food coloring, and the spice grinder—in a black trash bag. She carried it out to the curb. Tomorrow was trash day.

When all of that was done, she sat and waited to feel something. Guilt. Sorrow. Horror. She rummaged around in her mind, almost expecting something to jump out at her. Instead, the feeling dawned slowly, just as the sun might ooze across the glassy ocean. It took a while for her to recognize, and it wasn't until she was drifting into sleep that she finally did: peace.

SUNDAY, AUGUST 9

I arrive back at Mina's cottage by two, and I take a long, hot shower. I move like I'm in a dream, my limbs heavy and loose.

Flashes of the day knife through me at random moments.

I reach for the tap, and I see my hand reaching for Phillip's face. I hear myself saying, very softly, "Good boys are quiet boys."

I step out of the tub, and I step back into that kitchen and meet Scott's eyes. "Did you touch anything?" I ask. He shakes his head. I take the cake carrier off the top of the fridge.

I wipe the steam from the mirror, and I wipe the doorknob on our way out the back.

I walk into the bedroom, and I walk into the Richardses' house. There's Rose, ashen on the couch, mascara streaked on her cheeks. "I heard a gunshot," she says. "I didn't know what to do."

I look in the mirror, and I see Scott. "Wait until I'm gone to call," I tell him. He nods, and in those solemn, sad eyes, I see that he will never betray me for what I've done.

Because he knows I did it for her.

I float through the evening on a tide of Macallan. Waiting. Around nine, slightly more sober and still desperate to keep everything behind the walls holding me together, I begin to go through the cottage. I don't touch her desk, her rings, her notepad.

But I do fire up her laptop and try to erase her search history. She's already done it, though. *I love you*, I think.

I find her cake decorating kit after combing the kitchen. That's where I discover the little brown pill bottle, label scraped away. I put on my shoes, planning to take a walk down Commercial and quietly dispose of it in a public bin, but then I think better of it.

I busy myself cleaning, my mind blank, my heart blank. I scrub that cake carrier until it's spotless and put it back in the pantry.

She comes to the door just after eleven. "Mr. Zarabian," says the detective, her voice mournful. "I'm sorry to come by so late."

"I forgot to drop off my phone," I mutter.

"That's not why I'm here."

I know. I take a step backward. I brace a hand on the wall.

She sighs. "This afternoon, the Truro police were called to investigate a report of a possible domestic dispute at the home of Phillip and Sharon Rawlings. They searched the property and found a body buried in the yard. About an hour ago, Scott Richards formally identified the body as that of his daughter."

My back hits the coatrack. I close my eyes. "How did she—"

"We'll have to wait for the coroner's report, but it looks like she was hit pretty hard on the back of the head."

Detective Correia says other things, but I don't hear them. I can't. Because the dam inside me, the one that has held all these things at bay, has broken.

I will never touch her face or make love to her again.

I will never hear her voice, her laugh.

I will never be able to hold her and tell her I know what happened to her, and all I feel is awe and admiration at her strength.

I will never watch her eyes brighten when I tell her I love her.

I will live the rest of my life with a fragile hope that she already knew and that maybe, somewhere, she's a little more at peace in the knowledge that I finished what she started.

But right now, that hope isn't enough. I slide down the wall. My head falls into my hands. And I start to sob.

EPILOGUE

Maggie had thought that night would be the end, but it turned out to be the beginning of something she'd never been able to envision before. She had wondered if the guilt would bubble up or if the police would show up at her door and shout, "We know what you did!"

Neither of those things happened. Instead, it was Ivy who called Maggie up two days after the fact, sobbing, to break the news. Lawrence had a problem mixing the pain pills with alcohol, and this time, he'd taken too much. He was gone. Maggie had said she was sorry to hear that. But when Ivy had demanded she come home, Maggie had said no. And when she demanded Maggie show up at the funeral, Maggie had said no. And when she'd begun to scream at Maggie, Maggie hung up.

And then Maggie had done something she'd never thought she'd be strong enough to do. She had shown up at Ivy's door. Face-to-face, within arm's reach. Her possessions were all stuffed into the Corolla, and the tank was full. She left the engine running. Her heart pounded as she rang the doorbell.

Ivy opened the door, wearing black, which looked wrong and strange amid the backdrop of garland and Christmas lights sparkling all around her home, immaculate and oh so tasteful. "I knew you'd come crawling back," she snapped.

"I'm not coming back," Maggie said. "I'm saying goodbye."

"I suppose you expect me to give you money? If you think you can get your hands on a single cent he left behind after treating us so—"

"No. I'm going to take care of myself from now on. You never did a very good job of it."

"You're ungrateful," Ivy sneered. "You always have been."

"And you are a terrible, warped person," Maggie said to her mother. "I don't forgive you for what you did to me. He might have abused me, but you did, too. You helped him."

Ivy's eyes glowed with rage. "You little—"

"Stop it," Maggie said. "You'll smear your lipstick."

"The next time you show up here—"

"If I ever do, please slam the door in my face. I'll be better off that way."

She stepped back as Ivy let out a screech of rage and did exactly that.

Wearing a savage smile, she headed back to her car. When she got inside, she pulled out her phone and blocked her mother's number.

She'd read a lot of stuff about forgiveness. She and Lori had discussed it at length. But what she'd come to, after all those months, was that it wasn't her job to offer these people who had hurt her any kind of comfort.

Instead, it was up to her to get to her own kind of peace. A peace that involved justice. It flew in the face of everything she'd been taught growing up—turn the other cheek and forgive and forgive and forgive until there was nothing left of you but a shell—but perhaps that was why an alternative was so easy to embrace.

Maggie drove to the beach, and she parked her car. She pulled her coat tight around her and held the hood over her head to keep the wind from knocking it back. Her boots crunched in the ice-crusted sand as she leaned into the wind and trudged toward the lapping waves.

Someday, she'd graduate from college.

Someday, she'd meet a wonderful man and fall madly in love.

Someday, she'd have a child, whom she would love more than herself.

But at that moment, it was just her, here on the beach, at the edge of the world and the rest of her life. She spread her arms and turned her face to the starry sky. She was weightless as a ribbon in the breeze, carried up and out over the ocean, dancing with the waves.

She kept her feet anchored in the sand, but nothing was holding her down anymore except her own desire to be exactly where she was.

THURSDAY, SEPTEMBER 10

I leave Waltham just before three, hoping to avoid rush hour. I shouldn't be leaving the office this early, not with everything that's going on, but I don't have another meeting until tomorrow, when I have my first one-on-one with the new CEO of Biostar. Blake Pierce assured me the guy has already steered two other biotechs to IPO, so we'll be in good hands.

Drew texts me as I'm getting on the turnpike. **Let's get together this weekend. New opportunity I need to discuss with you.**

I smile. He's nothing if not resilient. I knew he would back down and do the right thing, and he did. The Monday after Mina was found, Drew signed the agreement with Pinewell—and then he gave his notice. He's gone out of his way to make sure the transition was smooth.

It's also been nice to have my best friend back. The day of Mina's memorial in Provincetown was not easy, with Scott and Rose sitting on opposite sides of the chapel, me not really wanting to be near either of them, Devon and Caitlin huddled on one side of me, and my mom sobbing uncontrollably on my shoulder as if Dad had died all over again. I was grateful that I had Drew there to hold me up and manage things; otherwise, I might have gotten in my car and driven it straight over the pier. More than one night in the last month, I've crashed on Drew and Caroline's couch, unable to face going back to the condo where Mina and I lived during our first and only exquisite months of marriage. It's on the market now. I'm closing on a new place in the South End next week.

Mina's cottage is already under contract—it was snapped up less than a week after it was listed. I can't be there knowing she'll never walk through the door or write another page while looking out at the sea. I hope the next occupant loves the view as much as she did.

I exit onto 93 South. It's all familiar now, the turns automatic. But I think this is the last time I'll drive this way for a good long while. There's just one final thing I need to do.

While I drive, I let myself think about her. About us. It's something I still need to avoid most of the time if I want to keep functioning, but each day, I give in a for a few minutes. I owe it to her.

I took a risk. A not-so-calculated jump into the great unknown. That's what Mina was, right up until the end. Huge parts of her, kept hidden from me. I still feel like I knew her, though, and reading her book helped me understand her better.

I don't regret loving her. I will never regret it.

But I will always wonder if I could have saved her somehow. Different words, different actions. I will always fear that I pushed her into motion that Monday morning, but maybe it was inevitable. She'd already decided she couldn't move on until she'd taken Phillip out of this world. It might have been just a matter of time.

Could I have stopped her? *Should* I have stopped her? I'm not sure on either count.

She died quickly. Instantly, the medical examiner told me. Something, a cast iron pan, they think, slammed into the back of her head at just the perfect place. Massive fracture, catastrophic hemorrhage, lights out. She didn't have time to be scared or feel pain.

I'm still glad Sharon is dead, though. Two days after they found Mina's body, the forensic results came back for the Prius—the investigators found some of Sharon's silver hairs on the headrest of the driver's seat. She probably moved the car the day she first met me. The temptation of revenge might have been too difficult for me to resist if she were still alive.

I wonder if Rose provided the flowers for the funeral of her daughter's murderer, just to look gracious.

I walk into the Mariner just after five, another risk I've decided to take.

It's off-season now, not crowded. I take a seat on a stool and wait for him to recognize me.

I can tell the moment he does, because a weird array of emotions crosses his face in less than a second—fear, confusion, defiance. I meet his eyes. "The Mayflower, please."

Stefan glances around at the nearly empty bar and then obliges. "Didn't expect to see you in here again."

I sip my beer.

"I'm sorry," he says. "I mean, I know you probably think I was happy when I was cleared, but I was still sad to hear what happened to her."

I draw in a long breath through my nose. Then I set the little brown pill bottle on the bar.

Stefan blinks at it. Scratches at his jaw.

"Figured this belonged to you," I say.

He swallows hard. "I don't know how—"

"Did you really think she was going to use it on herself?"

He says nothing.

"Her plan would have worked if his wife hadn't come home," I tell him.

The fear in his eyes is unmistakable now.

"She asked for help, and you gave it to her," I say. In another world, another life, he might have said no. But she still could have gotten what she needed. In this world, though, she made herself a list, including *Stef*. Including *cash*. She drove to Harwich on Monday, July 27, and used the money she withdrew from that ATM in Barnstable to pay Stefan Silva for what she wanted, which is most likely why her wallet was empty when they found it in her car. She already had the plan. She just needed the means.

"If it helps at all, it was more about the future than the past," he says in a low voice. When I don't reply, he continues. "She said she'd tried everything else—therapy, her writing, all that shit—and it wasn't enough. She wanted a fresh start, with you. Kids, living the dream. Clean slate. I didn't ask a lot of questions about what she was doing. I told her I didn't want to know."

"But you knew."

"I knew her back *then*. Part of her, at least." His nostrils flare. "What he turned her into."

The part she never wanted me to know. Would she ever have told me the real story? Maybe she didn't want to, for the same reason she never planned to write about our relationship. She wanted to protect us. It's probably why she left her rings behind, too. I wasn't the only one who walled stuff off. She wanted to keep me safe behind one of those walls, thinking I had access to her whole world when I only had a piece.

I wish she were here. I'd tell her we were stronger than that.

"Did she leave the phone behind on purpose?" I ask.

He stares down at the pill bottle on the bar. "She was going to come back for it. Afterward."

She didn't mind being seen, but she didn't want anyone to know exactly where she'd been. After she left her parents, she could have claimed she drove straight back to Harwich, and he could have backed her up. He was her insurance policy, her alibi. "You were left holding the bag."

"One last favor, I guess."

"Did she tell you that you weren't the father? Is that why she wanted to talk?"

He nods. "I didn't know whether I was relieved or disappointed. I always wondered what would have happened if I'd refused to sign those papers, if I'd been too proud to take the money. Now I think it's okay, what happened. I hope that kid is in a good place."

"Me, too." I hope he never discovers that his biological father was a monster.

Stefan slides the pill bottle off the bar and tosses it in the trash. "So the guy's dead now."

I sip my beer.

"Got what he deserved in the end," he adds. "Dead at the bottom of the stairs, shot through with nails."

"Is that how it was?"

His eyes narrow. "I have a friend on the Truro force. He said it was a pretty fucked-up scene."

"One last favor," I murmur, staring until I see the understanding dawn. Then I pull out my wallet and lay a ten on the bar. "Thanks."

He peers down at the pill bottle in the trash and then at me. He nods. "Take care, man."

I head out of the bar, back to my car, and start the long drive back to Boston to pick up my daughter. There's a new voicemail on my phone. It's Mina's editor, Kyle. He's begging me for a decision. Says he needs it yesterday. In Mina's will, she gave control of her entire estate to me, and it turns out I have a say about whether *The Quiet Girl* will actually be published. Sure, it'll be under her pseudonym, but I have a feeling someone's going to leak the truth. They are, after all, in the business of selling books.

I don't know, though, how far it would go from there. Would anyone link the end of her book to the end of her life? Would she want the book to be her final testament, or, having acted out the end, would she want to keep it quiet? What clues did we leave behind, her and Stefan and I, and will anyone ever connect them?

What was it worth to her, to make her voice heard after so many years of silence?

I call Kyle back with my final answer. It's another jump into the unknown, with Mina's hand firmly in mine.

READING GROUP GUIDE

1. When we first meet Alex, he is heading to apologize to his wife after an argument. Why did you initially believe Mina wasn't responding to Alex's texts? What did you make of their relationship from this initial scene? How would you describe Alex?

2. Provincetown is Mina's writer's hideaway—a perfect escape. If you could choose any place in the world for your own retreat, where would it be? Why do you think Mina is drawn to Provincetown?

3. Describe Layla. What was your initial reaction to Layla and her spotty memory? If you were Esteban, would you have taken the girl in?

4. What do you make of Rose and Scott? How can you describe their overall relationship with Mina?

5. We learn a lot about Mina through her husband, her parents, and her manuscript. How would you describe her? What can you infer about her personality?

6. If you were to write a novel about your own life, what kind of story would it be? How much would you change or embellish?

7. Do you think writing the novel set Mina's revenge in motion? Or did Mina's plan inspire the novel?

8. Why do you think Stefan helps Mina? Do you find him trustworthy? How would you describe his character?

9. Why do you think Mina decides to write her story? Imagine what that process would feel like for her. If you were in her shoes, how would you decide to finally express yourself?

10. What ultimately drives Mina to confront her past? What role does Alex and their marriage play in this story?

A CONVERSATION WITH THE AUTHOR

The Quiet Girl **is a clever and intensely twisty story of revenge and suspense. Where did you get your inspiration?**

The first seeds of this story were planted when I was on Cape Cod in 2018 for a late summer weekend. We had ridden from Boston to Provincetown on the ferry, and we were staying with family in Truro. I was enchanted by the setting, a narrow, hauntingly beautiful curl of land that's only sparsely inhabited in the winter months but full to the brim in the summer. I remember staring out at the ocean when the idea came to me: What if a writer disappeared from this setting... and what if she left a book behind that offered some explanation as to why and how? From there, it was just a matter of the details. And because I am trained as a clinical psychologist, the twists and turns usually involve some sort of psychological injury or condition that affects how some characters view and react to the world.

Talk a bit about Maggie's fugue state. What research went into bringing this complicated disorder to life? How are trauma and fugue linked, both in the story and in real life?

The first time I ever read about what was then called psychogenic fugue was in my abnormal psychology class in college. I was utterly fascinated by the stories of how some people suddenly walk away from their lives and seem to forget who they are for a time; some even adopt entirely new identities before abruptly recovering. I knew this concept had been a topic in fiction before, and certainly amnesia is a popular trope—it's such a powerful, frightening, universally affecting idea. But as I considered a story that dealt with fugue, I was most interested in *why* my character had experienced it in the first place.

These days, the condition is called dissociative fugue. Some kinds of dissociation are normal and not linked to trauma, like daydreaming. It's a kind of mental disconnection from the world around you. However, the more disabling types of dissociation—where the mind completely walls off the memory of certain experiences—are pretty closely linked with traumatic experiences. This is Maggie's experience in the book: she had been sexually abused for years before she experienced a severe and prolonged fugue state, and it was her realization that her abuser had gotten her pregnant that finally triggered the event.

In this story, Maggie is at first quite intent on recovering memories of what happened when she was "away," but her psychiatrist, Dr. Schwartz, does *not* focus on memory recovery as part of treatment. Dr. Schwartz even points out that those memories might never be recoverable, and she's much more interested in uncovering and processing the trauma she believes triggered the fugue episode. This is consistent with many models and approaches to treating trauma and dissociative disorders.

It was very important to me to depict not only the condition properly, but also its aftermath, including potential treatment. For that reason, I asked an experienced colleague of mine who works with adults (my specialty is children and families) to read a draft of the novel and critique it with the goal of achieving a faithful and accurate portrayal that neither romanticized nor minimized fugue for plot convenience. And this is why, just as an example, I did not have Maggie suddenly remember what happened during her fugue, even if it might have been handy for my plot—in real life, memories of what happened during a true fugue episode are usually never recovered.

There's a really fantastic blurring between fact and fiction in *The Quiet Girl*, as readers try to discern the difference between Mina's novel and Mina's real experiences. How did you play with that line? Do you think authors often insert their own experiences into their writing?

The blurred and shifting line between invention and reality is one of the reasons I enjoy reading books in this genre, and it was one of the many enjoyable things about writing *The Quiet Girl*. I loved leaving tiny little clues in the Layla/Maggie story line, especially early on, that might make readers sit forward and wonder if they've hit upon something significant—or remember later and think, *So* that's *what that was!*

For most differences between Mina's life and the story she wrote, I wanted there to be a reason why she made the choice she did as an author. For example, she had just turned eighteen when she experienced a fugue episode, and it lasted for five months instead of ten weeks, and she actually had the baby instead of having an abortion. She chose to create a character that was a bit of a wish for her past self—the character of Maggie becomes angry and energized rather than continuing to try to suppress her past as Mina did. She is older and more proactive, more able to function as an adult in this world and make the choices that are ultimately best for her, and, in the end, takes a drastic action that until the very end Mina had only fantasized about. Mina gave her main character more advantages, and arguably less pain, and she wrote the ending she wanted for herself. And although she never gets to experience it, her character lives on in her own hard-won happy ending.

I think writers use their own experiences in different ways within their stories. Sometimes it's a deep understanding of a certain setting, world, or culture. Sometimes it's some life situation or relationship dynamic. For me, I often use my stories as a kind of processing of my own experiences, perceptions, and fascinations, and *The Quiet Girl* is a very particular version of that—no other book I've written veers closer to my real life than this one, which is a strange confession to make, all things considered...

How much do you think Mina changed or embellished her life story when writing her novel?

I think of Maggie and Layla as Mina's understanding of herself as a younger person, only with Mina controlling the history and course of events. In writing that story, Mina was trying to show herself some compassion and even heal by creating a more empowered character than she herself might have been when she was younger. Mina deliberately changed events in the story, not just to obscure details or protect people, but to allow herself to nurture and experiment with different pasts. In the end, of course, weaving that narrative isn't enough for Mina and might even have made that fantasy more real and necessary for her. I think that kind of revenge fantasy is not abnormal for someone who endured what Mina did, and I wanted to show the different ways it could play out.

Which character did you enjoy writing the most? Which was the most challenging?

I most enjoyed writing Maggie, I think. She's so incredibly raw, like an exposed nerve, but at the same time, her intellect is active and even aggressive. She's not an agreeable, easygoing character, and at times I think she's a bit hard to sympathize with. I enjoyed the challenge of making her not likable but understandable. Only my readers can tell me if I succeeded!

In terms of the most challenging characters to write, it was probably the mothers: Ivy and Rose. I was worried they risked being almost unbelievable in terms of their behavior, and I didn't want them to be caricatures. Social desirability and display can twist people up, and I wanted Ivy and Rose to be examples of how a person can lose sight of doing what's right when there's a possibility they might lose face or status as a result. And sometimes, when that need to protect one's image is deep and internalized, it can drive a person to develop their own alternative narrative or completely deny reality as a form of self-protection.

Was it difficult to keep track of the characters and how they were portrayed in Alex's world and in Mina's novel?

I didn't find it particularly difficult, in drafting, at least. It was in revisions that I'd read something in one of the narratives and nearly have a heart attack because it wasn't consistent...and then realize it was *supposed* to be a difference between the two. My editor, MJ Johnston, was particularly helpful during the revision process in encouraging me to highlight some of the differences between reality and fiction as Alex tries to understand how the book Mina wrote is linked to what happened to her, both to help readers keep track and to process the unfolding story. In my opinion, that made the story much clearer and more compelling—and probably much more enjoyable for readers!

What does your writing process typically look like?

These days, I usually fall in love with a concept—cult psychology, mass hysteria events, and impostors who can fool some of the most sophisticated among us are my most recent obsessions. With this book, it was dissociative fugue. Typically, I start to read whatever's available on the subject, and I usually get inspired by possibilities, which then morph into story and character ideas. After that, I create a stream-of-consciousness-type document where I begin to outline who the main character is and what might happen in the story— this is where things can easily branch off into creative places I never thought I'd be—which eventually evolves into the actual plot struc- ture with a defined three acts, midpoint climax, etc. That whole process of researching and outlining can take days...or even years. I have several of these rambling documents, and not all of them will become books someday—but many of them have. For those, at some point, anywhere from a few hours to a few years after I originally develop the idea, I begin to write. When I'm really into a story, that part might only take a month or two from start to finish, but it's usu- ally only the tail end of the overall process!

When you're not writing, what are you up to?

I'm a child psychologist who specializes in working with young children and their families, so some of my time is devoted to that. But when I'm not working or writing, I can be found walking, hiking, or running. I'm a huge fan of covering long distances under my own foot power (no bikes or scooters for me), and I am rarely happier than when I'm outdoors, particularly with my loved ones, enjoying the beauty of the world around me. I also love to travel, and I often get book ideas when I'm in a new place and meeting new people.

ACKNOWLEDGMENTS

I am so grateful to Dominique Raccah and the entire phenomenal team at Sourcebooks for making this book possible. Thank you especially to MJ Johnston, my fantastic editor, for being passionate about this story, for pushing me to add flesh to the bones, and for advocating for *The Quiet Girl* at every step. Thanks also to Sabrina Baskey, my copy editor, for straightening my wonky timeline and breaking me of my em-dash addiction (or, at least, moving me in the proper direction). Appreciation also goes to Heather Hall and the rest of the editing and production team for keen attention to detail and the reader experience. Finally, thank you to Ervin Serrano for designing a cover that captures the psychological experience of the main characters with one simple, arresting image.

I am so thankful for my agent, Victoria Marini, for helping me take a chance with my career, for believing in me, for challenging me to twist up the plot just a little more, and for navigating our course through the publishing world. And many thanks to the supportive team at the Irene Goodman Literary Agency for backing her up!

Thank you to my dearest friends, who each read a version of the manuscript at various stages and provided feedback as well as cheerleading: Lydia Kang, Jayne Tan, Claudine Fitzgerald, and Paul Block.

Lydia, once again, your consultations on the merits of one fatal poison versus another were endlessly helpful; I so enjoy our conversations about how best to kill people. And, Paul, thank you for applying your psychologist's eye to both the portrayal of dissociative fugue and the therapy sessions that followed.

I would like to offer my deepest thanks to Detective Supervisor Meredith Lobur of the Provincetown Police Department, who was incredibly generous in sharing her knowledge about the unique features and challenges of police work at the very tip of Cape Cod during the summer months. Any deviations in this novel from investigational procedure or mistakes in that regard are on me.

Family, thank you for loving me. To all my children, both the ones I gave birth to and the ones I lucked into: Asher, Alma, Evelyn, Erin, and T—I love you endlessly and am always aware of what amazing gifts you are. Thank you to my parents, Jerry and Julie, and my sisters, Cathryn and Robin, for supporting me, even from continents away, and thank you to my in-laws, Bruce and Donna, for supporting me from slightly closer by. It's hard for me to express, even with all the words in my head, just how grateful I am for each and every one of you.

And to Peter Kosa: thank you for spontaneous trips to Provincetown, biotech consultation, your confidence in me even when my own is flagging, your unrelenting enthusiasm for this story, sticking by me in dark times, and the constant joy you take—and share—in celebrating small triumphs. We did it, my love, and I know you've got the champagne on ice.

ABOUT THE AUTHOR

S. F. Kosa is a clinical psychologist with a fascination for the seedy underbelly of the human psyche. Though *The Quiet Girl* is her debut psychological suspense novel, she also writes as Sarah Fine and is the author of more than two dozen fantasy, urban fantasy, sci-fi, and romance novels, several of which have been translated into multiple languages. She lives in Massachusetts with her husband and their (blended) brood of five young humans.